Praise for
Rage of the Behemoth
~ ~ ~

"Old-school monster mayhem set in far-off settings that practically blister your hands as you read. Another fine anthology by editor Waltz in his growing heroic fantasy oeuvre."
~ E.E. KNIGHT ~
author, the *Vampire Earth* & *Age of Fire* series

"*Rage of the Behemoth*, the new anthology of Sword and Sorcery fiction from Rogue Blades Entertainment, takes as its theme the constant struggle between man and beast. Since Perseus first slaughtered the sea monster or Beowulf his dragon, the epic story of man versus beast has been a part of every mythology worldwide. And although in our modern times we do not believe in the monsters the ancients did, we still find a great deal of pleasure in reading about how a human David beat a monstrous Goliath…the authors chosen have managed to broaden the man versus monster theme and give it more depth. *Rage of the Behemoth* takes the best of Robert E. Howard and revitalizes it for the twenty-first century."
~ JOHN OTTINGER III ~
of Grasping for the Wind

"With hill-sized monsters and the hard-bitten warriors who must oppose them, *Rage of the Behemoth* will thrill all lovers of fast-paced fantasy action."
~ PEADAR Ó. GUILÍN ~
author, *The Inferior*

"*Rage of the Behemoth* is an intriguing glimpse into a multitude of savage worlds. The anthology is a throwback to the glory days of Burroughs and Howard, with an icy, ominous edge."
~ THEODORE BEALE ~
of *Black Gate* & author, *Summa Elvetica*

"...pure exultation, a heedless dive into [stories] where the monsters are epic in scale, and the heroes that face them larger still. The protagonists are uniform in one way: no matter the danger, they face it with unwavering confidence and panache. Whether armed with magic, finely crafted weapons, or a shard of gristly bone, these heroes are a testament to how much fun sheer audacity can be. Muscles are finely sculpted, and features chiseled. Minds are sharp, and actions clear and decisive. This sort of superbeing is a rarity in twenty-first century fantasy, perhaps seen as a throwback to the Conan era, so very long ago. But if these twenty-one stories are throwbacks, go ahead and throw me back, because these tales are uniformly fun reads…for each large-scale threat, we're given a large-scale hero to defeat it. How unlike life these stories are, and thankfully so."

~ AARON BRADFORD STARR ~
of *Black Gate*

"*Rage of the Behemoth* delivers exactly what it promises: full-throated adventure fantasy, traditional Sword and Sorcery full of action and magic."

~ RICHARD HORTON ~
of The Elephant Forgets, *Locus Magazine*, *The New York Review of Science Fiction*, *The Internet Review of Science Fiction*, & *Black Gate*

"Jason M. Waltz has created a great anthology in *Rage of the Behemoth*…perhaps the most impressive thing is that each story, within each section, provides a fresh vision of the anthology theme — and all of them constructed with true craftsmanship. And what a theme it is. Man versus Nature is one of the pillar themes of literature and within that theme man fighting against tooth-and-claw is the foundation of great pulp action whether written by Robert E. Howard or Jack London or even Hemingway, as in his *Old Man and the Sea*. The larger the savage beast the greater the instinctive fear imparted to the reader and they don't come much bigger than the Behemoths found in these pages. **For a thrill ride, for adventure across every clime and terrain, for a seasoning of fear which is built right into humanity's DNA —** *Rage of the Behemoth* **is a sure thing.**"

~ NATHAN MEYER ~
author, *Aldwyns Academy* & Gold Eagle Books action titles

Rogue Blades Presents

Rage of the Behemoth

An Anthology of Heroic Adventure

Numbered Edition
6 of 74

Edited by Jason M Waltz
Milwaukee, WI

Published by
Rogue Blades Entertainment
5234 S. 22nd Street, Suite 401
Milwaukee, Wisconsin 53221
USA
www.roguebladesentertainment.com

Cover Artist: Johnney Perkins ~ "Nessie", "Manticore" and "Conjured Protector"
Cover Artist: Didier Normand ~ "Ice Dragon" and "Griffin and Bear"
Interior Illustrations: John Whitman
Interior Graphics: Didier Normand

This is a work of fiction. All the characters, places and events portrayed in this anthology are either fictitious or used fictitiously.

Rogue Blades Presents
Rage of the Behemoth: An Anthology of Heroic Adventure
Copyright © 2009 Rogue Blades Entertainment
ISBN-13: 978-0-9820536-2-1 (paper)
ISBN-13: 978-0-9820536-3-8 (electronic)
Library of Congress Control Number: 2009924022

First Edition: June 2009
Printed and Bound in The United States of America
0 9 8 7 6 5 4 3 2 1

All rights reserved. No part of this publication may be reproduced or transmitted in any form or by any means, electronic or mechanical, including photocopying, recording, or any information storage and retrieval system, without the prior written permission of the publisher and the individual authors, excepting brief quotes used in connection with reviews.

Copyright for individual works reverts to the individual authors and artists.

Visit the RBE website to find out more about the contributing authors and artists through interviews and links to their personal websites and other works.

Rogue Blades Entertainment
Putting the Sword back into Swordplay; the Hero back into Heroics!

Rage of the Behemoth

Acknowledgments —————————————————————— 1
Artists ——————————————————————————————— 3
Forward: A Scattering of Jewels ——————————— 7
  by Mark Finn
Introduction ——————————————————————————— 9
  by John O'Neill

Tales

Under Red Skies ——————————————————————— 17
  by Frederick Tor

DEPTHLESS SEAS ————————————————————— 31

Portrait of a Behemoth ——————————————— 35
  by Richard K. Lyon and Andrew J. Offutt
  & illustration by John Whitman

Black Water ——————————————————————————— 51
  by Sean T.M. Stiennon

Passion of the Stormlord ————————————— 65
  by Robert A. Mancebo

The Beast in the Lake ——————————————— 73
  by Kevin Lumley
  & cover art by Johnney Perkins

FROZEN WASTES ————————————————————— 89

Serpents beneath the Ice ——————————————— 93
  by Carl Walmsley
  & illustration by John Whitman

The Wolf of Winter ——————————————————— 109
  by Bill Ward

Nothing Left of the Man ——————————————— 117
  by Jeff Stewart

Blood Ice ——————————————————————————— 131
  by Mary Rosenblum
  & cover art by Didier Normand

Scalding Sands — 149

Black Diamond Sands — 153
by Lois Tilton
& illustration by John Whitman

The Hunter of Rhim — 171
by Martin Turton

As from His Lair, the Wild Beast — 185
by Michael Ehart

Stalker of the Blood-Red Sands — 199
by A. Kiwi Courters
& cover art by Johnney Perkins

Mysterious Jungles — 215

Poisonous Redemption — 219
by Kate Martin
& illustration by John Whitman

Yaggoth-Voor — 231
by Bruce Durham

Runner of the Hidden Ways — 247
by Jason E. Thummel

Beyond the Reach of His Gods — 257
by Brian Ruckley
& cover art by Johnney Perkins

Ageless Mountains — 275

The Rotten Bones Rattle — 279
by C.L. Werner
& illustration by John Whitman

Vasily and the Beast Gods — 303
by Daniel R. Robichaud

Thunder Canyon — 317
by Jeff Draper

Where the Shadow Falls — 331
by T.W. Williams
& cover art by Didier Normand

Advertisements — 344

Acknowledgments

There is a monster for each of us to face. Some we conquer; some we flee; some we negotiate with; some we suffer; some we…become. At one point, this anthology was one of my monsters. Yet with the aid of the best of the people involved in its creation I triumphed over the worst of the beast.

It began easy enough: I chose the raging behemoth theme long before last year's *Return of the Sword* was even in layout (in fact, I already have the themes for the next three years as well). The interior design of five sections based upon habitat and headlined by professional writers quickly followed. Then came soliciting such authors. I eventually contacted twenty-one authors well-known in the speculative fiction genres. My goal was simple: spread the market interest. Heroic spec fic is not particular to sword and sorcery, after all — even fantasy for that matter. While horror authors weren't solicited, I did seek five established authors who wrote within different fantastical genres and whose past works indicated both they and their divergent fan bases could find a common appeal in this anthology. Other criteria existed as well, such as finding an old favorite and a new, a shared world and a non-shared world writer, and so forth.

I think I was successful. Thus far, I had faced my monster down.

Some of these authors I managed to invite in person; a few were recommended via mutual contacts; most were blind emails. Actually, I never did contact two authors directly — one I tried to locate through a forum master and one I never found. Of the twenty I did invite, nineteen replied. Eighteen of those — even if they declined — were extremely pleasant, thanked me for inviting them, and wished me well. Most of the decliners even went so far as to explain why they could not accept my offer, and a few said I could contact them again for a future project. Five authors did agree to join though, and suddenly we had the core of the book. Another monster defeated.

Then the call for submissions began the winnowing of the tales. It was interesting to watch the rate at which the different habitats were attacked and filled. I say *attacked* as it was extremely obvious from the start which were the preferred: Mountains and Seas. In fact, submissions to these two so outdistanced the others that I had to slow them down and several times announce that the other habitats (especially Jungles) were sorely lacking attention. As could be expected, Seas and Mountains were the first to find quality tales easy to accept. Sands and Wastes surged then, also filling rather rapidly, though I was sad to see a few stories escape my acceptance through various outside reasons. Then there was the lonely Jungles, all three of whose tales were the last selected. It wasn't easy, though, and it came down to the very end. I had seriously considered extending the submission period when I finally found that final tale. A monster narrowly evaded.

Yet another monster reared its ugly mug in the midst of all this: separation

~ Acknowledgments ~

from my previous publishing house and the creation of my own — Rogue Blades Entertainment. Unanticipated as it was, it came at an awkward time. Resources and time that should have been spent on the anthology suddenly were requisitioned by the demands of creating a new business and laying the groundwork for a new small press publisher. Despite these changes, all of the authors and artists herein have been wonderfully understanding and pleasures to work with. Throughout this long process of becoming a publisher and the at times troublesome burden it has been upon my time, attention, and skills, most every single member of this anthology has stepped forward and assisted or offered to assist in some manner. Talk about monster thwarted!

Other difficulties rose along the way: in addition to several personal challenges there was the sudden departure of one of the headlining authors, lost emails and electronic contracts, delayed art, crashing software, and the untimely death of Richard K. Lyon (be sure to read Andy Offutt's tribute to their friendship on page 34). Even as I type this, my struggle with layout continues. Yet I am proud of this work and of all its members — proud to have worked with each of them. Prouder still that over half of the authors and artists involved with *Return of the Sword* returned to work with me again, with seven of them finding their way onto these pages. I cannot begin to explain what an affirmation that is, and how grateful I am for their confidence in RBE.

Monsters suffered…and trampled beneath a unified front!

And so I offer to you, dear reader, a collection of thrilling tales wrapped in stunning art, and created by spectacular artists of pen and brush. I thank each one of them for their friendship and their contributions. I thank the many helping hands behind the scenes, from advance readers, to networkers, to encouragers, to proofers, to supporters, to counselors. To friends. And I especially thank my wife and daughters for their encouragement — as well as their tolerance — of a man who could easily have become a grouchy old monster by this story's end.

Jason
May 2009
Milwaukee, Wisconsin
USA

Artists

Cover Artist

Johnney Perkins

Johnney is a commercial artist by day — but only because he can't be a speculative fiction cover artist all the time. He has been a loyal fan of fantasy and sci-fi ever since the age of five, when he saw his first Frank Frazetta works. His paintings of fantasy locales and characters are spectacular, but it was his warrior themes that led me to him. Early in the process of creating the 2008 Rogue Blades Presents anthology *Return of the Sword*, I contacted him about an original piece of art depicting a mounted warrior returning to battle, sword raised on high. The rest, as they say, is history. Johnney delivered the spectacular and widely praised "Return of the Sword" in record time — and it's become the perfect complement to the opening title of a publisher dedicated to invigorating the short fiction form of heroic adventure and fantasy. It has been my pleasure to continue to work with Johnney. He tackled his three covers for this book in the midst of a busy schedule and with more input from me this time. He did a spot-on job rendering the art specific for three of the habitat stories inside — and rightfully earned the praise of their authors. I look forward to working with him on many projects in the years ahead. You can find Johnney's art — and even Johnney! — at numerous shows and conventions across the United States, or view more of his works at his websites: www.johnperkinsart.com (under construction at this writing), www.myspace.com/jperkins24, and www.fantasyartists.org/Gal30. Johnney's limited edition covers can be found after the Introduction on pages 14-16.

Cover Artist & Transitional Graphics

Didier Normand

I found Didier Normand's art while working on a wonderful project soon to be released by Cyberwizard Productions. Didier is one of several artists contributing to an epic verse collaboration between an American poet and a French poet. It was a delight to work with Didier, though at times the language barrier posed unique difficulties. Each time patience and natural artistic ability won through, and I think we worked well together. In addition to two of the covers, Didier provided the habitat-specific transitions scattered throughout the stories. Didier is a French primary school teacher by day and another Frank Frazetta-inspired fantasy artist at all other times. Didier had been passionate about drawing since an early age, but it wasn't until receiving a box of paints as a present in 1983 that he started to paint. He wasn't quite sure what to do with the oils until he remembered a book a friend had lent him. It was one of Frazetta's. One look, and that's what he wanted to do ("What a naughty vain child I was," he says now), for fantasy held everything: the human body, landscapes, unreal creatures, stories, different textures of rocks, trees, metals…So he began to reproduce the master's canvases. They weren't so bad…then. Looking at them now, he can see how far from the originals they really were. Then in 1990, he began to paint his first original works. Since that time, the passion has grown. Though self-taught and not dependent upon his art for a living (one day, he hopes), Didier sees a canvas as always in progress, just for fun, just waiting for better. Exhibitions of Didier's paintings have taken place in the South of France where he lives. He also works for an American comic book series, *Witch Hunter*. You can see some of his artwork at www.myspace.com/didiernormand. Didier's limited edition covers follow this section on pages 5 and 6.

Interior Illustration

John Whitman

The individual covers was John's idea — so blame him. Or thank him. Avid collectors of numerous things (such as John is) will recognize the concept comes for multi-cover collectible comics. Sound idea. Fun idea. Compounded workload idea. It meant the regular cover of the book had to wait until I had received, read and selected all of the stories — and chosen the cover behemoths. Then had to wait on those five covers to be created. This caused the book to be announced long before I had a cover to display. This also caused the angst-roiled gut ache I suffered early in the process. In the end, beautiful idea though, for all six covers are outstanding. Then came the interior illustrations. Neither John nor I had worked two-page art into a book before, so we experimented, he with the drawing and I with the layout. We finally settled on the bold forefront line art spanning from edge to edge that you find within. We think it properly reminiscent of much of the black and white art found both in many of the early pulps and in many of the paperback fantasies of the 1980s; assuredly appropriate for the tales gathered here. We hope you agree.

Ice Dragon
by Didier Normand

Griffin and Bear
by Didier Normand

Forward:
A Scattering of Jewels

Mock Sword and Sorcery at your own peril.

Oh, we all know the clichés, for they haunt us on late-night movie channels: overly-muscled bodybuilders in furry diapers, wielding thick swords with even thicker accents, trading ham-fisted dialogue with Italian women in metal bikinis…it seems like a parody, really. In fact, it's exactly that.

I'm not sure who thought it was a brilliant idea to compartmentalize popular fiction into all of the various 'styles' that we have now, but I've always thought it was a huge mistake. After all, if you have a historical character in a historical setting fighting fantastic creatures, is it fantasy or is it historical fiction? Consider that people in the Middle Ages actually believed in monsters before you make your choice. I'd argue that a dragonslayer book has just as much right to be considered historical fiction, if indeed the author did the research necessary to ground the tale in a believable setting. But I'm getting ahead of myself.

Why does Sword and Sorcery get such a bad rap? I'll suggest that it's because all anyone ever looks at is the parodies listed above, and in doing so thinks that all they have to do is copy the high points, and then — Violà! You're the next Robert E. Howard.

Well, as anyone who's ever tried to write Sword and Sorcery knows, Robert E. Howard was a genius, and writing Sword and Sorcery is particularly difficult to do. In the twentieth century, there have existed only a handful of real masters of the genre, and what traits they all share in common can be counted on the fingers of one hand: Robert E. Howard, Fritz Lieber, C.L. Moore, Michael Moorcock, Karl Edward Wagner, David Gemmell, Charles Saunders and several others perhaps less well known but equally celebrated. What they all brought to the banquet of Sword and Sorcery writing was a unique point-of-view. That's what really shapes and defines Sword and Sorcery fiction — it's not always the world, but the worldview (and what you do with it) that matters the most.

In *Rage of the Behemoth*, you'll find a number of different points-of-view; some political, some fantastic, and all offered up through a myriad of cultures and time periods. Notice too that the heroes of these stories aren't invincible. They aren't all imbued with destiny, nor the trappings of magic, nor even entitlement to greatness. They are usually people in a hard situation, doing what they can to overcome and survive.

Each of these stories, all carefully crafted, and lovingly presented, will give you a glimpse into new realms, bristling with steel and intrigue. Of magic, you will find an abundance (and the crafty folks who trade in it). For action, look no further. Swords flash and fists crash with regularity. You're in for an

~ Forward ~

exciting ride!

    I appreciate the dedication and effort that went into the making of this collection. With Sword and Sorcery still on the ropes, having lost so many of its forefathers, it's nice to see another generation of authors willing to step up and get in the ring and fight for the genre that they hold so dear. Keep it up, fellas. We'll beat 'em yet. And then maybe we can — finally — get rid of the furry diapers, too.

Mark Finn

Author, *Blood & Thunder: The Life and Art of Robert E. Howard*
April, 2009
Vernon, Texas
USA

Introduction

I get in a lot of debates about Sword and Sorcery.

When I tell people I edit a Sword and Sorcery magazine, normally I get a raised eyebrow. Frequently, two eyebrows. Occasionally, I get the distinct sense that if the person I'm talking to had a third eyebrow, she'd hoist it too.

"By Sword and Sorcery," she says, "you mean those books where some barbarian guy with a bloody axe is, you know, standing on a hill and there's a half-naked woman with huge breasts at his feet?"

That's it. That's it, exactly.

This is where it gets interesting, and not just because we're already talking about breasts. She'll swirl her drink for a minute, look around to see if the cute guy from Marketing has come back, notice Josh from Accounting is giving her the eye, and quickly say, "This is fascinating. Tell me more."

This is usually when I talk about my magazine, *Black Gate*. We've been around since 2001, purchased original fiction from writers like Michael Moorcock, Charles de Lint, Cory Doctorow, and Jason E. Thummel, are carried in bookstores around the country, maybe she's seen us?

Nope. Never. Not once in over a dozen office parties and business conferences across the nation has anyone actually recalled seeing my magazine. It's depressing. Magazine distribution in this country stinks. Nobody takes the time to peek around behind *Martha Stewart Living*.

Then Josh tries to make his move, approaching with a drink in each hand, and suddenly she'll take my arm and show renewed interest. "What's so great about Sword & Sorcery?" she asks, propelling me across the room and glancing nervously over her shoulder.

Well, that's easy. Monsters.

Genre fiction made up the bulk of my early reading. As Mark Finn observes in his excellent Forward, the twentieth century produced a handful of real masters of Sword and Sorcery, and I studied them all. I stood with Fritz Leiber's Fafhrd and the Grey Mouser as they faced weird horrors in the most lethal corners of fabulous Lankhmar, and thrilled as Karl Edward Wagner's Kane combated unkillable eldritch stalkers in the ruins of ancient temples.

To Mark's list I would add two more masters from the previous century, short story writers not always associated with Sword and Sorcery but who were nonetheless supremely gifted in creating unnatural creatures and unfathomable cosmic mysteries, and heroes who could face them: Leigh Brackett and H.P. Lovecraft. I walked with John Ross as he gazed in wonder at the decayed Martian splendor of Brackett's lost city of Shandakar, place of terrible secrets, and shuddered with terror as Nathaniel Peaslee encountered the timeless horror beneath the Australian outback in Lovecraft's "The Shadow out of Time."

When I was young, monsters were what it was all about. If it didn't have

~ Introduction ~

monsters and men who could stand up to them, it wasn't worth reading. (Except for Lovecraft, of course, whose stories had monsters and men who pointedly *couldn't* stand up to them, and who either went crazy or ended up as tasty snacks. Sometimes both.)

Like most young readers though, by the time I entered college my tastes had broadened considerably. Gradually I learned to appreciate Nathanial Hawthorne, Jane Austen, James Joyce, and F. Scott Fitzgerald — and eventually the modern masters who followed in their footsteps, such as Joseph Heller, Jane Smiley, Mario Vargas Llosa, and Gabriel Garcia Marquez.

Her eyes have been wandering since the words "decayed Martian splendor," but she perks up at Garcia Marquez. "I love him! *One Hundred Years of Solitude* was fantastic."

Indeed it was, in every sense of the word. Like a lot of modern fiction *One Hundred Years of Solitude*, with its casual portrayal of magic as part of history, embraced the fantastic as a component of the very fabric of story-telling. And as Mark astutely notes, if your tale is set in an era when the characters believed whole-heartedly in dragons and the supernatural, your story must too.

Today a lot of modern fantasy — and much of modern fiction in general — has followed Garcia Marquez's example, and overall I think the genre is better for it. Fantasy novels routinely climb the best-seller lists, something unheard of in the days when I read Fritz Leiber in bed with a flashlight. In a word, fantasy is more mainstream today, and our finest writers are being read by audiences that would have been unreachable not too long ago.

Still. I'm now in my mid-40s, and while I enjoy a great deal of the novels and short stories that come into my hands, I frequently find they're missing something. They're missing the creativity, the delicious tension, the high-voltage drama that turned me on to reading in my youth.

Specifically, they're missing monsters.

Jason M. Waltz understood this. Jason realized what the literature of Western Civilization has recently been lacking, and did something about it. In *Rage of the Behemoth*, his second anthology and the follow up to last year's *Return of the Sword*, he's picked a theme near and dear to my heart: monsters.

And not just any monsters — behemoths, the tippy-top of the fantasy food chain. In the submission guidelines he crafted for the book Jason wrote "*Rage of the Behemoth* will contain 21 stories about the biggest, baddest, boldest behemoths ever to roar across the pages of heroic adventure! 140,000+ words of monstrous mayhem recording the ferocious battles that rage between gargantuan creatures of myth and legend and the warriors and wizards who wage war against, beside, and astride them."

If you're like me, this book will fill a significant void in your reading diet. It is long overdue.

It opens with "Under Red Skies" by Frederick Tor, a fast-paced tale of urban adventure, and a behemoth that begins as an egg. But even new-birthed monsters can be terrible foes...even if this one turns out to be slightly less

~ Introduction ~

deadly to our protagonist than his own home, a unique city filled with powerful and vindictive enemies.

The first narrative section, Depthless Seas, promises titans from beneath the waves, and it kicks off with "Portrait of a Behemoth" by long-time collaborators Richard K. Lyon and Andrew J. Offutt, authors of the *War of the Wizards* trilogy. Richard passed away last year, and this story, featuring a cunning trap laid in sand, wizards locked in an age-old duel, and a plucky pirate princess, is a fitting coda to a long career in heroic fantasy. "Black Water" by Sean T.M. Stiennon is perhaps my favorite, a marvelous tale of a father waging a desperate battle to save his adopted son from an ancient horror, a creature conjured to destroy an empire…and now returned to wreak vengeance on the last descendent of its creators. It's one of the most original pieces in this collection, and I'm sure you'll enjoy it. Next is "Passion of the Stormlord" by Robert A. Mancebo, a gripping tale of a derelict ship, a treacherous djinn, and a fast-thinking captain just one wish removed from doom. The last watery piece is Kevin Lumley's heroic fantasy version of *The Old Man and the Sea*, "The Beast in the Lake," a classic matching of man-versus-monster in which Crow Thiefmaster pits both brains and brawn against a leviathan from a dark lake.

Next we switch venues to the Frozen Wastes, opening with "Serpents beneath the Ice" by Carl Walmsley, a terrific, action-packed tale of a journey though an arctic domain teaming with hidden — and deadly — life, and the splendidly-drawn characters who seek out the dark mystery at its heart. "The Wolf of Winter," from *Black Gate*'s own Bill Ward, is a wrenching tale of a black-hearted conqueror whose blood-soaked path leads him to a final confrontation on a frozen land. The final line of this one will stay with you for a long time. Jeff Stewart's "Nothing Left of the Man" begins as a classic monster tale, pitting hardy Valkyrion fur traders against a massive bear…but quickly becomes something very different indeed, as Sigurd the Valkyrion leader learns he must play detective to learn the truth behind the inhuman creature on the verge of destroying a remote village. The respected novelist Mary Rosenblum is next with "Blood Ice," a mini-saga of dragons, blood oaths, a kidnapped princess, a stealthy raid in the night, and family secrets that may destroy a kingdom…or save it.

The third quartet of stories is set in Scalding Sands, and it opens with Lois Tilton's gripping "Black Diamond Sands," in which a young sorcerous adept learns that not all behemoths need be feared…and that true power sometimes comes in strange guises. Martin Turton's "The Hunter of Rhim" is a potent horror story, with a uniquely original monster and a unique monster-hunter… one who has paid a terrible price for the ability to protect others. In "As from His Lair, the Wild Beast" by Michael Ehart, a warrior and her daughter are pursued by relentless enemies into an ancient marsh where a great beast slumbers lightly. Surviving both will take courage and cunning — and a plan born of desperation. And in "Stalker of the Blood-Red Sands" by A. Kiwi

~ Introduction ~

Courters, a young Queen and her small band of soldiers track a murderous manticore before it can reach a defenseless village — aided by a beautiful and mysterious warrior whose casual nudity causes a completely different set of problems.

Next up is Mysterious Jungles, opening with "Poisonous Redemption" by Kate Martin, an inventive tale of wronged royals on a quest for vengeance and redemption. But the true star here is the jungle itself, a vividly realized setting of venom-dripping vines and massive snakes — and a lethal creature right out of legend. "Yaggoth-Voor" by Bruce Durham is a real gem, an exciting narrative of a crew who stumble across a shipwreck, a young survivor, and an island whose ruins conceal a terrible mystery. Durham's dialog is spot-on, and he brings his crew of sailors and soldiers to life with style and vigor. Jason E. Thummel is next with "Runner of the Hidden Ways," a tightly-constructed marvel of relentless energy and clever world-building, in which we follow Ikuru the king's messenger on a suicidal mission as he seeks vengeance on the skinless men for the slaughter of his people…and finds instead a captured god who may hold the key to something far greater. "Beyond the Reach of His Gods" by gifted prose stylist Brian Ruckley may be the most splendidly written piece here. Ruckley superbly captures the oppressive alienness of a land far from home to Rhuan and his crew of northern raiders as they quest for gold deep in the jungle — and inadvertently serve as instruments of vengeance for their wily guide, who leads them to a tribe that practices brutal human sacrifice…sacrifice that earns them the service of a terrifying beast.

The final section is Ageless Mountains, and it begins with "The Rotten Bones Rattle" by C.L. Werner, which follows a masterless samurai to a secret mining operation atop fog-shrouded Cripple Mountain, a place haunted by a deadly sorcerous construct. A greedy Shogun, warring clans, and cold-hearted ninja all stand in his way, but that won't be enough to stop Shintaro Oba as he seeks to free the soul of his dead liege. "Vasily and the Beast Gods" by Daniel R. Robichaud begins with our hero in a cage, on his way to a sacrifice that will open the way to the Hidden Kingdoms of the mythical Ancients. The iron bars of the cage are only the first challenge for Vasily in this fast-paced and inventive tale of a dread sorcerer, a deadly game of wits, and not one but two monstrous opponents. Jeff Draper's "Thunder Canyon" is the relentless and bloody tale of Rath, who slips into the camp of the raiders who have killed his wife to exact a terrible vengeance…until he discovers their mountain giant captive and, even more astonishing, a reason to keep living. And finally, in T.W. Williams' "Where the Shadow Falls," John Humble is ejected from his mercenary band for blasphemy and disrespect right in the middle of a war zone, and it takes a combination of bad luck, martial skill, and sheer bravado to bring him face-to-face with the one creature who could put him, quite literally, on top of the world again. It's a rousing tale of an unusual partnership, and a fitting close to the book

As for my young companion at the party, who displayed such pointed but

~ Introduction ~

brief interest in Sword and Sorcery…she eventually wandered off toward the snack table, where she was cruelly cornered by Josh for forty painful, hard-to-watch minutes. Monsters come in many shapes and sizes. I felt sympathetic, but her fate was writ.

What's so fascinating about Sword & Sorcery? It's the literature of monsters. And it teaches us how to spot them, and sometimes to find the courage to face them. Perhaps if my young friend had shown more interest, she might have drawn a little inspiration from the great works of Leigh Brackett and C.L. Moore, and found a way to confront her own predator with more grace and fortitude.

I know you won't make that mistake. Enjoy the works that await you on the following pages, but take lessons from them too. Monsters are out there.

Keep your sword sharp.

John O'Neill

Publisher and editor,
Black Gate Magazine
May, 2009
St. Charles, Illinois
USA

Manticore
by Johnney Perkins

Conjured Protector
by Johnney Perkins

Nessie
by Johnney Perkins

Frederick Tor was born on July 1ˢᵗ with a pen in one hand and a falchion in the other. One dripped blood, but the other — the other! — ran black with ink. Fred entered this world with one purpose: to write tales of high adventure for Rogue Blades Entertainment. With him came the sprawling city of Skovolis, the cosmopolitan metropolis that dwarfed Constantinople in breadth and width, and Nineveh in depth. Skovolis. Home to the best civilized humanity could offer — in all its decadent glory and savage decay. Home also to Kaimer, the barbaric street warrior who knew the byways of her lowest levels as well as the corridors of her highest power mongers. A man of many stories. And so RBE is proud to introduce the first of Kaimer's tales as chronicled by house author Frederick Tor. Herein we discover that the veneer of civilization — even in a city as advanced and wealthy as Skovolis — is easily brushed aside by the brutalities and scheming of callous men and women. As is often the case among such places and people, a man of stalwart action willing to strike at evil without hesitation (and with only minor thoughts of profit), willing to deny flawed lords and gods blind obeisance (again with only meager thoughts of gain), and willing to defy the gross liberalities common to its pampered and pompous inhabitants (once more, at no cost to himself), rises to the fore. Such a man could be called a hero. Such a man is Kaimer.

Under Red Skies

A Tale of Kaimer in Skovolis

by Frederick Tor

The meaty *thwack* of a sharp blade parting flesh and greeting wood echoed in the vast darkness surrounding Kaimer. He snapped his head back, seeking the location of the familiar noise. Years eating among the live food vendors in the lower levels had tuned his ear to the regularly falling cleavers. This unknown butcher wielded an especially large and heavy blade.

Another *thwack* rewarded Kaimer's acute hearing, coming directly from the blackness he watched. He heard a shuffle of feet and saw the weak glow of candles or a hooded torch above the lip of the wall that penned him in. The red of Skovolis' morning sky winked at him through holes in a distant roof. A third *thwack*, and something dark lobbed over the wall to *thunk* in the dirt before him: a human leg neatly severed at foot and hip. Blood pooled on the packed dirt of the cage, searching for escape.

Kaimer knew the search was futile.

He shoved a thick-fingered hand through his black locks and pushed them from before his eyes. The careless move brought a wince — quickly replaced by irritation — when his fingers struck the barely clotted welt upon his skull. They came away damp and his head rang like a death collector's gong — low and vibrant, deep enough to shiver teeth. He did not know how long he had been a prisoner, penned in the oversized cage. From the size of the knot on his head he would not be surprised to learn it was several days.

He had searched the entire cage and found no clue as to who owned it or what kind of creature it was meant for. Something large was certain. A poured stone wall encircled the wide arena, its far side a good spear throw away. Steel bars thicker than Kaimer's waist and sunk into the wall towered side-by-side and arched overhead until they met in a gray mesh far above. Even at full height and stretching his arms high, he still came short of the wall's top by six hands or more. A simple jump for him, but one he saw no need to make yet.

An extreme amount of effort had gone into the building of such a cage. An equally extreme amount of effort had gone into throwing him inside it.

Unable to see anything but the steel bars and the roof above — and that only when the red sky was bright enough — Kaimer had been forced to rely upon his ears. Not that much of an adjustment: living in the depths of Skovolis necessitated keen hearing; surviving amidst the politics of the City of Thrones required sharp ears. Darkness was far more than simply absolute — it was often friend and advantage.

He knew men inhabited the building housing the vast cage. The low rumble of conversation, laughter, and, once, a scream, accompanied by wood smoke and roasting meat after the sun went down told him so. Yet not once had anyone spoken to him.

His green eyes darkened and he clenched his fists in frustration, unconsciously seeking the rough firmness of the hilts that normally filled them. A man of action, built for navigating the city's torturous byways above and below ground, this was the only sign of the anger that churned within. His powerful frame yearned for movement, demanded to face his foes head-on and finish this charade.

Another slab of human flesh — a torso — slapped against the earth. The red sun's light, though weak, infused the chamber, allowing Kaimer to see other pieces of butchered men scattered beyond the latest additions. A veritable feast lay spread across the dirt arena. Kaimer rose to a crouch, feigning a weakness he no longer felt. Welts and bruises covered his body and at least one rib grated, probably broken. He hadn't lived this long without learning to ignore pain. There would always be time to nurse injuries after he exacted his due. Escape wasn't his priority.

Kaimer had either worked for or against all of the major powers within Skovolis. All of the 'thrones' in Throne City; even the royal one. Hierarch to guild master to lord, criminal or patri, it mattered not; he knew them all. There was a remote chance a new party sought to enter the battle of thrones, but Kaimer doubted it. He suspected the person behind his capture would not be a stranger. It would explain why he stood alive in the cage, rather than in pieces across its floor. While many of the city's Patricians would rejoice at his captivity, an equal number would be angered. His captor feared outright killing him, so it seemed he would soon serve as entertainment, either as bait or at auction.

A low growl rumbled in the back of his throat: he did not appreciate becoming a pawn in any of the Patri's power plays. The thought forced Kaimer's head up and he studied the darkness beyond the edges of the wall with new intent. He wondered if seats rose there in the murky shadows; if this was but another of the city's gaming houses and he the game. He hadn't been a collector up here in the upper city in several seasons, so he supposed an arena such as this could have been built without his knowledge. After all, his own plans included larger prey than these gladiatorial matches usually offered. Though this cage was something different.

 He shrugged, turning the motion into a stretch and flex of his powerful shoulders. They'd pummeled him severely; he'd give them credit for that. Kaimer recalled the last mug of ale he'd raised to his lips, remembered wondering why he was already reeling on only the third one, and remembered the bottom of the clay mug crashing into his chin. He ruefully touched the tender lump under his jaw, then found the fresh scabs on either cheek where clay shards had sliced into him.

 He rubbed his square jaw and found another ache. Kaimer examined his memory of the blow to his chin as his tongue explored a tenderness around his teeth. He nodded at the remembered image of an open eye and curved blade tattooed on his assailant's wrist. At least one of his captors worked the lower levels as a router. Only routers could wear The Bladed Eye on their forearms. The undercity's guard-guides were a select lot who kept careful roster of their number. It wouldn't be difficult to determine who had hired one during the time of Kaimer's captivity.

 A voice from above interrupted.

 "And so the mighty Kaimer yet lives."

 Kaimer turned to his right, searching for the speaker, seeing instead, something dark and round hurtle over the wall. It bounced and spun in a lop-sided roll toward him, finally settling an arm's length away. A head.

 Dark hair matted with blood lay clumped about it, pink flesh and the white of the severed spinal cord gleaming within its strands. He stretched forth a hand, sure he did not want to see whose it was. A quick shove turned it enough to see the profile and the spider sigil on the right cheek.

 Toarch.

 Dammit. It was all Kaimer allowed himself. Attachments were unwise in Skovolis; he'd learned that early. But Toarch had been just a boy. He rubbed the scoured flesh on the inside of his left wrist. He may not be a recognized router any longer, but there were those who would remember and there would be an accounting.

 "So, bird got your tongue?" A chortle drew his eyes upward once more. Four boots, their toes curled in the distinctive manner of the Skriven clans, rested atop the wall. Their owners' bodies were shrouded in shadow. *Impossible.* Kaimer flatly dismissed them as being his unknown captors. Not that the Skri weren't capable of capturing him and the others, but they didn't own territory enough to house this cage. Not this high in the city. Even without the exaggerated size, the patches of red sky ensured they weren't in the undercity.

Without a Patri sponsor, their presence would not be tolerated.

"Speak up Kaimer, I know you are just dying to say something. Famous fighter like you? Skovolis' own 'Warrior King'? Tell us how you are going to get out of there and rip our innards up through our throats when you do." A hearty laugh followed, its echoes coming from further up and behind the motionless boots above him. His guess at the seats must have been a good one; someone watched from the darkness. On a whim, Kaimer tried one of the oldest tricks.

"Your mother lay with jackals and had more pleasure than your father gave her at your making." He spoke the insult in Skri, the native tongue he'd learned during his time serving beneath a Skriven captain in the Talons. Not one of the boots shifted.

"What did you say warrior? See," the voice turned away, "your knuckles have driven the sense from his head, Krendl. You've set Kaimer to babbling." Harsh laughter from several throats followed, cut short by a vile oath.

"Damn you Zrae, no names. Now he—"

"Aww close it. He's not getting out of there. Not tonight, not ever. Not until the Patri sends the muckers in and they shovel him out in the guano." A roar of laughter greeted this declaration, though Kaimer could still hear the grumbles of the one named Krendl.

So. Not Skriven. To insult the manhood of any Skriven male was an immediate death challenge never left unanswered. He had thought to entice one or two of them into the cage. The vanished chance at possible escape did not deter him. Kaimer recognized neither of the names, but that did not matter. He'd killed nameless opponents before. He had learned a few items of import though. Most of his captors were overconfident; they answered to a Patri; whatever this cage was built for was on its way; he was part of its feeding. And whoever held him prisoner didn't want Kaimer to know who they were. Which meant they also thought he could escape with the knowledge.

Kaimer ducked his head to the dirt and grinned. He hadn't felt better in days. Then he decided he wanted to be far away from the raw meat when whatever smelled it came to eat. He rose and stepped to his left. Crossbow bolts *thunked* into the dirt on either side of his feet.

"Sit down!"

"Stay there, Kaimer!"

"Stand still!"

Multiple throats yelled at him. He smirked at their obvious fear of him, but stopped moving. The voice belonging to Zrae drew closer and Kaimer fastened on it. The man yelled again — "Get in the dirt, bastard, now!" — his voice almost directly over Kaimer's head. Kaimer obeyed it, leaning forward and putting his hands out to lower himself slowly to the earth. Both hands touched down at the same time — one closing about the bolt that had been by his foot — and pushed him into a violent roll to the right.

While Kaimer's body rose and turned into its flip, he drew his right arm back, his eyes locked on the screaming face shoved against the bars of the cage overhead, his arm snapped forward, he landed flat on his back, knocking his breath rushing from his lungs, and never took his eyes from Zrae's. Kaimer smiled at the surprised look that entered the man's face immediately after the crossbow bolt entered one eye.

Zrae sagged into the cage and the sword in his hand slipped from his grasp and clattered against the bars. Silence dropped almost as fast as the dead man did; all heard the rattle of the bolt as Zrae's weight pulled him down and his head lolled between the steel bars. Pandemonium struck: loud voices demanded revenge, drawn swords and vambraced arms banged against the steel, shouts and stamping feet approached from further away.

"Hold!" A stentorian voice cut through the din, smothering it all.

And was obeyed.

A chuckle, low and mirthless, rolled across the chamber from the far side of the cage. Kaimer squinted into the blackness shrouding the rising seats to no avail. He pushed himself to his feet and the laughter rose with him. One step toward it, and it instantly cut off. No other sound followed, even after he had crossed half the cage. That voice. He knew it, or once knew one like it. One word wasn't enough to confirm it, yet still the distant memory of a face came unbidden—

Something scraped against the cage. Kaimer stood still; waited to see what happened next. Steel grated on steel, and torchlight illuminated the darkness above and to his left. Multiple hands held a section of bars open, while others lowered a ramp into the cage. Kaimer adjusted his position, and a voice from behind halted him.

"No more warnings, Kaimer. Not after that. Next bolts go in your legs and back, and you can lie there while the thing eats you—Hey!" A thud and more oaths cut the threat off. Kaimer bit back his retort and remained where he was, watching the parade descending the ramp. He eyed as much of the wall as he could and counted at least six crossbows aimed nonchalantly into the cage.

Kaimer returned his gaze to the ramp. Four men armed with bared blades led the way down the ramp, behind them a team of slaves pulling what appeared to be a circus wagon. Slaves held brakes on all the wheels, while a dozen more hauled backward on ropes attached to the rear of the high-walled wagon. They eased the wagon down the ramp and rolled it to the middle of the cage. The slaves dismantled the wheels and lowered the bed to lie flat upon the ground. Once finished ensuring its stability, they removed the wagon's high walls and exposed what hid inside. A gigantic ivory object nestled in mounds of hay sat in the middle of the wagon bed.

The slaves gathered all of the loose wagon pieces and turned to march back up the ramp. As the last slave passed the face of the object, a guard swung his sword. Once across the back of the man's legs, sending him to his knees; once again across his throat, spraying blood across the sparkling ivory. No one uttered a word and soon the ramp disappeared as the last guard crossed the wall and the bars slammed into place. An order rang out and silence followed the sounds of marching feet. A glance around the wall told Kaimer the crossbowmen had left as well. It seemed he was alone.

Slowly, he took a step, tensing for any indication that hidden watchers remained. When nothing happened, Kaimer walked along the wall until he was directly adjacent to the cage's latest addition. He stared at it, unsure. It reminded him of the eggs he stole from market vendors…only it was as tall as he was. He had heard of dragons and other wyrms, but he thought they had live births. He couldn't think of another creature that would hatch from something that large, but an egg it must be.

He reappraised the size and bars of his cage, his eyes following their steel paths until they disappeared into the dark recesses above. Better than twenty-five heights — taller than any monument in Skovolis save that of the First Hierarch. By decree, no single structure within the city could be built taller. Didn't mean much, when vying powers simply built new structures atop old.

Kaimer stood a hand above one height, and he'd climbed higher than twenty in the crevices and byways of the undercity, though not straight up. The steel bars would be slick, and he couldn't discern what waited at the top. It was too far and too dark for him to determine whether he could escape through them or not. He didn't relish finding out that he couldn't while hanging upside down from them after a long climb. He studied the wall again, the place where steel and stone met. The bars were spaced the widest there, though still set too close together for him to slip through. At least from his position. Leaping to the wall to confirm his suspicions wouldn't be difficult. He glanced at the gate and wondered at its operation. Trying to get a better look without appearing to do so, Kaimer pretended to lose his balance and staggered backward, flailing his arms to remain upright. His ruse took him too far. The back of his legs collided with the wagon bed and he fell; his trailing fist thumped against the egg.

Something inside thumped back.

Kaimer scrambled away and ducked beside the grounded wagon. He stared at the egg, expecting something to crash through its shell. When nothing happened he quietly crept aside, watching the egg and scanning the circular wall of the cage. A single torch stood at each of the four directions, but nothing moved between them. A glimpse of the darkening sky told him night fell once again upon Skovolis. Finding the closest wall with his back, Kaimer sat and waited.

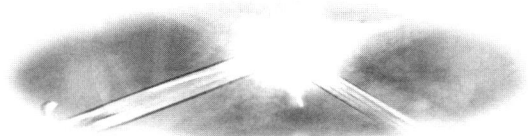

A shower of dirt clods peppered his body.

Kaimer sprang to his feet and froze. The feathered backside of a baby bird bobbed not twenty feet away. *Baby* seemed grossly incorrect, though a glance at the shattered egg informed him otherwise. It looked like a baby bird with its matted half-formed feathers, some plastered to its sides and others a ruffled mess. Its off-balance stance and spread-legged steps further proved it. Yet this baby was taller than Kaimer and looked to have forty pounds on him. It dug and scratched at the ground in obvious agitation. If he didn't stand where he did, Kaimer would have thought it comical. Until he realized the bird's wild antics were due to the blood-soaked dirt where the dead slave had lain.

Nothing remained of the body save a wad of phlegm-covered cloth, the gleam of fractured bone protruding from the sodden mess. In its frantic search for food the thing had fixated on that area; soon it would wander in search of more. Kaimer looked for and found Toarch's body parts in the gloom on the far side of the cage. The blood had long congealed, but food didn't remain fresh long in Skovolis' heavy and stagnant air. The smell of rotting meat and the drone of hungry flies hung in the cage.

The bird lurched forward, its sudden motion almost sending Kaimer into flight. Men with crossbows simply angered him, gave him an enemy to focus on. Giant birds were outside of his experience.

The bird's jerky steps took it left then right as it continued scrabbling at the ground. One lurch took it away from Toarch's severed head. The next took it to his leg. The bird stilled at the instant of contact, then pounced upon the meat, talons and beak shredding the flesh with zeal.

Kaimer squinted. The cold meat turned away the beak. Still soft, he realized, though the razor-sharp talons chased away any relief. In moments they had shredded the thigh and bared the bone within. Spearing a strip of meat on one talon, the bird turned its head sideways and stuck the morsel in its mouth. It continued doing so, hopping on one foot for each bite, eyes intent upon its next target. Each hop grew steadier than the one before.

Placing one foot slowly before the other, Kaimer crept toward the centered wagon. Two steps, four. The bird's head jerked toward him. He froze, one foot off the ground. Its head bobbed and weaved, obviously wanting to find its next bite, yet its opulent eyes never left him. Gritting his teeth, Kaimer watched its feet scrabble for its food, watched it kick the remains of the leg out of its reach. Just when he felt he couldn't keep his foot arched any longer, the bird squawked in frustration and scampered after its meal.

Kaimer planted his foot and propelled himself into the shelter of the wooden wagon bed. He peered through the scattered hay and saw the bird glance once at where he'd been then go back to its grisly feast. He sighed and glanced to his right. His eye fell on the spit wad remains of the slave.

The sharp edge of splintered bone gave him pause. Watching the bird, Kaimer moved along the wagon until he reached the edge closest the once mortal pile. He stretched out a hand and dropped it into the gruesome mess. He clenched and pulled it to him.

Behind the wagon, Kaimer sorted through the remains. Cloth, leather, guts — bones. Many were broken and crushed by the manducation of a giant craw. He found one mostly intact, its last few inches sheared off in a dangerous edge. It would do for now, but he wanted something longer. Frustrated, Kaimer turned toward the wagon. Hay and broken shell. He touched the shell and found it gummy and leathery on one side, rough like sandstone on the other. It crumbled in his fist. In his search for a weapon, he had stood higher and stretched further across the platform. A sudden squawk reminded him of his exposure. He dropped upon the flat surface too late.

The bird fixed both eyes on Kaimer now. He slid backward and it took two steps forward. He stopped; it stopped, canting its oversized head and staring at him. When he didn't move again, it squawked once more. Not satisfied, it squawked again and scratched at the dirt.

Kaimer refused to move, determined to outwait the bird. Its keen eyes could see him better in the descending darkness, and he wasn't about to ruin his odds now. The bird dug troughs in the dirt with its talons and bobbed its head back and forth, undecided. It alternated between looking at him and at the ground, hunger still driving its motivations. It finally spied another morsel and scrambled toward it. It ducked its head toward its next bite when something bit Kaimer's open palm.

"Arrgh!" He exploded from the hay, his fist clenched tight upon a squirming rat, his eyes only on the bird. The bird jerked backward, stumbling over whatever piece of meat it had found, and thumped to the dirt on its backside.

Kaimer sprinted toward the downed monstrosity, rat in one hand, bone shiv in the other. The thing rolled and hopped to its feet faster than he expected, but it hadn't regained its balance when Kaimer threw his body the last few feet and slammed into the bird shiv first.

The scream of a thousand mortally-wounded war stallions could not have sounded louder in Kaimer's ears. The long avian cry rattled his senses, and the collision sent him to his knees. The bird staggered, but did not go down; instead bounced off the wall behind it and back into Kaimer. He clung to the bone embedded in the bird's thigh muscle and fell between its legs. The bird's churning legs finally caught their balance and it raced across the cage, dragging Kaimer beneath it. Talons larger than the meager weapon Kaimer held scythed on either side of him.

Tilting his head back, he tried to see where the bird ran while keeping his head off of the ground. Suddenly Toarch's horrible rictus grinned at Kaimer from the dark. He let go just as his face slammed into that of his friend. The collision sent him sideways beneath the bird's feet.

Three talons pierced his body — right shoulder, right arm, left hip — before Kaimer tumbled free. Their ripping departure hurt more than their sudden impact and the momentum of his spin slammed him into the wooden wagon. With a groan, he pushed himself upward. Braced upon all fours, he panted for breath. He vaguely heard shouts as if from a far distance. He considered finding their source when something in his left hand squirmed. The rat.

Kaimer looked for the bird, saw it on the far side of the cage, scratching at the lodged bone. Torchlight flared beyond the walls, and now he could hear men call to one another.

Glancing left and right, Kaimer pushed himself to his feet. The bird immediately started after him. To his right was the gate he'd seen earlier; to the left, nothing but...

Toarch's leg bone.

Kaimer threw the rat at the charging bird and dove for the bone. He heard the bird squeal, then he landed face first in the dirt, both arms stretched for the bone. His hands found it, and he raised it above him as he rolled over, pointing it where last he'd seen the bird. Lying on his back, looking between his toes for the monster, he couldn't find it. He panicked and struggled upright, searching the dark. Angry squawks drew his attention, and he found the bird pecking and stomping at the ground in frenzy. He laughed.

"Thank Rezia for that damned rat!"

Kaimer rose to his feet, determined to end the fight fast. More light filled the chamber and he heard the sound of running feet. He didn't wait. Stealthily he advanced on the bird, taking advantage of its own noisome actions. He was almost within striking reach of it when it wrenched its head up. Intelligence flared in its eyes as it slowly lifted a foot: impaled on one talon was the rat.

The bird charged.

Kaimer thrust the leg bone before him but not fast enough. The bird rushed straight into him, bowling him over. He lost the bone and came up empty handed, dizzy and eyes clouded. The bird shook its head and circled toward him, wobbling on unsteady legs.

"Knocked you back, did I? Well come along you big bastard. Let's get this over with before they break us up."

Men lined the wall of the cage now, yelling and waving their arms. Both bird and man ignored them; faced each other with chests heaving, blood dripping from their bodies, and death in their eyes. Kaimer did vaguely wonder when the first crossbow bolts would strike him, but forgot the thought when the bird resumed its charge.

He threw himself backward, landing in the dirt at the base of the wall and covering his face with his arms. The bird couldn't slow its momentum; it ran full force into the stone. At the crunch and squeal, Kaimer dropped his hands into the dirt to push upward and sliced his fingers on something sharp. He closed them around the object and brought it close to his face. The second crossbow bolt the guards had warned him with earlier.

The bird staggered back from the wall, then spun, knocking Kaimer to the dirt with a spread wing. He rolled, the bolt clenched in a fist, narrowly evading the bird's stomping feet. He heard the *thunk* of other bolts landing about him, saw one magically sprout from the bird's closest foot, accompanied by its screech and increased yelling from above.

He grabbed the descending foot and twisted from beneath it. The bird stumbled as it tried to step and shake him loose. Grimly Kaimer refused to let go, each hopping lurch of the bird slamming him into the earth, further cracking his ribs and forcing his breath away. The crescendo of the bird's squawks vied with the blood throbbing in his head.

A dreadful scream abruptly rent the air. His adversary stilled mid-hop and landed leg-locked upon him. Kaimer's groans were drowned beneath the even greater bedlam erupting above. It sounded like full-scale battle, but he couldn't worry about whatever happened up there; he knew what would happen right here, now. The bird, overloaded and suddenly halted in its frantic attempts to escape, fell.

It slammed into the earth beside him and the impact lifted him from the ground. Kaimer rode the momentum of his rise and turned toward his foe. Fist-first, he sunk the bolt into the oversized amber eye closest to him.

A pain-filled screech shattered the night and sent him reeling from the bird's thrashing body, hands over his ears. Thunder on high shook the cage, and huge chunks of rubble fell against the bars. Screams from above were abruptly drowned by the *crack* of sundered stone. He stumbled away from the downed bird, trying to watch it and the flickering torchlight above.

Sudden powerful winds hurtled him aside. He crouched and ducked his head — but not before seeing talons the size of elephant tusks curl between the bars of the cage and pull.

Mumbling every prayer to every god he knew, Kaimer ran blind.

The ground lurched and he fell. Another tremor shook the arena floor, and he pushed himself up and made toward the center of the cage. Deaf, dodging crashing debris, tripping at each quake, he ran with single-minded determination for the wagon bed. Sudden wrenching of steel made him look up in time to see a gigantic section of the cage rip away and disappear into the darkness. He watched massive cracks run through the wall of his cell, saw chunks of stone and flailing bodies drop to the bottom of the cage — and further into the dark crevices splintering through the earth.

Kaimer dove onto the wagon bed and burrowed beneath the hay and shell just as a tremendous earthquake shook the chamber. The wagon tossed and twisted upon the heaving earth, but he refused to be dislodged. No protection from the rain of stone and steel that fell around and upon him; Kaimer sought only to hide from threats old and new. He rolled over and almost impaled himself upon the ragged edge of steel suspended just above him. The top of the cage had landed across half its base, smashing the stone into the ground and tearing down almost a complete section of the outside wall of the structure hiding the cage. The largest creature Kaimer had ever seen filled the sky, almost eclipsing the full moon-lit night. A winged monstrosity larger than the Hierarch's central palace lowered itself through the gaping hole in ceiling and cage.

It was too big. The awesome fury in its cry at its failure rattled the remaining foundations. Kaimer felt the earth shift beneath him; saw one of the crevices widen across the room and slither toward him. Flaring torches and screaming armed men disappeared into it. The wounded offspring — no denying the relationship — whimpered. The giant bird screeched in raging answer and stretched a foot into the cage toward its smaller version. Just as its talons closed around the bleating infant, the floor of the cage separated and the world fell away beneath the wagon bed.

Kaimer clung to its wooden slats as it fell and bounced. Bruising blows pounded against his back, and the wood splintered and shook beneath him. A final drop smashed him against something immovable; a splinter shoved through his calf. A dazed Kaimer slowly unclenched his fingers. Experimentally he wiggled each one: painful, yet functioning. Kaimer sat up. Cringing at his broken ribs, he examined his wounds. Bruised and bleeding, he'd live.

A rumble above reminded him not for long if he did not move. Shoving himself off the broken wagon, Kaimer crawled across the rubble of generations common beneath every topside building. More refuse fell from above, and a trickle of pebbles and dirt fell across his back. He made his way to the closest fissure and followed it to the outside air. He squeezed free and stood upon a narrow ledge on the exterior of the building that had housed the cage. Its roof was gone, as was half of the wall beside him.

He recognized an ancient monument to his left, and Artinea Fwainteta's residence to his right. With a nod of understanding, he realized where he was; who had owned his prison. The muted sound of applause reached him and he looked down upon one of the Artinea's well-known terrace parties. Dozens of the man's visitors stood gazing and pointing in Kaimer's direction. Further applause greeted their host's bow and placating wave of his hand. Kaimer heard the end of the man's speech.

"…and so the legendary roc answered the call of my mystics and came to smite my enemy. Even now the traitor Patri's home tumbles."

More heads turned in Kaimer's direction, and he deemed it wise to melt into the shadows. He glanced up and saw the giant roc leap into the sky, baby clenched in one massive foot, squirming bodies in the other. Faint screams reached his ears, and he smiled when one of the figures slipped free and fell back into the city. The Artinea continued to orate and Kaimer snorted at the absurd speech — then nodded in appreciation of the Patri's ability to capitalize on events. Fwainteta didn't sit with the ruling Table of Artineii without reason. The man hadn't orchestrated one part of tonight's events — but by tomorrow he and the roc would be the talk of the city.

A grim look settled upon Kaimer's face. He knew who had used him and Toarch for bird food. The boy had died simply because of enjoying a beer with Kaimer. Because of a powerful woman who felt herself scorned. No matter if she also sat at the Table. If the Patri survived the night, she would not survive the three-day.

Turning, Kaimer descended the outside of the edifice and headed for the nearest access to the lower city. He turned beneath an arch and leaped to his right as a small shadow detached itself from a dark alcove and plunged toward him. He dropped behind a pillar and waited. A soft laugh echoed in the small space.

"Glad to see you made it out, Kaimer."

Now Kaimer recognized the laugh as the one from the darkness above the cage…and one from his past. His hands dropped to his hips and hung uselessly, aping the gripping of his sword hilts.

"I hoped you would survive. So I brought you these." An arm extended from the shadows, a brace of belted swords dangling from its open hand. Kaimer knew they were his weapons. He stood, but remained behind the pillar.

"Come, come. We haven't all night; the Gold will be here soon. It's not our time yet."

"Epech?" Kaimer stepped forward.

"Ah, you do remember. Good. Now please, take these." The swords shoved forward, airborne. Kaimer met them midair, ignored one completely, grasped the sheath of the other in his right hand and drew its blade with his left in one maneuver. He landed on his feet, and even with the brief buckle of his injured leg, his sword tip extended into the shadowed alcove.

"Well done!" The voice rang out from above and to the right of Kaimer. He rose from his fighting stance and slowly turned to face it. A thickset man, shaven head luminous in the moonlight, deep-set eyes hidden beneath a thick brow, and gleaming teeth parted in mirth gazed calmly back. Kaimer sheathed his sword and rendered an elaborate bow.

"Epech Grey. A pleasure." He completed his bow and retrieved his other weapon. One by one, he looped each over his shoulders and across his back. "To what do I owe the honor?"

"Let us attribute it to stupidity." Grey gestured toward the dark object lying behind Kaimer. "My gift. A stupid man with an even more stupid plan. I heartily enjoyed watching you ruin it."

"And if I had not."

"Why, I would have lost the one hundred golden heroes I placed upon you." The man dangled a fat coin purse and grinned anew. "Fortunate for me I collected my winnings in person. Can't say anyone else will be collecting. It's over now." He added flatly.

"My thanks then." Kaimer shifted backward, closer to the darkness, ready to plunge into the hidden ways of Skovolis. Booted feet sounded behind him; a squad of Talons approached.

He stooped and scooped up Grey's present, its wet slickness and awkward shape revealing its nature before Kaimer even turned it toward the moonlight. Patri Deilic's head. The man Kaimer had intended to find. The man who had owned this fallen fortress. But not Kaimer's captor. Kaimer snapped his head up — but Grey had vanished.

Tucking the head under an arm, Kaimer slipped away into the night. *You are a strange foe, Epech Grey. One day we will settle our differences; one day you will push too far, and you will die.* Not this night. Tonight Kaimer had other plans. He thanked Grey's perverse humor for delivering Kaimer's swords and saving him a hunting trip by collecting Deilic's head.

He ducked into an alley that slanted downward and followed it into Skovolis' depths. A death collector's gong sounded from ahead and he waited for the Sons of Night and Darkness to come to him. He studied the men, then dropped the severed head in their cart and moved on.

Kaimer knew something Epech did not. Despite Grey's words, it was not over.

Patri Deilic had not devised this night's events on his own. He wasn't bold or clever enough. And he answered to Patri Spenzinna. She had been Kaimer's lover once. She claimed otherwise; that he had been hers. Regardless, their relationship had only lasted until Kaimer had obtained what he wanted: the names of her undercity contacts. He had left her; the contacts had left life.

He had heard that she was upset.

Depthless Seas

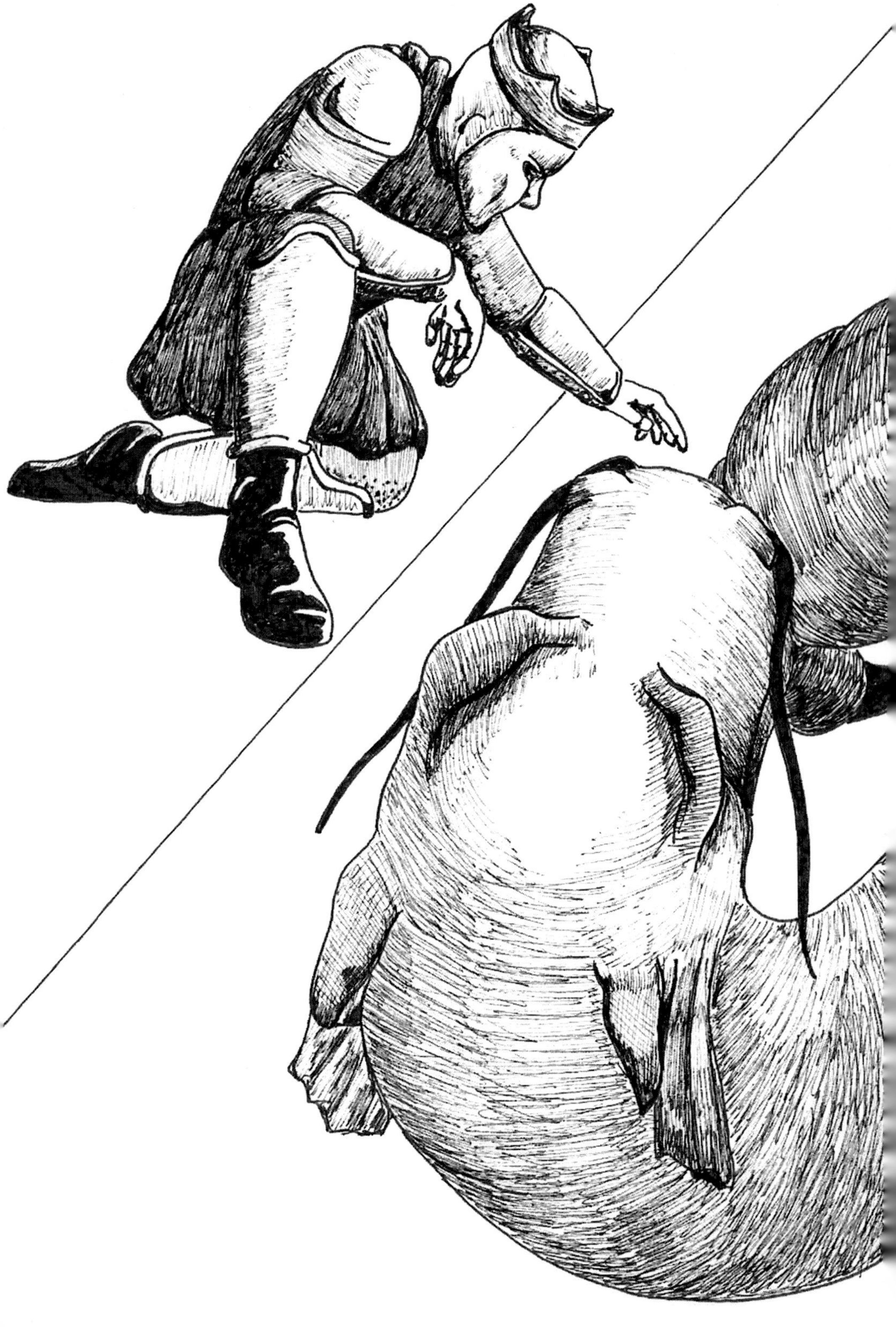

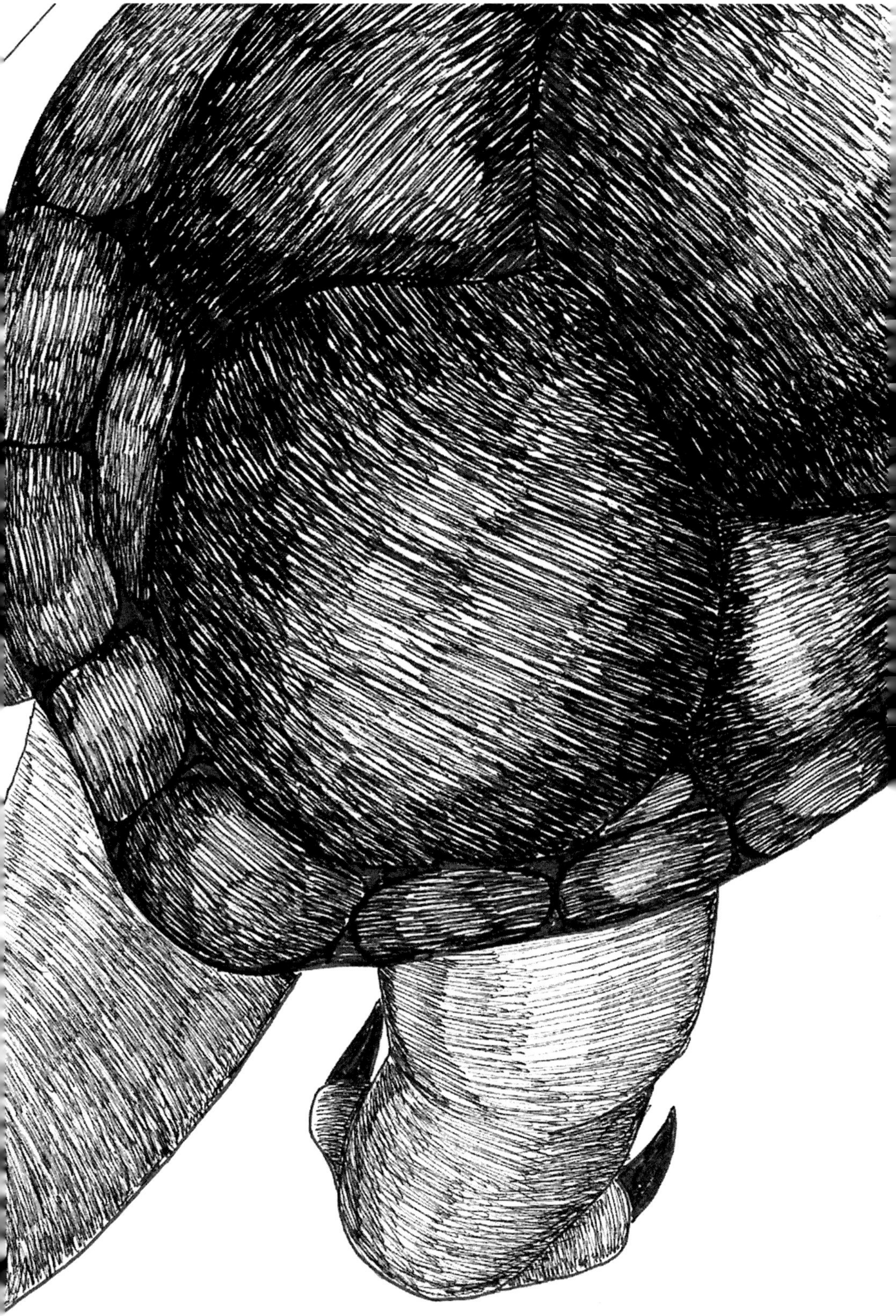

For my friend Dick

Dick Lyon and I were — I mean ARE — partners.

This — "Portrait of a Behemoth" — is our most recent, and maybe the last. Dick Lyon and I collaborated on a few stories and four novels, three of heroic fantasy and one of science fiction. We were the perfect collaborative team.

We never had that first argument. We seldom disagreed. (It's true that we worked together by mail and phone.) In fact, Dick and I did not meet until our first novel had been published and we were asked to form a two-man panel at a convention of science fiction/fantasy fans. Since that first novel about the dauntless — and shamelessly vain — Tiana of Rome, *Demon in the Mirror*, I have told many people across the counry that in our writing, the Lyonheart was the scientist and I the engineer. That is, nearly all the ideas were his in a first draft; and nearly all the writing was mine.

We respected each other even before we met. Who could fail to like and respect a big, easygoing, boyish-faced man with a smile that has to be called angelic, and more ideas, many of them truly far out, than any six or seven of us full-time writers?

Good grief, this is the man who invented the concept of the intergalactic railroad that we wrote about in the novel serialized in *Analog* magazine, *Rails across the Galaxy*. Dick convinced the science-trained editor that it could work!

And I've got to stop before my tears rust my keyboard.

So long, partner.

Andy
February 2009
Kentucky
USA

The science fiction and fantasy writing duo of Andy Offutt and Richard 'Lyonheart' Lyon was unique. Mr. Offutt was a prolific writer from the late 1960s to the mid-1980s, writing in the Thieves World, Conan, and Cormac MacArt series in addition to writing his own novels. In the late 1970s he edited the five Swords Against Darkness anthologies and served as president of the Science Fiction Writers of America (SFWA). As John Cleve, he wrote the 19-novel Spaceways series from 1982-84. However, he says that he is most proud to have been Guest of Honor or toastmaster at some 400 SF/Fantasy conventions, including one in Milwaukee, two World SF Cons, and a World Fantasy con. Dr. Lyon was a highly regarded research chemist credited with many patents and recognized with numerous awards for his contributions to pollution control and alternative energy. He also had quite a humorous imagination. A few years ago, I met Richard in the online Sword & Sorcery Critique Group hosted by SFReader.com. A kind and endearing man, I am honored to have known him. The Offutt/Lyon collaboration was unusual from the start, originating as it did without either party meeting until late in the game, and remaining so as they continued to conduct business via the phone and post office — even until Richard's death last year. They shared many stories over the years, but it's been over a quarter of a century since readers first were introduced to the War of the Wizards trilogy and a certain female pirate. Sometimes behemoths are of our own making — and sometimes they are made just for us. 'On a wing and a prayer' never sounded more appropriate then in this tale.

Portrait of a Behemoth

A Tale of Tiana Highrider

**by Richard K. Lyon and Andrew J. Offutt
& illustration by John Whitman**

Scene 1: Hanging by a thread

The spacious and richly — if too colorfully — furnished apartment could not be called kingly, for its resident was a prince. The prince, in fact, of Orvar, though not the Crown Prince, for it was not his father but his brother who wore the crown. Furthermore His Majesty had no heir, a fact of considerable interest to his younger brother. In fact that was why on this occasion Prince Edrimar was entertaining a visitor in his most private apartment, a building separate from the royal palace. In fact a man, even a prince, needed an important reason for hosting this guest, who was among the six ugliest men in all the world.

Prince Edrimar was definitely not among their number, a man as lean and richly haired of face and skull as his brother was fat and all but abandoned by his hair. In contrast with his nightmarish guest, Edrimar had the sort of face that was easily overlooked in a crowd. However he possessed a trait that made him stand out in even in a large throng. This royal's idea of clothing style and color was strictly his own. His choice of attire on this lovely summer's day was a violet jacket over a maroon tunic with hem of skirt and sleeves bordered with a turquoise band with a gold curlicue detail. His sash was lavender with chartreuse tassels — over pea-green leggings and salmon pink hose with a grass-green stripe. His soft roll-top boots were of burnt orange suede.

A highly detailed map of Orvar lay spread out on a polished oak table before Prince Edrimar and his visitor. The twinned rubies on His Highness's fingers flashed as he touched the map here and there, describing the events of the coming Festival of the Lesser Turtle. His guest, a short, bloated being who somehow put Edrimar in mind of a yellow toad, watched him from rather protuberant eyes that were pools of dark wisdom. He was loosely girt in an instep-long robe of yellow-green — not chartreuse, but darker. He spoke from an overly broad mouth when Edrimar finished his explanation.

Prince Edrimar, as Chief Wizard of Naroka, I require that you solemnly answer two questions. The first is this: have you arranged for King Philandrimar to come to view my painting?"

"Lord Ekron, by the Cud of the Cow whose ruminations created the world, I swear that I have," Edrimar told him. "I arranged for many people to tell my brother about it and he has promised one and all to go and see it. He is even enthusiastic."

The wizard stared at the prince for a moment from nightmarish eyes before nodding his satisfaction. "Good. My second question concerns the despicable woman who pretends to be the princess Shalisse. Have you made certain that she will be with the king when he comes to see my painting?"

"Yes," Edrimar said. "By the Back of the Great Turtle on which the world rests and is sustained, I swear that I have. The king is quite taken with her. True, she is a beauty, with a mass of mane like a fine roan horse. At my suggestion my dear brother has loaned her a gem-studded tiara, diamond necklace, several ruby and emerald bracelets and ornate drop earrings, and a gown sprinkled with sapphire chips to wear to the Festival tomorrow. Naturally, to protect these royal treasures, the jewels and Shalisse are under heavy guard. When my brother goes to view your painting, she will have no choice but to go with him."

Resembling a toad eating a particularly tasty fly, the wizard smiled. "Good. You have sworn the First and Second Oaths and I will respond in kind. By the Great Spider whose web-spinning created the world and sustains it, I swear that all that needs doing to set our trap has been done. Tomorrow King Philandrimar and the pirate Tiana Highrider will die."

That news brought an ill-fitting smile to Edrimar's face. He pointed away from the map table to a smaller, silver-trimmed one that held two glasses and a decanter full of dark crimson wine. "The occasion," he said, "calls for wine, a toast to the health of the new king."

"Please pardon me while I clear my mouth," the Narokan wizard said, and from his extra-wide mouth he spat a tiny dark something onto the eleven-colored carpet of woven silk.

Had Edrimar looked at the floor, he would have seen that the object so casually spat by the wizard was a small black sphere. The prince's attention, however, was fixed on properly serving the wine, a task that must be carried out without arousing the suspicions of the enormously clever wizard. The room's air seemed heavy, freighted with the tension between wizard and prince.

When both men were seated, Edrimar reached for the ornately decorated decanter, his hand steady and unhurried. The vessels into which he poured wine were simple goblets of unadorned crystal. While the decanter appeared to be equally innocent, the prince had paid a supremely skilled craftsman a considerable sum for it. Today it would again earn its price. If a man was to murder his way to a crown, he must not leave loose ends. Which of the two glasses Ekron chose was entirely up to the wizard and did not matter. The poison was not in either.

Busy serving the wine, Edrimar never glanced at the floor. Thus he missed the unfolding from the diminutive sphere of eight hairy legs. The unnatural creature began moving purposefully across the floor.

After guest and host had both sipped the wine and agreed that it was excellent, Ekron said, "Highness, there is something I do not understand that you may explain. Here on Orvar you hold turtles in much greater reverence than do other western nations. You go so far as to make it a capital crime to disrespect a turtle. Why?"

Behind Edrimar, the spider was ascending the wall.

Having emptied his glass, the nervous royal poured himself more wine. He did so carefully but without appearing to take such pains. "The Great Turtle," he explained, "whom you suppose does not exist, has a daughter, the Lesser Turtle. Orvar has the apparently unsafe honor of resting on the back of the Lesser Turtle. Although she has not submerged for countless centuries, she could change her mind and do so at any moment. Naturally the people of this island have long considered it wise not to annoy the Lesser Turtle! Hence we hold several different ceremonies and are careful to treat all turtles with respect."

The spider was stalking across the ceiling.

Sipping his wine, Ekron laughed, his contempt for Orvar and its superstitious people all too evident. While the wine in the wizard's glass was looking low, the prince knew he must not appear in a hurry to refill it. Instead he said, "I too have a question. How did you trick this Tiana into impersonating the princess?"

"Great traps," the wizard replied, "are tailored to fit the victim. The bastard daughter of an Ilan noble, Tiana was rescued from her father's murderers by Caranga, a black chieftain of pirates. When he adopted her and tried to teach the maidenly virtues on the deck of his ship, Tiana learned instead to be like him. Since it is not easy for a woman to gain leadership among freebooters, she went on to become what she must to achieve her goal. It was not enough for that beauty with hair like flame to become a skilled strategist and tactician, a capable battlefield surgeon, and competent navigator. She also had to be bolder and braver than any man."

His Highness flashed a smile. "You're saying the wench grew up to join the family business!"

The mage showed no appreciation of the royal humor. "Aye. Show Tiana of Reme a dangerous prize, and she will steal it. I arranged for her to find a wrecked ship. Letters on that wreck showed that your brother had proposed marriage to Princess Shalisse, that the princess is supposed to be a great beauty but no one here in Orvar has ever seen her, and that your brother would give his bride a fortune in jewelry. Someone as greedy as Tiana Highrider could not pass up an opportunity to commit a great theft."

Nodding his understanding, Edrimar asked, "But why are you so concerned about the exact manner of her death?"

The spider was directly above his head and had commenced to spin…something.

"Because the wizard Pyre and I are sworn enemies," Ekron said matter-of-factly. "It's an oddly limited war because neither of us dares commit an act of great wickedness lest the greatest of all wizards, Solon Tha, destroy the offender. In our last battle, Pyre made a tactical error. Believing that the wizard Lamarred would certainly kill Tiana, he swore by the Third Oath that he would avenge her death."

Mention of the Third Oath sent a slight shudder through His Highness. Everyone knew that the swearing of the Third Oath, the Oath by the Fires that Will Destroy the World, was never without consequence.

A cobweb drifted down from the ceiling to drape unnoticed on the pile of walnut hair atop the prince's head. Ekron's goblet was now nearly empty and his host refilled it, pouring with the decanter at a slightly different angle. Although it was completely transparent, it held two different wines, one wholesome and one poisoned.

After a sip of the second wine, the wizard continued his explanation. "As things happened, Tiana destroyed Lamarred, and that makes Pyre vulnerable. Suppose, for example, that Tiana does something blasphemous and the superstitious people of an island nation righteously stone her to death. Pyre would be obliged to sink the whole island beneath the waves, a most wicked deed for which Solon Tha would surely punish him."

Prince Edrimar's eyes widened in horror. "You plan to destroy my kingdom before I even take the throne!"

"Yes," Ekron said, still in that dull, matter-of fact way, "I promised you the crown and scepter. I made no promise that your throne would be above water." The wizard drained his goblet. "I really must compliment you on this wine. It has exactly the same aroma, bouquet and flavor as the first measure you poured for me. Worshiping the Spider as we Narokans do, we regard the setting of cunning traps as the mark of true civilization. I had not expected a Westerner to be so subtle."

The loop of spider's silk atop Edrimar's head slid down to surround his neck.

"You should be dead by now!" he protested — and then his eyes popped wide. A sudden painful tightness around his neck kept him from saying more and he was horrified to feel himself being pulled upward.

The suddenly dangling royal could not breathe and pain was starting to blur his vision. He had a moment of clarity in which he saw a hideous great yellow-green toad. Smiling up at him, it spoke, in Ekron's voice.

"Surely you did not really think you could poison a wizard of my brilliance and ingenuity!"

That was followed by the slipping down from the ceiling of a tiny spider. It dropped directly into the toad's mouth, where it was swallowed while darkness closed in on Prince Edrimar.

Scene 2: How a Wizard Kept His Promise

Radiantly bedecked with twinkling jewels and with her excellent figure emphasized by a tight-bodiced green gown besprent with flakes of turquoise, the flame-haired pirate Tiana of Reme fair glowed under a pale blue sky decorated with puffs of cloud. The fit of the garment was enhanced by the fact that she had had little to eat for too long. Dreams of food and the eating of it had dominated last night's dreams. As Princess Shalisse, Tiana pretended happiness and interest as she followed King Philandrimar of Orvar to one Festival event after another, most of them boring. As captain of the fleet ship *Vixen*, Tiana was unaccustomed to the encumbrance of skirts, and the one she wore today added to her unvoiced complaints. At least she wore her own boots under the damned rustling, clinging yet egregiously too full skirt. This despite the fact that the king and his courtiers had done their best to insist that she wear the feminine shoes that she considered effete.

Philandrimar's city-state was a vivid sprawl of pastel buildings. Houses and places of business alike were painted with seeming whimsy all in sky blue and pansy yellow and lime and the yellow-green of early grass and several shades of pink. Oddly, the Azure Palace was mostly white. The people Tiana saw seemed happy. Presiding over Orvar might be pretty pleasant...

She was fascinated by only one Festival event, the one that featured a beautifully built young man. A golden collection of muscles in the sunlight, he stood poised on the edge of a cliff above the Great Salt Sea, which noisily boiled over the sharp edges of jutting rocks many feet below. The foaming waves promised certain death even for a youth so powerfully built. Yet the third such dauntless — or brainless? — young man had safely made the dive before even the keen eye of Captain Tiana of Reme spotted the secret of the feat. Each athlete made his dive just after the water crashed over the rocks, splashing high, and retreated. By the time the hurtling body reached the water, the sea had cleared the rocks and was rushing back. Again the incoming wave left those stones bare. As the diver hurtled down, the incoming wave again covered the rocks, protecting him. Tiana joined in the cheering and the shameless squeals of younger women and girls.

After watching the cliff-diving, Philandrimar wanted to introduce her to his brother Prince Edrimar. Tiana's stomach rumbled. "Your Majesty," the hungry 'princess' said timidly as they approached the prince's apartment, "are you sure this is a good time?"

"It's the perfect time!" Philandrimar assured her. "When he sees how beautiful you are, he'll be so jealous that he will—"

"Your Majesty, please go back!" The shout came from a soldier who was running toward them under a tall, silvery helm that rose to a point several inches above his head. This weapon-man in blue and green, Tiana realized, was part of the advance guard that had gone ahead to secure Edrimar's apartment. "It's horrible Sire! The Prince—Ohh! Dear Theba, my poor lord prince, he—"

The habit of command forced Tiana out of her role as frightened virgin. "Soldier!" she snapped. "Take a deep breath, and report what has happened."

Trying to do as ordered, the young man said, "Prince Edrimar is dead, murdered, and that's not the worst of it! His Highness looks like he was hanged but there's no rope! His body just floats in midair, and, and whoever killed him mocked him. His late Highness is wearing the ceremonial crown of Orvar and holding the sapphire scepter!"

And from behind them came the voice of Captain Arrias, a darkly good-looking man with a handsome gold ring in one earlobe. "Your Majesty, I must get you back to your apartments at once. You are not safe here. Once I have made certain of—"

Tiana was swift to turn on him with a chill stare. "Captain!"

Shining green eyes fixed the officer with a stare that combined shock and reproach. "How dare you issue an order to your king?"

Arrias, whose face was crowded by a thick dark beard, favored her with the slightest hint of a bow. "My lady Princess, I dare because the laws of this land give me absolute charge of the king's safety. It is my duty to do whatever I judge needful to keep my liege-lord safe."

He paused briefly before adding, "Furthermore, Princess Shalisse, once you are queen of this land, I will owe the same duty to you."

"Well, I'm not yet your queen!" Tiana snapped, hurriedly taking off her jewels and plopping them into the whaleskin bag she took from her bodice. "Right now your only authority is guarding the royal gems, so you can hold them while I investigate."

Then it was "Oh, drat!" as she dropped the bag of precious metal and stones. Hurriedly she bent to retrieve it, her short step making the hem of her lengthy skirt cover it briefly. She straightened accompanied by the jingling within the bag, and with one hand just within her bodice, extended the bag with the other.

She showed the staring Orvarese a thin smile. "Drat! This gown was definitely not made for bending over! I nearly popped out over the top!" The nonplused captain accepted the packet with a more profound bow, and naturally said nothing about the scintillant tiara still atop her bright red hair. Even his thick beard could not altogether conceal his blush.

His mouth open in surprise, meanwhile, her plump little betrothed was staring. "Shalisse, what are you planning? Can you not see there's danger? You can't just—"

"Dearest," Tiana told him gently, "I have to do this. If I'm to be your queen I must show myself brave enough for the office."

Philandrimar continued to stare, a bellied man with sparse hair the color of a good saddle around a too-round face marred under his lower lip by a silly little patch of fur just the size of his fingertip. Not giving the man a chance to disagree, Tiana slipped past the rigid guards and rushed toward the apartment of the late Prince Edrimar. A woman who had seen and touched many recently deceased bodies though she was not yet thirty, Tiana began her examination as soon as she entered the eye-distressingly furnished and decorated room. His late Highness did indeed appear to be floating in air. No thorough examination was needed to assure her that no struggle had taken place in this garish room dominated by the garishly attired dangling man. Nor was there any piece of overturned furniture that would hint that he had hanged himself. But here, eddying gently in air, he hung, surely hanged.

Tiana had a closer look. It revealed that Edrimar was suspended by a single strand of impossibly strong spider silk. The too-experienced foe of too many mages angrily murmured a single word. "Ekron."

Soon the disguised pirate was examining the map, the used wine glasses and the seemingly innocent decanter, doing her best to ignore the rumble of her stomach. Once she examined that decanter, she smiled grimly.

Ekron of Naroka, she thought, will soon learn that plotting against Tiana of Reme is a mistake.

Scene 3: Conversation with a Statue

After some discussion, King Philandrimar persuaded Captain Arrias that the Festival of the Lesser Turtle must proceed as planned. People could be quietly told that Prince Edrimar could not attend because of illness and, after the festival, his mysterious demise could be announced. Tiana, meanwhile, was trying to be unobtrusive in examining herself in one mirrored wall. She greeted her image with a little smirk and a wink that was more coquettish than piratic.

Philandrimar strutted in escorting his taller fiancée to the head table for the royal luncheon. Tiana was hungry, but, as he politely held her chair, he whispered, "Shalisse dearest, lunch today will be shernak. It's a great delicacy, even more expensive than sherbet. Please do not let yourself be misled by its appearance."

Before she and the hungry and complaining crew of her fleet ship *Vixen* had lucked upon the mastless, crewless craft of unknown origin with its fascinating documents about a Princess Shalisse of Shalanissa, they had been hard pressed and she had felt compelled to order half rations all around. Since then her dreams had been laden with food, and in quantity. Now, thinking that His Majesty's phrase "great delicacy" likely meant "small portion," Tiana quelled a sigh and instead forced herself to smile and nod. The point was that she had no need of delicacy, but of quantity. Tiana was, damn it, hungry!

Abruptly everyone in the hall froze — except Tiana. The odd eating utensils of no longer conversing guests were poised motionless in air, whether en route to or from their bowls. Their mouths were ludicrously open, eerily halted in mid-word. As for Tiana, surrounded by a sudden shiver-inducing silence, she slumped, her eyes closing — but only for a moment. She opened those flashing green orbs to see that she was in a different great dining hall, this one vast and somber, carpets as dark a red as blood, and tapestries as cold a blue as winter ice. She was sitting at one end of a long table of polished walnut. Seated at its far end, facing her, was Pyre.

The wizard said, "Welcome to Castle Ice, Tiana," in an amiable manner. "There is much about wizardly politics I want to explain to you and meeting in a dream is a convenient way to do so — particularly with you so in need of a good meal!"

It was then that Tiana noted that a large beef roast, hot and dripping its savory juice, occupied a serving tray directly in front of her. Plates filled with boiled potatoes and green beans with almonds and red peas with fennel and grishel were ranked next to the heroically sized beef roast. Her stomach gurgled at the sight beyond them of crushed green fertato with dalgias and onions, accompanied by a bowl of banana fired in honey. And beyond that mouthwatering array the rest of the long table was burdened with more!

"All right, I'll listen to what you have to say," a salivating Tiana told the wizard, "but I don't want to leave this table hungry. My meal stays in me, and the leftovers betake themselves directly to *Vixen*."

Even Pyre could chuckle, and did. "I agree." And Tiana ate, and ate, while all around her the courtiers of the king of Orvar sat motionless and silent. As she ate, she planned the rejection she would give Pyre, who surely meant to make improper advances to her. To her frustration, however, the dark mage accompanied her outré meal with his voice, explaining wizardly politics, the different factions, their intrigues, a vast ancient and ugly business in which the unpleasantness between himself and Ekron was only a minor event. And then Tiana sighed and sat back, her stomach not only silenced but well filled, and the spell ended.

To her relief, the plump young serving girl brought plenty of bread along

~ Portrait of a Behemoth ~

with a large bowl and an odd fork/spoon. Tiana's stomach did not snarl. Not sure how to use the utensil, the un-hungry pirate was studying it when an unlikely movement caught her eye. Startled, she transferred her gaze to look into her bowl. It was full of crawling white worms, writhing around each other in a squirming mass. Telling herself that she'd eaten worse, Tiana raised her fork/spoon — and stopped. The worms were more than squirming; they were spelling out words!

> TIANA, she read, THIS IS PYRE. YOU ARE IN MORTAL PERIL! MY ENEMY EKRON IS CARRYING OUT A PLOT AGAINST ME WHICH INVOLVES CAUSING YOUR DEATH! FLEE, TIANA! RUN AWAY NOW!

His Royal Majesty was gazing at her with concern. In another moment he would look in her bowl and see that she was getting messages from a feared mage! How could she explain that?

Since she could not, Tiana hastily dug her utensil into the worms and began shoveling them into her mouth. And Theba be praised — they weren't that bad! Rather like lobster the way the Calacians served them, live with the shell removed and their flavor enhanced by fennel and grishel. She was happy to store away the thick-crusted nut-stuffed bread, too, along with a fine juicy pear. The wine she passed.

When they had finished with lunch, a little time remained before the turtle races, and Philandrimar asked her to walk with him through the palace's statuary garden. There his chins waggled as he discoursed on his distinguished ancestry, pointing first to the statue of a great lawgiver and next to a fearless defender of the island kingdom.

Listening with half an ear and making the occasional impressed noise, Tiana studied one of the statues. It represented a tall man with a hawkish face, a tiny beard, and eyes hard as diamonds. Those eyes were looking straight at her, as if into her — and there was something familiar about the face.

She twitched and her heart leaped when the statue spoke, addressing her directly.

"Tiana. This cloaking spell gives us only one minute alone. Tell me, why have you not heeded my warning?"

"Because, Pyre," she snapped, "we are not friends! The last time we met, you tried to kill me."

"I did no such thing," the wizard calmly contradicted. "I am a conjurer and alchemist — that is, a man of science! I attempted to frighten you out of doing something that would have been dangerous for both of us. You would not have survived going against Lamarred, if you hadn't had the luck of Ambares."

"Well," she snapped, "you couldn't scare me then and you can't scare me now." Her lips tightened grimly.

"Woman!" The mage protested, "I'm only asking you to be sensible!

Ekron is planning—"

"Planning to kill King Philandrimar and me — yes, I already knew that! Can you tell me any of the plot's details?"

"No! That doesn't matter! This is a cosmic battle! Terrible consequences hang above us all! What you have to do is avert them! Flee this inconsequential island!"

"I can't do that. They won't let me take my jewels with me."

The dark mage stared at her in openmouthed outrage. "You're planning to take advantage of Philandrimar's assassination!" he accused. "You see yourself using the confusion to escape with those baubles!"

While this thought had entered Tiana's mind, she snapped, "I am not! I'm going to save Philandrimar's life and take the jewels as fair payment for services rendered."

Having had her say, Tiana stepped away from the statue. "But—" it said, displaying amazing thoughtlessness in trying to follow her by stepping off its pedestal. As it fell crashing to the floor, Tiana hopped out of the way and Philandrimar squealed in fright. He followed his belly to her side.

"Darling, are you hurt?" he asked.

"No," she told him, "but I fear me this statue is in need of some repair."

Far to the north, in Castle Ice, the wizard Pyre awoke from a trance. He was, he discovered, not sitting in his chair as he should have been. Instead he was lying, face down, on the floor. His nose felt as if it was broken.

Scene 4: The Painting on the Sand

At the turtle races, King Philandrimar explained to Tiana at length that this was truly royal sport, far more stately and dignified than dog- or horse-racing. He also promised effusively that after the races, they would view a wonderful painting, the one the toad-like little man had painted on the sand of the beach. Everyone, Philandrimar assured her, said it was magnificent. Through all this, Tiana fretted. In a moment of anger, she had said she was going to save this wretched man!

A mistake. It ruined a good robbery plan — and how was she going to do it? She didn't know, but wizards had their weaknesses. They had too much pride in their magic and too little respect for what sharp steel and quick wits could do. She would go along and see Ekron's painting and, when it showed its true nature, she would pull the dagger hidden in her right boot and Captain Tiana Highrider would act.

As she had feared, the races among fancifully decorated turtles were about as exciting as watching hair grow. When at last the final "race" had been "run," Captain Arrias and one hundred Royal Guardsmen trekked with Philandrimar and Tiana across the festival grounds and out onto a wide sand flat. The king could see little of the Festival because in accord with standard procedure he was in the center of the procession, surrounded by men in heavy armor. Claiming that Princess Shalisse must introduce herself to the people, Tiana walked with Captain Arrias at the head of the procession.

When they reached their goal, he looked around suspiciously and shouted, "Out swords! Stand ready to meet attack!"

The sound of swords grating between sharpeners mounted in a hundred sheaths was dramatic, menacing, and loud.

Though he was used to Arrias's cautious habits, Philandrimar demanded, "What hobgoblin frightens you now, man? You're worse than an old maid looking under her bed."

"Your Majesty," the captain replied in a tone of clear authority, "my suspicions were aroused when I first heard of this painting on the sand. Why artwork that cannot be moved unless it's a ruse to force Your Highness to come here? A picture this large and this new should smell strongly of paint, but does not. Now we arrive and the artist, who should be waiting to receive your praise, is gone. Instead here is a huge new painting without the slightest odor. I regret spoiling your outing, sire, but we dare not risk your person in what may be a trap. We must return to the palace immediately."

Inwardly Philandrimar moaned. As ruler of this realm he made great decisions, did things that touched the lives of all his people, but he was powerless in the small things that made up day-to-day life. To enjoy this moment's diversion, he must beg. "Good Captain Arrias," he said reasonably, "What harm can it do just to look at the painting before we go? You can spread your men around it so that I can see it and still be within your protection. Besides, we are in the middle of a sand flat. How could danger approach without our seeing it?"

To Philandrimar's relief, Arrias reluctantly nodded agreement. His guards began to spread out to encircle the painting…and they kept spreading. He had never dreamed that any artist created to this vast extent. Arranging his even one hundred men under arms in a circle around the painting left them standing three feet apart. Even though the artistic creation on the beach was immense, minute details were faultlessly rendered. Nothing about the painting of the thing called Garnog was handsome, but much of it was indisputably colorful. The creature about to rear from the sand was blood-red and golden yellow and charcoal, with a lengthy blue tail and the great angry-looking red eyes of a bird of prey. Yellow were the claws and beak that looked capable of monstrous bloody work.

Unable to comprehend the painting at a glance, His Majesty walked around the sprawling monstrosity in astonishment. It was, he realized, a life-size rendition of some huge beast, a veritable behemoth. It seemed impossible that any artist could have made coarse sand look so perfectly like sharp white teeth and claws. The sinews of those powerful legs were perfectly drawn. Philandrimar and the others could almost feel the heat of the painted orange red fire that poured out of that fearful mouth.

What a shame that such a truly fine work should be so impermanent! The impossibility of preserving this painting was particularly painful because now the king recognized its subject, Garnog, the son of the Lesser Turtle by a dragon father. An important figure in Orvar's pantheon, Garnog was often artistically rendered, but never before this well, this perfectly. Philandrimar could easily imagine the beast starting to move.

Of course the motion of that razor sharp claw was only an illusion caused by shifting shadows…except…

King Philandrimar stood stock still, holding his right arm straight out. Since he wasn't moving, neither was the shadow of his hand but the claw was drawing closer. As he stared in fascination, the gap between the shadow of his hand and the sharp tip of that huge claw disappeared. Instantly His Majesty felt a sharp stabbing pain and he was bleeding from a hideous hole in his right hand.

Forgetting his intended, he ran, slipping behind the guardsmen. Once he had waddled safely beyond them, he yelled for his physician. While the man should have been nearby, Philandrimar didn't see him when he looked around. Instead he saw that the painted monster was moving across the sand, slipping under the mailed feet of the Orvarese soldiers.

It's coming for me! I've got to run or die! Philandrimar ran — not for the first time cursing his short legs — with the painting following at speed with its eerie flowing movement. The panicky monarch looked for his guards to spring into action but they were busy milling about and yelling in confusion. Their liege-lord was getting farther and farther from their protection, and the monster was gaining on him.

Name of the Lesser Turtle! Good steel armor flashed in the sunlight as armed men were a move, running after Philandrimar, their swords, upper body armor, bracers and greaves shining with their movements. But the monster was flowing faster than they could run in their heavy armor and helms. What was a plump, crowned man to do?

Scene 5: A Turtle Race

As she sped after Philandrimar and the monster, Tiana heard Captain Arrias shout, "Men, I want every sword on the ground! The creature is Garnog! Striking the son of the Lesser Turtle would be blasphemy, an offense to both the Lesser Turtle and her sacred sire!"

A frightful clanging arose as tall-helmed men in glittering cuirasses threw down their weapons, presenting Garnog with a defenseless gaggle of prey in useless shining armor. Tiana clamped her teeth. Drood take it! She had planned to snatch a good steel blade from one of those soldiers as they milled about, and put sharp steel to work. Now to save poor Philandrimar, she must battle a monster of incredible size with only the dagger that no one knew she had.

But…maybe Garnog wasn't really that huge. Wide and long as he was, perhaps the beast was no thicker than a coat of paint?

Heedless of exposing her bare legs, Tiana hurriedly pulled up her encumbering skirt in front and tucked it through her cloth-of-gold sash. The act of sliding a long and quite broad dagger out of its special sheath in her right boot was so well practiced as to be almost automatic. Ahead of her the panting pirate could see the long, powerful tail of the outré horror slashing back and forth over the sand in a blue blur of destruction. If this were normal combat with a three dimensional monster, that tail would knock down anyone trying to attack Garnog from the rear. The thing was as thick as her waist. What would it do to her if Tiana raced across it to get at the monstrosity's back?

Instead of finding out, she hurled her eminently sinuous self into the air like a great pale cat, in a dagger-first dive onto the turdragon's thrashing tail. Her blade, longer than her foot, jerked in her hand as it bit into paint-covered sand. For a moment the sand beneath her roiled as a live thing, so that Tiana was hard pressed to keep a two-handed hold on the hilt.

Instead of subsiding, the strangely mobile sand moved out from under her. Getting to her feet, she saw Garnog's severed tail eerily writhing and flopping like a decapitated snake. Black blood leaked from one end and a trail of that foul ichor led across the sand to the monster itself, still in pursuit of a seemingly panicked King Philandrimar.

Turning toward the sound of running feet, Tiana saw Captain Arrias and a host of guardsmen running toward her. "Good news!" she shouted. "The monster can be killed!"

"Blasphemer!" the horrified Arrias yelled back. "You have dared maim the Sacred Son of the Lesser Turtle! You must be put to death by stoning!"

For a moment Tiana stared at the captain as if he were mad. *The idiot is supposed to defend his king, not the stupid superstitions of this island! Isn't it enough that he has foolishly disarmed a good half his force? Stoning her for trying to save their king made absolutely no sense…except that it might be exactly what Ekron wanted.*

"Sir! Look!" a soldier shouted, pointing.

Glancing back, Tiana saw that Garnog was changing, growing out of the sand. For a brief time the thing had the appearance of a turtle-dragon that had been flattened like a pressed flower and was flowing up out of the sand. Quickly however, it swelled, gaining the thickness normal for a beast of its width and length. It was also moving much faster than it had before, tail or no tail. If it were still after King Philandrimar, he was doomed. Instead, however, it had turned and was coming straight for Tiana. She watched in horror as the great yellow beak chomped a shrieking soldier in half, good coat of woven chain and all. Paying no heed to the monster that was rushing toward them like an avalanche, Captain Arrias pointed at Tiana and bellowed his command:"Seize her!"

Over half the guardsmen had heard and obeyed his prior order to discard their swords. Their armor and those too-tall helmets flashed under the bright sun as all of them moved like automatons into battle formation. From behind an armored wall, the fire-breathing ghastly spawn of a turtle and a dragon was rushing at Tiana while the men in front of her had become a wall of steel four soldiers deep and twenty-five wide. They were charging her at rapid march. Their commander, she decided, was either having a panic attack or was in Ekron's dark power.

This, Tiana thought, is too easy. Two enemies, both coming at me as fast as they can, and neither able to turn quickly! She shouted, "Is none of you little boys willing to help a poor helpless girl in distress?"

And then she was off at the run, red mane flying and bare legs flashing. Some fifty running paces away from the soldiers, she made a right angle turn and with churning legs sped from between them and the approaching turdragon. While the soldiers halted, the thing did not.

Garnog swerved its huge body this way and that, knocking down and stepping on several howling men. Orvarese blood spurted and splashed as unarmed men died or were maimed. Tiana saw that horrid now-red beak chomp and rip the legs off a wailing warrior.

Rounding the behemoth, Tiana raced toward the festival area, about half of which was still intact.

Behind her she could hear the ghastly outcries of the monster's victims seasoned with a lot of profanity, while a nice little breeze assaulted her nostrils and esthetic sense with an odor that might be dragon-turtle excrement. With the behemoth between her and the guardsmen, she was unable to see what had befallen them.

Agonized or terrified or both, mothers' sons shouted and screamed, howled and squealed…and were maimed or slain, thanks to the preference of their commander for superstition rather than logic and plain good sense. Mangled, profusely bleeding, weaponless weapon-men strewed the glittering sand like the red-streaked petals of a huge flower.

While she ran through the ruins of the festival grounds with fiery hair streaming loose in her wake, Tiana tried to sort things out in her head. She had saved the life of that silly Philandrimar, she was wanted for a capital crime and pursued by a preternatural monstrosity. Clearly it was time for an honest pirate to get herself on her ship and sail away with the jewels she was earning with each passing moment.

Behind her, Garnog was smashing its way through the festival area. Booths cracked and snapped like splinters and gaily colored tents and awnings dragged from the body of the destroyer. For a creature that was part turtle, Garnog was amazingly fast, but he was also broad and bulky and the city ahead of her had a lot of narrow streets. Spotting a particularly close-walled alley, Tiana made for it.

As she sped down the alley, she heard a horrible crashing behind her, ear-offending crunching noise amid the snapping of timbers and the crashing down of roofs. A quick backward glance confirmed her fears. Most of Orvar's buildings were flimsy structures that were rebuilt after every hurricane season. Garnog was going through them like a bear through a chicken coop.

As she raced farther down the alley, she heard a horrendous crash behind her, followed by furious roars. Another rearward glance showed her the turdragon stuck between the fragments of two buildings both of which were made of logs that were huge oaken rectangles thicker than a man.

Smiling in self-congratulation, Tiana took half a step toward her helpless foe. As she gave it a mocking bow, it roared. With a cloud of fire rushing toward her, Tiana Highrider continued the bow by falling flat — with a splash as she was so unfortunate as to land in a mud puddle. The cloud of burning red and yellow fury rose as once again the enraged behemoth hurtled toward her. For a moment she was staring up at searing heat…and then it was gone. The hot stench of the monster's breath, however, threatened her consciousness.

Parts of her gown had escaped the mud bath and were smoldering. As she extinguished the flame, Tiana considered her options. Mud was at least a form of armor against a dragon's flaming belch. For the moment her foe was immobilized. Did she dare seize this opportunity and try to kill it? With only a dagger, how can I—

Another roar from the turdragon and this time it wasn't aiming at her. Not so mindless as it seemed, the awful creature was setting ablaze the buildings that held it trapped! Oh Blessed Theba! This whole city was much too flammable!

At the next corner Tiana turned left and Garnog followed at a speed it should not have possessed, smashing buildings and burning anything that was in its way with billowing dragon-breath. Spread by a hot dry wind, the fires grew, eating more and more of the city. Orvar was being destroyed and all Tiana could do was run.

Against a foe like Garnog running was a losing strategy, but what about cliff diving? Despite growing fatigue and shortness of breath, she turned, ripped off her muddied skirt, and reached into her bodice to check on the whaleskin bag of royal Orvar jewelry — the real sparklies, not the false bag she'd prepared last night and had handed to dear, dear Arrias the ass. Assured of the security of her booty but wishing she could have added that nice twinkly circle of gold in his ear, Tiana headed for the cliff at the run.

No point in going through all this and losing my loot!

As she neared the cliff, she did not give Garnog even a swift backward glance, though her ears told her that the colossus was lumbering down upon her. It was her sincere wish that if it followed her off the cliff, the horrid thing would splatter his immensity all over the jagged rocks at its base. At the edge, she looked down, saw the wicked-looking rocks become bare of water, waited a few seconds — feeling Garnog's heavier than heavy footsteps and flinching at the heat when dragon-fire roared past on her left — and leaped.

In midair she wondered belatedly if there was more to cliff-diving than Philandrimar had explained…

The water struck her a terrible blow. Despite the pain-stars that filled her head, she began swimming rapidly away from the rocks. Before she had gone far, a great wave struck her, pushing her farther out to sea. Tiana swam on, assuming that Garnog had just come plummeting into the water. If it survived the fall, her only hope was to get far away before it revived. Tiana swam. And swam. As she stroked desperately for a ship she hoped was sorcerously laden with victuals with the murderous behemoth surely close on her trail, she was forced to do that which she did not want to do: take a brief rest by treading water for a little. And then without looking back, she resumed swimming.

When Tiana climbed aboard *Vixen,* she was strangely stained with streaks of color. Paying no heed to the burning city behind her or to the persistent snarl of her belly, she pointed out to sea and ordered her astonished crew to set sail. Once they were clear of the harbor, she retired to her cabin.

Exhausted, she collapsed into her chair. Though sleep came quickly, she realized that she was becoming strangely cold.

Next morning, Tiana awoke with a strong suspicion that someone had put mashed potatoes in her bed, but, when she sat up, she banged her head against a hammock that had not been there last night. While the mashed potatoes shared her bed with a considerable quantity of mushroom gravy and four fried chickens, the hammock held three roast ducks, two boiled turkeys and a plucked but uncooked ostrich. While all this left her little room in the bed, she could not get out of it because her cabin was piled high with spit-roasted pigs and oxen, along with baskets of boiled vegetables.

On deck and again swaggering as her crew was accustomed to seeing her, she was much surprised not to see a pursuing turdragon or its corpse but a vast multicolored smear upon the sea. Ah! No wonder Captain Arrias hadn't smelled paint! To ensure that no evidence remained of the murders he had intended, Ekron had painted with water colors.

Sean T. M. Stiennon is a creature known to lurk around the campus of University of Wisconsin—Madison, though he has been spotted in other parts of the city. Residents should beware his fascination with bound volumes, Japanese cartoons, and his curious identification with fictional hero Don Quixote. When not brooding, consuming pizza, or talking with family and friends, he can be found sleeping. Somehow, though, he manages to spend quite a bit of time writing. He is the author of the collection Six with Flinteye *and the space opera novel* Memory Wipe. *Occasional posts at his blog Wordperfect Alchemist (http://seantmstiennon.livejournal.com) and a sometimes updated www.SFReader.com Author's Page keep his fans updated. In this story, Sean again writes of his character Shabak and the kabrisk's human son. It is a continuation of an interesting examination of relationships and roles that he has obviously invested much thought in. Here the past rears its very ugly head and threatens to wreck everything Shabak has striven for...unless he faces his behemoth head on.*

Black Water

A Tale of Shabak the Kabrisk

by Sean T.M. Stiennon

When he returned from the village of Stamfir, Shabak the kabrisk found his home on Talon Point in ruins. His best fishing net lay in shreds upon the sand, which was churned as if by a furious battle. A glance into his cave revealed that the hearth fire had been doused by the overturned water pot and that several of his traps, fish spears, and other possessions had been destroyed. His foster-son Drace's sword was gone from its place upon the wall.

Shabak crouched outside the cave and studied the sand. There had indeed been a struggle here. He saw human footprints that matched Drace's, but if bandits or corsairs had attacked the cave in Shabak's absence, he could find no sign of them in the sand. It seemed as if Drace had fought against a whirlwind.

Shabak stood five feet in height, his whole body sheathed in a gray-green carapace with thick, short limbs, a stubby, finned tail, black eyes set deep in a boxy head, and a pincer appendage that sprouted from the shoulder above his left arm. He used that pincer now to poke at the sand while he gazed around at the wasteland of stone and water that was Talon Point. As always, the sky was the color of tarnished iron, and the sea churned in mossy green waves, smashing itself into shards of white upon the jagged boulders of the shore. A short beach extended to the water from the mouth of Shabak's cave, and just offshore rose the tor of white limestone that served to direct men to his dwelling. With a pang, Shabak realized he might find his foster-son's corpse just beyond the next rock. Perhaps it had been foolish to leave him alone while Shabak went into the village to trade crab shell ornaments for ale and bread.

Shabak stepped back into his cave. Judging from how much of its fuel the hearth fire had consumed, Drace had been away for at least three hours. Shabak entered his sleeping chamber and ignited the magical glowstone that provided him with illumination. This room had also been ransacked: the thin blankets upon his cot were torn, his few books scattered, and other possessions broken. He had taken his steel dagger with him on his journey, but his other weapons — the great mace, its head over a foot long; the square pointed sword; and the bow, carved from the shell of an emperor crab — lay undisturbed in their racks. A bandit would have taken them. The black cloud of fear that had begun to well around Shabak's heart grew thicker. He slung his bow and quiver over his shoulders and hooked the mace onto his belt.

Outside, he looked up and down the shoreline. Drace appeared to have been carried off by force. *South or north? Inland, toward Stamfir? Or perhaps across the sea to any place in the world?* Shabak stalked along the rocks that bounded his little beach on both sides, searching for any sign of travel over them.

He found a dark stain splashed across a chunk of storm-swept stone on the north side of the beach and bent down to study it. A splash of blood, he decided. *Drace, or another man?* He scraped a little away with one finger and brought it to his pointed tongue.

Shabak spat. This blood tasted more foul than anything which had ever passed between his lips, like rotten fish pickled in salt water and seasoned with sulfur. Shabak gagged and felt as though he should seek a rock to scrape his tongue clean. When he had recovered, Shabak set off across the rocks of Talon Point, tracking the kidnapper by small signs: a scraped barnacle, a splash of wet sand on a dry rock, a starfish dislodged. Dread like noxious smoke filled his thoughts.

Shabak's thick, gray-green exoskeleton protected him from the sharp edges of stones, barnacles, and mussels, while his pincer appendage helped him navigate around them. He splashed through dark pools, scrambled over massive boulders, and picked his way over rocks like the horns of ancient dragons, using his tail for greater balance. He passed one of his traps and found a meaty black crab caught in the net. He killed it, peeled its carapace away with his pincer, and ate raw chunks of its soft meat. He threw it away after the grumbling of his stomach had settled a little and continued on. He couldn't afford the time to forage for more.

Shabak traveled between sheer cliffs on one side and churning sea on the other, heart pounding beneath a shadow of fear. He couldn't guess who had taken his son, or for what purpose. Many men nursed grudges against him: Slaug Brokentooth, who had already sent one assassin; Alzius Krog, the corsair who had escaped from Shabak with a mangled hand; the sorcerer Laciosso; numerous others. Any one of them might have sent men who, finding

Shabak absent, had decided to use his son against him, perhaps to draw him into a trap he couldn't help but spring.

Shabak ached to know that his son was safe. For nearly sixteen years they had lived together on Talon Point, staying alive with fishing and crab-trapping. Shabak had taught his son to be a warrior since the age of six, and together they had fought many battles in defense of the weak. *If Drace were dead...*

Miles and hours passed. The rocky expanse between cliffs and sea became narrower, and in places Shabak had to wade through miniature inlets of frothing water and salty waves, his feet crunching the shells of tiny mollusks and slipping on clumps of saltwater weed. He saw black holes worn by the sea in the side of the towering cliff, caves where he sometimes stayed a night when his wandering took him far to the north. Waves frothed at their edges so that they looked like the mouths of rabid wolves. Shabak picked his way over the rocks carefully. To an untrained human, this journey would have been nearly impossible, but the All-Father had made Shabak and all kabrisks for water and stone.

He rounded an outflung spur of the cliff that sheltered a larger bay and found another of the black crabs — this one transfixed on a sharp stone. He bent to examine it. It looked as if the creature had been impaled, still writhing, on the stone, then had each of its legs pulled out so that only a thin string of muscle connected them to the body. Shabak shuddered. Would he find Drace splayed out in a similar fashion?

The crab's pincers pointed toward a cave at the base of the cliff whose maw spanned the length of three horses. Shabak took his bow off his shoulders, braced it against his strong legs, and strung it. It was short, only three feet long, but it had as much power as a human bow twice its size. Shabak set a steel-tipped arrow to his bowstring and crept forward. An inlet of dark water separated him from the cave, and Shabak shivered as he waded through it. Although he recognized the inlet from other journeys up this coast, something felt wrong in the very air and water of the place. A faint scent like sulfurous smoke drifted into his slit nostrils, and Shabak felt glad that he hadn't filled his belly. The odor grew stronger, and he felt his bowels begin to churn. A rotting whale carcass would not produce such a stink.

Shabak stood before the mouth of the cave, gazing into its black depths. Kabrisk eyes were good in darkness, but Shabak could see nothing within. "Drace!" he called out.

There was no answer, but the noxious scent continued to waft out. Shabak advanced, keeping his arrow aimed at the ground. He didn't want to risk shooting his foster-son.

Cold, moist stone smacked beneath his carapace armored feet. The air felt even colder than outside, and the roar of the waves faded from hearing. Shabak cursed his lack of foresight in not bringing a torch, but it would have been nearly impossible to keep it dry during his journey. He stood in the darkness, waiting for his eyes to adjust properly, keeping his bow half-drawn and listening carefully for any sound. He thought he heard breathing ahead.

Shabak's gaze followed the curve of the cavern's walls upward and found something pale in the darkness. A moment later, he made out two bright eyes. "Drace," he gasped. "Drace, it's me. Shabak."

He began to step forward, then realized Drace wasn't alone. The rotten odor pervading the room surged against Shabak, so strong he felt weakened by it. Something black slid from the darkness to lie across Drace's neck. "Come no closer, Shabak son of Orak, or this boy is dead."

The voice spoke Wenthalic, Drace's native tongue, but rather than its normal pleasant rawness it sounded like plates of rusted iron grating against each other. Shabak clacked his fangs and drew his bow.

"Careful, Shabak," Drace rasped.

So the boy lived, and was well enough to get a few words out. Shabak's heart lightened, but the words of Drace's captor sent a cold rush through his bones. No living man besides Drace knew the name of Shabak's father. The outline he perceived in the darkness began to take shape.

"Who are you?"

"One who knew Orak well," the voice answered. "I am neither human nor Ancient, though I know much of you kabrisks."

Shabak kept his bow drawn and aimed towards the voice. The sulfurous odor seemed to intensify. "Tell me why you've taken my son."

"Your son? Most would think that odd — a kabrisk of over two hundred years begetting a gold-haired human boy. But I should know better than any that like can create unlike. Lower your bow, Shabak. The arrow could not kill me before I broke his neck."

Shabak glanced at Drace. He saw the boy's eye whites bob down in a nod, and he slackened his pull on the bowstring and unnocked the arrow.

"Better," said the voice from the darkness. "But you truly do not know me, Shabak?"

Shabak thought of every creature he had ever encountered that fell outside human and Ancient. He had spoken with a golem and seen the bones of titans and dragons, but this thing was none of those.

"I've never met you," Shabak said. "Tell me why you have invaded my home and taken my son."

"I will in my time. First, let me say that you have never met me, but you know my name. I am Black Water."

Recognition came to Shabak, and it was as if he had woken from sleep to find a great spider clinging to his face. He did know this thing. *All-Father have mercy.*

"My father is long dead," Shabak growled. "You cannot want anything with me."

"But I do," said Black Water. Shabak heard a clattering as the thing shifted. "That's why I have brought you here, through the boy. I will kill you, Shabak."

Shabak didn't fail to notice the certainty in its voice. "Then why not take me now?"

Again Black Water shifted. "I am old, Shabak, older than you. I would prefer to fight you without weapons. You can have your son. Take him now, for he is not my prey. But swear to me that you will return to this cave without so much as a stone to strike me with, or I will kill him."

Drace started to speak, but his voice trailed off into a gurgle. It was hard to think, with Black Water's stench so close by. Shabak wouldn't know where to send an arrow in this darkness, and he couldn't be sure that one arrow anywhere would be enough to kill this monster.

"You truly have no interest in Drace? You will let him go free?"

"Yes."

Shabak knew that Black Water would not lie unless he thought it essential. He nodded in the darkness. "Then I swear by the Granite Throne of Ocean's Heart that I will return in an hour with nothing but what the All-Father has given me."

"Done."

Shabak heard a loud skittering as Black Water withdrew deeper into the cave. Drace collapsed upon floor of the cave, groaning. Shabak dove forward to kneel by his son.

"Can you walk?" he asked.

Drace levered himself up on his arms, shook for a moment with the effort, and then dropped back down. "I'm sick," he muttered. "Thing smells."

"Don't curse," Shabak said, slinging his bow over one arm. He knew that Black Water still watched them from the rear of the cave, but he didn't fear the creature yet. It knew that Shabak's oath bound him tighter than any chains.

Shabak bent down and lifted Drace onto his shoulders. At fifteen years, he stood a foot taller than Shabak, but the kabrisk had little difficulty hauling the boy out into the weak daylight. A drizzle had begun to fall while Shabak was in the cave, making every rock slick with moisture and allowing a deeper chill to settle in the air. Shabak entered the inlet at the mouth of the cave, placing each step carefully. Drace's feet dangled in the water.

After a few minutes, the boy recovered enough strength to walk with one arm around Shabak's shoulders. For over a quarter of an hour the two made their way south toward Shabak's cave. At last, Shabak stopped. "Are you feeling better?"

Drace nodded. Shabak saw with a pang that his golden hair and bronze face were filthy, as if Black Water had dragged the boy through sand along the way. Shabak eased his son down against a boulder. "Are you hungry? Thirsty?"

"I had just finished eating when the monster came," Drace gasped. "I'm fine. I'm sorry…I'm sorry I couldn't kill it. Managed to get a little blood out before it took me, though."

"I'm proud of that," Shabak said. "Black Water is an opponent far beyond you."

Drace snorted. "I've killed many men."

"You know that Black Water is no man."

The boy shivered and lowered his head. "What is it? It stinks, and its tentacles...its tentacles feel like ice, and the way it moves..."

Shabak sat down beside his son and gently laid his closed pincer on Drace's shoulder. "I'll tell you. You should know, because when I leave you, I may not return."

"They don't call you the Stone of Masmok Hill for nothing, Shabak," Drace said with a tinge of his usual sarcasm.

Shabak closed his eyes. The darkness behind his lids swirled like the ocean in a storm, and he remembered his father, and the stories Orak had told him, both light and dark, during his childhood on the island of Ocean's Heart. He remembered the specter that had haunted his father for years, the evil that Orak had helped create.

Shabak began to speak, eyes still shut. "My father lived in his prime more than two hundred years ago when the human empire of Amost was decaying and the world of men was growing increasingly lawless, as tribes of savage men came from north and south to take lands that the Amostian legions could no longer defend. Even the kivashar from the Waste beyond the Icicles made some raids on the Northlands. The city of Amost itself was riven by squabbling between contenders for the throne, and the empire fell into pieces.

"These were hard times for kabrisks. My people had lived on Ocean's Heart since the earliest Days of Ancients, but they had made peace with the Amostian empire for most of its existence. However, two hundred years ago, a new emperor named Dogaius took the throne in Amost, and he was hungry for new conquests that he hoped would rally his broken empire. He planned to sail against Ocean's Heart with whatever legions or auxiliaries would still follow him crammed into the last of his triremes."

Shabak opened his eyes and looked out over the Green Sea. Somewhere, far to the east, Ocean's Heart lay among the waves, and the king still sat upon his Granite Throne.

"The kabrisks were weak then. Many of our warriors had been slaughtered in a battle against a pirate fleet. The king said we... kabrisks...would fight the Amostians with all we had, and that we would win. But many of the Granite Lords were fearful. Some fled Ocean's Heart to take refuge elsewhere. Others readied their warriors for battle. One chose a darker path: Kriskal, my father's lord. He thought of a terrible plan to create something that would kill Emperor Dogaius and turn back the invasion. He turned to an ancient text scribed on tablets of bone by the kabrisk sorcerer Gothrak many centuries earlier. Kriskal found a spell that would allow him to create a dark creature, a monster from the Days of Death. He gathered together other kabrisks to aid him, including my father, one of his greatest warriors. Together they conducted a dark ritual, each offering their blood for the creature's strength, and they created Black Water.

"But it wouldn't obey their commands. It killed Kriskal and the others were forced to flee. My father managed to escape and warn the king's mages, who succeeded in banishing Black Water from Ocean's Heart. My father never recovered from his guilt…and of the fear of the thing that now walked the world, seeking kabrisk blood. He warned me of it when I left Ocean's Heart for the lands of men, and now it has found me. Because it never killed my father, it will take vengeance on me in his place."

"You really think this Black Water can kill you?"

"Perhaps."

"Then you'd be stupid to return. Get help from Lord Traver, or Haeglo — enough spears, and you can kill even a dragon."

"Silence! My word is my bond," Shabak growled. "And Black Water has no interest in humans. He came for me."

The kabrisk stood. "I must go now. If I don't return, go to Stamfir and find work. It would be better to settle down with a craft and a wife than to live as a warrior, but I won't command you. Remember everything I've taught you."

Shabak dropped his bow and quiver down on the sand, then threw his mace and dagger beside them. He stood. Thirst burned at the back of his throat, but there was no way to quench it in the little time he had left.

"Wait," Drace said. "Didn't Dogaius invade?"

Shabak shook his head. "No. His commanders conspired against him and murdered him on the night before the fleet sailed. Kriskal's crime was pointless, in the end.

"Farewell, my son," he said, turning away.

Shabak left Drace still resting against the rock and made his way back to the cave where Black Water waited.

Before reaching the cave, Shabak removed even the sturdy cloth that covered his loins to completely fulfill the terms of his oath. He went to battle stripped of all but those things which his nature granted him. Shabak knew there was great strength in his arms — he had snapped chains and battered down doors that humans couldn't budge — and he was heavy enough to knock down a horse. He also knew that Black Water was powerful, although it had rebelled before Kriskal had finished its gestation and strengthening.

The sulfuric stench returned to Shabak's nostrils as he looked out over the little inlet. He waded in and slapped his broad tail on the water's surface.

"Black Water!" he roared. "I have returned."

"Good, Shabak son of Orak. Good," came the monster's voice.

The first thing Shabak saw of Black Water was a sinuous black tentacle that reached out into the drizzle as if testing it for poison. Then, Shabak heard a clattering upon stone, and the monster emerged into the light.

Six legs supported it, three on each side, shaped roughly like those of a crab, but strangely warped so that none looked exactly like any other. The armor that sheathed them was a deep violet color mottled with black and the darkest of greens. The body itself was a mass of flesh covered with chitin plates, no two of which were the same shape or fit with the others in the same way. Gaping holes showed gnarled flesh beneath, and writhing tentacles sprouted from the cracks to lick obscenely at the air. Some of them were withered, dangling limply over the monster's sides. Two grotesquely mismatched pincers with blades like executioner's axes sprouted just below its face.

Shabak's eyes locked with Black Water's. They were dark with rims of purest gold, set in deep holes within the monster's face, one slightly higher than the other. Beneath them yawned a mouth of saw-edged teeth set in rotten black gums from which a pair of tongues emerged to taste the air. Shabak shuddered to look upon it. Black Water was the size of a small ship, large enough to fill the main chamber of Shabak's cave and more.

It spoke, both tongues slapping against each other inside its mouth. "As you see, Kriskal was not skilled in his work…he made me poorly."

"Aren't you going to kill me?" Shabak asked.

"First, I'd like to know who the boy is. Why does Shabak, champion among kabrisks, raise a human child?"

"Because I choose to."

"No answer. Tell me why."

"Because his father died in a battle I fought in."

Black Water's tentacles entangled themselves with each other in complex knots that somehow chilled Shabak to his marrow. "Ah…and this father…was he perhaps the Amostian, Valedarius?"

"How do you know that?"

"I know many things, Shabak. I know that you led an army of peasants against Valedarius' legion at the battle of Masmok Hill, and I know that you defeated him, killing Valedarius himself in single combat. So you took his life, and then you took his son."

"What do you mean?" Shabak growled. Black Water's odor made him lightheaded.

"You couldn't be content to kill a man who opposed you. You also had to corrupt his legacy."

Shabak ground his teeth together. "I have raised Drace to be a good man."

"A man loyal to Ancients, not his own people. Look upon me, Shabak, and see what Ancients have done. Kriskal and Orak made me to kill humans. In the Days of Ancients, the raothi of Salathran and the kivashar of Lokhor broke the world between them and ravaged it with their sorceries. Humans were nothing more than slaves to build their monuments…or grace their tables."

Black Water advanced slowly, with a lurching gait that made his whole body sway. "I am of you, Shabak. But for the hunger of Ancients for power, but for your desire to crush humans beneath you, I wouldn't blight the world."

Shabak curled his hands into fists. "I kept the people of Wenthal from tyranny when I led them against Valedarius."

"Valedarius, the Amostian, who might have brought order to the Northlands. Valedarius, who opposed the will of Ancients."

"He tortured to death every kabrisk he caught. Few of us remain in the Northlands because of him."

Black Water's mouth seemed to turn in on itself, sucking its own tongues. Then it said, "So you killed him. And how many humans died in the war? Humans who now live in savagery when they might have lived in peace beneath some vestige of Amostian order?"

"Valedarius was a murderous tyrant."

"But who gave you any right to decide who would rule the humans? Who granted you guardianship of his son? Who gave you power to rule the men of Jothornis, those hundred years ago?"

Shabak kept his expression fixed, but the monster's words slipped under his carapace and wormed into his heart like biting flies. He remembered clearly how twisted Valedarius had been, and knew that the people of Jothornis had accepted his rule freely. But the crimes of the Ancients were many…and Black Water himself had been made in an attempt by Ancients to harness black powers in their wars against humans.

Shabak began to walk forward, laying each foot down carefully. "Enough talk."

"I am old, Shabak. When I have killed you, my work will be finished, and I will be able to die at last."

Black Water skittered forward, splashing into the water and swinging its many tentacles in twisted arcs. Its two great pincers snapped at the air.

Shabak met it in the center of the inlet, up to his waist in brackish water. He ducked beneath the slashing pincers, immersing himself in salty water for a moment, and used his legs to drive himself up at its underside, both fists extended to punch. He swung his pincer and hooked it into a patch of soft flesh while his fists hammered at chitin. The stench filled his nostrils so thickly it felt like liquid, but Shabak ignored it. His armored fists cracked against the carapace of Black Water's underside.

But the monster had tentacles below as well as above, and they whipped out to snatch his limbs and force them away. Drace had been right — they felt like bands of liquid ice as they licked over his armor, and they were strong. Then the stinking bulk of flesh and armor above him crashed down, pressing him into the water with terrible weight. Shabak threw himself back and thrashed away from Black Water's body, but he felt himself crushed down until his carapace scraped the rocks and rough sand of the bottom. He pushed up with all his strength and struggled with legs and tail to force himself away. Black Water's tentacles gripped him, but his strength was sufficient to break their hold. He thrashed beneath Black Water's bulk and emerged at last into open water.

Shabak came up, shaking water out of his eyes, and leapt back barely in time to avoid a beheading sweep from one of the monster's pincers. "How long can you fight me, Shabak?" it hissed. "Your blows are like the bites of gnats to me."

Shabak backed away from it, moving toward deeper water. More water would increase his advantage in maneuverability.

Again, Black Water charged, white water spraying up around it as it reached its pincers out to crush and slash. The longer tentacles at its front groped towards Shabak. He reached out with his hands as Black Water's pincers swung and managed to grab one of them just above the wrist. Tentacles snapped at his face, trying to pry out his eyes and get around his neck, but he warded them off with his own pincer and his fangs while he worked his fingers into the cracks of the pincer's armor and pulled on it, bracing his feet in the muck of the bottom. Muscles bulged beneath Shabak's carapace, and Black Water screamed in pain. One of its tentacles wrapped around Shabak's neck and squeezed at his windpipe, cutting off air. He pulled, feeling tendons and muscles within Black Water's arm stretch to their limits.

Black Water moved sideways like the crab he resembled, and suddenly Shabak found hundreds of pounds of warped chitin, muscle, and stinking flesh ploughing into him even as the monster's cold tentacles held him in place. Shabak released the pincer and struggled to stay ahead of Black Water's rush, tearing at the tentacles grasping him with his hands and pincer. Black blood spattered onto him, clouding his mind with its hot stink.

Then, instead of retreating further, Shabak reversed his course and charged to meet Black Water's advance. One of the monster's thickly armored legs punched his chest, cracking the carapace and drawing a splash of Shabak's red blood. Then Shabak clambered up onto Black Water's back, digging his fingers into every spot of soft flesh in its ill-fitted plates. He snapped his pincer at tentacles that seemed as numerous as hairs upon a human's head. He found a larger patch of exposed flesh that had once sprouted a tentacle, braced himself with his hands, and sank his fangs deep into it.

A single taste of Black Water's blood had been enough to sicken him. Now a fountain of it gushed into his mouth, plunging his tongue into a burning hell as he fought not to swallow or release his hold; fought instead to work his fangs deeper into the monster's flesh, striving to open a wound into whatever diseased organs filled its body. Icy tentacles pulled at him, but Shabak clung on with all his strength even when a pair of them found his neck and squeezed until his airflow was cut off entirely and the blood vessels deep in his neck were constricted. But kabrisks were made for water, and Shabak could go without air far longer than any human. He kept his hold and Black Water writhed. Shabak's stomach heaved, trying to eject its contents, but Black Water's grip blocked the upsurge of half-digested meat and bile.

At last, he could tolerate no more. He tore his fangs loose, spitting and snarling. His jaws had dug a black pit in the monster's flesh. He fought the pulling tentacles to raise an arm, then forced his hand into the wound he had created, digging through muscle and burning black blood. The lingering taste was so horrible his mouth seemed to have withered to ash. Shabak struggled harder and harder to keep his hold even as he felt the meat of Black Water's insides and tore at it with his armored hand.

The monster gave one last heave with both tentacles and body and pulled Shabak free. The writhing tentacles lifted him into the air even as the two around his throat continued to squeeze. Shabak began to feel the need for air, and he pulled at the bonds of ice gripping his throat, struggling to loosen them. He managed to pull one up within range of his fangs. The flesh was lithe with muscle, but he gripped it with all the strength of his jaws as that blood, like bile from a dragon's liver, filled his mouth once again. His teeth met in its center and the tentacle went limp. Shabak's pincer hacked at the other, nearly severing it, and at last he dropped and struck the water of the inlet. Shabak opened his mouth, letting the salty water scour his mouth clean of Black Water's blood. Then he came up, neck high in water, and drew air into his lungs. His throat ached with bruises and seared with the pain of his stomach erupting its contents.

Black Water had retreated a few feet, but now it advanced on Shabak again, clacking its pincers. "You are strong, Shabak. The last kabrisk I slew succumbed quickly, and few can endure my blood."

Shabak felt strangely leaden in all his limbs, and his carapace seemed to burn where blood had smeared it. *Was the monster's blood poison, and had he just ingested his death?*

"No," Black Water continued, "it won't kill you. But it might make you easier prey."

"Why all the talk?" Shabak gasped, blinking water from his eyes. "Didn't you come to kill me?"

"I want to savor you, Shabak. You'll probably be my last. I don't have many years left in my body. Kriskal made me poorly, may darkness take his soul. May darkness take all you kabrisks, toying with the lives of humans and seeking to dominate them with sorcery."

Had all his work for humans been nothing more than an attempt to maintain the power of Ancients? Shabak knew that the crimes of kabrisks and other Ancients were many. He had once seen a kabrisk warrior kill an entire family for the bad food they had given him. His father had told him tales of the Days of Ancients, when primitive humans had been hunted down and enslaved by kabrisks, raothi, and kivashar.

But Shabak had fought for the humans, against tyrants who would seek to enslave them…and he knew, deep in his heart, that he had raised Drace not from any lust for power, but because the baby had been helpless, still bloody from the womb as his mother lay dying. Shabak remembered clearly the first time he had held his son in his arms and the boy had smiled up at the harsh chitin features of his face.

And that son still lived, growing into a man. And he still needed Shabak. Other men needed Shabak. Many times, the weak and the small had called upon him to defend them from rogues and oppressors. There was much good yet for him to do. He couldn't die in this battle.

Shabak moved further out into the sea until the stone vanished beneath his feet and he treaded water to keep his head up. Black Water advanced on him until only a few whipping tentacles showed above the waves. The kabrisk filled his lungs with cold air, straining his aching throat, and submerged himself in the water. Through the green waters of Talon Point, Black Water looked not so much a tangible being as a dread ghost of past crimes. In many ways his form was like that of a kabrisk, but terribly warped and mangled. Shabak saw something of himself in those burning black and gold eyes. Black Water had led a long life filled with violence and pain. The kabrisks — and Shabak's father — were responsible for that.

But as Shabak swam to meet it, he did not think of Orak his father, the crimes of his ancestors, or any of the evils done by Ancients. He thought of Drace — Drace, an infant who demanded food nearly every hour; Drace, a toddler just learning how to mend nets and clean fish; Drace, a boy setting out in their little boat to fish on his own; and Drace, a young man, tall, strong, and brave. Shabak had raised him well, but he knew that the boy still needed him — had needed him from the day of his birth. He was truly Drace's father.

Black Water's pincers shot out and snapped at Shabak's carapace. The kabrisk swerved around them, propelling himself through the frigid water with legs and tail, and went for Black Water's throat, only half-concealed by plates of twisted chitin. The monster backpedaled and Shabak felt a great pincer close upon his right shoulder, snapping through his exoskeleton and slicing away a chunk of the underlying flesh. He surged forward, ducked under the beast's maw, and seized Black Water's underside in his hands as he braced his feet against the bottom. Tentacles coiled around him, squeezing and tugging. Black Water's pincers couldn't come near enough to close over him, but their blunt ends beat at his back, hammering on his armor.

Shabak opened his mouth, releasing a flood of air bubbles, and stretched his fangs up towards a patch of exposed throat. Bitter salt water filled his mouth. He sank his fangs into rubbery, greasy flesh and felt the hellish taste of Black Water's blood once again. Shabak's senses recoiled from the agony of that flavor, but he thought of Drace, and drowning out all his revulsion, he bit for Black Water's throat. His teeth met and he pulled away a chunk of flesh. He had lost too much of his air, but there was no way to refill his lungs with Black Water's tentacles holding him. Shabak could only bite again, gnawing deeper into Black Water's noxious flesh. He closed his eyes to the water filled with stinging blood.

Black Water roared and thrashed. Its tentacles squeezed at him so hard his carapace began to crack, and its hammering pincers opened wounds in Shabak's back. Shabak reached both hands and his pincer into the growing wound even as he pushed himself up from the bottom with his feet, digging deeper and deeper.

A racking shudder went through Black Water's entire body, and Shabak felt the tentacles weaken for a moment before they squeezed again, harder than ever. Shabak clung on even as his own blood misted the water. His whole body ached and his joints popped as Black Water pulled at him with the strength of desperation. The monster kicked wildly at the seabed with its legs, throwing up clouds of silt as it tried to pull away from Shabak's grip. All sensation besides pain vanished until Shabak could barely tell if he felt his own or Black Water's pain.

Dimly, he felt his gnawing teeth and tearing hands come into an open space. He had torn into Black Water's throat. The beast roiled. Massive strength pounded at Shabak's body, further cracking chitin and pummeling the naked flesh beneath. He felt ribs crack as pincers smashed into him again and again. The water around him was black as night. He felt his lungs heave and knew that he was drowning.

Shabak forced himself up from the bottom, straining with arms, legs, and tail, surrounded by a column of black blood. He felt his head break the surface, felt cold air rush into his throat, just moments before darkness choked away his consciousness and the water came up around him once more.

Shabak woke with cold water up to his waist, sand beneath him, and a cold rock against his back. His body ached as if a landslide had passed over it, and he could see his blood staining the water around him. His eyes stung horribly, but he forced them wide and looked out over the Green Sea. He saw no sign of Black Water.

Something splashed off to his right, and Shabak snapped his head around, searching for his foe. Instead, he saw his golden haired son coming toward him with a handful of gray clams. The boy's chest was bare, and Shabak realized that his worst wounds were bound with strips of cloth from Drace's tunic.

The boy knelt in the water beside the kabrisk and held out the clams. "Hungry?"

"No," Shabak croaked. His throat burned, and the horrible taste of the monster's blood lingered in his mouth. "But I'll eat."

Drace drew his knife, pried the clams open, tore out their gray meat, and offered it to Shabak. Chewing and swallowing was painful, but Shabak forced himself to eat nonetheless.

"Are you feeling better?" Shabak asked.

Drace nodded. "Once I got away from the smell, it hadn't hurt me too much. But you're badly cracked up. What did you do, hug it to death?"

Shabak closed his eyes and groaned. The salty seawater, bound over his wounds by the makeshift bandages, only magnified his pain. "Black Water is dead."

"Were you planning to eat him? He looked a bit like a crab."

The very thought nearly made Shabak retch up what little his stomach contained. He saw his son's smile. "I just hope he doesn't poison the crabs and fish," Shabak said.

"Hm," Drace grunted. "Can you walk back to the cave?"

"A few more minutes," Shabak said, closing his eyes and slumping down against the stone. Before he went to sleep, however, a question came into his mind.

"Drace, didn't you go back when I told you to?"

"No. I watched the fight, and when you came up for air the last time, I swam out after you and brought you to shore. Nearly broke my arms — you're heavy, even in water."

Shabak smiled gently. Drace might need him, but sometimes it was easy to forget how much he needed his son. He wouldn't be well enough to trap and fish for several days, but he knew that Drace could work hard enough to feed both of them. Shabak had trained his son well.

Still, something worrisome occurred to Shabak. "Drace," he asked, "did you hear what I said to Black Water?"

The boy shook his head. "I came just as the two of you were starting to fight."

Shabak sighed. So the boy hadn't overhead his father's identity. Good.

Drace crouched on a rock at his side and contentment warmed Shabak's heart as he allowed sleep to creep over him. With his last thought, he thanked the All-Father for today's victory and for his son.

Rob Mancebo is a husband of 30 years and father of four. Whether standing guard on the German border during the cold war, repairing video and alarm systems for a defense contractor, quelling riots in LA, or just working as a guard at a local retail store, he always seems to end up in some facet of security. He's had stories published in Electronic Tales, Amazing Journeys Magazine, Cyberpulp, Ray Gun Revival, Flashing Swords, Spacewesterns, *and* Alienskin. *He also edits for Cyberwizard Productions and his personal website at www.geocities.com/robmancebo has more stories and information. Rob possesses an amazing ability to create a complete tale that requires little effort from an editor within days. What follows is actually Rob's third attempt at cracking the* Rage of the Behemoth *lineup. Both of the previous submissions were excellent tales that simply did not meet my vision of the anthology's theme. Third time was the charm however, and I believe every reader will be glad that Rob did not lose interest. As is often the case, things aren't always what they seem...even the larger-than-life things that seem insurmountable. A burst of ingenuity at the right time can deflect even a behemoth.*

Passion of the Stormlord

A Tale of the Seas

by Robert A. Mancebo

"Make haste to furl the sail!" Asad al Din bellowed into the raging wind. His crew of Nabataean sailors struggled to haul down the billowing cloud of striped silk, but the power of the wind threatened to drag them off the ship's wooden deck.

"The might of the storm is too great, Captain!" Jalil called back. "It will cast the crew into the sea!"

"Ease off the main sheet, you great lout!" Asad al Din roared as the knotted muscles of his arms and shoulders heaved against the sweeping tiller, keeping the ship's nose pointed into the crashing waves. "Carefully now, carefully!"

Three men dragging mightily eased the sodden line through a tackle, allowing the great triangular sail to release its hold upon the storm winds and flap wildly. That done, the rest of the sailors lowered the boom and bound the loose sail.

"We make great speed, even with a bare mast," Jalil called. "Surely this passing tempest is the retribution of Allah!"

"Ha!" Asad al Din scoffed loudly. "The retribution of Allah is swift, but only against the unrighteous. This is but a storm in the season for storms."

"There is a fell voice echoing in the sky," Jalil warned. "And I have glimpsed the dark bulk of a monster within the clouds. I fear this is no earthly tempest."

"Bah, save your tales of monsters for the children in the bazaar," his captain replied. "For this is no more than a quick squall. I see the clouds clearing ahead. We'll be free of this storm yet."

"Ship ahoy!" Saqr, who watched the ocean from the *Rasha's* bow, called back.

Already the storm winds were quieting and it was easier to make out the men's voices across the deck.

"I see no masts," Asad al Din called forward. "Is she a derelict?"

"Nay, captain, her masts are snapped, but I think I see a man upon her deck."

"Jalil, take the tiller," Asad al Din ordered. "I would see this ship."

With his first mate at the helm, Asad al Din strode forward, bare feet gripping the rain-slick deck. He rested a firm hand upon the curving dagger thrust through his bright, silken sash, loosening it for any coming action. The white caps of the waves were calming and the *Rasha*'s sleek bow made easy work of traveling through the churning sea.

They approached, but not too close lest the churning sea slam the hulls together and wreck both ships. The crippled vessel had been a good ship, a powerful trading galley. Now her masts dangled by their rigging, sagging alongside her starboard rail and pulling her midsection within reach of the waves. A single man — near naked, shirt and turban lost, his dark hair dripping with rain and spray — strode her listing deck.

The *Rasha's* crew could see the cold fire of madness burning in his eyes. The man stalked back and forth along the rail like one preparing to jump, unable to decide where.

"Where is your crew?" Asad al Din called to the man. "Will you come over? We can cast you a line."

"My crew is dead and I am damned," the other man called back. "I make this my final farewell to life, may Allah be merciful." He drew back his arm and tossed an object in a high arc to land upon the *Rasha's* deck.

"What is it?" Asad al Din called back.

"It is the wealth of the world!" The sailor shouted across the gap widening between their ships. "Allah grant that she serve you better than she has served me!"

Curious, Asad al Din crossed the rolling deck and picked up an engraved brass bottle from where it had jammed into a coil of line.

"Run now, Nabataean," the man shouted wildly. "Raise your sails and run for the coast, for *he* will pursue with storm and thunder!"

"Whatever is the madman shouting about?" Asad al Din mumbled, looking at the bottle. "Surely the man is mad for such a little thing to cause such great concern."

He heard Saqr gasp."Mercy of Allah!"

When he looked up, the ocean was empty save for the churning waves that washed across the endless expanse sending up spray to blow in the wind.

"Where did the ship go?"

"It went under, Captain," Saqr called to him. "A rogue wave simply tipped it over and it sank like a stone.

"Allah be merciful," Asad al Din said with a bowing of his head.

"What did the fellow throw across to us?" Mundhir, one of the other sailors asked eagerly.

"Yes," Saqr, said. "What did the mad one think the wealth of the world is that it would fit into a small bottle?"

Asad al Din looked to the wondrous craftsmanship of the small vessel he held. Etched bird of paradise figures flowed around enameled panels and settings of pearls and small, faceted stones of aqua.

"Some exotic perfume of India, blended to turn an old sheik's withered passion to fire, no doubt," he told his men.

"Take care not to spill any upon Hamzah then," Saqr warned and pushed the crewman's shoulder playfully, "or we'll have trouble in port!"

The rest of the men laughed coarsely, and little Hamzah snorted at his loss of dignity.

Asad al Din pulled at the figured metal stopper. Instead of the gentle wafting of perfume, a great explosion of brimstone made the gathered crew choke and cough.

Upon the deck before them knelt a young woman. Silks of azure and saffron stitched and patterned with silver thread draped her in the filmiest of veils. A twining gold band restrained her headscarf and when she raised her hands to Asad al Din in supplication, they saw that her nails were unnaturally long and painted with shining gold to match the polished manacles that encircled her wrists.

In an uncanny whisper that somehow roared above the subsiding storm and sea she asked, "How may this one serve, Master?"

"Allah protect us," Saqr exclaimed. "It is a Djinn!"

The astonished sailors snapped their fingers and made signs against evil.

"Truly," she answered without raising her head. "This one is Wasimah, princess of the desert Djinn, slave to the holder of Sülyman Pasha's seal. What power or riches does my new master command?"

When Asad al Din would've spoken, Fakih, the eldest of the crew stopped him with a curt gesture and a warning. "Beware, Captain, the Djinn are servants of the corrupter. No good will come of any wealth offered by their hands. You saw her previous master! Save us all by throwing the bottle into the sea!"

The kneeling figure dropped her outstretched arms, and her low laughter held the sting of poison in it.

When she raised her face, they found it was perfectly formed with dark, daintily painted lashes and full, ruby lips. Yet her eyes, Asad al Din saw, were empty and haunted.

"The old man is wise," she told him. "For though this one has granted many gifts throughout many ages of the world, seldom have they given happiness."

"Creature of the devil!" Fakih accused.

"This one is no child of the fallen," she replied. "This one sprang from the loins of Lilith, before the creation of Eve, mother of humankind.

"That the son's of Adam command this one to deliver unto them powers and treasures that are their downfall is the choice of humanity, not any corruption of the Djinn."

"What are the terms of your service?" Asad al Din asked thoughtfully.

"One wish, my master, one wish and then my ownership must be passed to another."

"Wish for a shipload of gold!" one man suggested.

"Or of frankincense!" said another.

"Wish for a palace—no," another stuttered, "Wish to be the Pasha of Persia!"

"All these things are simply done," the Djinn assured the men. "Each man may have all his heart desires. Such is this one's power."

"And what will happen," Asad al Din interrupted their elation, "if these wishes be granted?"

"This ship already has a full hold," she replied. "Were this one to grant a shipful of gold, this *fulk* would sink and you should all drown. A shipload of frankincense would do the same. Were this one to make one of your men the Pasha of Persia, he would be a lord without friends or supporters, quickly murdered and replaced by a man with more political power."

The sailors murmured at her answer. Asad al Din waved down their mutterings and told them, "See my friends, we must be cautious with our wishes."

"Cautious," she agreed, but then added, "and hasty."

"Hasty?"

"Yes, for the Stormlord Azim, Prince of the desert Djinn, follows close upon this one's path as he has for all these centuries of imprisonment. He shall send storms and waves to crush you.

"For it is the nature of this one's prison to be found by men, and it is his will that it be quickly lost again."

"Then it was his wrath that crushed the last ship?" Fakih accused.

"And many more before it," she admitted.

"We are far from land," Saqr said. "Yet perhaps we can make a run for the coast."

"If that is your will," she said with a nod. "You may try."

"Or we could wish him away!" Asad al Din suggested.

"Nay," Wasimah told them. "Earthly gifts are within this one's power. Yet Lord Azim is this one's husband and no power to withstand his wrath abides in this one's hands."

"Why does he follow?" Fakih asked.

"The world has changed about us," she said. "He awaits this one's release from bondage."

"How then, if we release you?" This from Asad al Din.

"Then this one and her lord shall take out their revenge upon mankind for subjugating our people!" she snapped, and fire shown in her eyes. "We shall harry the earth with storm, wind, and wave until nothing lives within our reach!"

"You are a bitter spirit," Fakih told her sadly.

"Bitterness distilled from the rancor of centuries of imprisonment and slavery, aye," she spat. "Were these binding chains loosed from this one's wrists, she would rend this ship as a farmer shucks an ear of Egyptian corn." She stood and her golden nails clashed as her fingers convulsed with frustrated passion.

"Dogs and sons of dogs," Asad al Din bellowed, breaking the spell of horror that had mesmerized his crew. "Are you all going to wait for this cataclysm to pour out upon your miserable heads? Raise the sail and let us run before this arch Djinn lest the surging sea drink our bones!"

With her sails raised, the *Rasha* ran before the fringe of the storm like the gazelle she was named for. The clouds boiled and the storm winds lashed at their stern, but the *fulk* coursed on through the sea.

"I see him!" Fakih shouted and pointed back at the pursuing maelstrom. "There, in the clouds!"

"A tale for the children in the bazaar indeed," Asad al Din said with wonder. As lightning flashed, they could all perceive the shadowy figure that seemed to be driving black clouds like a chariot drawn by plunging stallions. Below the giant figure a dark waterspout rose from the sea like a monstrous pillar of rippling death.

Slowly, ever so slowly, the storm overtook them. Rains and wind battered the ship, and the frightened sailors could clearly see the Djinn lord driving the clouds while the ravaging shadow of the huge water-spout rushed ever closer.

"He is gaining!" Hamzah warned them.

"Lighten the load!" Asad al Din ordered. "Cast away all but our water and weapons!"

The crew made a human chain and hoisted bail, tub, and casket from the ship's creaking hold to pitch them overboard. Yet even then the Djinn drew closer, rearing up like a mountaintop above the clouds, his naked chest shining with rain, and his bearded face set in a snarl of determination and wrath.

"Only the fastest ship ever to sail the sea might hope to keep ahead of Azim," Wasimah told them with a cruel laugh.

"Captain," Hamzah sallied. "Perhaps a small wish to help." He took the seal from Asad al Din's hand, closed his eyes and said, "I wish our ship, the *Rasha*, was the fastest ship in the world!"

A jolt ran through the ship making its timbers quiver and the deck lurch beneath their feet as its speed redoubled.

"A wise choice," Fakih lauded his shipmate's wish.

"Aye, now we'll keep ahead of the stormlord's wrath," Hamzah said.

"We shall see," Asad al Din answered, and watched with measuring eye the form of the raging Djinn slipping further behind.

The *Rasha* pulled away from the center of the storm at wondrous speed and the crew cheered. Yet still were they driven by the wind. No matter how fast their ship, they could not escape the unnatural storm entirely, only run before it.

Soon came Mundhir, rushing to his captain and shouting, "Water in the hold! The stitching is being torn asunder. We're sinking!"

"A trick!" Asad al Din accused Wasimah.

"No trick," she replied coldly. "The wish was fairly granted. Speed is not in the strength of a ship's hull."

As they took on water, the *Rasha* bogged down and the rippling black waterspout roared closer behind them. In the churning clouds above, they could see Azim's savage smile as a taloned hand greater than a spreading forest oak reached down to rend them.

"Fetch me my sword!" Asad al Din ordered.

"You cannot fight this prince of the Djinn, Captain!" Fakih screamed.

"Better to die fighting than as slaughtered lambs!"

Mundhir took hold of the seal and shouted, "I wish the *Rasha* be sealed against the sea and unsinkable!"

Wasimah bowed her head and suddenly the ship floated high once again, breasting the waves lightly. The roaring wrath of the frustrated Djinn in the clouds was terrible to hear and fierce lightning split the heavens as they pulled away from his grasping hand.

Yet soon after, the bright sail began to rip in the storm and they slowed, easing back toward the crushing grasp of the Lord of Storms. Another man wished the sail untearable. Then the mast began to splinter under the strain…the rigging to fray…

Each time they were slowed and brought near to the power of Azim's terrible wrath. One-by-one the crew was forced to pass on the seal and use up their wishes to keep ahead of the pursuing Djinn until only Asad al Din's wish remained.

And then the black sorcery began.

"There's something floating in the water ahead," Saqr called from the bow. "It's—it's a corpse!"

Jalil swept the tiller to avoid it, but Saqr called again, "There's another one—and another!" They felt a thump as the *Rasha* struck something yielding in the water.

The crew ran to the rail in time to see boney fingers scraping and scrabbling to catch hold of the ship's sides.

"Allah be merciful," Fakih prayed. "The sea is giving up its lowly dead! They seek to board!"

"Gather swords and spears," Asad al Din ordered. "Repel boarders!"

The men broke from the spell of horror to arm themselves and hack and beat the collecting corpses from the ship's rails.

"They are gathering even as we travel," Jalil called desperately. "Soon there will be too many to drive back! They will load down the ship and the Djinn will catch us!"

"Captain, use your wish to fend off this deathless pestilence!" Fakih begged, for the sea's dead were loathsome and ghastly of aspect.

"Only to be overwhelmed by the next trick?" Jalil demanded as he drew his scimitar and cut the head off a hideous bloated corpse that sought to crawl over the rail. "This is an endless nightmare of evil!"

Wasimah laughed in dark amusement at their quandary. "Yes, next he shall call against you the sharks and whales of the deep, or perhaps calm the wind and leave your fast ship in eternal doldrums while you starve unto death."

"I should cut your misleading throat!" Jalil threatened.

At that, she laughed again. "The weapons of humanity have no power over the Djinn."

"Wish her human, Captain, that we might revenge ourselves before we perish!" Saqr suggested while he cut off the fingers of a clinging corpse with his sword.

"Aye, let these cursed corpses tear at her flesh as well as our own!" little Hamzah agreed, backing away from the unstoppable wave of crawling corpses that scrabbled over the rail.

At that Asad al Din saw a shadow of fear awaken in Wasimah's dark eyes.

"That is within your power, is it not?" he demanded of her.

She began to answer but, before she could lie, he held before her the imprisoning seal of the great Sülyman Pasha, King of the Hebrews and scourge of all the Djinn and demons of the desert.

She lowered her eyes and admitted through clenched teeth, "It is within this one's power."

"We could rid the world of a great evil by killing you," Asad al Din told her with a threatening sweep of his sword.

"This one," she replied bitterly, "who has suffered centuries of imprisonment and slavery at the hands of the sons of men, expects no less."

"Kill her!" Jalil shouted as he tried to keep the threatening legion of undead at bay with his swinging sword. "Make her human and let her at least die with us!"

Asad al Din raised her chin with a gentle touch, looked into the dark eyes of the Djinn, and saw what the wise Sülyman Pasha had seen centuries before. Not a monster, but a woman. A fickle woman with very dangerous powers, yet a woman all the same.

In the midst of storm and black sorcery, Asad al Din began to laugh.

"I am Asad al Din," he shouted into the wind. "Lion of the Faith, Nabataean swashbuckler, captain of the seas, traveler of the world. I do not murder or abuse women!

"Hear now my wish, Wasimah, Princess of the desert Djinn." He looked into her confused, questioning eyes. "I wish that you were free—"

At his words the golden manacles fell from her wrists and the golden sheaths fell from her fingernails which became like the claws of a beast. The woman smiled an inhuman smile of blood-lust and passion unleashed as she turned upon the crew to rend them.

"—to do only good throughout the world," he finished.

She turned back with a hiss like a threatening cobra. Her face a mask of violence, her eyes burning with frustrated vengeance.

"It would seem *good* to this one to destroy all men!" she snarled.

"Good in the eyes of men and demons is subjective," he said. "Only in Allah is there truth."

"You are a hard-hearted master," she lowered her claws with a sigh. "You would release this one from the slavery of humanity only to make her a slave to the unyielding will of Allah."

"That is my wish," Asad al Din lowered the tip of his sword to touch the deck next to his foot.

The Djinn waved a hand and a glowing bubble of fire appeared before her. She cast it upon the deck and it burst with a flash of pure light that broke the dark enchantment of Azim. The sea cleared, bloated bodies sinking once more below the waves. Then she stepped off the deck to hover above the white-capped waves.

Raising a slim hand to her lips, she blew a gust of wild wind that carried the unsinkable *Rasha* far out ahead of the storm that had pursued it. The crew grabbed onto lines and the mast to keep from being pitched overboard as the ship bounded wildly over the ocean.

The dark, angry waterspout moved to follow them. Wasimah vanished and a smaller, white waterspout rose and swept playfully, enticingly, across its path. The men watched the dark torrent follow after the light in an awe-inspiring dance of storms sweeping off into the trackless seas.

"It is as I suspected," Asad al Din said as the storm retreated. "She had no power to withstand the wrath of her husband, but she possesses the wiles to entice him."

"If only we could have saved another wish," Hamzah mourned. "We could have had a hold full of gold."

"Bah, Allah has blessed us with health and strong hands." Asad al Din smiled. "If you, sons of dogs, cannot fill the hold of the fastest ship in the world with gold within the year, you are not fit to ship with Asad al Din, captain of the seas!"

Kevin 'Jaqhama' Lumley lives in Sydney, Australia, and writes pulp genre fiction for various webzine, magazine and book publishers. He keeps a personal blog at http://kevin-jaqhama-lumley.blogspot.com, and can be found on numerous online forums such as those at SFReader and Brass Goggles. In addition to adventuring through writing, he is an avid motorcyclist who just so happens to be motoring around Europe with his ladylove as this anthology hits the shelves. Kevin enjoys being involved at all levels of writing and riding, and he is always ready to offer advice, opinion, and information on either. His tale deals with settling debts and honoring friendships, and taking advantage of opportunities to do so no matter the cost…or the size of the problem faced.

The Beast in the Lake

A Tale of Crow Thiefmaster

by Kevin Lumley
& cover art by Johnney Perkins

Now it happened, as I arrived in Creggan, a small town on the edge of the northern Borderlands, that the story started to spread like wildfire amongst the populace.

"The lake Beast has slain Lord Udy's son!"

I stopped a couple who were walking by.

"Excuse me, good sir, m'lady. I heard you speaking of some beast that has killed Lord Udy's son. Might I trouble you to tell me the details?"

And so they did.

Staith, the firstborn, killed by a mysterious creature that haunted the lake, ten years before. Sten, the second son, grown to manhood. Seeking revenge on the beast he had set out to slay it…and was slain in turn. A sad tale indeed. Lord Udy grieved, as well he might.

Putting aside the business that had brought me to Creggan, I hastily resaddled my horse and took the road that led to Uldach Castle. Some years ago Udy had performed a favor on my behalf, at some risk to himself. I was indebted to the man; I always repaid those debts I could. Uldach Castle was less than half a day's ride from Creggan. It gave me time to think.

I arrived at the castle mid-afternoon and was taken to Lord Udy. My friend looked twice as old as when last we had met. The death of his son, Sten, weighed heavily upon him. I offered my condolences. We talked. I mentioned a way I might repay my debt. Reluctantly, Udy accepted my proposal. We agreed I would rest before I spoke more of it.

A servant showed me to a room.

Before resting, I stood upon the wide balcony three stories above the castle grounds. From there I had a panoramic view across the lake. The lake

flowed into a wide river, and that river all the way out to the sea beyond.
From what little I knew of the tales of the Beast, it was said to swim back up the river and thence return to the lake before me once every ten years. I suspected that those who said it returned like a salmon to the place that spawned it spoke true of the fabled monster.

The sun had all but set when finally I closed my eyes. It seemed mere moments later that a knock upon the door awakened me. I rolled off the bed and onto my feet. "Come."

The door opened and a head of tousled hair poked around it. "M'lord Crow. Lord Udy said I should wake you for the main meal in the hall."

"Thank you, lad. I shall be down shortly." I smiled at the youngster.

"Very good, sir." Soft footsteps walked away.

I pulled on my black leather boots — making sure the slim daggers were in place inside them — and my black vest of many pockets. I did not bother to take up my short sword nor my crossbow. There was little chance I would need them here in Castle Uldach.

A guest in the castle once before, I had no trouble locating the great hall. Lord Udy and most of his clansmen were already seated about a long table laden with much food. Good, I was famished. Most of the men were northern clansmen, loyal to, or affiliated with, the Lord of Uldach Castle. The majority wore the colors of the Uldach Clan.

"Ah. Crow. Good of you to join us. Some of my men believe you to be naught but a legend."

I smiled. "I am Crow. Called Thiefmaster. Your Lord did me a great service once. I am here to repay it, if I can."

Those assembled looked at me. One coughed. "I thought you'd be…well…bigger," he said.

There was some laughter. I chuckled myself. I knew they saw a slim, wiry man dressed all in black: knee-length breeks of soft leather, high, flap-topped boots, a shirt of silk beneath my waist length vest. I had left my archers cap in my room, so thus the men could take in my lean face and short cropped blonde hair. And the black patch over my left eye.

Ah, that magical eye of mine. Useless in daylight or any kind of bright light, but when I remove the patch in dim light or darkness I can see as well as any cat, or other night creature. A secret I share only with the man I shave each morning. Doubtless these men expected someone more imposing, having heard the tales associated with my, shall we say, somewhat nefarious activities.

"Judge not the contents of a book by the cover it presents," I told them.

"Here, Crow. Have a seat beside me," said Udy. "Eat what you wish. We make a fine drop of mead hereabouts. Will you have some?"

I accepted a goblet handed me by a servant. Udy was correct; it was good.

"Let's talk whilst we eat, Crow. What say you?"

I nodded. "Who here can tell me of the monster? Who knows best the history of the creature you all refer to as the Beast?"

Lord Udy pointed to an older man with pure white hair. "Arrin here, he knows most of the tales, served my father, he did. And I'll send for Hamesh. The man who escaped the Beast's clutches t'other day." He turned and nodded to a retainer, who hurried off.

"How did he survive?" I asked.

"I understand he swam so fast that onlookers swore he ran atop the water," Lord Udy replied dryly.

"And who can blame the poor man," another pointed out.

Grim nods from those assembled.

"I've heard the tales since I was a boy, but I confess I know not what be truth and what be myth." a man stated.

"I know most of the stories," volunteered Arrin. "I am not the oldest at the castle, but I'm close enough to those who are methinks.

"There have been tales about yon monster here in the lake since before Castle Uldach stood upon these shores. They go back centuries as I know.

"The Beast, the Creature, the Monster…many titles does the thing have. Some stories say how 'tis a sea serpent. But other tales tell that the Beast can walk on land. I well recall one story that had it gobbling up a family from a crofter's hut some way up on the moor. The Beast's footprints have been found around the shores of the lake many times. Every now and again the beastie's tracks have been found in the forest. Four footed they say. The marks of its long tail easily seen, being dragged along behind it. For myself I am not convinced 'tis a sea serpent. I've heard too many tales of the thing swanning around on the surface of the lake, head held well above the water. I don't think a sea serpent or a fish of any kind would be breathing air. Nor would a sea creature be able to roam about the land. Something different is this beastie. Not a fish and not an animal. Mayhap a little of both." The old man stopped and reached for his goblet.

"So it can travel on land as easily as it can swim about in the lake then?" I mused. "Tell us about the creature's looks, Arrin, and invest us with how it hunts and kills men."

The old man smacked his lips and banged the goblet back down on the wooden table. "Aye, then. Most stories agree it looks for all the world like a sea serpent, such as we might imagine one. A long neck and a long tail it has. A big head, with a wide jaw and rows of razor sharp teeth. The mouth's big enough to bite a man's head off they say. This much I saw myself once, many years ago. I was fishing down at the lake's edge, and I saw it pop up out of the water not far away. I dropped my line and just stood there a'staring at the thing. It didn't take any notice of me, just swam around for a time before disappearing beneath the surface again. Not that I'm awful sorry about that as you can imagine.

"I would not think yon beastie was a fast runner on land, but I've heard it said it kind of walks and slides along, all at the same time like, upon four short legs and webbed feet. As for how yon nasty hunts and kills, well I'm afraid I would not have the first idea."

I inclined my head to the old man. "Thank you for your information, friend. One thing puzzles me—"

"Only one thing, Crow?" interrupted another. There was chuckling amongst the assembled Uldach clansmen. The potent mead was having its effect on them.

I joined the mirth. "One thing about the Beast," I continued. "The tales of the creature go back centuries as you say. Yet how can this be? How old can it be? Surely no animal can live for so long?"

The old man who had been recounting the history of the creature looked at his Lord and then me and shrugged. "I cannot offer an opinion on that, gentlemen."

"I've heard the thing comes back every ten years, at this precise time," another man told us. "They say it returns to mate."

"Ten years between matings?" asked another dubiously. "I don't think the beastie can be a real clansman?"

We all laughed aloud at that.

"Know you how big the thing is, Arrin?" another asked.

And as that worthy opened his mouth to reply a different voice preceded him.

"It's big. It's very big!"

All heads turned to he who had spoken. I saw a man in his early thirties, his long hair wildly tangled and his shirt opened and stained. He wavered as he walked closer to the Lord's table.

"Hamesh," exclaimed Udy. "I see you've been at the nectar, man?"

"And why would I not," replied the other, raising a clay jug for evidence. "I cannot get the horror of it out of my mind."

"I'm sorry to ask you to repeat the events of that morn, friend Hamesh," I apologized in advance.

"Crow here is working on a plan to slay the Beast," explained Lord Udy.

"Is he by the Gods?" Hamesh made an attempt to steady himself. "And would this plan involve swords and spears and other sharp, pointy things?"

"I wasn't thinking to throttle the Beast to death with my bare hands," I admitted.

"Then let me tell you this Crow Thiefmaster. From what I could see, yon monster is scaled from nose to toes. I don't think a sword or a spear is going to do aught but annoy it."

"Tell me all," I demanded.

"And so I will. There was Sten and myself. Jolf and Rigor. Sten had sworn to slay the Beast, after it had taken his brother," here Hamesh inclined his head in Udy's direction, "the lord's firstborn son. Killed by the monster when he was fishing in the lake, ten years before.

"Aye, ten years had Sten waited to get his revenge on the Beast. And we three had sworn to aid him. Sten was a clever man. He'd had the castle blacksmith make him a crossbow. No little thing such as I've heard you carry, Sir Crow. No. This was a bow such as the southern pirates use to pierce the sides of the ships they prey upon. The blacksmith did a fine job too. We affixed that crossbow to the front of our boat. We knew it was about the time of the creature's return. Clansmen all up and down the lake, crofters, forest workers, all were instructed to keep a keen eye out for the Beast. So it was that only a few days ago word came to us of a sighting. The very next morning Sten and we three took our boat and our bow out into the center of the lake. And we waited. For hours. We tossed the carcass of a freshly killed piglet over the side on a rope, hoping to whet the monsters appetite, to draw it to us."

Here the man drew in a sharp breath and took another draught from his goblet. "Well we certainly did that," he said. The drinking of the mead seemed to steady him.

"Up it came. Up out of the depths. Swallowed the bait we'd used down whole, it did. Sten fired the great arrow at it. We all saw it strike full into the creature's thick neck. We cheered. We cheered before we started screaming."

Tears had begun to trickle down the poor fellows cheeks. I wasn't sure he was even aware of them.

He continued. "First it took Rigor. It snapped down at him and all but bit him clean in half. Sten took up a spear and cast it at the Beast. I don't think it even penetrated the monster's scaled hide. Jolf was next. Down came that great head, the maw wide open. It snatched him up in its jaws and gobbled him down in two bites. Sten yelled at me to swim for my life and pushed me overboard. He waved his arms to distract the monster. I struck the water just as the Beast smashed that great head down onto our boat. I heard Sten cry out. I couldn't see him. Then the creature raised its head and I saw Sten clasped between its jaws. He was screaming. I could take no more. I turned and swam for the shore. I prayed to every god I knew of to let me reach the safety of land. I was terrified."

Hamesh buried his face in his hands and Lord Udy, whose cheeks were also wet with tears, was moved to reach out and touch the poor fellow's shoulders. He patted the man as one might a favorite pet. "It's alright, Hamesh. It's alright."

"I'm so sorry, M'lord."

"Wasn't your fault, man. Nothing you could do. Nothing anyone could do."

The lord looked over at me. "Do you see what you're up against, Crow?"

I nodded solemnly.

Udy shook his head. "Crow. I would have no man die on my behalf. I release you from your debt. Forget about the Beast. Let the creature return to the sea for another ten years. I've lost two sons now, I would not lose a good friend into the bargain."

There was some grumbling amongst the assembled clansmen. They clamored for revenge. I guessed that if I did not take up the challenge, one of them would.

"What happened to the crossbow that was rigged to the boat?" I asked.

Arrin answered me. "The remains of the boat drifted ashore some hours later. The bow was still in one piece. The boat itself is useless."

"Working throughout the night, could the bow be affixed to a new boat?" I inquired.

Arrin rubbed his chin thoughtfully. Lord Udy stared at me. Even Hamesh looked up.

"What point in repeating Sten's plan?" asked the Lord. "It failed once. I would not expect it to work a second time."

"The plan was sound," I told them. "But it lacked a few small details. I believe I can succeed where Sten failed. Indeed, if your son was sitting beside me now he would listen to my idea and nod in agreement."

"You really think you can slay the Beast…and not be killed yourself in the doing so?"

"Yes," I said to him.

I explained to Udy and his assembled clansmen what I had in mind. I asked for and received parchment and quill and a fresh pot of ink. With quick strokes I sketched two drawings.

"Do you see how this will work?" I asked the Lord. "A length of solid iron will suffice. And I'll need the strongest rope to be found in your castle. And it must be long, even if we must tie one piece to another."

I described my plan in some detail. Udy listened and looked at my sketches and rubbed his chin. "'Tis a bold plan, Crow."

Indeed it was. Although there was one part of my hastily thought out scheme that I had not shared with him. Nor would I.

"The barrels will be no problem," he assured me. "Plenty of those in the castle."

I stood up. "If all this can be made ready by the rising of the sun, then I will set out early."

"I'll have the men work through the night. Who knows how many more days it will be until the Beast makes its way back down the river and out to sea?"

"Aye," I agreed. "The sooner the better. Less it slip away and not return for another ten years."

"What do you now then, Crow Thiefmaster?"

"Return to that soft bed you provided me and get a good night's sleep."

Lord Udy and others stared at me.

"I would not be able to sleep a wink," Arrin exclaimed, "if I knew that on the morrow I would be rowing out upon yonder lake to face the awful creature."

I smiled and shrugged. "A man might trip on those long stone stairs of yours and do himself a mortal injury. But would he lose sleep thinking on it?"

"You're a strange man, Crow," Udy told me.

"Everyone says that," I admitted.

I had no trouble sleeping that night; I am seldom troubled by dreams or nightmares. Dimly I was aware of a pounding and clanging somewhere below, but it was not enough to bring me to full wakefulness — and I knew the cause of the noise.

The sun was rising over the waters of the lake when I opened my eyes. Again I stood on the balcony that adjoined my room. Again I looked out over the placid waters. I thought I spied a distant movement, far out on the calm surface, of something thrust upward from the water for a moment. I shrugged. No matter. I would find out if the Beast was still in the vicinity soon enough.

From my saddlebags I removed a small clay jar. I made sure that its lid was still secure, then wrapped it in a bit of cloth and tucked it carefully away in a pouch on my belt.

I would have to leave my vest behind. I was not happy about that, as it had saved my life many times. Few knew that the inside was lined with the finest and lightest chain mail it was possible to have made. This day, though, if I had to take to the water the weight of the vest would hinder me. I folded it and thrust it into one of my saddlebags, then closed the thick leather flap and locked the buckles. I wanted no one to investigate my secrets whilst I was away. The leather could be cut of course, but then I would be aware of it. I doubted any wanted Crow seeking them out. Picking up my small crossbow and the quiver of quarrels, I left the room.

The few retainers I passed nodded at me in silence. I hadn't even ventured forth yet and already people thought that I was on a doomed venture. All looked at me sadly.

I entered the courtyard and spied Lord Udy talking with a man I judged to be the blacksmith from his leather apron and blackened hands and forearms. They watched me approach.

"You're a cheery lot in the morning here, aren't you?" I asked.

A wan smile in return from the Lord. "People think I'm sending you to your death, laddie."

"You're not sending me anywhere," I pointed out. "I am doing this of my own free will."

"I fain you would reconsider."

"Be assured I have considered carefully Udy. If I did not think my plan would work, then I would not be pursuing it. I say again…your son, Sten, had the right idea. Had I been here when he set out, the head of the Beast would even now be sitting atop your castle's turrets."

A deep sigh. "I cannot change your mind then?"

"No. You set me on this path, but it is I who have decided to continue along it."

"Very well, Crow." He turned and introduced me to the man at his side. "This is Argus, my blacksmith. All night he has labored on that which you requested. And a fine job of it he has done, I must say."

I clasped hands with the big man. "I made it just as you wanted," he told me.

"So it works?" I asked.

"Aye. Works exactly as you want it to. Ingenious. I'd not have thought of such a canny thing."

I tried to look modest. "I merely came up with the idea. You are the one who put it into practice, Argus." I turned back to Lord Udy. "Is the new boat prepared?"

"Indeed it is. We've attached the barrels as you wanted."

I smiled and rubbed my hands together. "Lead the way."

A group of men and women were assembled near the shore of the lake. I followed Lord Udy as he walked past them and stopped short of the water's edge.

There on the sand sat my boat.

Barrels were tied all around it. A huge crossbow was mounted in the bow. I climbed into the vessel and took hold of the weapon. It swiveled from right to left. I wound the cocking mechanism and watched its smooth workings. I nodded in satisfaction.

"Oiled it this morn'," Argus said from behind me.

I checked the metal spear, or arrow, that Argus had spent hours modifying throughout the night. I fiddled with it. It worked just as I had described it to the blacksmith. He was an excellent craftsman. I said as much, and he grinned back at me.

I stepped back out of the small boat and addressed Lord Udy. "Does everyone know what they must do?"

He smiled grimly. "Aye, Crow. The men are ready."

I spied the tousle-haired youngster who had awoken me the day before. "What's your name lad?"

He smiled shyly and kicked the sand at his feet. "I'm Perkin," he told me.

"Come here."

Startled he hesitated, then approached me. I handed him my own small crossbow, and the quiver of bolts. "Look after this for me. Go with Argus and the others. Return it to me when I'm back on dry land."

He took the proffered items and hugged them to his chest. "I will," he said. He looked proud that I'd chosen him, out of all those assembled, to look after my equipment.

"Right then." I spread my hands. "Let's not be standing here all morn. Do some of you men push the boat into the water and I will be on my way."

"Crow." Lord Udy stared gravely at me. "May the Gods favor you with the luck of a devil."

I winked at him with my un-patched eye. "They do. Frequently."

Back into the boat I stepped. Argus and some of the others pushed it into the waters of the lake.

~ The Beast in the Lake ~

It was an ungainly thing, surrounded as it was with all those barrels. But they served a purpose.

I sat down in the middle of the boat and checked that the burlap sack between my feet contained that which I required. Satisfied, I lifted the oars and made my first stroke. There was just enough room between the barrels on each side to allow them movement.

"Wish me good hunting," I said to those on the beach.

Some waved and mumbled. Some shook their heads sadly. Lord Udy bowed his.

The stoutest and longest piece of rope to be found within the castle trailed from my boat and back into the hands of a small group of men on shore. Together with a pair of horses, they began to walk around the southern side of the lake, keeping directly opposite my position.

On my end, the rope was threaded through a steel shackle on the boat and securely attached to the great arrow that Argus had made.

I rowed into the wide expanse of water, staying always on the southern side. It was slow going, for the addition of the barrels tied to my vessel made steering difficult and the handling of the boat sluggish. When I reached a suitable point I laid down my oars and stretched. Then I stood up and carefully tested the stability of my ungainly craft. The barrels stopped the boat rocking from side to side, as it might normally have done.

I took hold of the giant crossbow and turned it toward me. Reaching into the pouch at my belt, I removed the clay jar and opened it. Being careful not to get its contents anywhere near my skin, I tilted it over the arrowhead and watched as a thick brown liquid ran slowly out. I moved the jar backward and forward, making sure that I coated the entire head of the arrow and some of the shaft with the deadly poison. After carefully inspecting my handiwork, I replaced the seal on my jar, re-wrapped it in its cloth, and tucked it securely back in my pouch.

I then turned the handle that operated the cocking mechanism of the great bow, partially setting the weapon. I did not tighten it, lest the terrific strain placed on the drawstring caused it to fray and perhaps snap.

While still standing, I opened the burlap sack at my feet and removed the blood-slicked body of a dead piglet slain that morning. Tying a knot around a dangling leg with the line tied off on an oarlock beside me, I tossed the deceased creature overboard and sat back down.

I ate some bread and cheese and drank from a flask of water — and wondered if the Beast would show itself today. Perhaps it had already concluded whatever business it conducted on its ten-year visits and had taken itself back out to sea.

The promise of a fine, sunny day abated as the morning progressed. The sky grew darker and a wind sprang up. The lake here was too deep to throw an anchor overboard, so I was forced to keep my position by frequently moving the oars about.

I had brought a tiny hourglass with me. I set it on the bench before me and watched the grains of sand trickle down.

An hour I sat there, using the oars to paddle back and forth. I turned the sand glass.

Another hour.

Then another.

The wind had increased and had created small waves upon the surface of the lake. A faint rain had begun to fall, and the sky had further darkened above me. I was starting to get cold. I had not thought to bring a warm coat along; one cannot think of everything.

I glanced toward the southern shore. The small group of men had taken shelter inside the edge of the tree line. The rope lay loose between us.

I was getting bored. Bored and cold.

For the hundredth time, I looked over the side of my small craft. A few small fish nibbled at the carcass of the dead piglet. Below them moved a shadow.

Was it a reflection of the dark clouds moving about in the skies overhead, or was something else down there, deeper in the water? Bending over the edge of the boat, my face close to the surface of the water, I lifted up the patch over my left eye and peered into the depths. In the darkness of the rising storm I could see quite well with my strange eye.

I closed my right orb.

"Ye Gods!"

I threw myself backward as a monstrous head burst from the dark depths, the piglet clasped in a mouth filled with teeth as long as daggers.

The Beast had taken the bait.

It reared above me, yellow eyes glaring down.

Even with the barrels surrounding me, the waves caused by the massive creature's arrival nearly swamped my pitiful craft. I leaped to the bow of the boat and wrenched the giant crossbow around. Pointing it at the creature I cranked the cocking handle to its maximum, until the drawstring vibrated, so tightly was it wound.

The Beast tilted its head and the tasty morsel it had been supplied disappeared down its long, sinuous throat with one swallow. I saw a small piece of jagged wood sticking out the side of its neck. Sten's arrow, no doubt. It did not seem to bother the creature.

Finished with its repast, it looked down at me once more. It opened its mouth.

I fired my own arrow, likewise aiming for that long neck.

The crossbow arms snapped forward. The arrow, propelled with terrific force, shot across the short distance that separated me from the monster.

My aim was true.

The arrow pierced the thick, scaled hide. Such was the force that it penetrated all the way through and emerged from the other side of the Beast's neck. As I had hoped it would.

The creature went berserk.

It reared up, out and out of the water. Then the great head drove downward, maw agape, seeking my soft flesh.

I threw myself over the side of the boat.

The mouth snapped at the spot I had stood in. I hugged the underside of one of the barrels, looking in the direction of the southern shore, hoping the men there were paying attention. They were. The rope that had been floating slack in the water suddenly went taut. Aided by the two horses, they began to reel it in.

I felt my vessel move shoreward.

The Beast must have felt the tugging also. It jerked its neck in the opposite direction. Thanks to the excellent work of Argus, the arrow could not be worked loose. Two steel wings had Argus fashioned onto the sides of the spearhead; wings that opened outward after piercing their target…wings that would only spread wider and dig deeper as pressure was applied against them. The more the creature tried to pull away, the more the steel wings locked against its scaled flesh.

It was impaled and like a fish on a hook, it could not free itself.

Enraged, the Beast drove its head down again. The eyes glared about and the snout twitched, searching for me. Its mouth was opened wide and those dagger-length teeth sought for me.

I ducked below the water as the Beast snapped at my small vessel and sent up a rain of splintered wood. This had been the reason for the barrels. I knew that no ordinary boat would survive an assault by such a creature. It would have been holed and sunk within moments.

The boat moved more quickly toward the southern shore. Argus must have been exhorting the men and the horses to their limit.

The creature screamed. I would have covered my ears if I could.

It was a horrifying sound. At once animal, but mixed with something else. Something almost human.

It shook its head frantically from side to side. It tried to resist being pulled in a direction it did not want to go. To no avail. Slowly and surely, the men and the horses drew it toward the shore.

The barrel obstructed my view of what the Beast was doing. I stuck my head up for a quick peek.

It saw me.

Down came that great, scaled head. Those awful yellow eyes and that terrible mouth full of sharp-toothed death. It smashed through the side of the boat, instantly turning good timber into matchsticks. The mouth snapped at anything and everything, tearing my small vessel to bits. Wood burst apart every time the Beast closed its mouth. A barrel shattered. The boat listed to one side.

How long would it take for the poison I had liberally coated the arrow with to work? I had applied enough to kill a small army. Yet the Beast seemed unaffected.

Another tremendous blow.

Half of the boat was underwater now, only the barrels keeping it afloat.

The head reared back again and struck once more.

Such was the impact of the last blow that the boat was thrown bodily out of the water. Clinging to my barrel still, I was flung into the air. I splashed back down and something sent a lance of agony up my right thigh. The pain was incredible. Treading water I looked for the source. A long splinter of thick wood, sharp as a stake, had stabbed into my leg. Even in that desperate situation the irony of me being likewise impaled did not escape me.

I reached down, grasped the offending object…and wrenched it out of my leg. I gasped as my blood spurted out and turned the water around me black.

Again I looked toward the southern shore. It was but a short distance off. I started to swim as fast as I could. I glanced over my shoulder and saw the Beast nosing about in the shattered remains of the boat. Then its head jerked up. Either it had seen me or it was able to scent the blood trail I was leaving in the water.

It came after me, sliding smoothly through the choppy water. It swam at an angle, and I saw that it strained against the men still pulling on their end of the stout rope. The Beast drew closer to me, but for every forward movement it was also dragged to the side.

I made sure to swim at an opposite angle.

My right leg was on fire. I didn't know if I was actually moving it or not. I could feel nothing but pain from the hip down. I swam over-arm, my hands clawing through the water. My left leg began to cramp from the unexpected exertion.

The skies were dark and storm-tossed. The waters of the lake had become endless waves; I lost sight of the shore. I did not know if I even swam in the right direction. Nor how close behind me came the Beast.

I heard a voice. "Crow. Crow. Come on. Come on, man. You're almost here!"

The voice belonged to the boy, I was sure of it. But what was his name? I couldn't think properly. Perkin. That was it.

"Here," he cried. "Here, Crow."

I could barely see through the water in my eyes. My lungs labored, my heart pounded. I was swallowing mouthfuls of lake. I followed the sound of his voice, no longer even looking back to see where the Beast was, or how close it was to me.

Suddenly I felt arms around me, trying to get me on my feet. I lurched and staggered, waist deep in water, not sure where I was or what I was doing.

I heard another voice. "I've got him, lad. Quick now, back into the trees. The Beast has reached the shore."

Angus was it?

My vision blurred, and blackness spun in my head. I vomited water.

Strong hands half dragged, half carried me up the beach and thence into the tree line. I blinked, suddenly aware of my surroundings. I pulled the patch back over my left eye.

The blacksmith tore a strip of cloth from his shirt and used it to bandage the wound in my right thigh. "That needs stitches or a hot iron," he said.

"Later. Help me to my feet. Where is the Beast?"

"The men have dragged it into the edge of the forest," Perkin told me excitedly.

The two of them supported me. I tried to stand on my own, but my right leg buckled. I had no feeling in it.

"Show me."

With the two of them half carrying me, we moved along the shore, following the tracks of the creature. The shouts of men, of cursing and yelling, came to our ears.

"Into the trees," directed Argus. We moved off, through the forest, winding our way between the tall pines. Closer to the sounds of consternation.

"There." Argus pointed.

The trees grew close together here, preventing the men from pulling the Beast any further inland. It was still tethered by the rope attached to the spear I'd fired through its neck.

The creature was truly large. I saw that it was indeed four-footed and taloned, and that a long tail swept about it. The slim and sinuous body supported a head that was sharp and angular. Long, lean jaws framed a wide, fang-filled mouth. Scaled all over the creature was, and those scales a greenish color, perfect camouflage in the water.

Finally realizing that it was the stout cord which ensnared it, the Beast twisted its head and snapped clean through it with those razor-edged teeth. It hissed and turned among the trees, its tail lashing out in all directions. It struck an Uldach spearman and threw him backward. The Beast reached for the man, maw open wide. A second clansman ran forward, hurling another spear at the monster. It struck the side of the armored snout and bounced harmlessly off. Others fired arrows at the creature. Few penetrated the scaled hide.

The Beast hesitated, its head wavering between its foes. Was it my imagination or were the movements of the Beast becoming slower? More sluggish?

I suspected that the poison with which I had coated the spearhead was beginning to have an effect; yet still too slow. I had not anticipated that.

The Beast chased after a man who had moved too close. Barely did he evade it by running between the clustered pines.

"In my pouch," I said urgently to Perkin. "A small jar. Take it out."

The lad wasted no time with needless questions. He fumbled at my waist and dug his hand into the pouch.

"I have it, Crow."

"Good. Now open it very carefully. Let not a drop of the liquid within fall onto your skin. It is a deadly poison."

I watched the boy gingerly open the container and then hold it well away from himself.

"Now take a bolt from my quiver and dip the head into the jar. Be very careful."

He did as I asked.

"Argus, hold me up." I could not stand unaided. The strong blacksmith held me steady. "Give me my bow," I requested.

I accepted the small weapon, and in a moment I had pulled back the drawstring and locked it in place. "Give me the quarrel, Perkin."

He handed it to me, wary of the sharp end now coated in the dark brown liquid.

I was careful myself, despite the shaking of my hands. I placed the tainted bolt into the runnel and made sure it was secure.

"Take me closer to the Beast," I ordered.

"As you wish, laddie," grunted Argus. Together he and Perkin guided me between the pines and nearer the enraged monster.

The Beast had grown tired of chasing the men that dashed back and forth about it, and had begun to retreat in the direction of the lake. It was almost out of the dense forest when we three came abreast of it. We were still between the boughs of the trees, where it could not strike at us.

"Let me go," I instructed.

I reached out with my left hand and took hold of a strong branch. I hopped forward, grasping another. In this fashion did I move even closer to the monster. It saw me and stopped. A pale yellow eye peered down. Did it recognize me as being the cause of its distress? Perhaps so, as instead of continuing its progress toward the lake, it lurched in my direction.

Balanced on my one good leg and using my free hand to support myself against a tree, I waited. The sinuous neck wound between two pines, and the wide maw gaped open. Wait, I told myself. Wait. Once more, the snout rose up.

Down snapped the head.

I fired my quarrel upward, into the open maw, up and into the roof of its mouth, hoping that my bolt would penetrate the soft flesh and lodge in the Beast's brain.

I threw myself to one side and crawled on two hands and one knee behind a tree, dragging my other leg behind me. I rolled and crawled some more. Then Argus and Perkin were there again and they lifted me up and hurried us away.

Behind me the Beast howled and shrieked. It threshed about, barging into

~ The Beast in the Lake ~

the trees, ripping up huge clods of earth with its talons.

We stopped and watched it.

It turned about and began to slither back to the lake, but slowly did it move. It seemed uncertain. It stumbled, then righted itself; stumbled again.

The men of Uldach Castle came up beside us. "Have we killed it?" they asked.

"Crow has killed it," Perkin said excitedly. "He fired a poisoned arrow into its mouth. Did you see that? Did you see how close he was? Right underneath it he stood. The nerve of it."

"Poisoned did you say?" one clansman asked with distaste.

"It was the only way," growled Argus. "Did you not see how little effect our spears and arrows had?"

We all saw the Beast fall.

Its legs collapsed beneath it.

It rolled onto its side and attempted to push itself back upright. And failed. The great mouth opened and the red tongue lolled out. At last the poison I had placed in its blood was working.

"Take me closer."

We made our way out from between the closely packed trees and down to the shore.

"Let me go," I told my two helpers.

Surprised they did so, I was barely able to balance myself unaided.

I hopped forward, as close to the Beast as I dared. Its breath came in gasps.

It was dying.

It turned its mighty head and looked at me.

We stared into each other's eyes. For a long time.

Then I realized that the powerful chest had stopped rising and falling. The eyes had lost their luster. The great head slumped upon the sand and did not move again.

The Beast was dead.

Frozen Wastes

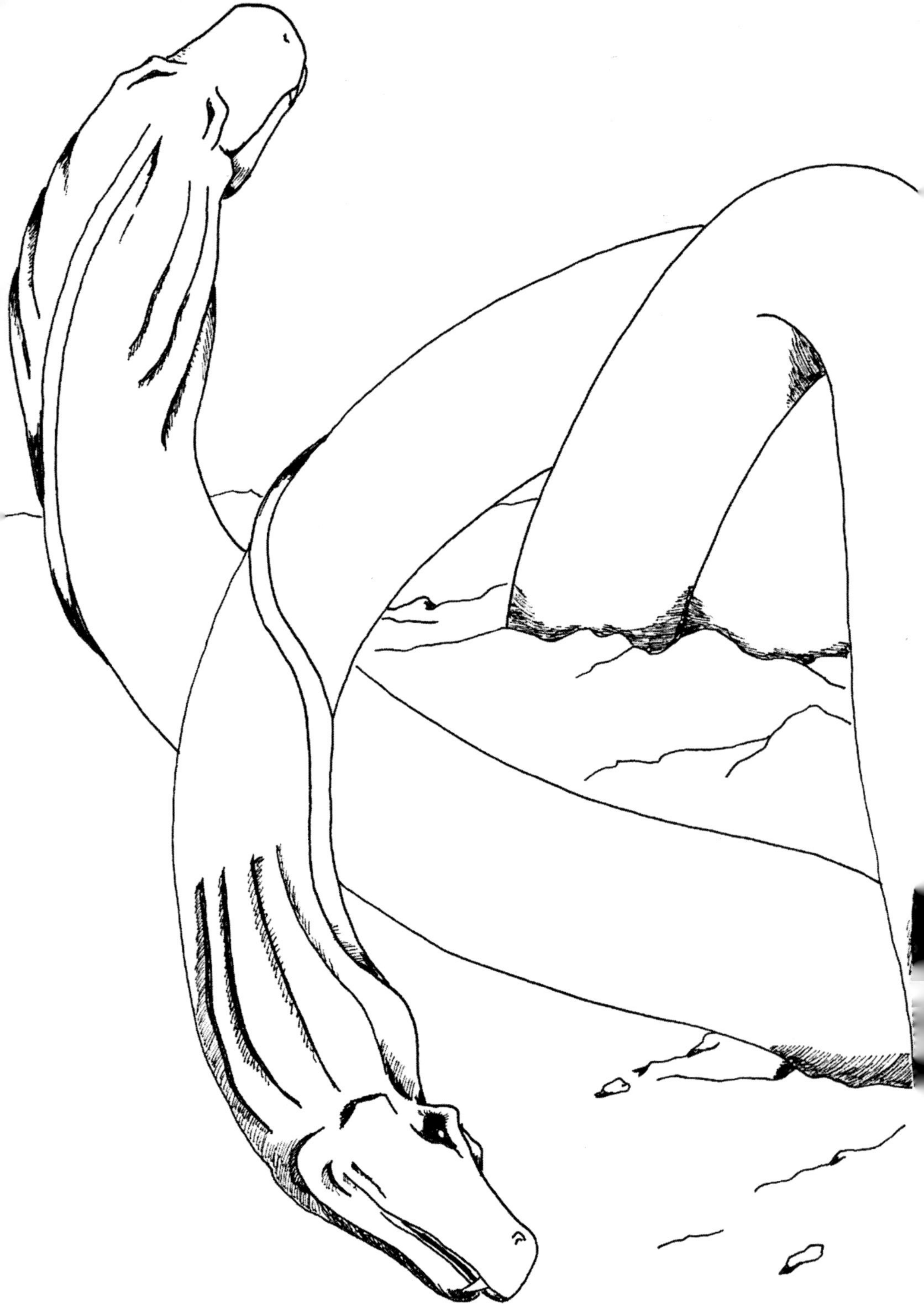

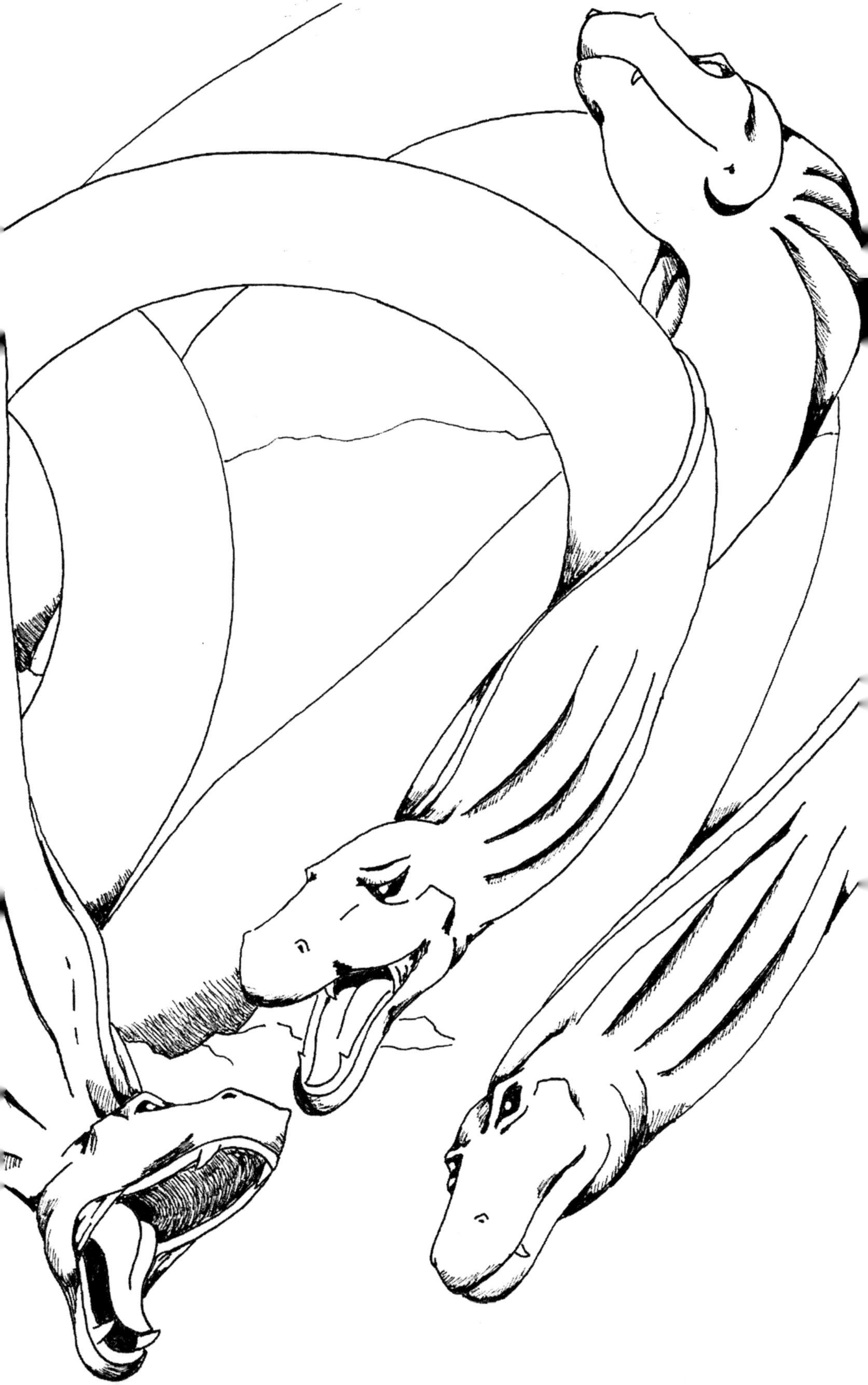

Born in deepest Hertfordshire (England), Carl Walmsley proceeded to change schools with startling regularity before uneventually settling in Portsmouth, where he studied for an English degree. He has his mother to thank/blame for a lifelong love of all things fantastical — and now finds his head full of characters and adventures, all clamoring for a place on the page. He currently teaches English at a small private school in 'The Midlands.' Carl's tale is one of returns and responsibilities. Sometimes accepting the necessity of a return is momentous enough — or at least so significant that we simply fail to see the true size of the reason we left in the first place…and the responsibility we incur by our return. Not seeing can often be a blessing…

Serpents beneath the Ice

A Tale of the Wastes

**by Carl Walmsley
& illustration by John Whitman**

Like a whetted blade, the ice-cutter cleaved through the frozen sea. Behind its iron-shod hull, a path of shattered ice trailed all the way back to the warmer northern waters. Southern sailors, well-used to the frozen straits, attacked the ice before the prow, hammering spikes deep into the crust. To each spike was cloven a chain, and winches — a dozen strong upon the foredeck — hauled these up, forcing the ship ever onwards towards the south.

Though the sails were furled and the oars stowed, those aboard *The Ice Maiden* still had much to do. Tireless crews cut ice from the hull and used it to cool the smoking winches. Others kept watch on the spikesmen below as they struggled to stay ahead of the fracturing ice and the hollows of black sea that appeared around the hull. Only five figures seemed removed from the struggles around them. Their clothing and manner marked them as passengers, as did their probing gaze which was fixed beyond the vast, snowy wastes on some unseen destination.

Above the tumult of splintering ice rose a grinding squeal, and greasy black smoke streamed from one of the winches. The deck crew poured ice hastily across the overworked machinery, but too late: wood and metal twisted and buckled, and in a cascade of riven gears and belching flame, the machine tore itself apart. The great ship slowed and stopped.

"What's the damage?" asked Fenn, once the smoke had cleared and those caught in the blast had been tended to. He leaned heavily upon a curved staff, a gift from his master many years before.

"Three dead, twice that injured," growled the captain of the sea-cutter. "Four of my winches reduced to kindling. We'll make it no closer to the shore—not without repairs."

Fenn cursed and spat, watching his spittle turn to ice moments after it touched the deck. "If I double your— "

The Captain shook his head. "No amount of coin will move this ship. Not unless your magic stretches to fixing broken machines."

Fenn turned and called to the two Orachiri hunters helping clear away the debris. "Can you guide us from here?"

The Orachiri exchanged glances, only their eyes visible among the thick furs and hides covering their bodies. A flurry of blinks and eye-brow movements — the secret language of their people — followed; then Lang-shau pulled down his mask.

"We can."

"But we must be quick," added Sey-ku. "The ice here is not safe—and with each day, it melts a little more."

Fenn nodded. "Give us a week, captain. If we haven't returned by then, we never will."

Long, counter-balanced planks were extended from the deck, and the five wanderers shimmied down an ice-crusted rope. The Orachiri led the way, cutting back and forth around areas of thin ice, sensing dangers none of the others could see as they trudged southward. After half a day of walking, the hunters informed Fenn that they had crossed the ice field and now stood above the southern continent. *The Ice Maiden* had vanished from sight many hours before.

There would be no sunset here — not at this time of year. A silver twilight, crisp and still, settled over the snowlands. The small party fashioned a simple hut of snow roofed with treated hide and settled in for the night. Lang-shau and Sey-ku prepared a fire using whale fat and some of the precious wood they had brought. Soon the little shelter was warm enough for the travelers to take off their outer-layers of clothing and heat some food.

Jawing at a tough string of meat, Conner leaned over and scanned the words that his servant entered into a thick ledger. "I think you'll find there were a few more of them than that," said the swordsman, tapping the page.

His hulking scribe nodded solemnly and altered the account.

"And *dashed* is a far more evocative word than *ran*." Conner stroked his neatly clipped beard. "Yes, let's have dashed."

His servant once more adjusted the record.

"What does he write for you?" asked Sey-ku. For the first time the two Orachiri had both uncovered their heads. Their faces were startlingly similar: angular and strong-boned, perfectly straight noses, unlined and pale — except the tanned and weathered skin around their eyes.

"Some of my more recent exploits," answered Conner, clearly relishing the question. "Before I signed on with Fenn here, my scribe and I had a run in with some cannibals."

Sey-ku stared at him blankly.

"Where I come from, people will pay a great deal to read about the exploits of brave men. Not everyone can be an adventurer." Conner smiled, teeth glinting like the walls of the shelter.

Sey-ku shrugged. "My people have no need for books. If a man cannot remember something and then teach it to his children, what use is it?"

Conner waved a hand dramatically. "There are some civilizations which have learned too much for any one man to remember."

"And, at the same time, have forgotten much that is important."

Conner seemed surprised by his servant's comment, and even a little put out. "You can be morose, Nomo. Focus your efforts on capturing my heroics, I think."

The servant nodded and resumed his writing.

"So, Fenn," Conner rumbled, self-consciously changing the subject, "what more can you tell us about this creature of yours?"

The conjuror tore his eyes from the flames into which he had been staring and gazed fixedly at the swordsman. "Why, are you particular about which monsters you kill?"

Conner shrugged, taking no offence if any was intended. "Not so long as Nomo records it—and I get paid. But I do like to know what I am up against."

"I have never seen the thing myself, but it is said to have appeared two years ago, attacking merchants en route to the port of Kapa-nuwat. Since then there have been sightings as far afield as Sa-ket and Rimehold. It roves all across the southern continent but each spring it returns here."

Lang-shau nodded. "Many among the Orachiri have seen the mess it leaves behind. It slaughters the bears and snow lions that we hunt."

"*Shenlat ro kane* we call it," said Sey-ku. "Serpents beneath the ice."

Whether for his own benefit or that of his companions, Conner unsheathed his sword and guided a whetstone along its glistening edge.

"What of the wizard?" Again, Nomo's contribution was unexpected.

Fenn stared at the large scribe for some time before answering. The man rarely spoke, but when he did, he invariably showed a keen intellect. And the large mace tucked into his belt suggested he could do far more than just write. "Gone."

"Killed by the beast?"

"Most likely. Now the monster uses his lair."

"And you know how to get there?" asked Conner, lifting his sword so that the blade seemed re-forged in the firelight.

"I will—once Sey-ku and Lang-shau guide us to the springs near the ice hills. Which they will do tomorrow."

"And why do you want it dead?" Conner asked the question in a casual enough way, but Fenn frowned at him nonetheless.

"Does it matter?"

Conner tested the edge of his blade, sucking a ruby of blood from his thumb. "Not greatly."

"Good." Something about Fenn's manner made it clear that he considered the discussion at an end. Lifting his blanket, the conjuror rolled onto his side.

"You should get some sleep. We'll be on our way again in a few hours."

Fenn had forgotten how desolate the snowlands could be. No breath of wind stirred the sparkling surface snow, and the only sound was the crunch of footfalls as he and his companions pressed on toward the south. He had thought never to return here. But then again, he had thought many things.

Sey-ku and Lang-shau were some way ahead, scouting for invisible landmarks or guiding them around thin-crusted snow hollows that might swallow them whole. The swordsman, Conner, and his servant, Nomo, brought up the rear. Conner had tried a few times to strike up conversation, but the two Orachiri had hushed him, warning that sounds travelled far over the ice and that, despite appearances, there were things here that it would be wise not to disturb. Fenn knew that to be true: unfortunately, his goal was to find and kill one such thing.

Lang-shau and Sey-ku had stopped, and were waiting for the others. As Fenn drew alongside, his freezing breath caught and chilled his throat: they stood upon the lip of a precipice — a great canyon hewn from the earth, gilded in ice and snow.

"This is new," said Sey-ku. "The ground has moved."

Fenn strained to make out the dimensions of the rift, gazing off in both directions to gauge its length. The snow made it impossible to discern.

"Can we go around?" asked Conner, peering down into the icy chasm. "It looks like a tricky climb."

They marched for more than a mile, trailing the edge of the rift. In places it narrowed to just a few dozen feet, suggesting that they were nearing its end, but every time it widened out once more. As they walked, Fenn became increasingly aware of the magic that pulsed from the ground — from the rock and the snow. This was not a natural occurrence — it was caused by the monster. *To stop me? How could it even know that I am coming?*

Perhaps I should turn back? The idea needled its way into his thoughts. A part of him wanted to — wanted the expedition to fail. It wouldn't be the first time he had given up — as his old master never missed an opportunity to remind him. *You give up too easily, Fenn. You must be willing to take risks if you are ever to fulfill your potential. Caution and fear stand but a few paces apart.* From across the years, the words came to him once more.

"Enough," he said suddenly. "We will climb down."

Sey-ku went first, slithering down a rope that his brother and Nomo lowered to the canyon floor some fifty feet below. At the base, Sey-ku lay flat and edged out over the densely packed snow. At the midpoint, his elbow punched through the crust, and flurries of soft snow began to tumble away through spreading cracks. Smoothly, the Orachiri slid away from the pothole

~ Serpents beneath the Ice ~

and waited. The snow settled. Once more he advanced and before long he had reached the other side.

The ascent of the far wall would have been impossible for a lesser climber — any handholds had been smoothed away by layers of ice, none of which could be relied upon to bear a man's weight. Many times, Sey-ku was forced to hang by his arms and to haul himself from one hold to the next. Panting heavily through his hide mask, he finally lowered a rope from the opposite summit, easing the passage of those that would follow.

Both Fenn and Conner were strong-limbed and steel-nerved and, with the aid of the ropes, they each crossed without much difficulty.

Lang-shau motioned for Nomo to begin his descent, but the hulking scribe shook his head, ponderously. "That ice may not support my weight. And you aren't strong enough to lower me. Go—I will hold the rope for you." Reluctantly, Lang-shau made his way down and across the chasm. At the foot of the far wall, he waited and gestured for Nomo to follow.

The scribe's descent was perilous. More than once he lost his footing and hung suspended above the ice-polished rocks. By the time he reached the bottom of the chasm, his palms were gashed and his thick woolen hose had been torn at the thigh.

"Here!" Lang-shau hurled across one end of a coil of rope. Nomo wrapped it about his wrists, and hesitantly set his belly upon the ice. Sledge-like, his great frame slid across the snow, leaving a far deeper groove than had the passing of his four companions. Within reach of Lang-shau's extended grasp, he reached out gratefully to accept it — and the ground fell away beneath him.

In a cascade of ice and billowing snow, the scribe vanished. Lang-shau flung himself back, grasping the rope and bracing himself. Even so, the sudden surge of weight hauled him forward, his feet jutting precariously over the newly opened fissure.

Sey-ku scampered down to help his brother, moving with reckless speed between slippery holds. By the time he grasped Lang-shau's back and heaved him away from the gaping snow-hole, the fracture had begun to widen. Despite the danger, and the scything of the rope through his flesh, Lang-shau refused to let go. Grasping the line together, both Orachiri began to pull and, inch by bloody inch, it rose from the hole.

When Nomo's hand grasped the edge of the fissure it was blue with cold — though runnels of red welled between his enormous fingers. In a titanic effort, as only those facing death can muster, he hauled himself from the hole and sagged upon the icy rock. A cloud of gasping breath-mist hung above the three men. It was some moments before any could talk.

"Thank you." Nomo's lungs heaved. "I thought I was—"

At that moment, a great section of the cavern-floor fell away, dropping down as far again as the rock walls rose above them. The falling snow turned and tumbled in its descent and then refused to lie still — twitching and shuffling upon the gulley floor. The three tired climbers were left stranded upon a small precipice, not daring to move.

From their vantage point, looking down upon the chasm, Fenn and Conner were the first to catch sight of a new danger, and called out a warning to their exhausted companions. Nomo and the two Orachiri heard their words — though they had barely the energy to listen — and a chittering sound that clicked and scraped from the stone below. Sey-ku craned over the edge, now only a foot or so from the shelf where he lay. There was movement against the white, but it was hard to make out. Above, Conner and Fenn continued to shout.

Then something sprang up the cliff wall, moving on powerful spidery legs that pierced the ice like pitons. A single bound brought it to within a few feet of the plateau, and Sey-ku cried out in alarm and leapt away.

"Climb!" he ordered, drawing his short curved sword.

The thing was over the edge before either his brother or the scribe had even made it to their feet. It had a segmented, insectoid body that glistened like new-made steel, and four opposed mandibles clicked together, twitching around a circular mouth.

Taking advantage of its position, Sey-ku swung at the creature's legs hoping to force it from the ledge. It reared up, avoiding the blow, and stabbed out with its appendages like four dagger-quick lances. Rolling forward, Sey-ku kicked away its hind legs and it fell, clicking and squealing from the lip of the plateau. Its scream came to an abrupt halt as it struck the chasm-bottom, but a chittering noise rumbled forth to take its place.

They climbed then — far faster than was safe, with the knowledge that to fall was to die. Sey-ku and Lang-shau moved ahead of Nomo, whose strength was almost spent before the climb began.

Two more of the devilish ice insects bounded up to the plateau, and now skittered up the rocks toward the fleeing men.

Raising his rod, Fenn began to turn it in his hands. The still air of the snowlands vanished as a swirling wind began to whip through the pass. He knew he risked dashing his companions from the walls if he lost control of his spell, but it was clear they could not outpace the ice spiders.

A funnel of wind snaked from the rod, sending a spiral of snow down into the chasm. Fenn drew the funnel back like a whip, then lashed at those spiders which had moved to within a few yards of his companions. With a jarring crack, snow and stone and kicking, screaming spiders exploded from the rock face and fell tumbling away. Fenn used the funnel-whip to drive back more of the things as they raced up and over the plateau ledge. It was clear they had disturbed an entire nest. Only when his friends — even the lumbering, exhausted Nomo — had scaled the cavern wall, did Fenn allow the winds to fade and die. He groaned and sagged, leaning now on his staff like an old man with a stick.

Without pause, propped against each other for support, the five warriors hurried away from the snow-filled gorge.

"I just don't see how it's relevant to the tale so far," said Conner, defensively. "It was over so quickly."

Nomo nodded, though his quill continued to hover pregnantly over the unwritten page.

"Just make a brief note, perhaps," added the swordsman. "For the sake of authenticity."

Nomo nodded, dipping the nib into the warmed-through ink for at least the fourth time. Still, he didn't write.

Sey-ku, Lang-shau and even Fenn were smiling now. Finishing the shelter had lifted everyone's mood, but Conner's discomfort had really helped to chase away the trials of the day.

"Mighty Fenn and hero Lang-shau," said Sey-ku mischievously, as though pondering what should be added to the journal. His brother nodded solemnly, turning his head theatrically in a more than passable impression of their swordsman companion. A moment later the two Orachiri exploded with laughter.

"Oh, write what you like!" scoffed Conner. "Honestly, what was I supposed to do from atop the cliff? How could I…" He trailed off, his words lost in the general mirth.

Finally, he smiled himself, conceding the humor of the situation. "Very well. I see that this is a chapter where I shall have to surrender the spotlight to my companions."

"Graciously done," said Sey-ku, patting his brother proudly on the back.

Without further pause, Nomo began to write.

The companions passed a further hour with good humored banter, and ate half-thawed supplies, warmed over their modest flame. Outside, for the first time since they had left the ship, it started to snow. Lang-shau assured them that this would help insulate the shelter and keep them warm.

Tucked into his blanket, Fenn gazed beyond the flickering embers that half-lit the shelter, his mind elsewhere. After the encounter at the gorge — which he was convinced had not been mere chance — they had not been able to move far before Nomo had needed to rest. He had been exhausted and half-frozen from his tumble into the ice-hole, and it had been clear that if they had not stopped hypothermia might have set in or the black stain of frostbite. They had pressed on for another mile or so, just to be clear of the ice-insects, and then struck camp. As it turned out, Nomo had recovered quickly once in the warmth, and the gashes to his and Lang-shau's palms from their battle with the rope had not proved too serious.

Tomorrow they would reach the springs. Sey-ku believed they were perhaps three hours away. From there, only a mile or so separated them from Fenn's former home. The place where he had spent almost a third of his life. Where he had learned his craft. Struggling not to think overmuch about what he might find, Fenn gradually surrendered to the lull of sleep.

Droplets of water, formed where the steam cooled in the chill air, glistened above the hot springs like frosted diamonds.

"Is this it?" asked Conner, peering down into a bubbling pool. "Are those steps?"

"Aye." Fenn knelt and dipped a hand in the hot water, and then brushed away the snow to reveal a cracked mosaic-covered stair. "There was a settlement here once. The people harnessed the warmth beneath the ground." He traced the line of a long crack in the mosaic and then sighed. "Long since gone."

"This way," he said, rising. "We are almost there."

This close to his former home, Fenn could not mistake the runnels of energy which pulsed through the rock beneath him. Few ever came to understand its draw, its addiction, and thoughts of the untapped fuel surged within him. Digging his curved rod into the snow before him, he marched purposefully onward. Behind him, none of his companions noticed. He dared not speak yet, lest his voice betray him. He had to trust that they were focused upon the task at hand, their senses primed; it would not do to approach such a place unwary or unwatchful.

The ruins were encased in ice, rising up like an opaque city of glittering glass within a wide, sloping valley. Snow had settled on the peaks, veiling whatever spires or towers once crowned this frozen metropolis, but a large triangular doorway was visible at its base.

"Shit," said Conner. "From a distance, I thought it was just a hill—or a small peak."

"That is how it has remained hidden," said Fenn. "Most of the year, it is buried beneath the ice. Even when it isn't, you would need to be inside the valley itself to see the base—and the entrance."

Sey-ku stared at the ruins in wonder. "I had no idea."

"Why is the doorway uncovered?" asked Lang-shau, pointing.

Fenn had already started marching downhill, but called back over his shoulder. "Because something has been inside."

The enormous door rose to more than five times the height of the tallest man. Again, Fenn considered telling his companions what they should expect…but there was little point. They would find out soon enough.

Instead, he instructed them to gather a large pile of snow, which they heaped before the opening. He then bade them stand well back. Hefting his rod, he allowed the tide of magic to rise up, to fill and flow through him — carefully siphoning it off and into the rod. His muscles trembled with the effort of containing it — of channeling such primeval, untapped power — of denying its yearning to overwhelm him; to consume and change him.

The snowy mound trembled and began to move. A rough, ill-formed head rose up, then long powerful arms and short, solid legs. Within moments a man of ice stood erect upon the threshold.

Fenn took a moment to force away the unused power — though the effort of doing so left him giddy. *It would be so easy to become swamped here. No wonder... No.* He forced the thought away.

"Stay behind the golem," he said, and a moment later the iceman began to lumber forward.

Something large had hewn a path through the ice, clearing the triangular tunnel into the city. Long gouges were cut deep into the ice on either side. All weapons were drawn; all eyes scanned the darkness that gave way reluctantly before the light from their torches.

"Wait." Fenn's voice echoed eerily in the murky passage. Just visible at the edge of the torchlight rose a wall, a door, again many times taller than a man, set seamlessly within.

Fenn produced a black glove from within his robes and slid it on. Its jet surface rippled in the half-light as if woven from the fabric of night. He reached once more inside his garments and retrieved a set of lock picks, then closed his eyes.

Even Nomo gasped when the hand floated free of the conjuror's wrist, and glided through the air toward the door. Fingers, deft as any still attached to the arm of a master thief, began to work at the lock. Fenn's eyes remained shut and his features twitched with the effort of concentration.

The click echoed in the stillness of the tunnel — only to be consumed by the swooshing roar of giant blades that fell from the ceiling, rose from the floor and exploded from the walls. The air around the door was rent with blows that would have sliced apart any creature standing before it.

In a second the blades were gone, returned to their hidden recesses — the disembodied glove undisturbed. Fenn, eyes still closed, allowed himself a faint smirk; with a thought, he willed the glove back onto the end of his arm. Nomo caught Fenn's eye and tapped his journal bag meaningfully as he accompanied the others through the now open doorway.

The atmosphere beyond was warmer than the chill air of the snowlands, and something about its smell and its stillness made it seem old. Both Langshau and Sey-ku began muttering a protective prayer. The hulking ice golem shambled forward, Conner a pace or two behind. A short way ahead the passage opened onto a much larger area, which seemed already to be dimly lit.

What little warning came gave only Conner time to react. Fenn saw the swordsman spring away and roll across the ice toward the wall. Then he heard the man's startled oath — and the snow beneath the rest of the companions exploded like a geyser, filling the air with a fine mist. Unseen blows fell and voices split the air, but through the white haze none could make out what happened. Then Sey-ku appeared, surging high above the plume, kicking the air and screaming. His left arm seemed held above him, supporting the weight of his struggling form — pinioned within the jaws of a monstrous white serpent. A crunch of bone and the unmistakable tearing of muscle, and a section of the white fountain turned red as the maimed Orachiri tumbled into the cloud, roaring in pain.

A second serpentine head, jaws gaping, surged from the settling snow and sought to close about Conner. Even as he again dived away, he sliced the air about him and the monster's head snapped back, leaving a trail of gore and an enormous, flopping tongue behind.

Fenn — rod in hand — swept the dissipating snow cloud away with a blast of wind. He and Nomo both still stood, though the latter had an arm curled protectively around his ribs. Lang-shau knelt over the body of his crippled brother.

Three giant snakes, scales white as deep-winter frost, eyes black as hate, loomed above them. Sliding rhythmically through the snow — their bodies half concealed beneath the surface — they circled the men. One serpent had an Orachiri sword lodged between its scales and blood bubbled from the mouth of another.

"Hey!" Twirling his blade, Conner thrust the point through the dismembered tongue and held it aloft like a trophy. "A snake with a lisp? Does that mean you'll just go *ttthhh?*"

A hissing roar answered from below and a fourth snake erupted from the snow beneath the swordsman. For an instant Conner held his balance, feet braced on either side of the serpentine skull. Then he toppled wildly and landed in a heap, losing his sword in the fall. The nearest serpent dipped its head toward Conner and spread wide its jaws. He smelt the beast's chill breath and saw the stump where its tongue used to be.

A snow golem's fist cannoned into the gaping maw, and a shockwave rippled along the length of the snake. A second time, and then a third, the huge ice paw hammered against the serpent's mouth and skull. Drooling blood and shattered teeth, it lolled drunkenly and then settled on the ground. There was a final crunch as the golem's foot stamped on its head, the lower jaw splintering away.

The hissing from the other snakes receded and they disappeared as one beneath the ice. A faint trembling from their slithering stirred the loose snow as they fled.

Everyone held their position for several seconds, then Fenn turned to regard the wounded Orachiri. "How bad?"

Lang-shau was packing ice around his brother's stump, numbing the nerves. Reaching into his pack, he pulled out a bandage and began to bind the wound. "He can't fight. Not like this."

"Give me your throwing axe," Sey-ku grunted. "I can fight."

"What the hell were they?" asked Conner, retrieving his sword, and shaking off the snow. "I came here to kill one monster—not four!"

"They are one monster," insisted Fenn. And, anticipating the further question, added "You'll see."

Once Sey-ku's wound was tended, the companions advanced slowly to the end of the passage. The chamber beyond was vast. It rose in the shape of a pyramid — a great hollow within the ruins of the city. Walkways and galleries were cut into the rock, encircling a multitude of levels that rose up and up into the icy gloom. Here and there, the stonework had fallen away, allowing the snow to seep in. A few shafts of light crisscrossed the immense vault, making the ice shine wherever they touched.

"It's changed," Fenn muttered, and seemed ready to elaborate when he fixed his gaze upon the snow-covered ground in the center of the cavern. "There."

The ice golem began to advance, the others fanning out behind it.

Not for the first time, Fenn questioned his decision to return. *Was it necessary? Might things not yet be resolved some other way?* A glance at Sey-ku, cradling what remained of his arm, suggested not. The monster had to be stopped.

A shaft of sunlight illuminated a sunken area of snow near the cavern's center. The faint outline of steps visible beneath a covering of frost led down into the recess.

"It knows we're here." Fenn's voice sounded small in the yawning space. "It knows…we mean to kill it. It will show us no mercy. We must do the same."

All around the group, making them twist and turn and adjust their weapons warily, the packed snow rose and fell as unseen things moved beneath the surface. Lang-shau stabbed repeatedly at a rolling surge which moved by his feet, but the tip came away unblooded.

"Wait," ordered Fenn. "It is still gathering. No one is to attack until I say so."

"What if—"

"No one." Fenn set his iron gaze upon Conner, and the swordsman shrugged.

The surface of the depression trembled. Brittle ice cracked and broke. Snow hissed and shivered. And then it rose — whole and monstrous — from beneath the snow.

Its body was elephantine — swollen and large-limbed, with thick leathery hide the color of aged ice. It had no obvious front or rear: the four stout legs jutting out at equidistant points from its monstrous bulk. Crooked ridges, like crenulations upon a fort, rippled around the upper part of the body and from between all but two of these protruded a long, sinewy snake: six in all. Each moved of its own accord, hissing and spitting and snapping — sounds that formed a chorus of serpentine voices which filled the echoing vault. A dozen black eyes glistened with malevolent rage as they scrutinized the men before them.

It was Shenlat ro kane. The serpents beneath the ice. A hydra.

Fenn raised his staff and it vibrated in his palms. A moment later flames ignited, crackling and melting, running in a circle around the beast. From beyond the undulating blaze, the six heads roared their defiance.

"I give you this one chance!" Fenn shouted. "Your last chance!"

The monster did not respond — other than to raise an enormous leg and step across the wall of fire. Mottled grey hide blackened and crisped, and one of the snake heads screeched in fury.

There could be no more hesitation. No more false hopes. Fenn signaled the attack.

The hydra was already halfway across the flames, though its footing was uncertain on the melting ground. The golem strode forth to block its path. Fists the size of boulders — with knuckles still stubbed with broken teeth — ground together like millstones, pounding the nearest snake from either side. A ruined head, twitching on the end of a sinewy body, slumped to the ground. A moment later, it fell away from the bulging shoulders, like a finger torn from a knuckle joint.

Side-by-side, Connor and Nomo attacked the creature's legs as they emerged from the flame. Sword and mace hacked and bludgeoned, drawing streaks of ichor and crunching flesh. A serpentine head came suddenly through the flame, knocking Nomo from his feet and turning upon the swordsman. Conner plucked a short heavy blade from his belt and hurled it into the throat of the gaping monster. The head jerked back, gagging and gargling on its own blood.

Conner raced to where Nomo had fallen, but an enormous leg — thicker than a tree — crashed against his back and he tumbled to the ground and lay motionless.

Holding his spear at full length, Lang-shau fenced with a snake-head, darting back and forth like a mongoose with a cobra. A sudden strike from the serpent tore a gash in his side, but a retaliatory thrust pierced the beast's eye and left it reeling in agony. Sidling to the left — the side where the creature was now blind — the Orachiri sought to gain the upper hand. Without warning, the serpent-head detached from the hydra.

The fully-formed snake slithered toward Lang-shau, forcing him to scurry back. He started to overbalance when an axe — thrown with all the force his wounded brother could muster — hammered against the snake's skull and left it stunned. Recovering his footing, Lang-shau resumed his game of cat and mouse, circling always to the left into the creature's blind spot.

Fenn had strung his staff like a flaming bow, and lashed lines of fire at the body of the hydra. Each crackling shaft scorched flesh and muscle, and the stench of burnt hide hung in the air. Even so — even with all the injuries his companions inflicted — Fenn knew they could not win in a straight fight. The hydra was too powerful: the magic that had birthed it too strong. Already, two of the remaining serpent-heads had pinned the golem from either side. By turns, they snapped at its frozen form, gouging out holes and scraping away chunks of ice. Conner and Nomo were both down, and Sey-ku and Lang-shau had been drawn away from the main fight by another of the hydra's detached heads.

Fenn twirled his rod, summoning a whirlwind that swept Connor and Nomo away from the hydra, and then drove the beast back a few paces so that its hind legs were once more scorched in the circle of flame. He forced himself to cut the spell off, fearing the exultation of power it threatened to incite.

Within moments the creature recovered and it surged forward, turning its full fury upon the ice golem. Like the tip of a crossbow bolt, a serpentine head ripped through the body of the ice warrior; moments later, another wrenched off an arm. Resiliently the single-purposed golem used its remaining limb to deliver a sledgehammer blow that lifted a snake up and over the body of the hydra so that it lolled lifelessly across its back. In the next instant, it was crushed beneath the advancing form of the monster.

Fenn knew what must happen now — knew what he must dare if they stood a chance of victory. He became aware of a dazed Conner rising beside him. The hydra, reduced now to three heads but as ferocious as ever, thundered toward them.

Conner raised his sword groggily. "Stay behind me." It was a futile gesture. He could not hope to stand against the hydra alone. It would make a good end to his story, however.

Fenn raised the rod that had been given to him on the day he earned the name conjuror, then thrust one end deep into the snow. His will flowed through its rune-etched form, fingering the power that surged and swelled beneath his feet. Power too much for any one man.

Yet, he invited it in. All the safeguards, all the discipline, all the years of training that allowed him to wield the treacherous power of magic were set aside. *Take me*, he said. *I am yours.*

Fenn was dimly aware of his changing form — of limbs and muscles that stretched and grew, realigning themselves into something new and terrible. He heard a maniacal growl erupt from his throat. His tongue licked teeth long and sharp. Far below, a man that had been his companion turned and looked at him in horror. *Conner. So small.*

Fenn fought to maintain himself; to hold on to that part of him still a man, still human. He knew he had only moments before the magic consumed him forever. His one chance lay in expelling — if only for a short time — the great reserves of power that filled this place. He concentrated upon his rod, using its presence like an anchor.

The gloom of the great cavern vanished in a flare of boiling flame that rose like a fountain from beneath the hydra. The plume lifted all the way to the apex of the chamber hundreds of feet above, then rolled back and down the walls like liquid fire. In its wake, ice turned to steam, swirling in vortices where it sought to escape from the rivers of flame.

A wind, fierce as any in hell, tore through the chamber. Ripping icicles from the lower walls, it sent a hail of jagged teeth against the scorched monster, then swirled up and up into the sheet of flame that assailed the ceiling. The elements met with a howl of melting rock and hissing steam. The earth groaned and shook, and jagged fissures snaked along the walls and sloping roof.

Magic — raw, untamed and unleashed.

Fenn felt exultant — supreme. Nothing was beyond his reach. He was—

Like a well abruptly grown dry, the magic vanished. The hydra and the thing that Fenn had become began to ebb and diminish. The sizzling sea of flame and the roaring winds snuffed out and a heavy, scorched silence settled over the cavern.

Fenn felt arms beneath him, felt Conner's strong grip lift him to his feet. Every part of him ached.

"Here," the swordsman offered his cloak to Fenn. The conjurer discovered his nakedness and gratefully accepted.

He looked about the debris of buckled rock and bubbling pools and saw the remains of his rod — scorched at both ends and split down the middle. The strain of channeling such power, and of shielding him from its touch, had proven too much.

"Check on the others," he said to Conner — though he could see that Lang-shau and Sey-ku's foe had vanished and that Nomo was up on his feet. This last part, Fenn had to do alone.

Picking his way through the rubble, he climbed over the up-thrust rocks and toppled stone. In the center of the chamber he found a man, naked and broken, lying in a growing pool of blood. His ashen skin and throaty breaths made death obvious and imminent.

Fenn knelt beside the man, and he opened his eyes. "I told you, you'd come back…one day," he coughed through the blood and bile filling his throat.

Fenn laid a hand upon the man's cheek. "And I told you I was a better mage than you gave me credit for."

"I'm sorry," the man said. "The magic—it's just so powerful here. It…"

"Consumes you. Changes you. I know." Fenn did not need to try hard to express his understanding.

"Don't just leave them here," the man said with a final effort.

Fenn nodded, but the man was already gone.

The conjuror limped from the giant chamber and through familiar tunnels until he found what he sought. He returned to his companions carrying the books from which he had studied as an apprentice — and from which his master had learned too much and dabbled too greedily.

Conner, Nomo, Lang-shau and Sey-ku waited for him. All of them gazed down at the body of the dead wizard.

"A man?" Conner asked. "The monster was— "

Fenn stopped before the swordsman and fixed him with such a gaze that the words caught in his mouth.

The conjurer then turned to Nomo. "Find another ending to your story, scribe," he said.

Nomo nodded. "Of course. The monster died. The end."

Without a word more, they began the long journey back to the north.

Bill Ward's fiction and a few nonfiction articles have appeared in numerous magazines and anthologies, including RBE's Return of the Sword. *He has also written background material and serial shorts for science fiction and fantasy tabletop game publications. To find more of his fiction or read his book reviews, please visit http://billwardwriter.com or find his weekly post at www.BlackGate.com. Bill's writing — often dark and possessing a dangerous edge — is raw. At its best, it is bloody and emotional. When it's even better it forces his characters and his readers to question their choices...examine their actions...evaluate their lives. Self-assessment is usually not so desirable; through it we often discover we are not the men we thought we were — and sometimes we learn we are the very monsters we fear.*

The Wolf of Winter

A Tale of the Wastes

by Bill Ward

Ice cracked beneath Krhanik's boots with a sound like the breaking of a man's skull. He took another step, and another, and the cold sheet beneath him groaned in protest. Krhanik walked on, heedless of the snapping sounds of fracturing ice, his face upright in the sleeting gale that pushed against his forward progress. Before him rose the image of the wolf, enormous, world-spanning; the beast that had haunted his earliest dreams and filled his blood with poisonous rage. Somewhere ahead of him, in the darkest part of the north, the wolf awaited him — and Krhanik walked unbowed into the storm to meet it.

To meet his destiny.

Beneath him bone-white fissures snaked in all directions with each careless step, rivulets of spider-silk-fine cracks marring the gray surface of the pack ice. Krhanik did not look down, never looked down. Keeping his eyes fixed on the line of flattened hills in the distance — the only landmark he could see in the swirling wet of the storm — Krhanik walked on under a twilight sky fat with rain clouds the color of damp felt.

Beneath him, beneath the creaking ice, the fathomless salt depths of the ocean rolled cold and hungry.

Krhanik could not recall how long he had been walking along the floe, or just when he had left his home south in the Thaws. He was old. His thoughts dwelled more in the past now than in the present, and he was often uncertain of the passage of time. But that did not matter, for time was mere illusion, as the wise men of the shamansal taught. Each moment contained all things, all people, all deeds — all existing within a single, instantaneous flash in the mind of the Eater God. Krhanik cared little for their flights of imagination, but shamanic notions of time had always appealed to him from the earliest age when he had begun to see his life take shape in his mind's eye.

He had seen this moment long ago, had lived with it for decades. Alone, numb with cold, clothed in stitched elk hide beneath a dingy white bear pelt, one mittened hand clutching at his pack strap as he leaned into the wind. The other hand, the right hand, squeezing the shaft of his ice-lance hard enough to feel it through the mitten's thick padding. The lance was of rarest southern hardwood but far rarer still was its tip, a conical spearhead of frozen blood colder than any earthly ice. It was the mark of a great man, a hero, a king. Krhanik had been all three.

And now he would be greater still with the meeting of the wolf.

A sound like the sundering of granite boomed above the gale, and Krhanik felt a shudder in the ice below and checked his balance to avoid falling. Behind him, directly in line with his tracks, a vast slab of gray split off from the main body of ice and twisted along its fault line, raising spumes of frothing seawater along its length and filling the air with the sounds of its grinding. Krhanik felt its gnashing power, felt it deep at the level of his bones, deeper even than the cold that deadened his every other sensation. There was a time when he would have run from that screaming twist of ice, not out of fear but of a cool appraisal of his own vulnerability. But the wolf was close, and Krhanik strode resolutely over the breaking sea ice and kept steadily on his course while cracks the size of a man's finger slithered below him and he could almost hear the low, subtle tearing sound of the failing ice above the sounds of his own laughter.

To laugh in the face of danger, to meet any challenge squarely, had always been his way. Krhanik had clawed his way from outcast cutthroat to King of Nine Tribes with only his own guile and strength to aid him. When the armies of the Guotai Hordes ravaged the Southlands and turned north for fresh conquests he had humbled them at the Battle of Snathak's Pass and slew their Great Khan. Krhanik had sent the Khan's head, its gold-toothed mouth stuffed with the man's own genitals, back to distant Orghaz Koi as a token of his contempt. As a younger man he had fought ritual poison-stave duels for coin and had defeated fourteen champions and a cleric of the Iron-Eyed God in one single, glorious year. Now his holdings stretched from the Ribreak Inlet to the Sunken Towns, his fortune was measured against the weight of the paving stones of ancient Rorrosant, and his armies had blackened the Southlands in nine successive seasons of raiding that would leave his name forever remembered there as the blackest of curses.

Beneath him the ice split. Salt water spilled along the crack and instantly froze. Solid land lay close by, just ahead — but Krhanik did not increase his pace.

At the meeting of Three Armies in the winter of his thirtieth year he had personally killed fifty-nine men over a half day of slaughter. The heart of the Kabra champion known as Bear Skull he consumed while that lord's own men looked on in horror, and he smiled a crimson smile at each retainer as they dropped to their knee and swore allegiance to their new master. The wolf laughed with him as he burned town after town in his campaign to bring all the lands of the Snow Lizard people under his heel. Krhanik smiled as he recalled the slaughter and ruin he had wrought the length and breadth of the Thaw.

He strode on oblivious to the sounds of the ice breaking in his wake, his every footfall shattering the friable surface just ahead of the thinning ice. The ocean splashed his boots and still Krhanik walked serenely forward, his mind on the glories of the past.

For the slaughter of the Snow Lizards they had called him Castigator. Other names, too, he had earned. In the south he was Eater's Shadow or Northern Devil, but to the tribes of the Thaw he was Red Limb, or Blood Star. The Guotai called him Black Heart, and Krhanik liked that name a great deal. Yet none of these names could he truly call his own.

Beneath him only a hint of ice remained. All around the cold surge of the sea rippled over the leaning shards of the pack ice, but Krhanik thought only of his true name as he walked. That which named his destiny.

The Kabra people had known. Possessing powerful shamans, they had seen the shadow that loomed just over Krhanik's shoulder. The wolf at world's end, Fenrax World-Devourer, a monstrous giant whose fur glistened with jagged spikes of frozen-air, and whose jaws steamed with the hot blood of its victims. The Kabra had known Krhanik for what he was, and called him the Winter Wolf after his spirit animal.

Krhanik did not so much as pause when his boot bit into the wet snow at the edge of the ice flow, and he did not turn around to see the vast expanse of ocean that had surged up to fill the world in his wake. He did, however, stop some long-spans further inland and look upward at the purpling sky, and strain to see the shape that suggested itself there. The cold assaulted him, and stinging flecks of ice pricked his exposed face, but still Krhanik stared for a long time at the roiling rain clouds. One, darker than the others, the color of a newly made blood-bruise, contained within it a pale shape. He watched the shape grow to fill the sky, as if it moved toward him just as he moved toward it. He marched on.

That night, in the dugout shelter he had made for himself, cradling the bit of burning punk he had carried with him in a fire pot beneath his jerkin, Krhanik thought of that shape and knew it for what it was. He had seen this too, as a boy, just as he had seen his future Kingship and his victories …and his inevitable sorrows.

Fenrax was coming to meet him, and behind the wolf blew the cold wind of destiny.

Krhanik awoke with a start, his hands clutched in front of him as if around a slender throat. A shadow waited outside the thin snow wall of his dugout and, with a roar, the Winter Wolf snatched up his lance and burst from his meager shelter in an explosion of crystalline powder.

The man was not afraid, but raised his gloved hands wide as a sign that he meant no harm. The slurry of the storm had abated, and the fresh snowfall — itself brighter than the sky — reflected light enough to see for many long-spans in all directions. The fur-clad stranger, framed by the scrawl of low hills on the horizon, smiled and gestured for Krhanik to put down his blood-tipped spear.

Krhanik kept his weapon level with the man's heart.

"Last boat. Last chance to flee this place," the man said, his accent hard to place. His youthful features resembled those of the Kabra people, but his voice had the lilt of the far south. "Please," he said, "do not stay here. You have a choice. Last boat." He pointed back along the path Krhanik had come the day before, though his tracks were long buried by the snows.

Krhanik glanced south, and saw a small craft moored on the precarious shore some long-spans distant. He squinted at the man and said nothing.

The man smiled and pointed to his chest, just where Krhanik's aim would take the frozen point of his lance should he attack. "Moas," he said, smiling again to show his bright teeth. "My name is Moas."

"Be on your way, Moas." Krhanik snarled, turning his back on the man to gather his things. He had decided Moas was not a threat.

"Do you hear that, Krhanik? That sound above the wind?"

Krhanik wheeled, dropping his fire pot in the snow and raising his lance. He took a full step toward Moas, yet the younger man did not flinch. "How did you know my name?" Krhanik said through barred teeth.

"You told me. Can't you hear the wailing above the wind? Please listen when I tell you that you do not have to be here. You do not have to chase this horrible dream of yours. You think you march forth in challenge—I tell you now you will be consumed by the thing you think to best."

"By the Eater's Guts I never spoke my name to you. Tell me how you come to be here, and come to know my name, or I'll stick you low, and leave you a long time dying in the waste."

Moas's smile wavered. "Time is all one thing, Krhanik Winter Wolf. You know that. That is how I know—"

Krhanik did not wait to hear more, but thrust his ice-lance swiftly forward into the man's chest. Moas fell to the ground with a cry of anguish.

Krhanik stood above him, spear poised to strike, wolf-snarl on his lips. "What do you know of my dreams, whelp? What do you know of the thing I seek?"

Moas groaned and blood darkened his lips. "He wails for you, even now, and there is still a chance. Listen above the wind." Moas panted, his face a mask of pain. "You can still leave this place. The ship will wait for you."

Krhanik stuck him again, low and cruel. The crimson of Moas's blood froze along the darker head of the ice-lance. The young man wailed — a sharp, barking sound — then his features settled into a beatific smile.

"I go now to dwell in the divine shadow of the Encompasser," Moas whispered to the overcast sky.

"Tell him Krhanik sent you." The Winter Wolf stabbed downward with all his strength and the stranger lay still, the black tendrils of his spreading blood creeping along the snow like the legs of a spider. Hot blood steamed in the cold air.

As Krhanik retrieved his extinguished fire pot he realized he had indeed told Moas his name, just before he slew him. With a growl he flung the useless pot from him and stalked north, never once turning back to look at the dead man or the dead man's ship.

He tried, too, not to listen to the sounds above the wind.

Day and night were much the same, for only weather mattered here. Krhanik moved implacably forward, through frozen spit and silent blankets of snow, through stinging hail and skin-cutting wind. On occasion he found himself in a world gone still; the only thing moving in the clear air brittle with cold and alive with the light of the stars. He had no fire and so did not stop to rest, only pausing now-and-again to gnaw on the strips of dried meat and seal blubber he had packed as provision. He paused, too, whenever the wolf seemed near.

He had lived his life in the shadow of the wolf. Long before he had met with the shaman and priests and wise men of the northern world, long before he had been told that the World-Devourer was his totem, or kindred animal, Krhanik had seen the wolf in his dreams, and felt him over his shoulder or loping just alongside as he moved out to make war or bring vengeance upon a town or tribe.

Fenrax had been there on his first raid, as Krhanik smote the defenseless serfs of some nameless village along the Viber. He had raised his bloody axe in salute as the beast loomed over him, big enough to blot out the moon, its eyes glinting with the unwavering light of distant planets. The beast had roared with Krhanik's own voice as he took the Kabra by surprise and put the men of their villages to the sword and impressed their whelps into service and made slaves of their fine-boned women. And in the Southlands he had seen, distinctly as anything in life, Fenrax rise up from the steam of the hot pools around Coralre to scatter the men on its walls just as his own besiegers had rushed forward with their ladders and stormed the town.

Had he really come all this way to slay it? To kill his totem? Krhanik did not think so, but could not remember ever setting out on this journey, or ever having decided to do so. Did it not make greater sense that he moved ever northward to bask in the beast's power, to relish its all-consuming spite?

Others had seen the giant wolf that dwelled within the shadows of his life. Others had felt its anger. An argument — the boy had been a fool and a coward — rage, pure rage and a striking fist — the boy had been his only son, his only heir — dark blood on his ring of office, the sick sound of bone cracking, of a skull cracking like pack ice with the thaw — the boy had been just a boy, he had taught him so much, he had loved him — blood on the floor, on the throne. Blood on his hands for all time.

Krhanik threw his head back and screamed. It was not the howl of the wolf.

His son lay dead before him, a senseless argument over a girl. Over marrying the wrong girl. Krhanik had wanted to behead the girl, had wanted to slaughter the world, but his wife must have hidden her, spirited her away. His wife had hidden herself in exile, not long after. With her gone, Krhanik could better hear the sounds of the wolf's breathing echoing through the halls on nights of the bright moon, and he remembered the sound, now. Remembered hating the sound.

Above the wind now, the cries of a woman. Of a child. It did not matter. "Fenrax!" the Winter Wolf roared, his ice-lance clenched in one outstretched hand. No longer cold, Krhanik boiled with the heat of his own rage. The shape in the sky had grown larger, and above the shrieking, above even the raging of the storm, swirled cruel laughter — laughter no longer his own. Krhanik raged his promises for revenge, and damned the beast that was his kindred spirit. He ran north, toward the blackest part of the sky, hearing nothing but his own screams, remembering now it was not union he sought, but vengeance for a life poisoned and defiled.

The wailing had been that of a child. A baby, swaddled in rich furs, waited for Krhanik upon a spit of blue ice in a sea of dead gray snow.

Krhanik froze.

After a still time filled only with the babe's sobbing, he moved closer to it, uncomprehending. It caught sight of him and shrieked anew, slender plumes of steam piping from its tiny mouth. Krhanik rushed to its side, shushing it as best he could, cradling it in hands that bore the stains of a thousand deaths. He did not understand. Alone in the wastes, it could not be here. Nothing could be here.

He did not understand.

He did not name it, would not give it a name. He thought to leave it behind, but could not. Toward blackest north the Winter Wolf marched, the tightly wrapped and sleeping babe sealed beneath his jerkin, pressed against his old heart for warmth. He wore the babe where once he wore the fire pot.

~ The Wolf of Winter ~

"You are not my son," he said to it. It was a boy child, and familiar to him, and for a thrilling moment he had thought it had been the child he had lost. The child he had murdered. But it was not. "You are not my son — be glad of it."

If time was as the shamansal say, as Moas had hinted, then at this moment Krhanik's boy still lived. At this moment, too, Krhanik was about to slay his son; was slaying him; was howling over his corpse. Over every instant loomed Fenrax, always watching, watching Krhanik all of his days. At this moment Krhanik was dashing the brains from a babe just this size in a burning farmhouse in a nameless village. In the very same moment he was deciding not to. In every instant a thousand thousand lives were extinguished and a thousand thousand lives remained whole — ever fate-bound to the bloody purpose of the Wolf of Winter.

The child began to cry, and Krhanik tried to comfort it. They were alone in the white world beneath an angry sky, and for the first time the ship of Moas entered into Krhanik's mind. "I would like to put you on that ship, little one," he said, and meant it more than any proclamation of kingship or oath he had ever made.

"Would you indeed?" A voice like breaking ice boomed out of the dark sky. Krhanik shook with the sound of it.

"Will you not look at me, my kin?" Its voice was many voices, hundreds, thousands, all roaring and rasping and grating and shouting down at Krhanik out of the sky. When he did not look up it howled a howl that set the world to shaking. "Look at me!"

Krhanik looked. The World-Devourer was bigger than the sky, ice-furred like a jagged mountain of glass. Its maw dripped a rich, steaming crimson. Krhanik could see it clearer now than he ever had in life.

"Are you me?" he asked and, as he did, he knew it was the wrong question.

Fenrax laughed, its thousand voices piping and bellowing their amusement, sending great flakes of ice shivering off its flanks to crash on the white earth below. The beast now filled all of Krhanik's vision, though through it he could see the glitter of stars.

"Am I you? The opposite is closer the truth, but not the whole story. Do you think I could be mistaken for that same frail mortal lying on his death bed, his head full of the confusion of remembered joy and bitter regret that you see before you?"

And it was before him, the whole scene. Just as Krhanik had seen his life as a boy, known he would carry the ice-lance and eat the heart of Bear Skull and defeat the Guotai and take the city of Coralre and unite the Nine Tribes under his kingship and rule all the lands of the Thaw — just as he had known those things and seen them, so too had he seen the image before him. The old, broken man, dying alone while his servants ransacked his palace, and his generals and chiefs schemed for succession and counted down the hours until his death. He saw it clearly, each labored breath of the dying man, as if it were happening before him at that moment.

Krhanik realized that it was happening, exactly that. It was all happening right now, at this particular flash in time. He was dying.

Fenrax World-Devourer smiled broadly and spoke in its many voices, "Now, come to me, favored son. Be one with us, your kith and kind. The black vengeance in your heart is a gift from me, embrace it as you have embraced me all your days."

A stirring at his chest, and Krhanik looked down at a familiar face. The babe regarded him, as if waiting for a decision. He bent his face down to nuzzle it, and kissed its forehead, and whispered to the child that was every possibility he had ever denied. "Your name is Krhanik. Krhanik only. Allow no other."

Krhanik raised his ice-lance, aimed its tip of frozen blood at the heart of the World-Killer that loomed colossal over the frozen plain, and threw with all his might.

Jeff Stewart knows what it is to hunt an unseen prey. He is a government employee who roams the globe looking for trouble, and usually ends up making it for himself. He constantly battles the forces of evil and bureaucracy, which may explain his limited career progression. He is owned by a Labrador Retriever who runs the house with an iron fist. He enjoys pirate movies, comic books, historical fiction, and long walks on the beach. Jeff also enjoys delivering a fine tale of mystery and marvel. Here we again meet Sigurd, and learn with him that blind fears gain their power in ignorance. The more they are fed, the larger they become and the more deadly their effects. Despite that, love can still survive and triumph…if given the opportunity.

Nothing Left of the Man

A Tale of Sigurd Grimbrow

by Jeff Stewart

The tracks outlined in the fresh snow indicated a monstrous bruin.

Sigurd Grimbrow grinned at their luck. Tired of just sitting aboard ship and watching the shoreline pass, he craved something to do. That was why he had debarked today; to stretch his legs and do a bit of hunting. The whole crew was weary of salted cod and porridge. Fresh meat would be a welcome reprieve, as would the sport in hunting it. He did experience a tinge of concern at the massive size of the paw prints, but the thrill of the discovery quickly overcame any anxiety

Sigurd glanced at his companions. Ketill Snake Eater watched the woods intently, an arrow nocked on his bow. Ketill was the best hunter among the Valkyrion crew. He had earned his name by slaying one of the giant Wyvern single-handedly, the only Valkyrion in living memory to do so. His accuracy with his powerful bow provided most of the meat that supplemented the crew's rations.

Chiangkin, the renegade Nevarine, knelt and studied the bear tracks. Smaller than his companions, Chiangkin had the olive skin, raven hair and high cheekbones of the Nevarine people. Sigurd had never met a man more at home in the woods. Chiangkin had been trained as a Keldan March Warder before being declared outlaw. Fleeing his homeland, the little man had joined Sigurd's Valkyrion crew and never looked back.

Chiangkin abruptly stood and without a word loped off along the beast's trail. Sigurd looked at Ketill. The blond hunter merely nodded and followed his friend. Sigurd grinned again. Another reason he had chosen these two to accompany him; they did not waste words.

The trio followed the trail through the dim woods, winding through the towering trees and great boulders. Hours passed as they pursued their quarry. Once they stopped at a rushing mountain stream to slake their thirst and chew some dried meat. They began to hurry as the shadows lengthened into afternoon. The days were short this time of the year, and there would be a lot of work in butchering the beast and hauling it back to the river.

Sigurd came around a bend in the trail to find Chiangkin studying the banks of another stream. Ketill was off to the side, scanning the ground. Sigurd moved to his comrades and saw instantly what the problem was. The plate sized tracks were plainly evident up to the edge of the stream, but did not emerge on the far side. The trail ended abruptly at the flowing water.

"Why would a bear move into the stream?" asked Sigurd. Chiangkin merely grunted, clearly puzzled by this behavior.

"Maybe it was looking for fish?" Even Ketill did not seem convinced of his own theory.

"Better question," quietly asked the Nevarine, "why this bear not sleeping?"

Sigurd felt a brief chill of foreboding at Chiangkin's words. Although it was not unheard of for a hibernating bear to awake periodically during the long northern winters, they would usually venture only a small way from their lair. A short exploration would convince them that winter still held the world in its icy grip, and then back to blissful sleep they would go. The trio had followed this monster for a long time over difficult terrain. It was a very long way from its lair.

"Well, we must make a decision," announced Sigurd, focusing on the problem at hand. "We cannot split up and we don't have time to search both ways. So which way do we go, upstream or down?"

"If it was after the fish, it would move upstream," offered Ketill.

"I think it knew we followed. I think it go downstream." The Nevarine looked thoughtful as he contemplated his suggestion.

"We have to get back to the ship before dark. This stream will flow into the river. Since we have to go that way eventually, we'll go downstream." The other two nodded at Sigurd's announcement and turned to follow the gurgling stream. Sigurd fell into the rear, but not before looking around uneasily. His shoulder blades twitched with the distinct feeling that they were being watched.

The trio moved steadily along the watercourse. The little stream obviously flooded during the spring thaw and the run-off had cleared most of the obstacles in the narrow flood plain. They made good time and were nearing the river channel when Chiangkin leapt the narrows and knelt on the far side. His companions jumped the constricted stream and joined him.

Fresh tracks clearly led from the rushing stream off into the woods, headed back into the hills. Puddles of stream water had frozen solid in the tracks, proof that at least half an hour had passed since they were made. The trail started abruptly at the water's edge. The trail's maker had clearly been following the stream bed before turning into the forest.

"Wind and Wave!" Ketill's whispered oath broke the silence.

"Yes," agreed an awestruck Chiangkin.

Sigurd merely looked into the forest, trying to pierce the gloom. Once again he had the uncomfortable feeling that they were being observed. "Come on, lads. Let us get back to the ship." He would feel less on edge when they were surrounded by their shield brothers back at the river. The trio turned and trotted along the flowing stream toward the river, leaving the ominous tracks behind them.

None of them spoke a word about the prints outlined in the snow — clearly made by a bare human foot.

The three hunters were met with good natured jeers when it was discovered that they returned empty handed. The crew spent the night along the riverbed and continued upstream the next morning. Still uneasy after yesterday's eerie hunt, Sigurd elected not to put a hunting party ashore.

The ship had been plying upriver for almost three weeks now, and was deep into Kazak territory. The heavy winters this far north made travel difficult, and most of the isolated villages were dependent on river traffic for news and trade. The Valkyrion crew traded its way from village to village, gathering the thick furs that Kazakstan was famous for. Soon the ship would be full and they could head downstream to the rich markets of the Confederation or Aragon.

An isolated village hove into view along the river's edge when the sun was at its zenith. The crew beached the longship and received a warm greeting from the lonely villagers. Sigurd held a hasty consultation with the village hetman, a fat Kazak who looked like he drank too much.

"Greetings, great Eorl."

"I am not Eorl here, merely a ship's captain," answered Sigurd.

The Kazak shrugged. "We are anxious to see your wares. It has been a long time between visitors this winter. Might I suggest that the ale and the vistock be withheld until the trading is complete?"

"I wholeheartedly agree. Your vistock is a heady brew, and some of my crew are younglings who have not had to brave such potent beverages before." Sigurd had seen too many of these happy trading fairs turn ugly, and if there was trouble his crew would be outnumbered by the locals.

Blankets were spread on the snowy ground and wares were displayed. Thick furs of mink, otter, beaver, elk, moose, and bear were hauled from the Kazak homes. The Valkyrion unloaded bales of rich eastern cloth, warm Keldan wool, pots and cunning metal work from the Confederation, Fiernan whiskey, tools and weapons of Keldan steel. Trading began in earnest and carried on late into the afternoon. Valkyrion and Kazak alike love to bargain, and brief trading fairs such as this gave a welcome respite to the slow days of the northern winter. The sun was low on the horizon and the cooking fires lit before the last bargain was sealed with a crushing handshake.

The Kazak men rolled a barrel of ale into the village square and bottles of the fiery vistock appeared. The victorious traders on both sides celebrated with a toast while the women of the village scattered to prepare the evening meal. The hetman approached Sigurd once more.

"Would your crew honor us by sharing our homes tonight? We do not have much, but visitors are always welcome and we would like to hear news of the outside world."

"Gladly, my good man, although I am not sure your liquor will be safe," Sigurd joked with a wink. "It would be nice to spend the night next to a warm fire rather than on the freezing ground."

Sigurd moved through the village, making sure each of his men were paired with a family for the night and watching for anyone drunk enough to make trouble. The crowd in the village square began to break up and drift to their homes, driven by the gathering chill. Sigurd noticed that the Kazaks glanced nervously at the setting sun. Wives returned to the square and chivied reluctant husbands home. People began to move quickly, as if fearful of being caught in the open by the darkness.

Sigurd found his thegn, Thorfinn Ironskin, with a bottle of vistock in one hand and his arm around a pretty Kazak girl.

"Thorfinn, tell the men to watch themselves. Something smells wrong here." Sigurd laid his forefinger alongside his nose to emphasize his point.

"What is it?" asked the red bearded giant.

"I am not sure. Just keep your eyes open."

The two leaders spread the word among the Valkyrion crew. Soon the village square was empty as the crew moved to the homes of their host families for the evening. Sigurd found himself at the home of the hetman. "Come in, come in. No strangers here." The stocky bald Kazak ushered Sigurd in. Producing a fresh bottle of the fiery vistock, he commenced drinking it as if it were water — only occasionally remembering to splash some in a glass for his guest.

The hetman rated a larger house than most Kazaks, and this one was three rooms built of stout logs and chinked with mud. Sigurd basked in the glorious warmth. The thick walls held in the heat from the central hearth which lit the common room. The other two rooms included one bedroom shared by a gaggle of children and the hetman's aged father, and another presumably for the hetman and his wife.

Sigurd and the hetman talked during dinner, discoursing on trade and the weather, topics dear to sailors and farmers alike. They had a delicious meal of rich stew and fresh bread, washed down by winter ale and vistock. The hetman's children watched wide-eyed and listened to Sigurd's sailing tales, fascinated by the gray-eyed outlander. The hetman's father, a senile old man, sat in the corner oblivious to the stranger at his table. The family seemed honest and happy enough, but Sigurd noted how the wife frequently glanced at the barred door, as if assuring herself that it was locked. Once, when a log on the fire popped unexpectedly, the whole family gasped in fright. The hetman laughed nervously, explaining, "We are not used to having visitors." But Sigurd didn't miss the frightened looks on the faces of the children.

After Sigurd had told all he knew of the western kingdoms, the family prepared for bed. The children were bustled into their room with a minimum of complaints. A pallet was laid near the hearth for the guest. The wife took the elderly father by the hand and led him toward his room.

Suddenly the old man looked up at the ceiling and a terrified cry burst from his throat. "It comes! It comes tonight!" The wife threw a frightened look at her husband and ushered the old man into his bed. Drawing the curtain across the doorway, she turned and left the room without a word.

The hetman sat at the table with Sigurd, staring pointedly at his glass. Clearly he hoped his guest would ignore the old man's outburst. Yet Sigurd saw no reason not to satisfy his own curiosity.

"What was that about?"

The hetman sighed and poured another glass of vistock. "Nothing. Just the ramblings of an old man." Sigurd sat quietly, waiting for more. The Kazak squirmed under his guest's scrutiny and gulped his drink. Filling the now empty glass, he looked his guest in the eye. "It is just…Well, there has been some trouble lately," he finally admitted.

"What kind of trouble?"

"Animals. A bear, actually. A huge monster, the largest ever seen in our memory. We think it has woken early and is hunting for food. There have been several attacks."

"Where?"

"In the woods at first. But lately here in the village," admitted the hetman.

"Why not just kill it?"

"We have tried. But the damned thing will not die. We have put a dozen arrows in it, but it does no good."

"Have you tracked it to its lair?"

"We tried, but have had no luck. Our best hunter was one of the first killed. He left to track it after the attacks began. But it found him first."

"How many attacks have there been?"

"More than a dozen. At the beginning they only happened in the woods, but a couple of weeks ago it came into the village. Since then it comes every third or fourth night. It batters down the door of a house and kills everyone inside. Then it leaves." The hetman downed another shot of vistock as if trying to wash a sour taste from his mouth.

"Does it eat its victims?"

"No, it just kills them. We have tried leaving food out for it. The food disappears but the killing continues. We do not know what to do."

The room was silent save for the crackling fire as the two men sat, each deep in their own thoughts. The hetman shifted several times in his seat, and finally mumbled something into his beard.

Sigurd leaned forward. "What was that?"

"Some say it is our penance."

"How so?" asked Sigurd.

"Last summer there was an ugly incident. Svetna, one of our local girls, had married an outsider a couple of years before. Oh, he was still a Kazak," explained the hetman, waving his hand, "but he was from upriver. Exiled from his own village for some reason. He was a fine hunter though, and we needed fresh meat, so I let him stay on."

"Anyway, the pair of them had a daughter. Everything seemed fine, except the girl had an evil eye."

"What do you mean?"

"You know, an evil eye. She had one brown eye like a normal girl and one evil eye, as blue as the sky. We tried to ignore it at first, but as she got older it began to affect the village. Cows went dry, hens wouldn't lay, accidents happened. Things that were more than just natural bad luck."

Sigurd nodded. The Valkyrion and the Kazaks shared a deep belief in luck and its impact on daily life. A man with bad luck was cursed, and a village with bad luck was damned. Entire settlements had been abandoned because the location had become unlucky.

"So what happened? Did you banish them?"

"No, although some argued for that. I considered it, but then things came to a head, very sudden like. Dmitri had a run in with the little girl. He caught her playing near his cow shed and feared that she had put a spell on his cows. He cuffed the girl and chased her down the street, switching her with a willow stick. He only stopped when the girl hid behind her mother's skirts. Dmitri cursed the girl and threatened to flay her hide if he caught her near his cows again. Svetna glared at Dmitri and swore that he would pay for his actions. Then she stormed inside with her daughter."

"Likely there would have been a fight right then, but the husband was away hunting. Anyway, Dmitri went out woodcutting with his brother. But his axe turned on the very first tree and cut his foot off. His brother carried him back to the village, but it was no use. He bled to death before they arrived. The village was upset enough by that, and when his brother revealed that Dmitri had damned Svetna and her daughter with his dying breath, it was too much. A crowd gathered and dragged the two of them from their home. They stoned them, right there in the village square. They were both dead by the time I got there."

Sigurd nodded grimly at this sorrowful tale. "How old was the girl?"

"Three. A bit more maybe."

"What happened to the man?"

"Radvik? I was waiting with some strapping boys when he got back from the hunt. It took five of us to hold him when he found out. Finally I broke a chair over his head. We put him in a hut to sleep it off, but the next morning he was gone." The hetman drank the last swallow of his vistock. "Never saw him again. But the attacks started two weeks later. Some say Radvik enchanted himself, others say he talked to the bear and asked for its help. My wife thinks the little girl's spirit has possessed the brute and come back to take revenge. Who knows?" He shrugged as if to explain away the mysterious ways of the universe.

"What happened to the people who stoned them?"

"Nothing! What could I do? Half the village was in on it. It was not as if the girl did not deserve her fate. She had an evil eye. She was bad luck!"

"What has your luck been like since then?" Sigurd softly asked.

The hetman averted his gaze and noisily cleared his throat. "Time for bed," he rasped as he stood and moved into the adjoining room.

Sigurd stoked the fire and contemplated the hetman's story. Killing a child was a terrible act, even a child with bad luck. He decided that he and his crew would leave first thing tomorrow, right after sunup. This village had bad luck, and he didn't want to be a victim of it. Rolling himself in his cloak, he lay on the pallet.

But sleep was a long time coming. He thought of his wife and son, remembering how much he loved them and how much it had hurt when he had lost them. He remembered with satisfaction the revenge he had taken on their killer. As sleep finally claimed the Valkyrion warrior, he found himself thinking that perhaps this village deserved its nemesis.

He awoke to a thundering roar. The terrible growl seemed to be right next to him and he rolled from his pallet grasping for his weapons. But the room was empty. Frightened cries from behind the children's curtain assured him that the roar had been real.

"Where is he?" The hetman's bald head poked through the doorway to his bedroom.

A mighty blow crashed against the barred door as if in answer to his question.

"I think your guest has returned," laconically commented the Valkyrion.

The bruin outside roared its rage at being balked in its hunt. Sigurd watched the door shudder as the bear began to savage the wooden barrier with a series of devastating blows. The thick logs of the door shuddered but held under the onslaught. A solid wooden beam — fully as broad as Sigurd's thigh and settled in iron brackets braced against the doorway lintels — supplemented the thrown bolt. Sigurd noted that the bar had been reinforced with iron and wondered if the hetman had anticipated such an attack. Whatever the reason, his preparations were well justified, and the thick plank held against the powerful blows being rained upon it.

The hetman's wife scrambled through the common room and herded the children into the corner of their bedroom, firmly drawing the curtain shut behind her. Sigurd briefly wondered what she thought the flimsy fabric would stop. The half-dressed hetman stumbled into the room, holding a long bladed knife.

Sigurd slipped his arm into his shield and hefted his war axe. He had doubts about their ability to kill the ravening monster outside, but even this door couldn't hold forever against such an assault. Scarcely had he finished the thought before a fist sized portion of wood splintered and flew inside. The bear immediately focused its efforts on this area and began to claw long strips of wood from the door.

"Won't the other villagers come to help?"

"No," said the hetman, nervously clutching his knife. "They are too afraid. They will simply huddle in their homes and hope the beast passes them by."

"Well, my men won't hide in the dark like frightened children! If we can hold the door a few moments, they can take the beast in the rear."

A splintering crash cut off his speech as two of the planks in the door buckled under the pressure. A huge paw, as broad as a man's chest, plunged through the gaping hole and swept menacingly at the two men. It cut the air inches from the terrified hetman. The bear roared in frustration at being stopped so close to its prey.

Sigurd leapt forward and his axe flashed. The blade struck the bear's massive front leg, but the glancing blow did not go deep. Still, it was enough to cause the bear to withdraw its limb and begin hammering the door again. Seconds passed with infinite slowness as the trapped men waited for some sign of rescue from without. But the only sound was the deadly boom of the bear's attack on the door, reverberating through building. Suddenly a mighty blow crashed into the door. The tortured wood splintered as, with hinges popping, the top half of the door caved in.

Instantly a snarling maw of dagger-length teeth crammed the opening. It was easily the largest bear snout Sigurd had ever seen, dwarfing even the white giants of his homeland. The head filled the open doorway and the bear's breath steamed in the cool night air, filling the room with a fetid stench. It leaned forward, unable to enter the room because the iron bound bar still held the lower half of the door in place. The lintels creaked ominously under the weight of the bear's massive shoulders. The head twisted with impatience as it tried to force its way into the enclosed space and the gaping muzzle roared its fury into the victims' faces. Its teeth snapped viciously and the monster's eyes blazed with hatred.

Sigurd feinted with his axe, trying to draw the animal's attention from the stunned hetman. Suddenly the Kazak shook himself and charged the beast. He ran under its snapping jaws and began ferociously stabbing the bear's exposed neck. The bear swung its snout and knocked the Kazak into the doorframe, stunning the hetman who slumped to the floor. The colossal head swooped and mighty jaws closed on the helpless form, engulfing the hetman until only his legs protruded from the snarling lips. The bear shook itself from side to side, crushing the limp body between its teeth. Liquid gore poured from its maw and steamed upon the floor. With a final shake of its enormous head, the bruin threw the broken ruin against the far wall.

Sigurd backed away from the snarling beast as it turned its attention to the remaining human. The head retreated and a massive paw swung into the room. Razor-sharp claws swept the air, inches from Sigurd's flesh. The snarling behemoth threw itself against the remnants of the door, trying desperately to reach its prey. Sigurd could feel the heat of the fire at his back and could hear the cries of terror from the children behind the curtain. He danced around the flailing paw, trying to measure how close he would have to be to strike the throat. Too close, he thought.

Then he heard a new clamor from outside. The noise rose and fell in a litany of curses and oaths. Sigurd grinned in spite of his predicament. Thorfinn had joined the battle.

"Come on out, you great hairy monster! By the Great Spear, I'll wear your coat for dinner tonight! Ketill, put some arrows in this pin cushion. Turn around or I'll chop my way through your damned hind end!"

The bear pulled itself from the hut and turned, snapping viscously at its enemies. Beyond its massive back, Sigurd saw Thorfinn jump back just in time to avoid the snapping jaws. Thorfinn leaped in with his axe and struck again, dodging back out as the bear spun to face him. Sigurd could see more of his crew surrounding the monster, brandishing weapons and torches. Like a pack of highly trained hounds, the men would attack from each side and then dance away, hopefully before the brute could react. But the massive bruin was dangerously swift, and two men were brutally clawed before they could get away.

Sigurd dashed forward and smashed his axe into the monster's back. After several blows, he realized it was useless. The low ceiling of the cottage and the narrow opening of the broken door prevented him from swinging a full blow at the bear's exposed back. The beast was armored by its thick matted fur which turned Sigurd's weakened blows. He realized that his axe could not cause significant damage to the creature in this situation.

Backing away, he scanned the room for a more effective weapon. He spied the long knife dropped by the ineffectual hetman, but rejected it immediately as unsuitable. Looking again, Sigurd finally spied a possibility in the hearth. A spit, four feet of sharpened iron, hung from its hooks above the smoldering fire. Dropping his axe and shield, Sigurd grabbed the spit, ignoring the pain as the hot metal seared his palms.

The bear was still snarling and striking at the semi-circle of Valkyrion that surrounded the door. It had turned until its colossal side leaned against the open doorway. Holding the stake at chest level to clear the remnants of the door, Sigurd charged his enemy. The sharpened spit hesitated briefly when it struck the bear but then continued with a small pop as it penetrated the thick hide. Throwing his weight onto the shaft, Sigurd pushed the spike as far as he could into the living flesh.

A deafening roar shook the night as the bear reared to its full height, towering over its tormentors. Dropping to all fours, the bruin charged the surrounding circle with lightning speed. Men were bowled over in the rush, but Thorfinn leaped in front of the fleeing creature, blocking its escape. A crashing blow from a massive paw swept the brave Valkyrion from its path like a rag doll. The red-bearded giant flew through the air to crash against the logs of a nearby house.

As suddenly as it had appeared, the monster was gone, leaving only the mangled bodies of its victims in the street. Sigurd clambered through the broken door and rushed to Thorfinn's side, fearful of what he would find. The thegn was bloodied and gashed, and thick blood oozed from between his lips, but he was alive. Thorfinn's eyelids fluttered and he looked up at his leader. His face broke into a bloody smile. "You…never told…me there was…a party."

Sigurd looked into the face of his injured friend and chuckled. "I knew you would crash the door. You dance rather poorly, you clumsy oaf."

"Your mother…did not complain. Could at least…offer me a drink," croaked the fallen man.

Ketill appeared at that moment with a mug of vistock. He helped Thorfinn to gulp it down while Sigurd moved off to check the rest of his crew. He found two of the Valkyrion dead, cut to ribbons by the razor sharp claws of the beast. Another had a broken arm and one of the local Kazaks had been crushed by a platter-sized paw when the beast fled. Thorfinn's life had been saved by the bronze scale mail that he wore, but he likely had internal injuries and could not be moved for some days. Counting the hetman that made four dead and two badly wounded.

And the beast had escaped.

Haakon the navigator took over the fallen Thorfinn's role as thegn. "What shall we do, Eorl?"

Sigurd looked around at the assembled men. Even if Thorfinn had been able to travel, he knew in his heart he could not abandon the village to face this threat alone. Yet if his fears were true, the beastly rampage was justified.

"We will bring the beast to bay and end this once and for all. It is sorely hurt. I do not like trailing a wounded beast, especially at night. We will leave at dawn. Ketill and Chiangkin will go with me. If we are not back by tomorrow night, then Thorfinn is Eorl and Haakon is thegn." Sigurd knew that three hunters were scarcely the force necessary to bring such a monster to bay, but he was loath to risk more of his crew. The three of them were the most experienced of the uninjured crew and stood the best chance of survival.

Angry shouts greeted this announcement. Men clamored to accompany the hunting party. Haakon merely looked at the Eorl. Sigurd stared back, his lips a thin line and his gray eyes dark with deadly intent.

"Shut your meal holes! The Eorl has spoken!" Haakon stared down the dissenting crew members. "Now get to work cleaning this place up. Rolf, you've got first watch. Take Thorwald with you. Get moving, you gutter trash."

Sigurd smiled and walked away from the bustling activity caused by the steersman's acid tongue. The younger men tended to forget that Haakon had been thegn for Sigurd's father for almost thirty years. The old wolf still had teeth when he needed them.

The trio of hunters set out from the village at dawn.

Sigurd approved the weapons each had selected. Ketill carried his bow and sword while Chiangkin took a bow and a short hatchet together with his long knife. Sigurd had left his war axe and instead carried an eight foot spear and his shield. His success with the spit last night had inspired him, and he wanted a little more distance between himself and those snapping jaws. Not normally a pious man, Sigurd nonetheless hoped that choosing this token might appeal to Wothen the Spearman.

The trail was easy to follow in the morning light. The tracks were heavy and broad, easily seen in the snow. Occasional spots of crimson marked the trail and told of the injured bear's suffering. They had barely entered the forest when Chiangkin stopped and knelt beside the trail. The others gathered around him.

"The beast is hit hard."

"How can you tell?" asked Sigurd.

"See how dark the blood is?" explained Ketill. "The smaller spots are bright red, but this dark splotch indicates an injured organ, possibly a liver or a kidney."

"Good. Maybe it will drop dead and save us the trouble."

"Something else," continued the Nevarine, "this is the same bear we tracked two days ago."

"Are you sure?"

"Yes, he is right," nodded Ketill. "Look at the left front paw. See how one of the claws is angled in? That is the same sign we followed last time. Besides, there cannot be two animals that large. This bear is twice the size of a normal beast. There is something unnatural in this." The whites of Ketill's eyes shown with fear in the morning light.

"Well," answered Sigurd, his face hardening with resolve, "let us hope the chase does not end the same way." The other two hunters fell silent and exchanged uneasy glances at this reminder of their strange encounter. Sigurd continued. "We know that it bleeds, whatever it is. And if it bleeds, we can kill it. We have men to avenge." They continued on without further conversation.

The trail continued through the woods, away from the river, and up into the hills. An hour later they came across the iron spit, lying across the trail.

The first two feet of the stake were covered with dried blood and matted hair. Sigurd nodded grimly at the other two and they resumed their march.

The nature of the trail changed as they moved higher. Instead of climbing straight up the hills, the trail wandered badly, and occasional bloody patches of wallowed snow revealed where the beast had fallen. The tracks became more erratic and the blood splashes fewer. Broken saplings and torn brush marked locations where the tortured beast had lashed out in agony, venting its rage and pain. Vicious claw marks appeared on tree trunks, well above the head of the tallest Valkyrion. Although sorely wounded, the great bruin still seemed capable of malevolent power.

"By the Maker, it is happening again."

Sigurd moved forward to see what caused Chiangkin's announcement. He scanned the signs on the trail and licked his lips nervously. His hackles rose with a primitive fear. The immense bear prints had begun to change. They twisted and shrank, tearing the snow into a shapeless mass. Ten feet further on the trail continued, but the clawed imprints had been replaced with a five-toed human footprint!

"Come on! We must be close!"

The three hunters spread out and moved swiftly along the forest floor. Sigurd, spear held before him, followed the signs in the snow while the two archers covered him on either flank. They had only advanced a hundred feet when Sigurd spotted a naked figure hunched over and scratching in the snow.

Warned by some primitive instinct, the hunted man whirled to face the newcomers. Yellow eyes blazed with inhuman hatred and blood stained teeth snarled through his matted beard: an animal brought to bay. The Valkyrion hunters were frozen by the alien spectacle before them. Sigurd's breath steamed in the frigid air while hunter and hunted silently faced each other in an awful tableau. Long moments passed as each party waited for some mysterious signal to break the spell.

The crouched brute abruptly launched itself directly at Sigurd, trampling the snow on all four limbs like some hairless beast. Bowstrings twanged as Sigurd knelt and braced the butt of his spear against the ground to receive the man's charge. Chiangkin's arrow skipped harmlessly across the snow but Ketill's shaft flew straight and true, piercing the throat of the galloping figure. Crimson gore splattered the forest as the man fell heavily. The momentum of his charge left a bloody smear on the icy surface and carried his body over the snow to skid within reach of the patiently waiting Sigurd . The fallen man gave one low groan and laid still, a spreading pool of steaming blood blossoming in the snow beneath his head.

Sigurd expelled the pent up air in his tortured lungs, surprised to discover he had been holding his breath during the deadly encounter. Ketill and Chiangkin advanced, arrows nocked at the ready, bowstrings drawn back to their mouths. The Valkyrion remained expectant, still amazed at the ferocity displayed, prepared to unleash violence at the first sign of danger. Long moments passed as the three hunters waited for any sign of life in their prostrate foe.

Signaling his brethren, Sigurd advanced on the motionless body. Stopping yards away, he waited until both archers had moved to better vantage points with clear fields of fire. The figure appeared to be that of a large man, with red-brown hair and large freckles on his arms and shoulders. Numerous small cuts were visible on the body and a bloody hole gaped in its lower back. Sigurd stepped forward and thrust his spear into the exposed muscle of the shoulder. The blade pierced the flesh easily, but a mere trickle of blood flowed. The body hadn't flinched.

Sigurd knelt and turned it over. Sightless eyes stared at him from the dead man's face. Although still warm to the touch, the body had already started to stiffen with the piercing cold. Ketill and Chiangkin lowered their bows and approached. Sigurd straightened the dead man's limbs, arranging the body on the ground. As he did so he noticed that the man's left index finger had been broken and never set properly. It had healed at a funny angle, giving his hand a crooked appearance.

"Who is he?"

"If I'm right, his name was Radvik," quietly answered Sigurd.

"What was he?" asked Chiangkin.

"A changeling. A shapeshifter. I think he could change his body into that of the great bear we fought. I have heard that it is an ancient power, seldom seen anymore."

"Black magick!" Ketill spat on the corpse.

"Maybe. Maybe not. But it was enough to get him exiled from his home village. He came here and fell in love. Even got married and had a child. But those villagers thought his daughter was possessed. They stoned her. His wife too. Stoned them in the middle of the square."

"Maker preserve us," whispered Chiangkin. "No wonder he tried to eat them."

"No, not eat them. I think he just wanted to kill them. The beast never ate its victims, it just killed them and left the bodies."

"How do you know all this?" asked Ketill.

"The hetman told me, last night. He was drunk. I think he knew about the bear, and he felt guilty about it." Sigurd looked in the face of the dead man and felt empty, like a stone had dropped into the hollow pit of his stomach and vanished. "I think Radvik went crazy. Perhaps his grief swallowed his mind until there was nothing left but revenge." The husky note in his voice reminded Sigurd's companions that he too had lost his wife and child, and had followed the treacherous path of bloody revenge. "I think in the end there was nothing left of the man, nothing but the beast."

"Perhaps," agreed Chiangkin, "but what about this?"

Sigurd suddenly noticed that the Nevarine no longer stood beside him. Chiangkin gestured at the site where the dead man had been crouched. An open spot of snow had been cleared, exposing a flat slab of rock. A bloody hand had scratched a garbled message with a rock shard upon the slate. The runes were Kazak, but were clearly related to the Valkyrion runes Sigurd knew so well. He stared at the message, awed by the powerful drive that had caused the mortally wounded man to scrawl a dying message in the rock.

He noisily cleared his constricted throat. "Let's go," he ordered. "Cover the body and then we need to get back down to the river. It will be dark soon and I don't want Haakon stealing my crew."

They rolled the body into a shallow gully, covered it with fresh evergreen boughs, and then used Sigurd's shield to shovel snow over the whole thing. Finishing their exertions, the men paused for a moment in silence, each contemplating the events of the past three days. Turning downhill, Sigurd led them through the lengthening afternoon shadows, back along the trail toward the distant river and the Kazak village.

An hour later, Chiangkin quietly asked, "Sigurd, what did Radvik write on the rocks?"

Sigurd did not turn but looked straight out at the horizon as he walked. The sharpened rays of the setting sun caught a wet glimmer in his gray eyes as he thought of the three words scratched on the slate.

"It said 'Svetna, forgive me.'"

As a child, Mary Rosenblum never really wanted to have a nine-to-five job to pay for doing what she wanted to do on the weekends. Grownups kindly explained that this wasn't practical. So far, she has managed to actually fulfill that life ambition to be poor by writing. She started out at Clarion West in 1988 and published one of her Clarion stories, 'For A Price', in Asimov's Magazine. *Since that first publication, she has published well more than 60 short stories in SF, mystery, and mainstream fiction, (she stopped counting at 60) as well as eight novels. Her newest novel,* Horizons, *was released in November 2006 from Tor Books and came out in paperback in November 2007.* Water Rites, *a compendium of the novel* Drylands, *as well as three prequel novelettes that first appeared in* Asimov's *were released from Fairwood Press in January 2007. The hardcover collection of her early short fiction,* Synthesis and Other Virtual Realities, *is available from Arkham House. Her speculative fiction stories have also been published in* The Magazine of Fantasy and Science Fiction, SciFiction, *and* Analog *among others. Mary won the Compton Crook award for Best First Novel, The Asimov's Readers Award, and has been a Hugo Award finalist as well as an Endeavor Award finalist, an Ellery Queen Reader's Award finalist, and short listed for a number of other awards. She publishes in mystery as Mary Freeman, teaches writing for Long Ridge Writers Group and at writers workshops, and was an instructor for the Clarion West Writers Workshop in the summer of 2008. When she is not writing, she lives sustainably on a small acreage where she trains dogs, raises sheep, teaches cheesemaking, and grows all her fruits and vegetables. She managed to raise two sons who have turned out to be pretty cool people and has even done a bit of traveling in China. And she still doesn't have a nine-to-five job. Or a lot of money, but hey, you choose your priorities. You can find Mary and more information at her website at www.sff.net/people/maryrosenblum. Here you can find a strong tale of priorities and discovery. Finding the mettle to assume unasked for responsibilities is sometimes a more difficult beast to face than the obvious behemoth in the room. Sometimes the monster isn't the one seen before us…but one within — even one of our own making. The truth can be freeing.*

Blood Ice

A Tale from the Cold Rim

**by Mary Rosenblum
& cover art by Didier Normand**

Aron reined his ice stallion in as they neared the crest of the pass. The animal tossed his head, curved horn gleaming like blue ice in the level beams of the setting sun, pawing the traffic-hardened snow with a three-clawed foot.

The highway below was empty. It usually teamed with traffic in this season when no ice storms raged down from the Northern Wastes, tribute coming up from the warmlands, ice-agates carried southward by the traders. Aron frowned, his uneasiness increasing. *You must come.* Elinda's words replayed for the thousandth time in his mind. *The king is dying and neither Jorsan nor I alone have the magic to hold back the ice and keep the springs warm. We need you, Aron. Jorsan will intervene for you with the king.* Aron eyed the white fangs of the Barrier Mountains, the teeth that held back the raiders from the Northern Wastes. With the help and magic of the boundary kingdoms.

He had never meant to come back.

We need you Aron.

For one of the royal line, Jorsan's magic had been weak since birth. Aron shook his head. The prince, his own age, had often drawn on Aron's magic to pass the tests the royal bloods had to take. It had been their secret. Few outside the Bloodlines had enough magic to matter, so no one had guessed. Almost no one. The snowlanders sensed something about him, for they called him Magic-Eyes — but who listened to snowlanders? The wind shifted suddenly, knife-edged and smelling of northern ice, frozen and cold. The ice stallion squealed and reared, nostrils flaring, eyes suddenly wild. Aron reined him in hard, unease increasing to fear. *Smoke? Battle burn?* He cursed and spurred the stallion into a flat, striding run, its clawed feet spraying ice chips behind them. They reached the crest of the pass and the stallion shied, squealing in fear, fighting the bit. With a wrench, Aron stilled the frightened animal.

Below, the once-green valley, warmed by the royal springs and lush with orchards and rich farms, lay blasted and frozen, barns and farmsteads roofless and smoldering. Bodies dotted the ice-covered roads, half-buried in drifts of dirty snow. The castle's stone walls gaped as if split by an axe, weeping ice like frozen tears. Bloody tears, colored by the setting sun.

With a cry, Aron spurred the stallion into a dangerous gallop. The ice horse raced past tumbled bodies, men and women sheltering their dead children beneath theirs, faces and limbs waxy with cold, eyes frost-rimed, staring sightlessly as Aron charged past, his heart clenched in a fist of stone. Figures moved in the shadow of the castle's shattered gates, white-robed looters hauling furniture and gear from the castle. He spotted their sleds and ice deer tethered among the ruined stone cottages of the town.

Snowlanders. The nomadic herders that followed their deer across the snowy moss lands between the green warmlands and the wasteland beyond the Barrier Mountains. Two of the white-robed figures tossed a body onto a growing pile and Aron spied red hair. *Elinda!* With a howl, he drew his sword, the curved blade gleaming in the setting sun's bloody light.

The snowlanders scattered as he charged through them, fast as ice foxes. Blind with rage, Aron rode down the man who had dragged out the red-haired body. The snowlander dove aside as Aron swung and his blade sliced only through folds of loose robes. The ice stallion dug its clawed toes into the frozen road, ice flying as it spun around, striking with its front feet as three spear-wielding nomads blocked their path.

More of the snowlanders circled them, their light, deadly throwing spears in hand. Aron sheathed his sword, scooped magic from the ice. The snowlanders scattered as he flung razor-edged shards of ice at them on a gust of biting wind, covering their faces with their snow robes. Blood blossomed on white as some of the shards bit home, but as Aron reined the stallion around, scooping more magic from the frozen ground, one of the robed figures darted forward, whirling weighted lines around his head before throwing them.

The lines wrapped around the stallion's front feet and it fell hard on its shoulder, skidding across slick ice. Aron leaped free but another set of lines wrapped his torso, pinning his arms to his side before he could unleash the magic. Two of the snowlanders landed on his shoulders, bringing him down. He struggled, but tangled in the lines he was no match for the tough nomads. He managed to draw his dagger and slash one before they wrenched the weapon from his hand.

"You fight hard for one who sleeps in a warm bed." A man with a frost-dark face and ice-pale eyes leaned over him.

Xirith, leader of the local snowlander tribe. Aron stared at him, teeth bared.

"I know you, Magic-Eyes. You have no reason to die today. Not even your magic can defeat an entire tribe." A glimmer of humor lurked in the depths of those icy eyes. "You have spilled no life blood and your thirst for vengeance-blood we respect. But we could teach you common sense, youngling. Why die, Magic-Eyes? Waste of a good sword arm."

"You were our allies." Struggling against the hands holding him down, Aron spat.

The nomad's eyes narrowed and for a moment his face hardened. "Everyone is dead here, Magic-Eyes," he said coldly. "They have no use for their goods. We do. I exchanged blood with the king and I do not violate my blood. We did not do this, Magic-Eyes. But we are taking a fair price for tombing your dead."

No, they had not done this. Magic had done this and snowlanders did not have magic. Sanity returned, and the hands holding him slackened as he sat up and bowed his head, shame flushing through him. "I...I was reacting. Not thinking." No, Xirith would never violate his blood oath. "I acted...before I thought."

"That you did, youngling. You will learn better if you live to grow old." Xirith offered his hand, drew Aron to his feet. "Your mount is not injured and you are welcome to ride with us. We will welcome you, if you choose. There is no one left here for you. We will leave as soon as we have finished tombing your dead. Too much magic lingers here and the ice dragon may return with his power-man rider."

"Ice dragon?" Aron stared at him, shocked. "Ridden by a sorcerer? That could not be. The royal family shares a blood oath with Blenath, the ice dragon who rules this territory."

The snowlander shrugged. "An ice dragon did this. Which one I could not say. Maybe they do not honor blood."

But they did. Numb, Aron turned away, walked slowly toward the body pile. Dragons spoke only truth and a blood oath was forever. God help the human who broke it. He remembered bright winter days playing tag with Blenath in the snow — he and Elinda and Jorsan. They had tried to slap the dragon in a vulnerable place, and the dragon had nipped them if they were slow, or tossed them into the snow. Blenath had laughed at times. Elinda had been the quickest and the best, but Aron was almost her equal. He blinked as he found himself at the pile of bodies. Red hair gleamed like burnished copper in the last beams of the setting sun. Heart as frozen as the ground, he looked closer. A youth. His heart began to pound in a slow, steady beat. Not a woman. A young man with an apprentice warrior's shoulder-length crop. Relief nearly buckled his knees.

"What about the king?" He faced Xirith. "What about the…the royal family?" He could not speak Elinda's name.

"The king lies there. With his son beside him." Xirith nodded toward twin mounds of stone near the castle's entry. "We found one survivor. No." He shook his head at Aron's expression. "Not the king's red-haired daughter. An old woman. She was buried and hidden by a falling wall." The chieftain's voice was dark with compassion. "The wastelanders drove behind the dragon, slaughtering the folk the ice magic did not blast. Those who lived, they took as slaves to haul their sledges full of loot."

Wastelanders. Aron's skin tightened with a chill that had nothing to do with the frozen valley. The fearsome nomads lived on the far northern wastelands and hunted fur fish and sea lizards beneath the ice of the Northern Sea. "They crossed the Barriers?"

"You should ride with us." Xirith laid a hand on his shoulder. "The wastelanders are no match for our deer." He jerked his head. "Or your horse."

"They couldn't cross. Blenath…" But a dragon had blasted the valley. "Where is the survivor?" Aron straightened his shoulders with a jerk.

Xirith led him past the men and women efficiently looting the frozen castle. The nomads had built a small smoky fire of oilstone in one of the guard chambers that hadn't been shattered by the ice magic. Inside, a small figure lay wrapped in blankets, tended by one of the nomad women.

"The old one is dying." The snowlander woman looked up as Xirith strode into the low-ceilinged room. "Too many broken bones."

Aron looked past the nomad leader, saw a pale, drawn face haloed by wisps of white hair against the deer wool blankets. The royal nurse, old beyond count. "Doria!" He flung himself to his knees beside her. "What happened? Where's Elinda?"

"Aron?" The pale eyes blinked and a spark of recognition flickered in their cloudy depths. "Ah, our heart, our only hope." Her cracked lips faltered into a smile. "The gods heard me, answered my prayers." She clutched his sleeve as he knelt beside her. "He took her. He took my child, my darling, my princess."

"He?" Hope and fear clashed in Aron's chest. "Who, Doria? Who did this?"

"Evil…evil. He…chained the dragon's soul, he did, bound the family with his magic so that their blood oath could not free the dragon. You…" She pulled herself upright with sudden fierce strength, her fingers like claws digging into his arm. "You can undo this." For a moment, the pale, blind eyes were bright with sight. "You can undo this!"

"Doria—" Too late. He lowered the frail body to the blankets as her last breath sighed through her dry lips and her soul shivered free of her flesh. "Elinda." He said her name softly, as if it might shatter. Looked up to meet Xirith's ice eyes. "Did they take captives from the castle, then?"

"One." The chieftain nodded. "A woman with bright hair — the king's daughter. The rest they slaughtered." He put a hand on Aron's shoulder.

Elinda was alive. Aron stood, dizzy with the images flashing through his brain. "Which way did they go? I must follow them."

"In the dark?" The flickering light from the oilstone fire filled the chieftain's eyes with shadows. "The wastelanders took most of the food and livestock with them. They will not move far until they have eaten and drunk everything. I doubt that even a power-man can force them. Or the ice dragon." His lips curved with disgust. "They are like ice bears, thinking only with their stomachs and their bloodlust. Time enough for you to get hold of your common sense again, Magic-Eyes." He put a hand on Aron's shoulder. "You can follow them in the light, when you can see their tracks. I will send a guide with you, give you supplies. And meanwhile, you can use your magic to thaw the springs, eh?" He gave Aron a grim smile. "We are tombing your dead, Magic-Eyes. My people would like to drink spring water instead of snow melt."

Aron walked to the springs flanked by two torchbearers. Xirith walked with him, and by twos and threes the nomads fell in behind, dark shadows in the thickening dusk, keeping a wary distance. The springs were ancient, wakened by the first king of the valley, kept warm and vital by his descendents ever since, an emerald of lush warmth that fed the warriors who defended the boundary lands. Now the water had frozen where it spilled from the stone face of the spring into the deep cistern below. Aron stared at the waterfall's white tumble, its music stilled, the ice black and clear. It was unlikely that he could summon enough magic to thaw the springs if all the family had died. He took a deep breath and reached for the warm heart of the world beneath his feet, feeling for its heat, drawing it up, up, from the depths. It flooded into him, through him, hotter than he'd ever managed before. He spread his fingers, reaching toward the stilled water, imagining the ice thawing.

A crack sounded, sharp in the cold stillness, and a moment later icy water splashed him. The cold drops stung his face and he opened his eyes as the frozen waterfall disintegrated into chunks and cascaded into the dark, liquid water of the cistern. Aron let his breath out, exhausted by the effort, and watched the re-warmed spring bubble over the rock face.

Elinda lives then. Her lingering magic had kept the springs alive so that he could release them. The wastelanders must still be near. Behind him the nomads cheered and surged forward with water skins and bowls, none getting too close to him. Snowlanders had no magic and feared it.

"Thank you." Xirith bowed his head. "We appreciate your gift, Magic-Eyes." He put his hand on Aron's arm, steered him toward cooking fires glowing at the base of the castle wall. "Come eat with us and at first light, we will help you on your way."

Aron found his ice horse tethered with the sled deer in one of the frozen fields and retrieved his rolled snow cloak from the saddle. The stallion dug contentedly through the ice with its horn to nibble at the frozen young grain shoots beneath. Aron knew the farm family that had planted that grain. He turned away with a knot in his throat. The oldest son, Dalor, had trained with him as a teen, had no love for the soil and had become a Captain in the King's Guard.

Aron wondered which of the many piles of rock and frozen soil marked his grave.

They ate stew made from wind-dried ice deer meat and some of the frozen vegetables the nomads had foraged from the ruined gardens. Aron had no appetite but he made himself eat.

"Why did the king send you away, Magic-Eyes?" Xirith sat down beside him with a brimming bowl of moss beer. "I heard you warmed the land as well as any royal kin."

"The king…didn't send me away." Aron felt his face getting hot and he leaned closer to the smoldering pile of oilstone, hoping to hide it. "I chose to leave. I…wanted to see something of the world beyond the boundary lands."

Xirith took a swallow of beer and offered the bowl to Aron, who shook his head. "The skein of leadership can be a tangled one." The nomad spoke thoughtfully. "But a smart man does not cast aside a good blade." He looked sideways at Aron. "Although a trade is a different matter." He drank again and shook his head. "Bride politics, eh?" He slapped Aron on the shoulder, stood. "But you are now alive to seek vengeance and honor them all, so there is that. Sleep well." And he walked away into the darkness, draining the last of his beer.

So even the nomads know why the king exiled me. Aron stared into the pulsing red glow of the oilstone fire. She hadn't even been betrothed yet, and his family was an old one, as old as the royal line. He had magic. A lot of magic for someone not of the royal blood. It wasn't unknown for talented commoners to breed into the royal bloodlines. He had thought that might be why the king had taken him in, in the first place, when his parents, warriors both, had died in that wastelander ambush so many winters ago.

He had not understood the king's anger that night, did not understand it this night. *Nor will I ever, now.* He pulled his snow cloak around him and stretched out close to the fire.

In the morning, the spring still flowed, unfrozen. That delighted the nomads and surprised Aron. He had expected his magic to dissipate during the night, to find the spring frozen again. Even a few streaks of green showed in the frozen ground around the spring.

"The king's daughter is still close." His heart leaped as he scooped a handful of clear water from the spring. "It's her lingering magic that keeps it flowing." The king must have given over maintenance of the spring and the valley to his children as he neared death. Aron sipped the cold, clean water and thought of one of those children. *You were strong enough after all ...though I thank the gods that you called me back.*

"I send these people with you." Xirith gestured toward a trio of robed figures. "They are members of my family and they have sleds prepared." He met Aron's eyes, his own eyes reflecting the bright glow of the rising sun. "This is your quest for vengeance. My people will aid you, but it is not our quest. Do you understand?"

"I don't expect them to die for me." Aron held the chieftain's gaze.

"How far into the face of death they follow you is their choice." The chieftain clapped him on the shoulder. "We have taken our burial payment from this place and we will move on. If you live, my offer is open to you, to ride with us. My people will bring you back to us. May the gods grant you your vengeance — and your life." He jerked his chin in a salute, turned and strode away, calling out commands to the nomads who were already folding their snow-colored tents and packing sleds.

Aron strode over to the three nomads who stood with three deer-drawn sleds and his stallion. Two men, one woman, they gave him their names. The woman, Siona, face weathered by the cold wind into a leathery mass of wrinkles, was clearly their leader. "We won't have to travel far to find them." She made a sign of disrespect with her left hand. "They will stop to gorge no matter how hard the power-man goads them. Kira is our best scout. No one sees him when he does not choose to be seen." She nodded at a slender youth. "We will follow him." She handed Aron his horse's reins, and took the handles of her own sled.

The ice deer started briskly, covering the trampled snow and ice with long, flat strides, their clawed toes digging into the frozen surface. The wind picked up with the dawn, sneaking icy fingers beneath his snow cloak as the stallion paced alongside Siona's sled. She, like the others, ran lightly behind the sled, stepping occasionally onto a narrow platform behind the cargo bed to ride for a few minutes before stepping off to run. Here, low in the foothills of the Barriers, the land undulated in old, wind-worn drifts, polished to a glassy smoothness, the occasional black thrust of rock streaking shadows across the white glare.

Lean and long-legged, the nomads ran unencumbered. They had stripped off their robes and wore only long-sleeved hooded tunics, pants made of soft deer hide with the hair inside, and laced boots soled with tough, abrasive snow-root bark. Soon they left the fading magic of the valley far behind, and the air grew colder, biting Aron's exposed face so that he laced his hood halfway closed.

The trail wasn't hard to follow as it cut straight east across the foothills of the Barrier Mountains. Clearly the wastelanders were headed for the next boundary settlement, Queen Arinda's holding. Aron shaded his eyes against the hard, cold light of noon to peer ahead. Destroy three settlements before word could be spread and the wastelanders could cross the mountains en mass and cut straight into the heart of the warmlands. If the sorcerer had found a way to control Blenath, then perhaps he could control any ice dragon. Or he could send Blenath to fight the oath-dragon of Queen Arinda's settlement. They had oathed with a small female, very old, and she would not be a match for the young and powerful Blenath.

The wastelanders had trampled the snow, the tread of their boots, soled with the spiny scales of the sea lizards they hunted, crossed by the tracks of heavy sledges. If the ice dragon traveled with them, he flew. A short time later, they found the first body, a gray-haired man with an injured leg. His throat had been cut. Aron looked down at the man's staring eyes, his own throat tight. The spring had been flowing this morning. So Elinda still lived.

He chafed when Siona called a halt, but she was right — the animals needed to feed. And they were getting close enough to be cautious. Kira slipped away to scout as they turned the deer and the stallion loose. The animals immediately began to break through the crusted snow with their horns, scraping their way down to the nutritious mats of moss with their claws. The small encampment melted into the white of snow and ice. They were nearly invisible, the low tents no more than drifts of snow, the animals a wild herd. *Save for the stallion.*

"I should have used a sled." He looked back as Siona came up beside him. "The ice stallion gives us away."

Siona shrugged. "Wasteland raiders are sloppy with scouts when they have loot, especially when they travel in a large group. They will just set guards and trust them as they feast. And…" She grinned. "You would have slowed us down, Magic-Eyes. You don't just step onto a sled and keep up. No." She shook her head. "The ice horses often herd with the deer. The wastelanders will think it's a crippled stallion, driven off from its herd."

Aron barely heard her. Elinda was out there. He stared eastward, the sunset wind stinging his face, shaken by sudden awareness.

"Your magic senses her?" Siona spoke softly.

"I sense her. Yes."

"Then perhaps the power-man with them senses you? Or us?"

"I…don't think it's magic. We…just know. She and I."

"Ah." Siona was silent for a moment. "Your plans, warmlander?" She faced him finally, her eyes wary in her weathered face. "Or do you need plans? Xirith believes that you mean to die."

"I did not come here just to suicide." He gave her a crooked smile. "That isn't going to help Elinda." He drew a deep breath. "I am going to slip into their camp if I can. I have enough ice magic that the wastelanders won't see me."

She made a sign to ward off magic, her expression sour. "What about the power-man with them, Magic-Eyes? He will see you, will he not?"

Aron nodded. The weak point in his plans. "If he is looking for me, I'm dead." He held her eyes. "If he is not looking for me, I can hide from him, too. Up to a point." They had played that game around the castle, he and Elinda and Jorsan. Hide and seek. He had been the best at hiding behind his magic, better even than Elinda. Jorsan had been easy to find. Aron shook himself out of his memories, pain constricting his heart. "I don't ask you to help me. This is my vengeance, not yours."

Siona shrugged. "We will decide how much this is our vengeance. Xirith is right. You are too sharp a blade to cast away. Although your desire for vengeance here is worthy." Her tone was thoughtful and he couldn't read her pale eyes. "Kira returned while you were setting up your tent. As you felt, they are close. They camp on the far side of the ridge. They have posted few guards." Her lip curled. "They are so sure of their strength and their power-man. They are building oilstone fires and already getting drunk. Kira did not see the ice dragon." She glanced at the sky, frowned. "Maybe the power-man no longer controls him."

"Maybe." Aron frowned. The ice dragon — if it *was* Blenath — was an unknown quantity here. A deadly one. He drew a slow breath. "If they are feasting, this is the time to visit."

"I have heard you magic-users can see in the dark. Is it true?" Siona pursed her lips as he nodded. "Let them drink longer. They'll have no head for your warmlander wine." She looked back at the low hummocks of their tents already dusted with snow by the bitter sunset wind. "Darkness is the sister of stealth. You may trust your magic, but never leave an extra blade behind." She put a hand lightly on his shoulder. "We will not walk into the camp with you. We are not seeking death. But we will be close by. If we can aid you, we will." She gave him a mirthless grin. "Xirith would like us to bring you back alive. If it's possible." She turned and strode off through the camp, her white robes swirling around her.

A realistic promise. Aron's lips tightened. He had a feeling she didn't think it was possible. He slid his blade from its sheath, ran his fingertip along its gleaming metal until the magic forged into it with his blood responded, the blade quivering in his grip. It was not likely he would survive. He sheathed the blade. His magic might be strong, but it wasn't royal magic and a sorcerer who could control an oath-blooded ice dragon would see him in a second. *If that sorcerer thought to look.*

Aron squatted out of the wind in the shelter of his tent and forced himself to eat some of the dried meat and moss cake the nomads had given him as he waited for darkness and wine to work on the wastelanders.

The moonless night cloaked him as Aron worked his way down the wind-cleared face of the ridge and he blessed his luck. His summoned night vision turned the snowy wasteland to a colorless day, although his head would hurt if he kept it up too long. Below, the oilstone fires pulsed orange, casting wavering shadows across the tumbled forms of the drunken and snoring wastelanders. They slept in their ice suits, curled into balls on the frozen ground like animals, hoods protecting their faces. Even the guard at the crest of the ridge had been nodding. Siona had slipped up behind him, invisible and noiseless in her robes, and slit his throat before he had time to make a sound.

Aron placed his feet carefully as he reached the bottom of the slope. A wastelander slept a few paces away, his ice suit blending perfectly into the shadow and light of the fire. Aron slipped past him, crouching low, hugging the face of the ridge. The sledges had been parked at the far side of the camp in a half circle. He could make out huddled figures clustered next to the heavy frames. *The captives? Chained to the sleds?*

From time to time, he pulled magic from the ice in the frozen ground, weaving the chill strands of power into the barrier that hid him. No wastelander could see him. Aron hoped his snow cloak would hide him from the sorcerer, should he be looking. The man would certainly see through the ice magic Aron used.

Slowly, cautiously, he worked his way around the perimeter of the camp, shielding his night-sensitive eyes from the radiance of the fires. Two tent shelters had been erected at the far edge of the camp. The wastelanders seemed to be content to sleep on the snow in their ice suits. He wondered at the placement of the tents — as if the sorcerer feared to be surrounded by the wastelanders. Aron reached a small outcrop a few strides from the smaller of the two tents and crouched there, considering. He could tell where Elinda was if he reached for her. But it would be like a shout in the silence of the camp; the sorcerer would know that a magic-user was close. If he hadn't detected Aron already.

Breathing lightly, Aron regarded the two tents. Wastelanders snored and grunted in their sleep. One of the captives moaned but the sound was quickly stifled. The ground groaned and murmured with the heat from the oilstone fires and the ice in the ridge behind him whispered with the small sounds of cold. *Which tent?* A faint sound came to him, almost obliterated by the snores of the wastelanders. A sob.

It came from the smaller tent.

Aron slid toward it on his stomach, feeling cautiously for magic traps. He could feel the pulse of powerful magic ahead, but couldn't localize it. His awareness brushed a boundary spell and he blessed his lessons with Elinda and Jorsan as he recognized a simple warning spell — set against the wastelanders, he guessed, not a magic-user.

It was easy to open a passage through the spell shield without alerting its creator, and in a moment he stood by the door flap of the tent. Another guarding spell defended the knot, but again, it was a simple spell, set against people without magic. It obediently loosened at his touch, silenced before it could alarm the one who had set it. Certainly, the sorcerer did not expect attack from a magic-user. But then, Aron thought bitterly, the man had slaughtered all magic-users in the valley. He eased the flap open and squinted, focusing his vision.

A figure curled on the bare ground, dressed only in a torn tunic and leggings, barefoot, shivering. Hair the color of embers even with his night vision spilled across her face. His heart froze and for a moment, Aron could only look. Then he shook himself and probed the darkness, flinching as a powerful spell scorched his cautious touch.

Elinda gasped, sat bolt upright, her eyes wide as she searched the darkness. "Aron." She breathed the name, wild hope flooding her face, replaced instantly by fear. "Leave now." She clasped her hands. "Hurry. He's very powerful and he'll have felt you."

"Shh." Aron stepped toward her, arms aching to clutch her to him. Halted as the guarding spell heated his skin. Leave now, his mind screamed. The sorcerer must have felt this intrusion. "What happened?"

"Patrol riders brought him in." The words tumbled out, blurred by her chattering teeth. "D-Dying, we thought. He cl-claimed to carry news of wasteland raiders, asked with his dying breath to tell the king. Once in the audience ch-chamber…he struck." She shivered. "We were all there….to hear the news. He bound us all with the spell that holds me, it contained our magic so that…so that we could not call Blenath. Then he…spelled the dragon. And sent him to…to destroy the valley." Her voice caught and she shuddered, shoulders hunching as she bent forward. Aron stepped forward but the spell halted him, sheeting his vision with white fire until he stumbled back.

"He forced us to watch. The wastelanders came behind Blenath."

Aron could barely make out her whispered words.

"He wants our magic, Aron. If he owns our magic, he owns the blood oath that binds Blenath. The spell he used…I think it's just a powerful binding spell. That's why he silenced us. An oath-blood could break it with a single command. He wanted…all of us…alive." She lifted her head, her eyes wide. "But the wastelanders broke into the chamber where he held us and not even his magic could stop them. They…cut down Father, our mother, Jorsan…" A sob choked her and Aron stepped into the agony of the barrier as far as he was able.

"He kept them from killing me. I wish he had failed." She flung her head up, eyes burning, fists clenched. "Then he would never have control of Blenath. He's letting me die, Aron. No water, no food, no warmth. I've managed to steal snow to eat, but…" She closed her eyes. "If I die slowly, without a wound, he will have a moment to steal my magic as I die. So he keeps me safe…to die. He plans to do this to all the Boundary Kingdoms, Aron." Her voice was bleak, hopeless. "When he controls the dragons, he can unleash the wasteland raiders on the warmlands."

Aron stared numbly into the darkness. Of course. Control the ice dragons, control them with an oath-blood bond, and no one would be able to stand before them. No magic bested the ice dragons. Not for long. Not permanently.

"Leave now." Her whisper was fierce and low. "Alert the other boundary kingdoms, so that they know what is coming. Quickly, before he feels you and—"

"I know what I have to do." His heart tore with the words. "I…love you." He turned, unable to look at her again, probed the door for any change in the magic.

"I love you, too. I always have." The whisper from behind him, so low he barely heard it, nearly broke him.

The sorcerer was wakening. Aron felt it in the pulse of the guarding barrier surrounding Elinda, a brief alarm. He slid through the opening and ran, cloaking the sounds of his steps with ice magic that wouldn't fool the sorcerer, choosing the shortest, shadowed route to the edge of the drunken camp. The skin on his neck crawled, expecting a blast of magic. He would do what he must do. Warn the next kingdom. Tears blurred his vision and he clenched his teeth as he wove between sleeping wastelanders.

A low, ripping snarl froze him in his tracks as he neared the circle of sleds. A sinuous shape crouched on the trampled snow, chained to a stake driven into the ground. An ice lizard. Aron recognized the distinctive blue and silver pattern of its scales, recognized it as one of the pet house lizards that had kept watch on the castle. He recoiled in horror from its whirling, silver eyes. Blood-oathed, its removal from the castle had driven it mad. Wounds and broken, bloodied scales testified to its fate here, plaything of the wastelanders. Before Aron could step back, it leaped to the end of its chain and buried curved fangs into his thigh. The snow cloak blocked some of the lizard's gripping power so that it did not tear muscle free, but its teeth burned as they pierced his flesh. Aron wrenched himself loose, biting back a cry, warm wetness soaking his leggings.

Instead of lunging again, the lizard shrilled a tortured cry and flung itself on its back, writhing. *Oath-blood, oath-blood*, it whistled in broken dragonspeak. *Not know, not know. Oath-blood forgive?*

Oath-blood? Aron hesitated. He wasn't of the royal family. A footstep

~ Blood Ice ~

whispered on snow behind him and without thought, Aron whirled, his blade leaping from its sheath into his hand.

Almost too late. A burly wastelander lunged, dagger gleaming as he slashed at Aron's face, white hair and skin blazing in Aron's night vision. Aron shifted the blade to his left hand, caught the wastelander's wrist, spun him down and away.

Within the measure of the ice lizard's chain.

The man screamed as the ice lizard's fangs closed on his face, then shifted to his throat, choking the scream to a gurgle — but not before the dagger sank home in the ice lizard's side. Aron jumped over the dying pair and ran, hearing shouts behind him as the camp, aroused by the scream, erupted. Wastelanders might drink heavily, but they roused easily.

Two figures rose in front of him, wielding the favored weapon of wastelanders — long-bladed stabbing spears with poisoned edges. One of the grinning raiders stabbed at Aron, and he sprang sideways, whirling to slice through the shaft of the second spear as its owner tried to slash him with the toothed blade. Aron leaped into the first man's returning stab, and thrust between the man's ribs before he could recover his balance.

A dozen figures rushed at Aron. He scooped ice magic from the snow, flinging a handful of it toward his attackers. They howled and faltered as sudden wind blasted them with razor-edged bits of ice, shredding skin and flesh. Aron veered around them, again leaping over the tangled bodies of the ice lizard and the wastelander, their mixed blood dark on the ground.

Oath-blood. He slowed, the nurse's words echoing in his head. *You can undo this.* A spark of hope ignited in his soul. *If she was right...* He slowed, even though he had reached the edge of the camp and the safety of the dark snowfields beyond. *If he was right...*

And if he was wrong?

Aron stopped, turned back. Gathering magic from the untrodden snowfields behind him, he spun it into whirling blades of ice, spun them at the glow of the oilstone fires, screams and shouts testifying to their impacts. Confusion reigned. The wastelanders grabbed weapons, stabbing and slashing at each other in the near darkness. From the corner of his eye, Aron saw movement by the larger shelter, scooped more ice magic and flung up a shield just as a bolt of magic hit. His shield shattered in a soundless explosion. *If he was right...*

He had always been stronger than Jorsan. He scooped more magic from the ground and opened himself to its energies, shaping it into a spear of shimmering power that he hurled toward the larger shelter. For an instant he felt a sense of piercing surprise and thought, for a heartbeat, that he had succeeded. Then the spear dissipated in a flash of light.

Too strong. Aron retreated and his hope began to fade even as he hurled more razor-ice and wind at a handful of wastelanders who had spied him. He knew the ridge rose behind him now, knew he would have to turn his back on the raging wastelanders to climb it.

With whooping cries, the three snowlanders bounded down the steep face, blades gleaming. Siona landed first, sliced the head from the closest wastelander, gutted a second, and ducked a wild swing. Behind her, Kira cut down the remaining attacker. Aron closed ranks with them, hope once more in his heart.

A shimmering light appeared low in the sky and the wastelanders to the rear shouted and pointed. The massing wastelanders halted and began to back away, shouting to each other in their guttural tongue. Now, Aron could see the hard beat of huge, luminous wings.

Blenath.

The sorcerer had called him after all. For no human mage could stand up to an ice dragon.

But an oath-blood could.

Only Blenath doesn't know I'm an oath-blood. Like the ice lizard, the dragon would have to taste Aron's blood to know.

Without killing him.

"Get back." Aron rounded on the snowlanders. "Get away now. You can't help me anymore."

They fell back, faces full of fear and awe, then scrambled up the face of the bluff, Siona last, turning back near the top to watch.

The ice dragon circled, its eyes flashing gold and crimson as it eyed Aron. He was aware of the sorcerer's staring eyes as well, felt the man's satisfied certainty, his confidence in the outcome. To him this had become a show. Entertainment. Like the deaths of the smallholders in the valley. Rage boiled within Aron, and he controlled it with an effort. Rage led to carelessness.

He moved away as Blenath landed, preventing the dragon from pinning him against the ridge. "You have betrayed your blood oath," he shouted as the dragon folded its wings.

Blenath didn't answer and its eyes whirled as the ice lizard's had, a crazy mix of gold and blood red. The huge head snaked out, fast as the flip of a whip, and Aron leaped away, rolling and coming fast to his feet, leaping again as the head struck once more. He dove sideways, beneath the sleek neck, came up in the hollow between the dragon's front leg and chest.

This was the game they'd played with Blenath as children. Blenath had laughed, then. Aron scrambled sideways as the ice dragon shifted with a snarling roar, neck arching as it tried to reach him. Aron ducked beneath the muscular neck as Blenath whipped his head around and tried to catch him. Fangs longer than Aron's hand clashed a few finger widths from his shoulder. *Close!* Aron gasped in a breath, his lungs burning, leaped again to stay in that shadow of safety, his muscles remembering the old game as Blenath spun, trying to expose him.

The huge jaws snapped again, missing him, blasting him with freezing breath. Aron stumbled, caught himself, rolled as the fangs snagged his robe, slipping out of it as the dragon tore it free, shook it fiercely. The wastelanders cheered, then hissed as they realized it was his robe only. The cold chilled the sweat slicking him and Aron wiped his face on his sleeve, stumbled again as his bitten leg weakened.

Only one way.

Aron slipped beneath Blenath's neck once more, made himself wait as the head darted at him, eyes spinning wildly, narrow tongue lolling as the huge jaws opened to bite...

"I am oath-blood," he yelled into the dragon's blind fury. "You cannot harm me."

The dragon's teeth closed on his arm, bone snapping with the sound of a dry stick breaking. His feet left the ground as the dragon yanked him skyward to shake him like it had shaken the robe. Pain exploded upward into his head. Aron caught a glimpse of wastelanders crowding around, a sea of pale faces, dark mouths open, cheering, howling for the kill. Then he spun as the dragon swung its head around and the pain in his arm drove black shadows through his vision.

Suddenly he again stood on the ground, the world swimming back into focus. A huge golden eye stared at him, not more than two hand spans from his face. "Oath-blood!" The dragon's shout nearly drove Aron's senses back into the darkness. "Why do I not know you?"

"I am...the king's son. I did...not know." Aron tried to shout the words, but he had no breath and they seeped out. "The sorcerer has stolen Elinda. He has spelled you. I tell you to be free of it. As an oath-blood. Destroy these invaders."

Blenath reared onto its thick haunches and loosed an anguished howl that split the darkness and sent the closest wastelanders reeling. Then the dragon lowered its head and ice-fire blasted from its gullet and out its roaring mouth. The frigid breath frosted the closest wastelanders where they stood so that they turned instantly into human statues of frozen flesh, their eyes still wide with surprise. The rest scrambled away, dropping weapons, running for the darkness in utter panic. Blenath launched after them, its vast, shadowy wings blocking out the stars, repeated blasts of its white breath mowing down the fleeing wastelanders and darkening the oilstone fires.

A bolt of blue fire cut through the darkness and seared one of the ice dragon's wings. Blenath shrieked and swerved, wobbled, then landed heavily, shrieking again as another bolt of fire licked its other shoulder.

The sorcerer. He stood in front of the shelters, legs spread, blue fire flickering about him. Aron struggled to his feet, cradling his broken arm. He crouched low and circled back, using the parked sledges for shelter. The chained valley folk huddled silently, their faces bright with hope as he passed, and made no sound to give him away.

The sorcerer bared his teeth, his hood thrown back, expression intent. He had the pale hair and skin of the wastelanders, but his eyes burned like sea emeralds. He threw bolt after bolt of searing fire at Blenath, slowing the great beast's advance and obviously wounding it. The dragon roared and breathed ice at the sorcerer, but its breaths curled uselessly against an unseen barrier. Emboldened by the sorcerer's success, the wastelanders returned, snatching up spears and ice axes.

If the sorcerer could keep Blenath's magic engaged, the wastelanders could further wound the dragon. Aron eased his broken arm to his side and drew his dagger left handed. The blade quivered with blood magic, eager to be used. He crept forward, timing his movements to the eruption of the magic fire. Three more steps… two…one…he tensed to throw — The sorcerer sensed Aron's intent and spun toward Aron, fire trailing from pointing fingers.

A figure landed between them, blade gleaming. Siona. The blast of magic flung her backward, scorching Aron in spite of her protection. The other two snowlanders attacked from each side. The sorcerer snarled something in a guttural language, raising his hands as he turned to face them. Aron hurtled Siona's charred body, his own flesh searing to his bones, and closed the distance. At the last moment, the sorcerer again sensed Aron's rage and twisted toward him. Aron drove a shoulder between the man's outstretched hands and thrust the dagger into the man's right eye.

The point sank home in that sea emerald orb and the world exploded in white light.

He dreamed of the courtyard, the three of them on a childhood afternoon playing hide and seek, Jorsan crying with the frustration of being the slowest, the weakest. Then the warm stones and blue summer sky faded but the copper gleam of Elinda's hair remained. "Ah, you're coming back to us." She bent over him, her hair falling around him like a curtain. "Blenath said you would and snapped at me when I worried."

Aron sat up, his joints aching, muscles stiff, feeling as if he'd been beaten. His splinted right arm throbbed with a dull pain, while his skin burned and itched as if he had been out in the midsummer sun too long. He struggled to recall the fight, remembered the vivid emerald eye exploding as his knifepoint went home. He shuddered.

"A backlash from the magic you released." Elinda slid her arm around his shoulders and his need for that support surprised him. "We couldn't wake you. I thought…" Her voice faltered.

He was inside a tent, but not one of the snowlander's ice shelters. Sun streamed through the doorway and beyond he saw yellowed, frosted grass along a stone-flagged roadway. He stared at the new green shoots spiking through the flattened stems until a man lugging a handcart loaded with new lumber came into view. "The valley?" He tried to rise, didn't need Elinda's restraining hand on his shoulder to convince him that was not going to work. "The snow is gone."

"We're both here. The spring is flowing and the ice has retreated. I sent word to the warmland kingdoms and they've sent help — more people, supplies, building materials. We'll be ready for the cold season. We'll be ready to guard the boundary."

We're both here. Sadness lurked beneath those words. Aron turned, found her eyes gleaming with unshed tears.

"I didn't know," he said.

"Nor I. I don't think anyone did."

"Doria did." He sighed, his fingers finding hers. "That's why I could warm the spring so easily. I thought your magic was still affecting it."

She shook her head. "The binding spell the sorcerer used blocked it. The spring froze before Blenath even reached it." Her smile trembled on her lips. "That's why you could help Jorsan pass the tests. Oh, I knew. I never let on though." She blinked back tears, her gaze on the thawed fields beyond the tent. "Blenath has hunted down the last of the wastelanders." She shuddered. "Dragon-vengeance is…thorough."

"We have time then, to rebuild." He summoned his strength, got his feet under him.

"We do." She took his arm, helped him rise. The steps to the doorway of the tent were difficult, but he could feel his strength beginning to return.

Outside, sun glittered on the blasted fields, but everywhere life sprouted, green and new. Men and women hauled away the shattered remains of the farmsteads and already roofs were being laid on the stone-walled cottages and a few sheep and cows grazed the sprouting grass. Beyond the small oasis of warmth, the Boundary Land rose like a white wall, edged in the distance by the fangs of the Barrier Mountains. And beyond that, the wasteland and the northern nomads with their poisoned spears and their restless, hungry hearts.

"We'll do this together," he said softly. "Sister."

She nodded and looked quickly away.

For everything, a price. You could have told me. He turned to face the castle and the two stone mounds near the entry. *You could have told me when I said I loved her. I would have understood. We would have understood.* A small vine had sprouted at the base of the king's mound and a blue flower winked like an eye in the sunlight. *But I forgive you.* Aron turned away to join his sister and consider the rebuilding.

Scalding Sands

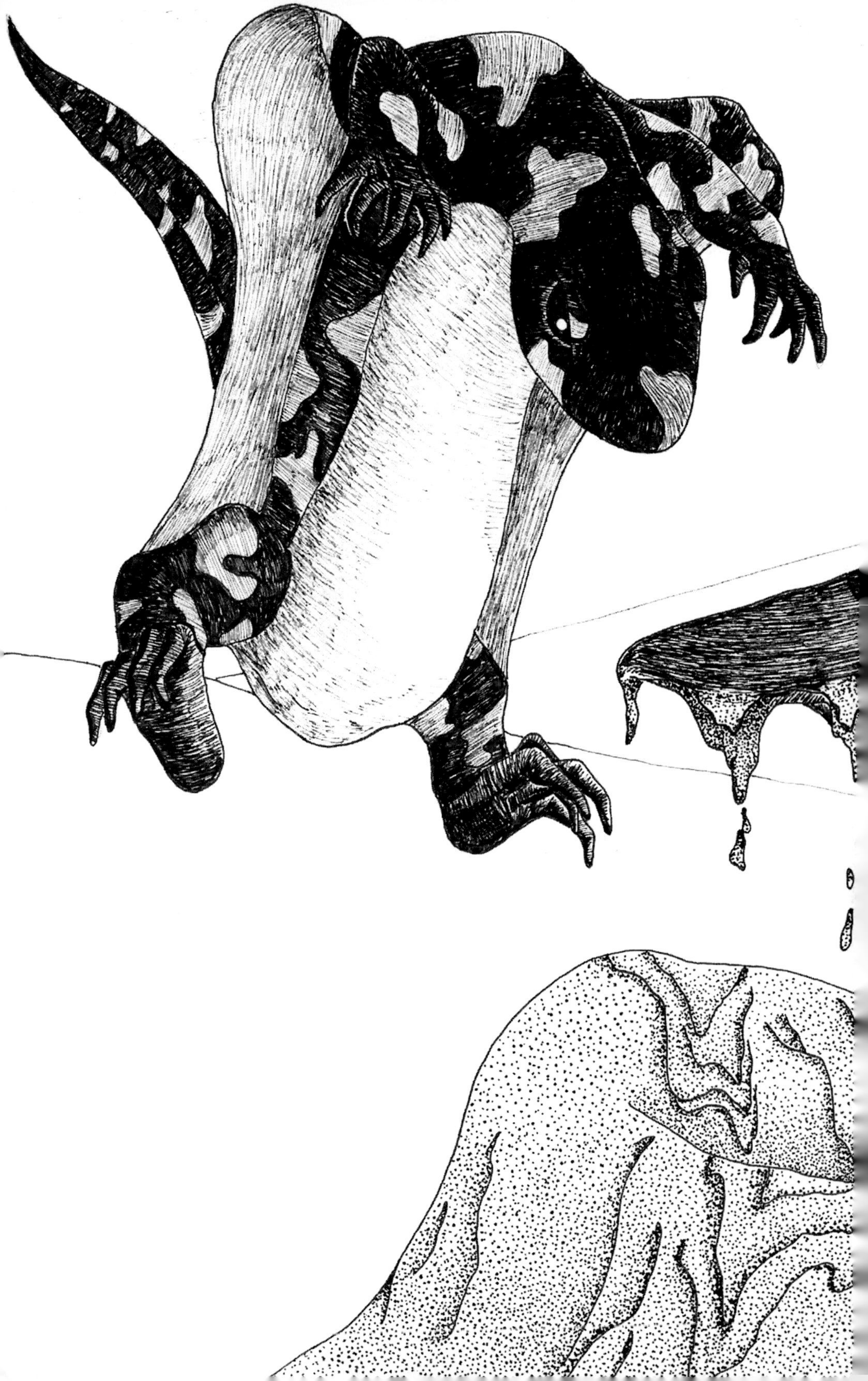

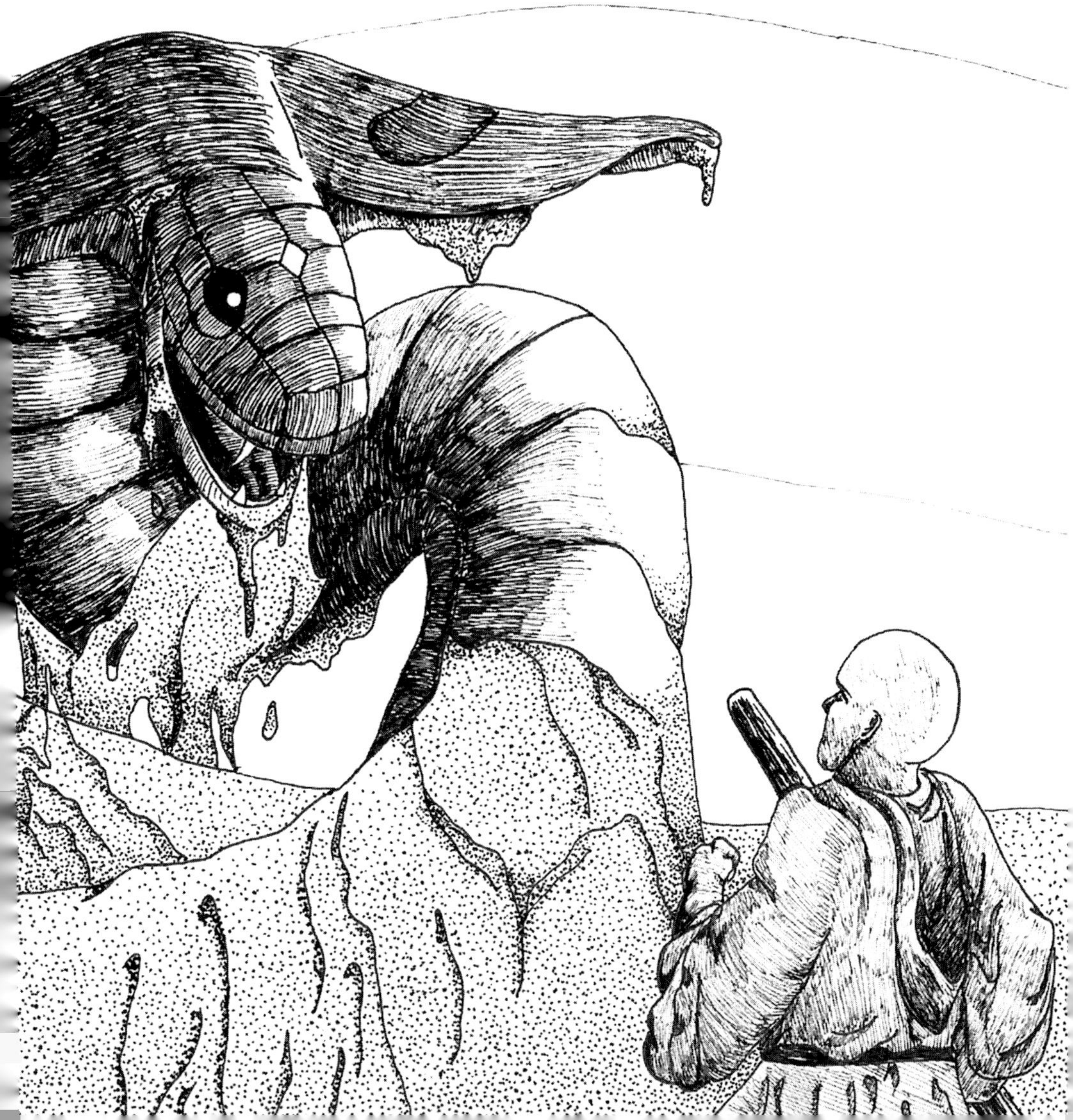

Lois Tilton is a Sideways winner and Nebula nominee. She's written Star Trek™ and Babylon 5™ books, as well as novels and numerous short stories of her own. When unfortunate events forced one of the professional authors to withdraw from the anthology at the last second, Lois agreed to headline Scalding Sands. This remarkable occurrence would not have happened without the help of another contributing member, Michael Ehart. Michael introduced us; I sent my emergency-situation proposal; Lois read it over…looked at RBE…and accepted. So it is only right that Michael penned the following introduction. Upon reading Michael's words, Lois remarked, "Can't really think of anything to add to it. Except maybe the night-blooming blood-drinking nightshade…"

Reliable sources tell me that Lois Tilton is a pretty serious gardener. This I am ready to believe, because her stories are planted, tended and grown with the same care as Nero Wolfe might have put into one of his orchids. I am not so certain I would feel entirely safe actually walking in her garden. Take her novel Written in Venom, *for example. A lot of writers have had their turn at the Norse myths, and some of them have done a pretty good job, too. But none of them thought of telling that story from the perspective of Loki, and that skewed view adds a flavor to the familiar tales that is particularly Tiltonesque. Unexpected turns. Surprising, often wicked motivations. A sort of garden path of the imagination that takes us to places we hadn't really wanted to go, but once having us taken us there, delight and astound. It doesn't matter what she writes, from Star Trek™ novels to her unique tales of vampires (no moping teenager bloodsuckers or ageless pretty-boys from her!) to the story you are about to read, Lois Tilton makes everything she writes seem like no one has ever seen things quite that way. It is a strange garden she grows, but a fruitful one, and you'll be glad that she has invited you in.*

Sometimes our behemoths really are as big as they appear. Sometimes our eyes mislead us. And sometimes we have it in us to be bigger than we ever thought it possible to be…or than we thought *we* could be.

Black Diamond Sands

A Tale of the Deserts

by Lois Tilton
& illustration by John Whitman

The body of the sorcerer Mehen was not yet cold, the cart had not yet come to bear him to the embalmers, when Urai heard a disturbance outside the front door of the house. Assuming that mourners were arriving, Urai left his father's body to greet them, but he stopped with the words of welcome still in his throat, for at the door stood the sorcerer Amit, accompanied by a man who wore a chain around his neck that identified him as an official of the civil magistrate's court.

Amit stood with arms folded across his chest as the magistrate unrolled a paper and read from it. "Be it known by all present that all the goods and property, household and chattels, of Mehen, Adept Sorcerer, are forfeit by reason of debt to Amit, Master Sorcerer. This judgment is attested by order of Tothep, Senior Civil Magistrate, and his seal affixed."

Shock rendered Urai speechless. He had known of his father's debts, but this — to come while the body was still in the house!

Amit glanced a moment at the body with a faint smile of satisfaction at the livid line of poison that ran from the web of Mehen's left thumb up to the heart, before turning to Urai. "Where is it?"

Urai knew what the master sorcerer wanted and went numbly to his father's workroom, to his locked cupboard, taking out the ivory box where Mehen had kept his most valuable objects. It was sealed and warded, of course, but Amit only had to make a sharp gesture with his hand, and the lid of the box flew open. "Yes," he said, removing an amulet of gold in which a small clear stone was set, incised with the glyph known as the Sorcerer's Eye. The same symbol was carved into the much larger diamond set in the ring on his right hand.

As Urai stood in helpless confusion, Amit looked around the workroom, displaying little interest in the rest of its contents. Attendants had followed him, and he ordered them, "Pack up all this trash." He then returned to the front room where the body lay and Urai's young sister Seshet stood nervously in a corner. The master sorcerer's face broke into an expression of greater satisfaction. "Yes," he said, giving the girl an assessing look. Then he turned back to the corpse, forced open its mouth and pulled out the piece of gold placed there, as tradition dictated, for the embalmers.

This act of desecration broke through Urai's numbness, and he lunged at Amit, crying in outrage, "You can't do that!" For if the embalmers were not paid, Mehen's body would be thrown into the common corpse pit for the jackals.

A gesture from the master sorcerer stopped him. "*All* the goods and property," he quoted, holding up the gold. "And chattels." Pointing at Seshet, he told his servants, "Take her."

Urai flung himself at them, fighting hopelessly to free his sister, who was crying out his name, but Amit only added, "The boy, too. Both of them."

Standing before his new master, Urai found himself perversely grateful for the copper slave collar locked around his neck with the metal tag that marked him as the property of Amit. It served to remind him that he was entirely powerless and without any rights, not even the right to his anger. He had sold it to Amit in exchange for the gold to give his father's body a proper embalming and burial. His vow now bound him more securely than any chains.

Were he not so bound, he surely would have attempted to tear Amit away from his weeping sister, whom the sorcerer was deliberately fondling in a manner meant to provoke Urai's outrage, a test of his submission. As if to remind him, Amit twisted the diamond ring on his finger, the focus of his power. "Your father was an ambitious and greedy man, son of Mehen. But worse, he was ambitious beyond his talent. I know this because he was apprentice to my own grandfather — you are aware of this?"

Urai managed to swallow the rage that was choking him. "So he told me."

"Mehen did you no favor when he decided to make you his own apprentice. And he certainly did you no favor when he went so far into debt. For this." Amit held up the engraved diamond amulet that had been the focus of all Mehen's ambition, pride and, yes, limited power. Shame washed over Urai's anger, for he could not deny the truth. "It was only because of his tie to my own family that I agreed to sell it to him at any price. He betrayed my trust, he tried to sell my secrets. Mehen was a fool, and now his children must redeem his debt."

The sorcerer abruptly changed his tone. "Tell me, boy, can you use this thing?"

Taking a deep, shaking breath, Urai replied, "He taught me. But he never allowed me to work with it, no."

"You are no adept in the craft."

"No."

"Do you know where diamonds come from?"

"From…the black desert in the south."

"Yes, from the black desert. Its name is the Harrara. Somewhere in the Harrara is the diamond mine. They call it the Alamaass. The only source of diamonds in all the world. I have an interest in this mine." Amit drew Seshet closer to him, stroking her body in a manner that brought renewed tears of shame to her eyes, but with his own gaze fixed on Urai as a snake might regard a rat. "I am going to sell you to the mine. The Alamaassin send a caravan every year to Qft, where there is a slave market. If you should manage to return from the mine with enough diamonds, and with the information that I seek, it is possible that I will release your sister to you. It is possible that I will have tired of her by then."

"How—"

"If you are worthy of the craft, you will find a way."

"And if…I do not return?"

"Then you may pity your sister."

Thus it came to pass that Urai found himself in chains on a barge headed south toward Qft, the last navigable port upstream from Xhem. From Qft the desert caravans came and went, lines of camels laden with bales of silks, with sacks of spices and incense, hammered metalware from eastern crafts masters, and gemstones from distant mines — jade, turquoise and rubies. But there was only one caravan that ventured into the black desert called the Harrara. Or so it was said. And no slave sold to the Alamaass mine ever crossed that desert again to return. So it was said.

Crocodiles lounged in the reeds of the riverbanks, showing their teeth in vast yawns that reminded Urai of Amit. He absently rubbed the tribal tattoo on his right forearm, the image of a cobra, coiled to strike. The flesh was still tender beneath the cobra's head, where the diamond was concealed in his flesh. A slave can not openly carry a sorcerer's focus gem. It had been Amit's sole concession to the difficulty of his task, to allow him the accursed diamond for which his father had mortgaged and lost his life. For Urai was by now convinced that Amit had brought about Mehen's death.

Amit's instructions had been coldly, relentlessly logical. The Alamaassin cross the Harrara when they come and go from the mine. Therefore the Harrara can be crossed. You will discover how. There is probably sorcery involved. You will discover the extent of their power. Most important, you will discover if they have learned how to engrave their diamonds, if they use them as focus gems. I have reason to believe they cannot. If they could focus their power through their diamonds, they would be able to rule the entire world. But I must be sure.

Diamonds were the hardest substance. Diamonds could cut other gems, nothing could cut diamonds. Not until Amit's discovery. Now he meant to gain control of the only source of diamonds in the world. The thought chilled Urai's blood. It would drive him mad, if he dwelled on it. He had no choice: he was bound to Amit's service. He had to concentrate instead on thoughts of his sister. He was her only hope.

When the barge came at least to Qft, Urai found himself part of a consignment of slaves destined for the diamond mine. They were a mixed lot — Xhemites, Punites, Qftians, and men from faraway lands that Urai did not know — but they were united in despair over their fate, of which they had heard many ominous tales.

"No one can cross the black desert."

"I've heard that no one has ever returned from the mine."

"They say that even a vulture will drop dead from the sky if it tries to fly over the Harrara."

"The men who live there are demons."

A leathery old Qftian with a gray beard shook his head at these remarks, but Urai, who was a sorcerer, would not dismiss the possibility of demons. If there were demons, it meant that whoever controlled them must possess great power, greater even than Amit's. He could almost wish it were true.

Their first sight of the Alamaassin only heightened the fears of the slaves, for they were clothed entirely in white robes that covered even their faces, except for a narrow slit for the eyes. Urai saw no way to tell if they were sorcerers. In his experience, sorcerers dressed much as other men, but the Alamaassin looked like corpses come from the embalmers, wrapped for the grave. And, like corpses, they did not seem to feel the heat. For while Urai's own headcloth, like the garments of all the slaves, was limp and grimy with sweat, the robes of the guards were pristine white with no stains of perspiration. Such a thing was not natural.

Even more unnatural, however, were the monstrous creatures awaiting them at the caravanserai. Urai had seen elephants and these were as massive, but their legs were shorter and splayed outward like lizards. Their color was black, mottled with a deep red. They had a thick, flat tail that twitched now and then as they lay sprawled on the ground with only their heads held alertly upright. Their eyes held a glow as of fire.

At the sight of these creatures, some of the slaves screamed about demons and many tried to flee. The Alamaassi guards appeared to be expecting this, for they went to work with their whips of copper wire, lashing the slaves into order.

Urai saw that the weathered graybeard did not exhibit such great fear, as if he were already familiar with the monsters. "You know what these creatures are?" he asked.

"The Alamaassin call them salamanders. They are the only creatures that can cross the Harrara. It is their birthplace."

"In Xhem, it is said that such creatures dwell in lakes of fire deep within the earth. In hell. It could only be sorcery that brings them to the surface. Are the Alamaassin sorcerers, then?" *Or demons?* And indeed, he could feel a slight tingling where the diamond was hidden beneath his tattoo, the closer he came to the salamanders.

Graybeard shrugged his indifference. It mattered little to him whether his new masters were sorcerers or not.

There were mountains of bundled goods heaped on the ground, and the slaves were ordered to load these onto the salamanders, which wore harnesses made for this purpose. It took more work with the lash to drive them to approach the creatures, and more than one slave attempted to flee again whenever a salamander would make a quick turn of its head in his direction. Even Graybeard, who claimed not to fear them, did not willingly come within reach of those jaws, for their breath felt like it came from a furnace. Urai was no more courageous, but the lash prevailed.

Besides the bundles, each salamander bore two pairs of large leather bladders, which the slaves had to fill with water drawn from the caravanserai's single well. The creatures could carry more than twenty times the weight of a camel. It was this water, Urai supposed, that was meant to sustain them all in the trek across the desert, so he willingly turned the winch that raised the dripping leather buckets, though the unaccustomed labor quickly blistered his hands.

There was a brief respite when the slaves were fed and finally allowed to drink their fill from the well, but all too soon, as the sun was setting, the Alamaassin mounted saddles fastened onto the necks of the salamanders. The laden creatures were goaded to their feet. The caravan was on its way back to the diamond mine.

Their progress was slow, kept to the plodding pace of the heavily-burdened salamanders. The slaves followed well behind the creatures in the clouds of dust raised by their muscular, undulating tails, and a single Alamaassi guard brought up the rear, with a long, thin sword suspended from his mount's harness. Urai's muscles ached from unaccustomed labor, adding to the pain of his blistered hands and the whip cuts on his back. This, then, was the life of a slave — toil and misery and pain.

At least they were traveling at night, when the heat of the sun was less. During the daylight hours, the Alamaassin erected large white tents and retreated into them, leaving only two guards on watch. The slaves found what shade they could, which grew more difficult every day they headed south, the temperature more intense, the land more arid. At last there were no longer any trees growing, not even the scrubby thorn acacias, or brown clumps of sand grass, only bare eroded ground.

But as he trudged behind the salamanders, Urai could not help wondering about the creatures. "It must be sorcery," he said to Graybeard as they followed in the creatures' dusty wake.

"What do you mean?"

"The salamanders. They don't eat or drink, they produce no waste. What else can it be but sorcery?"

"Are you a sorcerer, then, that you know this?" The other slave laughed curtly, then coughed and spat dust.

Urai felt alarm, that he had said too much, and forced a laugh of his own. "Would I be here if were a sorcerer? No, but when my father died, I was sold for debt to a sorcerer, to scrub out his chamber pots. He sold me to a camel merchant, who sold me to a carpet merchant, and here I am."

"So why are you asking me?" Graybeard demanded.

Apologetically, "Only because you seem to know something of these creatures. In Xhem they are legends. Do you know—"

Graybeard stopped. "Look, Cobra boy, I've seen your sort before, always asking questions. I can tell you have some foolish plan to run away. You think the Harrara is like the deserts of Xhem, that men cross on camels. I've seen the bodies of your kind on the sands, too dried out even for the vultures. Don't concern me with your plans. Don't ask me more questions. Don't speak to me again."

The leathery old slave turned and walked on, leaving Urai to follow in a state of near-panic. *Am I so obvious? Do the guards suspect me, too?* He would keep his silence from that time on, or so he told himself.

The land had been rising as they traveled, and soon they were obviously ascending to the top of a mountainous ridge. As Urai neared the crest, there was a sudden disturbance up ahead, the Alamaassin cursing and shouting commands at the salamanders, slaves crying out in terror and alarm, turning to flee back down the slope. Urai's forearm throbbed, detecting the action of sorcery as the riders attempted to control their unnatural mounts.

His curiosity overcame his weariness, and he continued to climb until he stood at the crest of a ridge that extended in both directions as far as the horizon and beyond, so that it seemed to be part of the rim of a vast bowl filled with black sand. The blazing starlight showed no outcropping of rock, no rise or fall of the land, no dunes, no stirring of wind. This was the Harrara, the black desert that no man could cross.

The leading salamanders had bolted out of their riders' control, and the massive creatures were now heading down slope. Urai had not imagined they could move so fast. As he watched, they reached the sand at the foot of the ridge and sprawled there like coals upon a bed of ashes. This was indeed their birthplace, he realized. They had come home.

Just then, another disturbance broke out on the other side of the ridge. One of the slaves, a stocky Punite they called Camel because of his split upper lip, had apparently decided to take advantage of the chaos to make a break and run. Perhaps he, too, had caught sight of the desert they were now about to cross, or perhaps the rampaging salamanders had sent him into a panic. But he had forgotten, or in his fear not been able to think, of the guard who always brought up the caravan's rear.

There came a sudden agonized shriek that rose in pitch and intensity, and Urai turned just in time to see the Punite's garments burst briefly into flame. The salamander's heated breath blackened the man's flesh as he writhed upon the sand. For several horrifying moments the charred thing on the ground continued to spasm, even after the screams had died away and the smoke and scent of roasted meat had wafted into the air.

The salamander ridden by the guard stood swinging its head from side to side with its jaws wide open, as if it were looking for another victim, and the slaves did not know whether to flee or stand motionless, to keep from attracting the deadly creature's wrath.

The caravan master gave up and ordered an early camp. As they sweated through the day, the slaves all spoke in horrified whispers among themselves of what they had just seen.

"It breathed flame!"

"I saw it open its jaws…"

To the other Xhemites among the slaves this proved that the salamanders and probably their riders were demons. Later, however, as they shifted positions to follow the meager shade, Urai confronted Graybeard in a furious whisper. "Did you know what they could do, those creatures? If someone had warned poor Camel—"

"No! I didn't know!" Defensively, lowering his voice, "People say things, there are rumors. Who knows if they are true?" Then, apologetic, "No, you're right, I might have said something, I don't know what…something. But what about you, Cobra, with all your questions? What do you know?"

"Nothing!" Urai insisted. "I only wonder if they are sorcerers. There are sorcerers who could burn a man to ash with a wave of their hands." He was thinking of Amit, but, seeing Graybeard's doubtful frown, "So I have heard."

"We're going to be crossing the Harrara now," said the old slave glumly. "Now we'll see what other legends are true."

The next night they descended to the desert basin. At every step, the temperature seemed to build. The black sands held the heat, even after the sun had set. It burned the soles of Urai's feet through his sandals. And the farther they went, the deeper the sand, until every step was an effort. It was Graybeard who pointed out that the broad, heavy footsteps of the salamanders compressed the loose grains to make a firmer surface.

Urai took a small swallow of water from his sack and concentrated on taking one step at a time. Another thousand steps, and he would allow himself another swallow.

Not all the slaves could restrain themselves, and before the night was over their sacks were empty. As they went on, some of them stumbled and fell, and it often took the lash to get them back to their feet. None had any doubt what would happen to any slave who could no longer go on. Urai had some concern for Graybeard, because of his age, but the leathery old slave seemed indestructible, even when younger men fell.

It was as much like a journey through hell as Urai had ever imagined, but he knew well that it would have been much worse to attempt the same trek with the sun high in the sky. With dawn beginning to color the horizon, a halt was finally called, and the slaves collapsed into the sand, sobbing and groaning.

At the same time, one of the Alamaassin held out his arms in the direction from which they had come and spoke an incantation that gave Urai's forearm a twinge. Seemingly from nowhere came a gust of wind that blew across the expanse of sand the caravan had just crossed, sweeping away their tracks, all signs of their passage.

"Now that was sorcery," said Graybeard, impressed in spite of his doubts.

Although Urai knew it had been a minor spell that he could have done himself, it was the first true working of sorcery he had witnessed from the Alamaassin, and he could now identify the sorcerer from the gold ring that he wore, although not the black stone it was set with — not a diamond, at least. It also occurred to him that if he ever did manage to make an escape from the mine, he might find himself lost in the middle of a desert devoid of landmarks. Yet while the Alamaassi sorcerer could sweep away their tracks in the sand, he could not sweep away the stars which illuminated the night like cold diamonds, and Urai began to take a fix on their position so as to mark the caravan's direction.

While the Alamaassin retreated to their white tents, the slaves had to spend the day huddled in the shadows they cast. Like the others, Urai pulled his headcloth over his face to keep the sun from blinding him. Both headcloth and loincloth, he noticed, now remained dry as the arid atmosphere of the desert thirstily absorbed his sweat. The furnace-heated air burned his lungs, no matter how shallowly he breathed, and blood seeped from his cracked lips. The sun also brought out a glint in the sand, as the light reflected off the grains. Urai idly used his finger to trace the shapes of serpents, of cobras, of spiders, always careful never to focus his power and bring them to life.

Night followed day, and day followed night. The rim of the mountains disappeared beyond the western horizon and their entire world was heated black sand underfoot and relentless sky overhead by day. One by one, the slaves fell. A man would faint, or his eyes would roll back in his head even while he remained wavering on his feet. The others would then attempt to support the victim but they rarely succeeded in reviving him, and guards soon came with the lash to drive them forward, while behind them a cloud of smoke rose into the air.

"If we had more water, we could have saved him," Graybeard complained bitterly, but the Alamaassin restricted their rations to a single sack, and no man would spare his own water to save another, not when his own life depended on it.

Then one day a Xhemite, whose tribal red-striped headcloth had by now faded to a uniform gray, stumbled and let his water sack fall. Urai saw the contents spilling into the sand and tried to save the water, but the sack was almost empty by the time he snatched it up. Acting on an impulse, he focused through the diamond beneath his skin, whispering the spell: *Increase*. At once, the water sack swelled, and he handed it back to the grateful owner, saying, "Lucky I got to it before it all spilled."

A few moments later, Graybeard came closer to him and said in a low voice, "I don't know what you did back there, but that guard may have seen."

"It was lucky most of the water didn't spill before I could pick up the sack," Urai said again, knowing how foolish he had been, yet also secretly elated that he had at last done a real working through the diamond. Still, he knew it would be too risky ever to try such a thing again, until it was time for him to escape.

A night came when it was possible to make out a faint shape on the eastern horizon, and as they slowly drew closer at the plodding pace of the laden salamanders, the shape resolved itself into an eroded mountain. The sight gave the slaves hope, for it could only be the location of the mine, which they had begun by this time to regard as their only possible refuge from death on the desert.

"It can't be worse," said Graybeard. "Nothing could be worse."

Yet it was with the mountain plainly in sight, perhaps only a day or two away, that the tough old slave suddenly collapsed with a sharp cry.

Urai ran to him. "What is it?" For while Graybeard was biting his lips with pain, his eyes showed he was still lucid.

"I don't know. My foot..."

"Come. Stand up!" Urai attempted to pull him to his feet, then, when Graybeard could not take another step, to bear part of his weight. The old man was not so heavy, sunbaked to leather and bone. "Lean on me! Walk!"

But it was evident from the swelling that Graybeard had broken or sprained his ankle. "Curse you, old man," Urai sobbed, "walk!" For he could now see the guard coming in their direction.

For a moment, the Alamaassi looked down on them from his seat on the salamander as Urai continued to pull-carry Graybeard. Then came the cut of the lash on Urai's neck. "Get away from him."

"No!" Urai cried, tightening his grip on Graybeard. "He can walk! It's only a sprain!"

Again the lash, harder this time, leaving blood running down his back. "Get away."

Urai stood defiant, refusing to relinquish his hold, until an unexpected blow struck him in the chest, sent him staggering backward. "Get away, damn you, Cobra boy!"

Then the searing blast of heat, the quick reduction of his friend to a mass of smoking char, and the Alamaassi, wrapped in his white robes so that only his eyes were visible, staring down at him in silence, daring him to react, as Amit had once dared him. Rage surged through Urai, the near-irresistible impulse to strike back, to see the Alamaassi's robes in flames, to hear his screams. He could feel the force of it growing, concentrating, intensifying. His fist clenched around the accumulating power, burning with the need for release, and in his mind he expended that power in a single bolt of focused energy.

Yet he managed to restrain the impulse, knowing that Graybeard, poor Graybeard was now beyond saving. And, like a half-remembered dream, seeing the image of a young girl with tears spilling out of her eyes, and a voice he hated: *Pity your sister.* Urai let his arm fall; he lowered his head in submission and turned to follow the caravan toward the mine. But in his heart he kept the rage still alive, smoldering, waiting.

The mountain had been worn away by the action of time until all that remained thrusting up above the sands was its inner core of hard black stone. From a fissure in that stone a portal had been cut, the entrance to the mine, now closed with a door covered in thick hides, to prevent the escape of moisture. This was a surprise to Urai, who had imagined a subterranean pool of fire where salamanders bred, but instead, as the door slid open, the scents of water and raw stone washed over him.

Inside the mountain, tunnels and chambers had been carved out. One tunnel led down to a cavern, and in its center was a pit. This was the diamond mine.

Slaves descended by ladders into the pit, where they hacked and chopped with picks and mattocks at the diamond-bearing matrix, then loaded the fragments into leather slings and winched them aloft to another gang of slaves, more experienced and trusted, who crushed the rock into finer particles and sieved the raw diamonds from them. There a guard was stationed to prevent theft.

In the pit, however, was only a single slave overseer, and Urai was content to labor there, not to attract unwanted attention. He rebuffed any attempts at friendship from the other slaves, for he was haunted constantly by the memory of Graybeard. His hands, blistered at first from the pick, grew calloused; his muscles grew hard from labor. His skin, that the desert had burned to near-black, began to fade, for the sunlight never reached into the mine, which was illuminated by globes containing some cool, radiant substance.

Urai's mind was now fixed on escape. He had acquired the information that Amit required. He knew that the Alamaassi sorcerer did not use diamonds as focus gems, and most of his attention seemed to be dedicated to the salamanders. Urai did not believe Amit would have any trouble overcoming him.

Nor should leaving the mine be difficult. There was only a single guard stationed at the entrance portal. The Alamaassin clearly believed that after their deadly ordeal in crossing the desert, no slave would dare leave the refuge of the mine. Yet first Urai must find the diamonds, stones large enough to satisfy Amit.

The work was slow. A ton of rock might not yield even a single diamond chip the size of a grain of rice. It was only the rarity of the diamonds that made them valuable. They were not used as gems, being too hard to cut and polish. Jewelers used them to cut other stones, alchemists to separate impurities in their solutions. Only Amit had realized their true potential.

Urai had been at least a tenday in the pit before he first spotted a bit of clear stone embedded in a broken piece of the matrix. *A diamond?* Other minerals, like quartz, looked much the same. He picked up the rock to take a closer look, but he did not know how to detect the difference. Then a thought came to him. Focusing through his own diamond, he dared a small spell of affinity, commanding *like to like*. Very faintly, he felt a vibration, as of two bells chiming the same note.

He quickly tossed the rock into the sling and returned with diligence to his work, fearing that at any moment the guards would come and seize him for using sorcery. But by the end of his shift, his apprehension had abated when nothing happened, just as his single working had gone unnoticed in the desert. Either the Alamaassi sorcerer's own power was too weak, or he did not bother to monitor the slaves. *And why should anyone suspect a slave of using sorcery?*

So Urai became more bold. The skill took some time to master, but gradually he became more attuned to the response as his own diamond reacted to the presence of others. Touching his fingertips to the rock matrix, he could feel the connection, and after a while he learned to distinguish from the strength of the vibration if another diamond were nearer or farther away, if it were large or small.

The first couple of stones, he folded into the waistband of his loincloth, but as his cache increased, he finally dared to use a spell of concealment to hide them under his pallet, although it was a permanent working and more likely to be discovered.

He began at last to think he had enough diamonds to satisfy Amit. The longer he delayed, the greater the risk. But he had detected a very strong vibration in a newly-exposed section of the pit, and its presence drove him to continue, one more day and another after that, determined to possess it. From time to time, he thought he saw the overseer looking at him with a suspicious interest and Urai had to make himself hold back, though he could sense so clearly that he was coming closer to something very large.

Finally a chunk of the matrix fell away under his pick, and he saw exposed the unmistakable shape of a raw diamond. He chipped away another flake of rock and more of the stone became visible. *It's the size of a crocodile's egg!* His entire forearm tingled with excitement.

Then he cursed, for a couple of the other slaves had noticed his persistent tapping at one piece of rock, and now the overseer was headed in his direction. Urai uttered a quick spell of concealment.

"What are you doing over here, boy?" the overseer demanded. "What are you chipping away at?"

"Oh, I thought I spotted something. It was nothing, though." Urai picked up a random broken rock from the floor of the pit. "You can see for yourself."

The overseer turned the rock over and back, frowning suspiciously. He took a globe of light and illuminated the section of the matrix where Urai had been working, but the spell held and he saw nothing.

"Take off your loincloth," he finally demanded, and Urai was glad that he had cached his stones away.

But he knew he would be watched now. The overseer might report him to the guards. He could delay no longer. Urai went directly to his pallet when his shift was over. After he had secured his diamonds beneath his loincloth, he began to recite a familiar spell.

This was the easy part. It had been his favorite exercise as a boy, and his mother had complained for years that she could not open a jar of grain without a cobra popping up at her and flaring its hood. He had made them large and small, in every color, in gold and jade and lapis to coil around his sister's arms and neck as ornaments. The memory caused a pang.

But those cobras had been happy, harmless creations. Into the spell he cast now, he poured all the venom and rage accumulated in his heart. Against Amit. Against his father's greed. Against the Alamaassin, and most of all the guard who had released the salamander's fury against Graybeard. If fate favored him, it would be that man on guard at the outer portal now.

The shape of the cobra tattooed onto his arm raised its head and began to separate itself from his flesh. A moment later, the serpent slithered rapidly into the tunnel on its deadly errand.

Urai's next task was more painful. With a sharp shard of stone, he cut into the scar on his arm. Working more by feel than sight, he extracted the diamond from beneath his skin. It was as if something had been severed, some extra sense cut off, nerves suddenly gone dead. The diamond, buried so long in his flesh, had become a part of him.

After wrapping the wound in a scrap of his ragged loincloth, he rose and followed the cobra into the tunnel. But when he reached the first branching that led down to the pit, he hesitated. Into his mind came a voice reminding him of the egg-sized diamond still embedded in the matrix. *You might cast a spell of concealment to render yourself invisible. You might descend into the pit unseen and remove the stone.* The voice went even further. *You might keep it for yourself instead of turning it over to Amit. With a diamond that size as your focus, you might perhaps even rival Amit's power.*

But Urai knew that voice. It was the voice of Mehen his father. I know the price is high, but it will be worth it. With a diamond as my focus, there will be no limit to what I can do!

Ambition. Greed. Debt. Murder. Slavery. Rape.

Pity your sister.

Urai turned his back on the pit and took the upper branch of the tunnel. When he reached the outer door, the white-robed body of the guard already lay collapsed in front of it, with the cobra coiled on his chest. Urai held out his arm and the serpent crawled onto it, then again became the tattoo.

Time was now urgent. Urai slid open the door and dragged the body outside. After so long in the cool, dark shelter of the mine, it was like walking into an open kiln. The sun was still high, but fortunately the portal stood at the moment in the mountain's shadow.

Urai rapidly stripped the dead guard of his robes. The man's naked skin was a pallid, unhealthy color, reminding Urai of the pale white scorpions that infested the tombs of the most ancient kings in Xhem. Once he was wearing the robes, he was pleased at how effectively they turned away the heat. More important, the guard's water flask was at least half full. Returning to the cavern to fill it would have meant a delay he could not afford.

Losing no more time, Urai began to trace the shape of a cobra into the sand, its length sixty feet, with a corresponding girth and a hood broad enough to shade him from the sun. When it was complete, he pressed his diamond into the sand between the serpent's eyes and began his spell. There was no holding back now. All his power was invested in that form in the sand.

At once, with a sharp hissing sound, sand began to flow into the cobra he had drawn, forming a vast elongated mound that rose at its midsection to almost half his height. Slowly the cobra raised its head from the sand, flaring its hood. Gleaming obsidian eyes flashed. Foot by foot, it rose from the desert floor, a sixty-foot black sandstone cobra with scales that glinted as they were struck by the sun.

Urai immediately mounted just behind its hood, and the giant serpent rapidly began to glide across the heated sands, soon leaving the mountain behind. A surge of exaltation rose in his heart. He had not only escaped the mine, he had accomplished a work of sorcery on the level of a true adept!

The cobra was far better adapted for movement across the sands than the salamanders, and being a creature of sorcery, it was tireless — as long as Urai's power did not fade. He hoped he would be able to go on without stopping through both night and day, and thus outrace any pursuit. To be even more safe, he raised a wind as the Alamaassi sorcerer had done, and obliterated his trail.

The Alamaassin might once have been powerful. They had tamed the giant salamanders and conquered the Harrara desert. But for all too long they had dwelled inside their mountain, only venturing out once a year as far as Qft. Qft with its dusty souk was the outer limit of their world.

Urai knew now that with a focus diamond the size of the stone he had left behind, a master sorcerer could pull the diamonds from their matrix with a wave of his hand. He would need no slaves, no caravans, no plodding salamanders. Infinite power — he would become like a god. Urai thought he might even pity the Alamaassin for what was going to befall them at Amit's hands, if he had not been their slave on that trek across the hell of the Harrara, if it had not been for Graybeard.

He managed to endure the first day and the night without rest, but at the height of the next day the heat threatened to overwhelm him. He halted the cobra and crawled into the shade of its spread hood, where he fell immediately into sleep. After that, he traveled as the Alamaassin did, only by night. By dawn of the fifth day he could clearly make out the shape of the mountains ahead of him on the desert's western rim. Beyond the mountains was Qft, and the river, the road home to Xhem where Seshet waited for his return, every day in torment that he could not stand to imagine.

By that time, he had given up expecting Alamaassi pursuit, so it was a shock that almost stopped his heart when he looked back and saw in the sky a distant object. Someone had once told him that even a vulture would drop dead from the sky if it tried to fly across the Harrara, but something was flying across it now, rapidly, and in his direction. This could not be happenstance.

Now there was no time to panic, no time to regret whatever mistakes he had made that allowed him to be followed. All his power was invested in the cobra, and he desperately considered how he could increase its speed or perhaps change it to a form that could fly. But he was not sure if he could accomplish this work in the cobra's present state or if he would have to first return it to sand, and he had no certainty that his creation would then actually be able to fly, and fast enough to outdistance his pursuit. He was not, perhaps, he realized, quite yet an adept in sorcery.

Accepting his limitations altered his resolve. He did not have the time for what he would need to do to escape. If he could not flee what was coming toward him, he would have to confront it.

He commanded the cobra to sink beneath the surface of the sand from which it had been born. Perhaps his pursuer had not yet seen it, or at least seen its size. Alone in his stark white robes, he stood on the black sands, awaiting the confrontation.

It was coming incredibly fast, obviously at the expenditure of great power. Urai was soon able to make out its shape, which seemed to be that of a ray or skate, swimming through the sky as such creatures normally swim across the floor of the sea. But as it came even closer, he realized that it was in fact a giant salamander, its form altered so that vast leathery wings now spread between the fore and hind limbs. The wings held it aloft, but it was propelled forward by the undulations of its huge muscular tail. So would such creatures swim through their lakes of fire, where they truly belonged. Urai thought it beautiful, with a sinuous grace unlike its ponderous gait on land. To be able to do such a work, the Alamaassi sorcerer who rode it must be a true master of the craft. Urai had badly, perhaps fatally, misjudged his power, but there was no retreat possible now.

He raised his arms and held them out in the gesture of challenge. Every moment he waited, the heat of the sands beneath his feet built up and the withering air sucked the moisture from his flesh. Thirst was starting to afflict him, but he could not abandon his stance now. He began to fear that the Alamaassi might reject his challenge and simply circle high overhead until the sun struck him down.

But no. It was descending. Closer. The salamander opened its vast maw, and the waves of heat that emerged from it were visible.

Closer.

Now!

Sand erupted into the air from the force of the giant cobra uncoiling to strike. Its shining fangs sank into the salamander's exposed throat.

The salamander faltered, falling, unbalanced and dragged down by the cobra's mass. Urai felt the impact as the two massive creatures struck the ground, still twisting and convulsing in their mortal duel. He ran for his life, lest the battling monsters crush him. The salamander lashed furiously with its powerful tail, but now on the ground the cobra could bring its full length into play, coiling around its foe, attempting to immobilize it. Heat blasted from the salamander's maw, while the cobra struck again and again with its venomous white fangs.

Suddenly the searing force of an explosion blew Urai to the ground. Gouts of incandescent matter fountained into the air, and a seething cloud of acrid smoke expanded rapidly. On his knees, Urai coughed and gasped, drawing up the hood of his robe over his face for protection as burning cinders fell around him. There came the too-familiar odor of burning flesh.

He rose shakily to his feet and groped inside his robes for his water flask, draining it almost to the last drop. The ground where the creatures had fought was now covered with unidentifiable black lumps and fragments, some of which had been his cobra. Nothing moved. Still shaken, he cautiously walked across the sands, in awe at the scope of the destruction. The harsh smoke still lingered in the air and his steps stirred up ash. Sixty feet of cobra scattered over more than a six hundred foot radius of sand, but Urai had only one purpose now: to examine as many fragments as possible, hoping to find a diamond the size of his smallest fingernail. Without it, without the ability to refill his water flask, he knew he would not live long enough to see the stars emerge. All his efforts would have been in vain and his sister would live out her days in slavery and degradation.

Already his head felt as if his skull had been cracked open from the inside. The world seemed to be going in and out of focus.

A ray of sunlight glanced off something reflective in the distance. Despite his blurring vision, Urai stumbled in that direction. When his sight cleared again the reflection was gone. *Only a trick of the light.* Again, he caught the reflection. *There!* It came from a shining, smooth black stone that he recognized after a moment as an obsidian eye of his cobra. He picked up the piece of black sandstone that had been part of the cobra's head. *Between the eyes...* He had placed his diamond between the cobra's eyes.

It was not there. Only a smaller black stone...

Urai rubbed at it and a black crust crumbled away. Rubbed again, harder, seeing the glint of clear stone beneath the black. He closed his eyes, focused his faltering power, and from the almost-empty flask the water came gushing out, spilling past the cap, overflowing, saturating his robes.

A short time later, in the shadow of a low black sandstone wall built from fragments of the broken cobra, Urai pried the diamond free and tried to clean it off. The incised form of the Sorcerer's Eye had been almost entirely worn away, its potency diminished with it. But Urai judged that it would be enough to bring him out of the desert, on foot, the way he had come in. Out of the desert and onto the road back to Xhem, to confront Amit with his success, to redeem his sister.

He bared his right forearm and took up a shard of obsidian, opened the old scab. With a push of his thumb, he slid what was left of the diamond into the wound. He flexed his fingers, made a fist.

A faint, very faint vibration trickled through his arm, a sensation so weak that he might not have noticed it before he became so much attuned to the presence of the diamond focus. The affinity spell must still be active. *What had it discovered, though, out here on the empty desert?*

He traced the sensation to its source, digging down into the sand until he encountered a broken-off segment of stone, roughly cylindrical, almost too large for him to close his hand around. He stared at it uncomprehendingly, thinking it resembled the tusk of an elephant, diamond instead of ivory, until he finally recognized it as part of his cobra's fang. Fangs of solid diamond. Not even Amit could have imagined a diamond of such size.

But how? How could such a thing come to be? He had formed the cobra from the black desert sand, transforming it to living sandstone. He had not the power to change one substance to another, sand to diamond; neither the power nor ability. *Where, then, had the diamond come from?*

Comprehension came. Urai stretched out his hand and uttered a spell of summoning: *Like to like.* An instant later his arm glittered with minute clear shards no larger than grains of sand.

A familiar voice spoke to him: *Here is wealth! Here is power!*

If he had used the crystals of diamond among the sand to form the cobra's fangs, he could form them in other ways, into potent glyphs. He could feel the potency gathering in his hand, ready for release.

No.

He had barely enough power remaining now to get him out of the desert, back to Xhem, to Seshet.

He rose to resume his journey across the black diamond desert that sparkled as far as the horizon and beyond.

Martin Turton lives in East Yorkshire, England, with his wife and three daughters. In the little spare time he has after working full time and looking after three children all under the age of four, he had been working on an unwieldy fantasy novel before turning to the shorter form in the hope of actually finishing something. His work has appeared or is forthcoming in Flashing Swords, Reflections Edge, Abandoned Towers, Allegory, Ray Gun Revival, Sorcerous Signals, Membrane SF, Afterburn SF, *at Sfzine.org and elsewhere. Find out more than you ever wanted to know about him at his livejournal Beyond Jerohim (http://monstewer.livejournal.com). Writing about characters allows the author not only to play at being a god but the opportunity to be someone else. Anyone else. Often it's fun being the hero; sometimes it's just plain nasty, and difficult to resist becoming another one of the monsters. It is one thing to stand determined before a raging fiend, quite another to quell the rage of the one inside.*

The Hunter of Rhim

A Tale of the Deserts

by Martin Turton

It was three weeks before his cries, before his pleas for mercy, fell silent. Hunter Jon waited another two days before he descended the steep stairs into the murky cell. The stench already hung heavy in the air.

He barely recognized the body when he found it curled up, fetus-like in a corner. Barely recognized it as the human it had once been. The skin was loose and sagging where it had been stretched over the mottled, heavy brow. The fingers were fractured and twisted where once they had been cruel talons. The teeth were broken and shattered. And, of course, the eyes were gone. The eyes were always gone.

That terrible, eyeless gaze turned toward Hunter Jon as he drew his knife. Its breathing was pitiful, coming in short, shallow gasps.

He rested a hand on its rough, scarred cheek. "Forgive me, brother. May The One have mercy on us both."

The screams were loud and dreadful as Hunter Jon began to slice at that loose, clammy skin.

For three years the Sagarki had been stealing souls. Nobody knew where they came from. Nobody knew what they wanted. Nobody knew who would be the next victim of a Sagarki possession.

A terrible, frightening time. Everybody waited in horrified anticipation of the next sudden, sickening burst of savagery as a Sagarki claimed a poor soul and went on a bloody, murderous rampage.

Murder became a common occurrence. The slightest change in a person's behavior triggered a frenzy of fear that turned entire towns into bloodthirsty mobs.

Rhim had once been a prosperous town, the last light of civilization before the Great Wastes.

Jon rode down the rough, filth-laden streets, ignoring the hollow stares, the flickering curtains, the silence of a town enthralled by its own misery. By a town which had watched nine of its sons and daughters be claimed by the Sagarki, beasts which stood as tall as a two-story house and were filled with rage and hatred and violence. Rumor had it that a woman in Gaaldine had been possessed by a Sagarki which had been twice that size. Jon had seen more of these beasts than any man alive and had dismissed the tales of horror sweeping across Ruritania. He didn't believe them. He couldn't believe them.

A scurry of feet on the wooden boardwalk and somebody shouted, "Murderer! Defiler!" before the feet hurried away again. Jon tucked his long coat behind the hilt of his sword and rubbed Risakin's ear to calm the skittish mare. He continued toward the tavern, a squat building standing alone on the main crossroads in the town.

Six pairs of eyes turned toward the door as he entered; six pairs of eyes which quickly returned to their drinks as they recognized the long black coat and broad-brimmed hat. He headed straight to the bar, removing his hat and running a hand through his thinning dark hair.

"I'm looking for a woman by the name of Addison." Jon could feel the six men staring at his back. He jingled some small silver coins in his hand as he regarded the tavern-keeper, an overweight man with curious stains on his vest.

"Ain't been in all day." The tavern-keeper regarded Jon suspiciously while rubbing at a glass with a dirty rag. "What you be wanting with her, anyway? We don't want any trouble 'round here, you know."

Jon tossed two battered silver coins across the bar. "A glass of Lysan Fire. And my business is my own."

He leaned back against the bar, keeping a wary eye on the others. *Come quickly,* the note had said. *The horror isn't ended. There is another.*

There was always more. Kill two Sagarki in Katrinamal and four more would appear in Gaaldine, kill three in Gondal and six more surfaced in Brenzaida. Each time the beasts were bigger, stronger. But no, the Sagarki in Gaaldine had to be a lie. They said it had slaughtered hundreds, even a thousand, before finally being slain. He drank some of the Lysan Fire, his eyes on the door.

Her writing had been squat and rounded, but Addison herself was a spare, lean woman, hard-bodied and sharp-eyed. "Hunter Jon," she said, stepping into the room. It wasn't a question.

"I no longer ride with my brothers. Jon is the only name left to me."

Addison's dark eyes regarded him levelly. "And yet you still wear the colors of the Hunters. And you still replied to my note."

"I no longer ride with the Hunters, but my skills are still my own. And we all have a part yet to play in this war we fight." Jon drank from his glass of Lysan Fire, a greenish liquid with a smoky head. "And if what you say is true, then we have no time to waste."

Bitterness tinged her hard smile. She considered his words. A faint shrug told him she had reached a decision. "Oh, it is true. Have no worries about that."

A sudden shuffling of chairs and the men left the tavern. Jon paid them no heed as he had another drink, taking the opportunity to study the woman in front of him over the rim of the glass. She wore a rough-checked shirt open at the neck and faded black pants tucked into brown boots that reached up to her calf. She looked like she hadn't changed her clothes for a week and the sand which clung to her boots and pants suggested she had been travelling through the Wastes. Two years of hunting the Sagarki had made him a wary man. "And why should I trust a woman who spends her days following a Sagarki through the Wastes?"

Addison smiled, a smile as dry as the endless Wastes themselves. "I have heard of you, Hunter Jon." She held up a hand as she saw him about to protest the name. "They say you are not held back by petty fears and superstitions, that you have no conscience to be troubled. That you will do what needs to be done. No more, no less." She took his hand in hers and placed something damp and wiry into it: the hair of a Sagarki. The stench, the dull-brown color, the thickness of it, all were unmistakable. That dry smile again. "They say if somebody offers you a Sagarki, you won't waste time asking stupid questions. You will do what needs to be done."

The hair felt loathsome and foul in Jon's hand. He gripped it tightly in a fist. "He has changed already?" He felt his heart quicken at the prospect of the hunt.

Addison brushed some sand off the arm of her sleeve. "I've never seen anything like it. He changes seemingly at will, or through some other influence that I can't determine. I only know that every time he changes, he is bigger. It is as though he feeds off the soul of the man who he possesses. The last time I saw him he towered hundreds of hands high. He would stride over this tavern in a step." She paused, a crease appearing above her small nose. "And that was three days ago." Another pause as she gauged Jon's reaction. "But whatever his guise, he always heads west, always west, barely stopping for food or sleep. I thought he would stop at the Wastes — nobody travels through the Wastes on their own, but he barely seemed to notice. Straight as an arrow he continued."

Jon felt a chill run down his spine. He thought of the tales of murder and horror in Gaaldine. If what Addison said was true, then they would be as nothing compared to what this creature could do. It took him a moment to consider the size of the thing before something else she had said made him pause. "He changes at will? No Sagarki can do that. The transformation is final — once the beast has control of the soul, that is the end."

"I can only tell you what I have seen. Though when he is in human form he seems little more than beast, so single-minded is he on his journey."

"And where is this journey taking him?" Jon wondered aloud.

Addison shrugged. "What is there to the West of the Wastes? Nothing. Nothing but the Sea of Sighs."

A shadow of a worry crossed Jon's mind but he shrugged it away. "Wherever he is going, we'll put an end to it soon enough."

For the briefest of times, Hunters had been looked upon as saviors, as the last remaining hope against the unrelenting horror of the Sagarki. Hunters were welcome everywhere they went. On the long, endless journeys they were forced to travel, never once did they go a night without a fire to warm them, a meal in their belly and a soft bed to sleep on.

That was before people realized what it meant to be a Hunter. Before they heard the screams of a loved one as a Hunter's knife cut into their flesh. Before they watched the skin being peeled away from a screaming child's face. Before they felt the cold, dead eyes of a Hunter following them down the street.

The Sagarki were a cruel enemy, uncaring of who they chose as their next victim — man, woman or child. Three years ago there had been no warning; no warning until towns and cities and villages had woken to a beast from nightmare in their midst, killing and defiling with a savagery never known.

And then the first Hunter, Hunter Raziel, discovered that the changes began inside long before the transformation and people began to fear the Hunters almost as much as they feared the Sagarki.

The room Jon had rented was clean and economical, a hard bed neatly made, a wash basin with a broken sheet of glass that served as a mirror and a single straight-backed chair in the corner. Addison lounged in that chair, her long legs crossed at the ankles. "So, do those things actually work then?" She nodded at his quiver of arrows. "Must get kind of expensive if you can't shoot straight."

Jon ran a thumb along the tip of a silver arrow-head. "They work as well as any other arrow." He fastened a belt around his waist, two daggers gleaming brightly in the morning light. He moved over to the wash-basin and splashed cold water on his face before bowing his head and reciting the True Prayer, all the while feeling Addison's cold green eyes on his back.

"You fear them," she said once he had finished.

Jon hung a necklace around his neck, the image of The One falling inside his black shirt. "Why do you say that?" He reached for his sword; the leather of the pommel was a worn, faded red.

Addison smiled, "You arm yourself with trinkets and superstitions. You delay our start. That's why I say you fear them." She rose to her feet. She was still wearing the same clothes, though she was now armed with a short, double-edged sword carried in a plain scabbard. "Do you deny it?"

Jon took one last look in the broken glass. His reflection showed him an aging, tired-looking man. "I've seen a Sagarki rip a man's head clean off his shoulders using nothing but its bare hands; I've seen a Sagarki leave six armed guards nothing but bloody shreds in a matter of moments. They are an enemy to be taken seriously, Addison."

Addison's smile was scornful. "Perhaps I have chosen the wrong man. I had heard you were the best of all Hunters. I had heard you were the man to slay the Sagarki. Or perhaps it was a different Hunter Jon who killed the Beast of Slasin?" Her eyes were dark despite the morning light spearing through the window.

An image of a dark room, seven small bodies curled on the wooden floor. Unmoving. Never to move again. "I will stop this Sagarki, Addison." His arms felt weary as he pulled on his long black overcoat. "Have no fear of that."

The Wastes. The vast desert which stretched all the way from the banks of the river Inarous to the Sea of Sighs. Few people travelled through the Wastes, and the few who did were known to return with tales of spiteful ghosts who roamed the sands at night; with tales of strange beasts who spoke in evil tongues and had teeth the length of a man's arm; with tales of a heat that scorched the skin.

Not a place for man or animal; Jon wouldn't take Risakin out there. Addison seemed unconcerned by his hesitation and was already striding ahead, her shirt sleeves rolled up to the elbow and her boots sending up puffs of the fine sand that rolled across the Wastes. One last look at the mare and an extra coin to the wide-eyed boy at the stable, and Jon followed her.

It looked like a red blanket had been laid over the landscape. She pointed to a hill, hazy in the distance, scraggly bushes clinging to whatever nourishment they could find beneath the sands. "There. I last saw him just a couple of miles past that hill."

The sun hung swollen and ripe in a sky of parched blue and those sands were already in Jon's shoes, in his black gloves; he could even taste them on his tongue. "So you saw a Sagarki and followed it into the Wastes, alone and unarmed." He nodded as though this was the most logical thing in the world.

Addison came to a sudden halt, looking at Jon from shadowed eyes. "Yes. Yes I did. And you know why? It was the screams I heard first. Terrible screams that seemed to shred the very air. It was in Garrowby, one of the abandoned settlements five days ride from here. A ghost town where the doors flap in the wind and curtains flicker as you walk the empty streets. I climbed the stairs in the old store and watched him from a window. He was writhing, squirming in agony; I never knew a man could suffer so much and still live." Her dark eyes were distant, unfocused. "And when it was done he wasn't a man anymore and he howled. A howl that shattered my window and sent me fleeing down those steps as though the Dark One himself was on my heels." She ran a hand through her ragged, rusty hair and began to walk to that distant hill, her boots scuffing the sands as she walked. "But then, when I realized nobody had followed me to my hiding place in that dark cellar, I wanted to kill that beast, to make it suffer the way it had made that man suffer so many agonies." She turned back to Jon, smiling shakily; the first sign of weakness he had yet seen in her. "Since that afternoon I have seen it go through that transformation seven times. Seven times he has gone through that agony, and you still tell me it's impossible?"

Jon adjusted the bow across his back. "I think the past three years have shown us that nothing is impossible, Addison. But if this beast is as you say he is, I think he could be important, both to us and to the Sagarki. I intend to be the first to reach him."

Their fire was a pitiful thing. The wild, straggly bushes that grew in the Wastes made a poor firewood. Jon and Addison sat close to the flames which barely fought off the chill of the wind howling across the barren landscape. The cold was as bitter as the heat of the day had been.

Addison broke their long silence. "Why did you become a Hunter?"

He looked up from the bootstrap he had been fixing. Addison's face was a mask of dancing shadows in the firelight, her skin a burnished brown. "Why? Because I was tired of killing my fellow man for reasons I didn't understand. Killing former friends for petty squabbles over who owned which field. When the Sagarki appeared I knew we had an enemy that had to be fought. We travelled half way across Ysandr, my friend Rastin and I, to answer Hunter Raziel's call."

Addison's face was impassive in those flickering shadows. "And what happened to him? Your friend, Rastin?"

Jon pulled the boot on, rising to his feet and stamping it firmly into place with a satisfied grunt. "You should rest. We have a long day ahead of us tomorrow."

The next day, Jon set a punishing pace and Addison was far behind him when he suddenly dropped to his haunches, eyes focused on the sand. She was short of breath when she reached his side, and could only raise a questioning eyebrow.

Jon pointed to the depressed sand beneath their feet, then swung a hand in a circle about them. Addison studied the packed sand and realized they stood in an imprint the size of a small farmer's field. Ahead, three smaller indentions — perhaps the size of Jon's room at the tavern — faced westward. A footprint.

They hurried on with renewed vigor, their faces grim and traced with lines of sweat.

The next time Jon stopped he laid his heavy coat on the ground and placed some hard bread and cheese on it. The ground here was rocky and uneven, sickly-looking weeds struggling through the cracks. The sun had just passed its zenith and Addison's hair was dark with sweat.

"I don't know why you insisted on coming with me." He sliced off a hunk of cheese with his silver dagger and handed it to her as she sank to her knees by his side.

She took the cheese from him. "I think you do. The same reason you still hunt even though your brothers are no longer by your side; when so many men hide and cower at the mere mention of the Sagarki." Her dark eyes looked west. "Once you have seen one of those beasts, once you have seen what it can do to a man, you can never sleep again knowing there is such a thing in the world." She finally looked back at Jon. "I want to see you kill it. I want you to show me its bloody corpse and tell me that it will never be coming back."

Jon nodded and chewed on the stale bread. Before long they were on their way again, the rocks hard on their feet and the wind driving the stinging sand into their faces. The wailing of that wind changed the further they walked and they began to hear voices behind it as the sun fell.

At first they put it down to nothing but the wind playing through the dark hills and the scraggy bushes, nothing more than the red sands rolling across the dunes. But when they made camp, the voices started referring to Jon and Addison by name; no longer could they pretend the wind whispered to them from the darkness.

"Hunter Jon....Jon the Betrayer..." the voices moaned, a hundred speaking as one. *"Waiting, waiting so long for you. Feed us, Hunter Jon. Feed us with your cruelties and deceptions. Tell us, Jon the Betrayer, tell us..."* A shadow flitted by a bush, barely seen in the flickering firelight. Addison's eyes were wide as she looked at Jon from across that pitiful fire.

"Why do they call you that? Jon the Betrayer?" Her voice was quiet, her face in darkness as the flames flickered and ebbed.

"Tell her, Jon the Betrayer. Tell of the night you stole into their room. Tell her what you did there..." The voices reached a pitch of moaning ecstasy.

They sounded closer.

Jon rolled his coat to make himself a pillow. He could feel watchful eyes on him. "Ignore them. I've yet to hear of a voice who can do a person harm."

"Oh, but we can, Addison...we can. Tell her, yes tell her what we can do..." The dry cracking of a twig sounded somewhere outside their ever-shrinking circle of light.

She came to him then, and he let her share his pillow as they lay together and watched the fire die before them. It was as the last flickering embers died away that he took her. Or she took him. Her hands were rough and urgent on him and sometimes they felt cold on his skin. Somebody cried out her name and he wasn't sure if it was his own voice and then again, when she came and cried out, loud in the night air. Even those voices in the shadows quieted their insistence just for a moment.

Morning brought with it a withering blue sky and an uneasy silence. Eyes were cast downward as clothing was adjusted and, as they left their little campsite, neither of them mentioned the footprints in the red sands.

The urgency seemed to have left Jon as they continued their journey westward. Instead of constantly ranging ahead, now he walked with Addison; his hand never far from his bow, eyes constantly scanning every direction like some protective jackal.

The footprints of their quarry were a constant presence by their side; sometimes a huge, three-toed imprint which seemed to take hours to pass, and then sometimes a neat human footprint smaller than Jon's own. And always headed westward, ever westward.

As the sun began to descend a third time and thoughts of the voices were heavy on both their minds, Addison finally broke the silence. It wasn't the question Jon had been expecting. "What happened to your friend Rastin?" Her hair was thick with sand and there was a dirty smear on her cheek.

For some reason that he couldn't understand, Jon felt that he owed her something. He fixed his eyes on the distant horizon. "I killed him. He had been taken by a Sagarki. I stopped him before he changed." The screams were loud in his ears and the smell of blood, so much blood, was foul in his nose.

Addison's footsteps didn't slow. "They say everybody knows of somebody who has been taken by the Sagarki."

There was a long silence. "And what of you, Addison? Do you know of somebody who has been taken?"

Before Addison could answer, the voices returned.

~ The Hunter of Rhim ~

The Sea of Sighs gained its name from the sound of the breeze which constantly rolled across the endless blue waves and out over the barren rocks and sandy dunes of the Wastes. It was a sigh of mourning. A sigh of loss.

A man stood at its edge, looking out across the waves before him. He turned to watch their approach. A wide smile spread across his face, though his faded blue eyes were cold. "You have found me." He spread his arms wide, the sleeves of his black shirt billowing in that mournful breeze. "I have nowhere left to run."

"Tristan!" Addison cried, trying to run past Jon, only to have him grab her wrist and pull her back.

"Addison, no. Stay with me." Jon kept a careful distance away from the stranger. The man laughed.

"What a fine couple you are! You haven't told her what I am, Hunter Jon? Ah," he shook his head, thick black hair ruffling in the wind, "but then, I don't suppose she told you about her Tristan, did she?"

Jon resisted the urge to look at Addison, fearing to take his eyes away from the Sagarki for even a moment.

Addison's struggles against Jon's grip weakened. "What have you done to him?"

The Sagarki's lips twisted in a mockery of a regretful smile. "He is still here. If I listen closely I can hear him begging, pleading for release, though it bores me after a while so I stop listening." He licked his lips as he looked at Addison. His lips were worm-like and his tongue was wet. "I did enjoy his memories of you, Addison; your cries of pleasure, the feel of your body under him—"

Perhaps it was the shock of the words or the faint sickness in the pit of his stomach. Jon's grip slipped from Addison's wrist and she flung herself at the young man whose eyes had suddenly turned a burnished gold.

Her sucking, rattling breath as the claws ripped into her throat was terrible to hear.

The Sagarki still appeared in Tristan's form; only his hand was clawed and scaled. He lifted Addison from her feet — blood gushing over his cruel talons as he lifted her off the ground — and watched her kick feebly, her hands waving uselessly in the air.

Jon's hesitation lasted only a matter of seconds — just long enough for her hands to stop waving and her legs to stop kicking. He dimly noticed the shaking of his hands as he nocked his bow and took aim at the slight young man before him tossing Addison dismissively to one side. Her body landed limply in a cloud of dust and dirt just as Jon fired his silver arrow.

He missed by ten feet, the arrow landing uselessly amid a pile of broken rocks.

"I was hoping we wouldn't have to go through this, Hunter Jon," the slender youth said from Jon's side. The claws were gone, but his hand dripped with blood.

Jon felt sick. He didn't dare tear his eyes away to look at Addison's broken body. "What are you? What do you want with me?" His voice was little more than a whisper.

Those lips twisted once more into a smile. "What am I? You could call me a student, Hunter Jon. I study your race as, I hear, you study mine. I study your race to ease the passage of our children." The smile widened as Jon stared at him. "Oh yes, those are children that are being born in your world, children that you hunt, Hunter Jon." He wrapped an arm around Jon's shoulders. The wind sighed around them, mourning the death of Addison, mourning the loss of hope.

"Unfortunately," Tristan continued, "the birth of our children can be a traumatic, frightening experience for them." Tristan grinned conspiratorially. "I seek to ease their passage."

There was no writhing in agony, no screams of pain. One moment Jon looked upon the face of Tristan, a youth with black hair and pale skin and a large nose, and then the face shifted, even melted, as the mouth widened into a wide red slit full of cruelly curved teeth. The eyes became golden and ancient.

Dull green scales spread over his body. And, even as the teeth formed, even as the scales spread, the beast soared into the air. He grew and grew. The wind howled as the creature grew, each scale the size of a window, every blemish, every hair magnified ten-fold as Jon looked up at a creature from the netherworld.

He had seen four beasts before, and always — always — they had been raging, they had been screaming, they had been butchering. The calm, watchful way this Sagarki looked down at Jon now frightened him more, was more terrible than any slaughter could ever be. It could have picked him up and crushed him with one mighty fist. And yet it stood there and looked down at him from golden eyes which seemed to loom as high as any sun.

The scales faded, the mouth narrowed, the creature…*folded,* and Tristan stood before him again, a knowing smile upon his face.

Jon stared at the man uncomprehendingly. "Why?"

"Why do I show you this?" The blue eyes flashed golden again. "Because you hunt our children, Hunter Jon. Because you lock them in cells away from the sunlight they need. Because you perform foul deeds on their dying bodies. Because I want you to know that your kind are to be no more. I want you to know this before you die."

This time Jon was prepared for the transformation. He staggered backward, spittle lashing his face as huge teeth snapped and missed. Jon's feet scrabbled in the dirt, propelling him away from the beast as he drew his sword, the silver bright in the dying light.

The beast towered over the Hunter and howled to the skies, a howl so loud that Jon screamed in pain. He felt something warm and wet trickle out of his ears as he struggled to his feet, the sword held out in front of him.

Never before had he seen a Sagarki so massive. It stood over four hundred hands high, taller than any living thing Jon had ever seen, taller even than any tower he'd stood beneath. The creature's scales were thick and hard and green. Dense, wiry hair tapered down its back and across those hulking shoulders so high Jon had to crane his neck to see them.

A huge, clawed fist shot out and batted the sword from Jon's hands. The foul mouth spread into a red grin as it loomed over its prey, each tooth as tall as a man.

He fumbled for his last remaining dagger but the beast hauled him from his feet by his shirt before he could reach it. A long black tongue oozed between yellowed teeth as the beast let out another howl of triumph.

Jon's own transformation was over in an instant — though it seemed to last an eternity. An eternity of cold, suffocating scales spreading across his skin. An eternity of black, ancient, evil thoughts battering the walls of his mind. An eternity of cruel, sharp teeth filling his mouth. An eternity of massive, battered talons tearing through the flesh around his knuckles. An eternity of the Sea of Sighs and of the Wastes veering before him and vertigo making his stomach roil sickeningly.

He felt a deep, burning sensation in his chest where the figure of The One burned a black hole into his scales. Only this constant pain reminded him of his humanity, of who he was. Reminded him of every other time he'd felt that same pain. Without that reminder he feared he would never return from the black pit of evil in which he dwelled.

The roar which erupted from his mouth was a cry of loss, a cry of pain, a cry of fury which mingled with the moaning of the breeze into a sound terrible to hear. So terrible that the beast released him, its ancient golden eyes widening in momentary fear.

That one moment was all Jon needed. His senses heightened, each second seemed an hour, each sigh a scream, each blemish on the beast's foul scales a weakness. He lashed out with a mighty fist, claws digging easily through the monster's scales and into the side of its neck, hot green blood spurting lavishly down his arm and into the roiling seas far, far below, even as his other fist slid beneath the beast's ribs.

Jon's howl of triumph ripped into the afternoon air, loud and dreadful as he tore greedily at the Sagarki's flesh. Blood ran down his throat, hot and sticky and ripe.

By the time the man's eyes slowly flickered open, the morning sun was just beginning to rise over the Sea of Sighs and the voices, the ecstatic, whispering voices had finally fallen silent.

The man tried to move, only to be held in place by stakes driven through his limbs and into the parched red sand. He struggled weakly, panic dawning in his eyes as the wounds across his chest opened and his blood seeped into the sand around him.

Jon sat by his side, drawing idle patterns in the sand with a small stick. "Struggling is no use, Tristan." His voice was quiet, almost sad. The man twisted his neck as best he could to look at Jon.

"You are one of us?" His movement opened a rent in his neck and his eyes glazed with pain.

"I don't know what I have become." Jon touched his chest. Underneath his shirt the skin had become blackened, the burn had reached almost to his breastbone. Tearing the figurine away from the scorched flesh had made him vomit with pain.

Tristan could only nod to that. He rested his neck and gazed up to the parched blue sky overhead for a long moment. "But why," he finally said, "why did you keep me alive?"

Jon traced some more patterns in the sand. "My friend Rastin and I. We made some discoveries. When we cut the Sagarki open, trying to find out what you were. Where you came from." Jon's eyes remained resolutely fixed on that stick moving through the sand. "He went too far, he overstepped the mark." Jon swallowed. "But I, I know that you have to wait for the moment when the Sagarki leaves the host to be able to control it. To control the beast, you have to feed as the host is dying."

Silence again from the shackled man as he learned of his fate. "You let her die. You couldn't let her see what you were."

Jon nodded. He had nothing else to say.

"You cannot win, you know. Every race we meet struggles against us, but they always fall. We will have farms of humans where our young can grow. We may even keep some of you for sport, Hunter Jon. And you. My brothers know of you even now, Hunter Jon. They will know what you have become and they will hunt the Hunter." It was all said in a dispassionate, almost conversational tone as the man lay in the red sands staring up at a barren sky of pale blue and a hazy yellow sun.

"I have no doubt." Jon looked out across the waves, the breeze singing its mournful song. "But I am afraid you will have bled dry before your brothers get here this time, Tristan."

Tristan nodded. "They will know of my fate, Hunter Jon. And you will pay."

That which had once been Tristan did slowly bleed to the point of death in those pale red sands. Sometimes it begged. Sometimes it gnashed its teeth, snapping at its shackles and issuing dire threats. Sometimes it was content, knowing there would be others to take its place.

Jon did not once leave its side. He watched it bleed out slowly, its skin becoming blanched and white, the sands around it black and sticky. And, as life slowly ebbed from it, as Jon began to slice its flaccid skin, peeling it away like that from a withered fruit, the waiting voices cried out in delight.

The sands were too thin and dusty to dig her a grave, so instead he had made her a shelter of rocks and pebbles. He tried to recite the True Prayer, though the blackened hole in his chest revolted at the words and he vomited over her gravesite instead.

It was a long walk back to Rhim. A long walk where the voices seemed to be a constant companion. And if he recognized two new voices among the thousands who spoke in delight of watching Jon's knife slicing through the skin, of watching hot blood trickle down his throat, he put it down to nothing more than his imagination.

The walls of Rhim finally loomed into view against a dusk sky of deepest, darkest blue. Jon paused and fell to his knees in the desert. Rhim, with all the accusatory stares, all the hatred, all the resentments.

You cannot win, the beast had said. And Jon knew it to be true. But it was a fight that had to be fought to the end. But not tonight. He was too tired to face the stares, the suspicions of Rhim.

Tomorrow he would continue the Hunt. Tonight he would rest. And, as the voices returned, he welcomed them with a smile. He lay back in sands of the deepest red and listened to their rapture, felt their hands clawing at his chest.

Tell us, Hunter Jon, tell us what it felt like, tell us of the taste, of the power...

Jon spoke long into the night, reveling in their rising ecstasy with each word.

And after — after he fell silent, after the voices fell silent — Rhim awoke to a roar that shook its very foundations. Awoke and screamed at the shadow that stood between the town and the newly risen sun; awoke and ran from the raging Sagarki that blotted out the morning light.

Michael Ehart's stories have appeared recently in Dark Worlds, Ray Gun Revival, The Sword Review, Every Day Fiction, Flashing Swords *and* Fear and Trembling, *and in the anthologies* Damned in Dixie, The Best of Everyday Fiction, Return of the Sword, Unparalleled Journeys II, *and* Magic and Mechanica. *His book* The Servant of the Manthycore *from DEP is considered by critics to be one of the best fantasy books of 2007. Michael Moorcock writes in the foreword, "It resonates with the authenticity of genuine myth, bringing a deep, true sense of the past; a conviction which does not borrow from genre but mines our profoundest dreams and memories; the kind which give birth to myths." The highly anticipated sequel,* The Tears of Ishtar, *will debut this fall. Ehart is married to one of the most beautiful women in the world and would offer "pistols for two, coffee for one" to anyone who disagrees but pesky laws get in the way and so offers instead to naysayers a referral to a good optometrist. You can find out more about what he is up to at http://mehart.blogspot.com. The following is a grand tale of persistence and perseverance against all odds and despite the size of the opposition.*

As from His Lair, the Wild Beast

A Tale of The Servant of the Manthycore

by Michael Ehart

The arrow hummed past Miri's head. It spent itself in a saw grass clump just a few paces ahead of her horse. She twisted in the saddle to spot the bowman who had loosed the arrow, caught a glimpse of his black robe as he scrambled down the side of the tall rock he had perched on. Most likely he had climbed it to spot her, and had taken the unlikely shot when he did.

She had a few moments while he remounted. Miri scrambled from the mare, tugging at the halter rope as she trotted forward to scoop up the arrow. The soldiers sent by the Priestesses of Ishtar to kill her mother, and incidentally her, were superbly equipped. Miri had been taught the fletcher's art by her mother, who after forty or more lifetimes had an amazing skill with anything having to do with fighting, death or destruction. But Miri had never seen anything so exquisite as these arrows. They were fashioned of some dark wood, nearly black, smooth and slightly oily to the touch, perfectly round and straight, with no trace of knife or draw. The feathering was slightly spiraled, and very long, almost a fifth of the length of the shaft. They were tipped with square patinaed bronze heads, barbless but covered with whorls and cuneiform etchings, prayers perhaps. This was the ninth black arrow she had collected.

She shoved the arrow into the quiver that hung from her saddle, grasped a handful of mane and swung back astride the mare. The horse spun toward where she had stood and nickered in complaint at having its hair pulled. Miri turned the mare's head in the direction of the marsh, away from the bowman, and kicked it into a trot. The trail was uncertain here. Any faster would be far more dangerous than the man following her, deadly though he might be. She hadn't far to go, anyway. The clearing with the small village was only a short distance.

The late afternoon shadows grew, making the trail even less certain. The villagers seldom came this way, spending most of their days in small round boats, fishing, hunting ducks, or gathering the wild rice that flourished in the slow-moving water of the Great Marsh. This corner of the marsh was studded with small twisted trees and occasional house-size boulders, washed here by some long-past deluge. The changing light and uneven ground made the growing shadows of trees and stones dance in slow, unnatural-seeming patterns; ahead, a stone became a lion, then slowly resolved back into a stone. Shadows, seemingly without source, formed figures that beckoned and urged her to ride this way, or that, and then dwindled into smaller, darker patches of deep black.

The soft, damp ground prevented Miri from hearing her pursuer's hoof beats. Even if she had, she would have had no idea how far they were from catching her. Sounds behaved strangely here in the marsh, transforming and changing volume and pitch, sometimes seeming to come from an opposite direction, or all directions, or even vanishing into sullen silence a mere arm's length from their source.

There was no mistaking the sound of a panicked horse, though. Miri wheeled her mare around and drew the knife she kept at her belt. The soldier's horse bellowed once more, and then bolted into view, riderless, eyes white in the growing darkness. Miri caught sight of a large splash of blood down the horse's flank as it ran past her. She snatched at the bridle, missed, and the horse vanished into the gloom of the village pathway.

Miri stared intently back down the trail. For long moments there was nothing. Then she heard the soft clopping of hooves, and a rider took form through the mist. "Ninshi," Miri called softly.

"Yes," her mother answered. As she drew near, Miri saw a splash of color across her tunic. Ninshi caught her stare, and nodded. "Not mine. When I cut his throat, his horse dumped us both on the ground, and he soaked me." She held out a fistful of black arrows. "He had these."

Miri nodded gratefully and shoved the arrows into her quiver. It was nearly full now, stuffed with deadly craftsmanship and beauty.

"How many followed me?" asked Miri. She had ridden out with the intention of being seen by their pursuers, bait to the trap. The soldiers of the Temple of Ishtar had followed them for nearly half a moon, herding them into this corner. Twice their scouts had caught them, and they had fought. Ninshi, who had been cursed some forty lifetimes ago, was impossibly deadly with nearly any weapon that came to hand, and under her teaching Miri had become a more than capable archer. Even though both times Miri and her mother were outnumbered, the fights were one-sided. Finally, their backs to the Great Marsh, Ninshi had decided to lure their pursuers into revealing their numbers.

~ As from His Lair, the Wild Beast ~

Miri had ridden in a flat loop across the mouth of the bend in the Tigris that cradled the marsh and Ninshi had lurked quietly behind to kill those she could and to count their enemies.

"I killed three. Not nearly enough. There may be as many as one hundred, perhaps more. It was hard to tell from where I could spy from. They have high opinion of us, it seems. Their camp has one great pavilion among the tents. They may be led by priestesses, which would explain their tenacity." She scratched at a streak of drying blood on the back of her hand. "They also have elephants."

"Elephants!" Miri had not seen the great beasts since her childhood in the Two Kingdoms, seven years ago. The pharaohs and their priests had used them in their processions.

"Yes. It seems they either want the jewel we carry, or revenge."

"Or both." Five or so years before, Ninshi had taken Miri to Nineveh to acquire one of the Tears of Ishtar, seven fabulous rubies, each of which had mystical properties. This they did in the service of the Mistress of Taverns, who desired all seven and would exchange for them the locations of the ancient herbs that might free Ninshi from her curse. In the course of things Ninshi had killed the High Priestess and set fire to the Temple. It was the second time in so many hundred years that she had done so. The Tear of Ishtar they carried now was a different one, but perhaps the priestesses didn't care about that.

"What will we do against so many?" They rode between twin hillocks, and turned their horses sharply to the right. A few paces more and they were in the village, a collection of low marsh-grass huts, fish drying racks and smoke houses made of driftwood. The few torches that illuminated it were low and small. The villagers, short men and women dressed in capes of brightly painted woven reeds, gathered to greet them. Their horses were led away, and wooden cups of willow beer were pressed into their hands. Miri gulped at hers, ignoring its amazingly pungent aroma. The aftertaste was dreadful, and only overcome by drinking more willow beer.

Ninshi shook her head as they were led to the Headman's hut. "We shall take council. We cannot stay here. It is only a matter of days before they find this place."

Eager hands pushed aside the mat that covered the door to the Headman's hut, and they were motioned inside. The hut was brightly lit by fire pit and fish oil lamps, and though small, there was plenty of room for the three of them. Miri was the largest of the three, and she was only fourteen summers old. Even Ninshi's small scarred form was larger than the ancient who sat in the corner. "We once again welcome you, Mistress of Sorrows, and you her daughter." The old man touched the center of his forehead with the forefingers of both hands in respect.

"Your welcome is most gratefully accepted."

This may have been the only village in all of the lands of the Tigris and

Euphrates, or of any lands which touched them, where Ninshi would be greeted with anything but fear. Her curse had given her long life in exchange for service to a Great Beast, the Manthycore, who required her to provide it several times a year with the flesh of men. For centuries she had led the young men of villages just like this one into the wilderness and slain them, but about a hundred years ago or so, she had instead led away a group of bandits who had taken up residence in this village and who had been terrorizing, raping and murdering the inhabitants. Instead of a legend of death, here she was remembered as a spirit of protection.

"Grandfather, we have numbered our foes. They are too many for us to fight, and so we must evade them. Is there a safe path through the marshes?"

The old man shook his head. "None may walk through. Though there are many pathways, all lead to bottomless bogs, or to nowhere at all. Have you not the power of flight, to soar above the reach of the arrows of your enemies?"

Ninshi shook her head. "I walk the earth, as do all born of woman."

The old man touched his forehead again with his forefingers. "Of course, Mistress of Sorrows. In that case I see only one course for us to take." He bent forward, dipped his thumb into his cup and drew an irregular half circle with beer on the mat between them. "This is the bend of the sacred River of Three, which men call the Tigris. It is at the mouth of this bend, which contains the Great Marshes where we sit, that your enemies, now ours, search for you, no?"

Ninshi nodded.

"They are not fools, for if they were, one such as you would have no need to flee them. So they will have spread their scouts across here." He drew a second line across the top of the first.

"I have slain those, but they will soon be replaced."

The old man nodded in return. "We will take you across the marsh, for though none can walk across, our people are great boatmen. Once out of the Great Marsh there is only the burning land to cross, and then you may travel the trade road to Eshnunna."

Ninshi leaned forward and tapped the makeshift map. "The trade road is here, no? I have seen the burning land from it. It is nothing more than a large stretch of sand, unusually fine. It will be hard to travel through, but not impossible. Anything heavier than a man will sink into the fine sand. I have traveled across smaller tracts of such, and it is impossible to lead a horse through. It will certainly slow pursuit."

The old man straightened. "I will send men to lead your horses away from the village, making false a trail. It may help, and we cannot carry them in our boats in any case."

"I do not like boats," Ninshi muttered under her breath. Miri smiled. In the seven years since Ninshi had bought her from slavers and adopted her as her daughter, she had seen her mother face soldiers, assassins, sorcery, beasts and demons without flinching. To anyone else, Ninshi's scarred and weathered face would have appeared stoic and unreadable. Miri could see something else. Everyone feared her mother, even Miri a little. It was somehow encouraging to see that there was something that Ninshi could not master.

The round boat scuttled through the water, driven by a small man from the village. He leaned, pushed and thrust their way with a long pole, forked at one end for thrusting, a woven wood paddle at the other end for when they covered deeper water. The boat looked as though it would come apart at any moment. It was made from strips of woven reed stretched over a wooden frame, plastered together and waterproofed with a pitch made from a thick black substance which bubbled up from pools found here and there in the marshes. The marsh man was perfectly comfortable in his conveyance, though, and seemed to give no attention to the creaking and pops the boat made as the frame flexed with each thrust of his pole.

"What is this burning land? Is it hotter than the surrounding desert?" Miri asked, partly out of curiosity, but mostly to take Ninshi's thought from the rippling fabric of the boat bottom.

"It is, a little I think. But mostly it is the very fine sand that makes it such a danger. It coats everything, finds its way through the finest cloth. To cross it is to suffer from constant thirst, and to be caught there in a wind storm is certain death, as the clouds of powdery sand are suffocating. I was told as a child that it was the site of the garden where First Man walked with his Creator, and when First Man was cast out, the Creator turned His face away, and all life there ceased. True or not, there cannot be a more lifeless place."

The boatman shoved the boat into the tangle of roots of an ancient marsh tree. "We will carry the boat now, for a few hundred steps. Save a quarter day of travel. Long, slender island." As he spoke, the boatman bowed, and touched his forefingers to his forehead. Miri scrambled out behind Ninshi, and by tugging and pushing, the three of them were able to get the boat free of the roots and onto their shoulders. It was hot, heavy work. The island was just barely solid, and the path between the marsh trees was narrow and twisted. By the time they had crossed it, they were filthy, sweat soaked and exhausted.

The boatman seemed not to notice. He took no time for rest, but started poling again as soon as they had set the boat into the thick brown water of the far side and clambered gracelessly in.

"Not far, now," the marsh man grunted. "Those rocks mark the higher ground. The Great Marsh ends there. There are a few hundred steps of rocky ground, ordinary desert, and then the burning land begins."

The rocks were indeed a boundary. Twice as tall as a large man, their long rounded shapes stood like sentries at the bottom of a slope. The water of the marsh lapped at their bases. They looked as though they had been placed there by design, dozens of them along the edge of the marsh, standing like the gapped and broken teeth of some great beast.

The marsh man slipped the small boat into the gap between two of the giant stones, and it shushed smoothly onto the reedy mud. They all climbed out, and Miri and Ninshi helped their guide pull the boat a few steps up the bank. A fresh, dry breeze from the desert beyond pushed the marsh odor of decay and stagnant water away.

"We will eat here, I have fish and beer. When we are refreshed, you will want to go that way. It is little more than a day's walk through the burning land to the trade road. We filled your water skins with fresh water from our spring. It will be enough to take you across."

They finished the meal of dried fish and beer quickly and with much higher spirits, they gathered their equipment to go. Ninshi reached out with one callused hand, and after a moment's hesitation, the marsh man grasped it with his own. "You have been a good guide, and we are grateful. Tell your Headman that I will look in from time to time, as best as I am able, and see that your people are protected from outsiders."

Miri watched in amazement as Ninshi yanked on the marsh man's hand, throwing him hard against the nearby standing stone. At nearly the same moment, a black arrow passed through the space where the marsh man's head had just been, to splash into the water beyond. Ninshi spun, her heavy-tipped sword appeared in her hand, and she dashed to the left to shelter behind the next stone over as a shower of arrows followed the first.

Even as Ninshi scrambled behind the far stone, Miri had her bow in hand and dived behind a clump of brush a step or two up the bank. She lay on her side for a moment, bent her bow, and strung it in one smooth practiced motion. She grabbed a handful of arrows from her quiver, placed them with bronze heads pointed in, and knelt with them under her right thigh. Her knife was thrust into the ground to her left, in case it came to that.

Over the top of the bush, Miri could see several figures moving at the top of the bank, outlined against the midday sky. She drew and loosed three arrows in as many heartbeats. All three struck center. Two of the archers who had ambushed them fell, transfixed by black arrows taken from their former companions. The third arrow *spanged* off some metal piece on the archer's chest, perhaps an armor scale, and shattered. Miri put the fourth arrow between his eyes.

She had lost track of her mother, but knew that whatever she was about, it was murderous and effective. There were several shouts from the top of the bank. A handful of men charged down it toward her. She dropped one with an arrow to the groin, and reached for her knife. Before she could bring it up a body slammed into her. They rolled, grunting and stabbing in a tangle down the slope to the edge of the swamp. Her mouth filled with blood, flesh, and beard as she ripped the man's cheek with her teeth. At the bottom she pushed him from atop her. He rolled and splashed into the marsh water, eyes staring sightlessly at the bright sky. She spat out a foul mouthful, and turned to face the battle, left arm useless and dripping blood, a sharp burning pain across her hipbone where the soldier's blade had scraped it.

Ninshi rose from a pile of bodies just above the clump of brush where Miri had knelt. Blood ran across her face from a cut at her scalp, and a slow blossom of red grew around a hole in the side of her tunic. "You live, then?" Ninshi said, her steady voice given lie by the tears which made clear streaks through the mask of blood.

"I think so," replied Miri, her voice squeaky and high. She turned, and sat down abruptly, shaking and cold.

"Can you bind your arm?" asked Ninshi. "I must find our boatman. From the top of the bank I can see that this was just an advance party. Many more are coming around the marsh, perhaps all of them. They are only a little way behind. We cannot stay here. We must go back into the marsh and find another way out."

Ninshi disappeared from the small circle of Miri's attention. Miri fumbled with her tunic, cut a strip from the bottom with her bloodied knife, and wrapped it around the slash in her upper arm. She tied it with the aid of her teeth, and had just finished when Ninshi returned with the marsh man. He was pale beneath his beard, and he tightly clutched a small fishing spear in his fist, its two-pronged head stained red.

"Good man, here. Sneaked up on one trying himself to sneak around us. Opened his neck right up with that toy. As I have often said, it is not the weapon which makes the warrior."

Miri stood shakily up. She half stumbled to where her quiver lay, and gathered the remaining arrows from where she had laid them. She pushed a little farther up the hill, and gathered a second quiver and as many arrows as it would hold from the bodies of the men who lay there. She did not look at them closely. She was not her adopted mother, who looked each man in the face as she killed him, and so was haunted each night by the faces of those she had slain. She had no stomach for that, and instead did her best to pretend that they were simple targets that she had shot in practice. It never worked entirely, and halfway back down the slope she bent and vomited fish and willow beer in a dribbling streak across the bushes there.

They loaded back into the boat, and the marsh man pushed off from the bank, alternately poling and rowing them as fast as he could away from the border stones of the Great Marsh. They were nearly out of sight of the stones when a large dark figure detached itself from the shadows at their base, its trunk raised high against the sky.

"We will have to get out of sight of whoever rides the elephant," Nishi grated. "And then decide where we might want to leave the marsh."

"There is a point where the burning lands spill into the Great Marsh," the boatman replied. "We will go deeper away from the soldiers, then I will take you there."

Ninshi nodded in approval. "You are a good man. I have not asked your name."

"I am Haaki Imtahas, Lady."

"Well met, then, Oh Fighter of the Great Fish. It is a strong name, fit for a hero."

"I am no hero, Lady," he said, but Miri could see he was pleased.

"How did they find us?" asked Miri.

Ninshi shook her head. "I don't know. It could be just bad luck. After all, there is no place that we can go except out of the marsh. There may be other companies than the one which chased us into the Marsh pursuing us. The cult of Ishtar is rich beyond measure, and has many, many followers. I am protected against sorcery by the symbol of my bondage to the Manthycore, but you are not, and we carry one of the Tears of Ishtar. It could be that through sorcery the Priestesses of Ishtar are able to see you from afar, or sense somehow where the Tear is."

"Yesterday I might have suspected treachery, but Haaki has proven his worth, as a guide and as a warrior."

Ninshi leaned over to check Miri's wound. Some of the feeling had returned, and she could move her hand a little. The slash was deep, but it had missed the tendons. Ninshi's wounds had already closed. The symbol of her bondage, the broken tooth talisman that she wore on a thong around her neck, not only protected her from sorcery and gave her an ageless life, it caused her to heal with amazing speed.

"You fought well. I am sorry I was slow getting behind them." Ninshi's eyes were, for a moment, transparent. Miri felt that she could see clear down into the heart of Ninshi's pain, emptiness and despair; for a heartbeat Miri felt all of the weight of that sadness. Like a suddenly unhidden stone, it settled upon her soul. Miri gasped, and the moment was past, but not the haunting memory.

Moments after they sighted the dune, they spied the elephant atop it. This was the point where the burning land met the marsh, and the soldiers of Ishtar were there ahead of them.

Ninshi grunted and shook her head. "They have many companies looking for us, then. We must find another way."

"Can we wait until nightfall, and perhaps sneak past them in the dark?" Miri asked.

"The sand is nearly white, and the moon is nearly full. We would be seen."

Haaki the boatman coughed. "Lady, we can go further along the edge of the marsh and hope they don't have enough men to guard all of it. But…" He coughed again and lowered his gaze.

Ninshi waited for him to continue. He poled for a moment in silence, then said, "There is something living in the Great Marsh, never spoken of to outsiders. It lies ahead. If we have good fortune, we will slip past it and never have it learn of our presence. It is…well, none really know. Some say a hillock or stone, come to life. Others call it a great beast, such as walked the earth before the Deluge. Whatever it is, few have glimpsed it. They say it slumbers among the willows, waiting for the End of Days when its Master calls it to battle."

Ninshi stared at the small marsh man for a moment, unblinking. "Then we shall have to avoid it."

They spent an uncomfortable night on a small spit of reeking mud and tree roots. They were just out of sight of the rise at the edge of the marsh where the elephant stood sentry. They loaded the boat in darkness, so that dawn's first hesitant fingers poked through the gloom to find them already underway.

This part of the Great Marsh was different. The trees seemed older and more twisted, and occasional moss-covered stones rose smooth and dripping above the water. It was darker, and quieter, and they found themselves whispering when they spoke at all.

A heavy mist rose from the tepid water, and even the marsh man seemed uncertain of the direction he must go. The promise of the morning sun burning away the mist went unfulfilled.

Gradually they became aware of a rhythm, a low pulsing of the mist and the water. With it came a low rumbling, barely audible.

The boatman stopped, and the boat slowly swung round in the feeble current. Miri found herself willing the mist to lift, peering intently into the gloom in the direction the sound and vibration seemed to come from.

As if in answer to the pressure of her gaze, the mist parted in long, ragged tatters. Shadows that had been deep and uncertain solidified, but into a form that her mind could not resolve. Like the shadow of a shadow, dreamlike but still real. She saw a large, rounded bulk. Its surface rose and fell slightly in the same rhythm as the water and mist. With each rise, bristles straightened, and lay back with each fall. At the same time the swampy air was filled by a powerful musk, a primordial scent of life, danger, and ancient beast.

"How big is it?" whispered Miri. She looked up to see the boatman's face white with horror. Ninshi shook her head, and motioned to the boatman. Quietly and carefully he poled back the short way to the spit where they had slept.

Miri had hated every moment on the spit that night, but it seemed like the firmest of sanctuaries when she stood upon it again. They sat in a circle, facing each other, for a while each lost in their own thoughts.

"I know what that is," said Ninshi finally. "I have seen his sister Leviathan who dwells in the middle sea."

"Can you kill it?" asked Miri.

Ninshi shook her head. "None can, save He who created him. There were songs, when I was a girl. Many things I have forgotten, but not that. His bones were said to be made of brass, and his tusks to be the size of cedar trunks. He is ancient, far more ancient than I, and will likely live on until, as you say, Master Fisherman, the End of Days. Sarsaok some called him, others Behemut. The Behemoth.

"Even mighty Gilgamesh himself could not slay him, for all the great king's might. It is said they wrestled for forty days, until the land was torn from Assur to Kish. Finally they battled to a standstill, and both retired in exhaustion, neither ever willing again to face the other."

Ninshi pondered for a moment, frowning. For a moment her hand strayed to the broken-tooth talisman that hung on a strap from her neck, and her frown deepened. "He has no special power other than his size, I think. Though what else a boar six men tall at his shoulder would need, I don't know. He will be cunning, for he has lived these long years and they will have added to the natural wisdom of his kind."

Ninshi shook her head as if to clear it. "I have a plan," she said. "Not a very good one, but a plan nonetheless."

"You were right. This is not a very good plan," Miri said.

Ninshi embraced Miri. "I know. I suspect it will fail. Still, there may be a chance if all works right." She stepped back and gave Miri an appraising look. "Should I fall, here is what you must do. Cut your hair, and travel as a boy. Go to Jermaish. He will welcome you as a sister, I think, and there are worse things to be than the sister of a king."

Miri spat. "You will not fall, and Jermaish is a lout."

Ninshi almost smiled. "Such a little girl you were when I found you." She turned and stepped her way to the boat where the marsh man waited.

Miri watched as the small boat slipped away. The mist was finally burning off, and she was able to see the boat for quite awhile. When it finally disappeared behind a bank of low reeds, she climbed one of the trees that helped make up the spit. She was surprised to discover that from that perch she could see the uncertain form of the Behemoth where it slept, and barely, the outline of the elephant atop the dune at the edge of the marsh.

After an eternity alone with her thoughts, the small boat reappeared, without Ninshi. Haaki said nothing when she clambered aboard, simply nodded as she lay flat so as to help hide their progress along the edge of the marsh and toward a small rocky bluff that lay a few hundred paces farther from the dune.

They made it to the bluff unnoticed. She slipped out of the boat and waded to the shore. Once there, Miri turned and waved to the marsh man. He touched the center of his forehead with both forefingers, then took up his pole and slowly pushed off, back into the marsh.

Her arm was very stiff, but she had regained most of its use. Still, the climb was slow and painful. She was as stealthy as she knew how to be, which was very stealthy indeed. She half expected to find a lookout at the top, but when she peeked over the edge she saw nothing but windswept rock, ground smooth by the sand which lay like a white ocean on the other side.

The soldiers of Ishtar had made camp in the lee of the dune. Three more elephants stood by a large blue pavilion, surrounded by smaller tents. She could see a number of horsemen riding along the narrow divide between desert and marsh, and here and there clumps of archers and spearmen.

"When you hear or see the Beast, you must make the elephants move," Ninshi had explained. "No boar would abide another in his territory, and we will hope that this one is no different. An elephant is not a boar, of course, but I doubt that it will matter. The creature may not have seen anything near to its own size since the Deluge. Boars have poor eyes, and this one is quite old. The elephants must move."

"They will," Miri promised.

"The elephants will not be any danger to you at any rate. They will not be able to follow you far into the burning land. They are too large, and the sand is too fine. Neither will horsemen. Men afoot will, and if they cast a wide enough net they will catch you. I have done them great harm, in the past and recently, so they will be eager to chase. So once the elephants are in motion…"

"Run," Miri finished. "I will run."

She carried her already strung bow over her shoulder, along with the two quivers of black arrows. Her pack, a small purse, her knife and a water skin were everything else she carried; for that matter everything else she owned.

It was hot, and the wait hard. She took a sip from her water skin, held the water in her mouth and let it slowly trickle down her throat. From where she sat she could just barely make out the hump of the great beast, and if she was still, was unlikely to be spotted by the soldiers just a few hundred paces away.

Ninshi's plan was unlikely, indeed. So much depended on her quickness, agility and ferocity. Miri had nearly limitless faith her mother, but could she even get close enough to The Behemoth without wakening him? And how much would it take to cause such an enormous creature to become enraged? Miri feared that it would not be as simple as Ninshi running up, climbing the great boar's shoulder onto his back, and then stabbing him with her sword until he was driven to frenzy.

Suddenly the great form in the marsh stirred. Something, a shoulder perhaps, twitched, like a horse bitten by a fly. Again it twitched, but this time the air was shaken by a great *chuff*. Miri glanced to the encampment. Every head was turned in the direction of the marsh. There was a second *chuff*, and the hillock form arose, black against the lighter brown and green marsh.

Even from this far away, the great boar was enormous, terrifying. His snout wrinkled the slash of his maw, dark red and dripping slaver. The ridge of his back rose impossibly over the stunted trees of the marsh. No mist obscured the great cliff of his shoulder. And most terrifying was the glimpse of one great red eye, flashing fierce as he twisted his head to *chuff* at his back. Miri tore her eyes away from him, as he started to spin, first one way, then the other, slashing at his own sides with tusks the size of trees. *The elephants must move!*

Miri knocked an arrow and drew, holding her left arm straight against the pain. It was an awkward draw, and she felt her arm spasm at the last moment, sending the first arrow unheeded into the sand between the bluff she was on and the dune with the elephant. It was a very long shot at any rate, but the elephant was a large target.

Her second arrow slipped smoothly from the string of her bow, and sailed swiftly across the afternoon sky to lodge in the hip of the elephant there. It was nearly spent, but it was enough to cause the elephant to bellow in pain, and spin slowly around to locate its attacker. Miri sent another arrow following for good measure, and though it missed the elephant it was met with a chorus of shouts, and arms and spears waved in her direction.

As she stood up and waved, so as to leave no doubt as to where the missiles had sped from, an answering bellow to the injured elephant's sounded from the swamp. This bellow was far greater, and of such volume that Miri staggered and dropped her bow to cover her ears. She felt something awaken from deep inside her, a fear so ancient and visceral that she could not put a name to it, only know that she should run, and keep running. She turned to see, dark against the sky, the great form of the boar, red-eyed and snorting, already nearly half the distance from where he had slept to where Miri stood.

A half-dozen arrows clattered around her. At least some of the soldiers had decided that she deserved some attention. It was time to run. Miri scooped up her bow and scrambled to the desert side of the bluff. The powdery sand of the burning land was drifted against the side. She dropped to the top of the drift and sank nearly to her waist. She struggled free, and was able to get a dozen or more steps before a second flight of arrows pattered into the sand around her.

Miri ran. The sand made poor footing, and was so loose that even the smallest rise was two steps forward, one back. Twice more arrows pattered into the sand near her. The second time she turned to gauge her pursuers. At the same time, the wind changed and her nostrils were filled with the heavy scent of boar-musk.

A handful of black robed soldiers struggled in the sand behind her. They had made less progress than she had, but she was tired and wounded. They would catch her, eventually.

She looked beyond them in astonishment. The elephant handlers had done exactly the worst thing they could have chosen. They had moved the remaining four elephants to the top of the dune. Even so, the great boar was taller, and now he bellowed again, this time in pure rage and challenge. The elephants bellowed back. The boar lowered its head and charged the dune, slamming into its base and knocking the elephants stumbling. The great form churned the dune with his forefeet, unable to climb the soft sand. One of the elephants bellowed back its own rage, and charged in turn. The boar caught the elephant behind the shoulder with one great tusk, and snapping his head to the side, threw the elephant to land bleeding in the sand.

The archers who were chasing her turned, and started peppering the great boar with arrows. They seemed to have little effect, except to cause the creature's eyes to glow redder. Another elephant was hurled to the side, knocking aside a dozen or more spearmen who had started toward the boar. The elephant didn't get up. Neither did the spearmen.

A small figure robed in blue stood up from the back of one of the remaining elephants, raised her hands. The air around her and the air around the boar changed. Miri felt her ears pop and her eyes bulge as some great force was pulled from somewhere — and then suddenly dissipated with no effect. The boar heaved itself to belly up on the dune, and its great jaws snapped, cutting off the priestess's shriek of rage. Miri was astonished to see a small form detach itself from between the shoulders of the boar and scramble down the near side of the dune. It was Ninshi.

The great beast roared into the encampment, scattering tents, men and horses. Ninshi ran at a right angle from the camp, directly at the archers who had pursued Miri. They stood for a moment, gawping, then dropped their weapons and scattered. They too must have seen Ninshi scramble down from the back of The Behemoth. It must have seemed like the great beast did her bidding.

Ninshi reached Miri's position and together they trudged through the sand, the bellows of the creature and the screams of men behind them. After a while the screams stopped.

For a moment, Miri thought it was over, that they could at last finish their journey, un-pursued and unthreatened. She turned her head to say something to her mother, when she heard a new sound, rhythmic and strange. She stopped, and turned, the whispering of the sand away from her steps lost in the approaching sound of the great beast, snorting and growling as it came for them across the dunes.

"Run," rasped Ninshi.

Miri did not need to be told twice. The pain of her wound forgotten, her weariness not even a memory, she put her head down and did her best to sprint across the powdery sand. Zigzagging between the dunes, always away from the approaching sound behind them, they scrambled, precious steps lost in the giving and unsupporting drifts.

She could not run forever. Soon, too soon her breath began to overtake her. Her feet began to slow, and soon she was able to count each heavy step.

"Up the dune, there," commanded Ninshi. "He may not be able to follow."

Miri pushed her tired legs, up, up, each step reclaiming part of the last as she slid back down. She could hear the Beast breathing, nearer now. She could not tell, but she was afraid to look back. Up, up.

A last she staggered to the crest. Beyond were more dunes, glimpsed as she fell onto her belly, and wriggled to turn at last and face the pursuing Behemoth.

Ninshi was not beside her! She stood instead at the base of the dune, sword drawn, waiting the charge of the Great Beast. Closer now than Miri had ever thought to be, she could see the bristles on its jowls, and the scars of forgotten scores of battles on its flanks. The Behemoth's tiny eyes glowed in rage, and his legs churned in the powdery sand.

His legs, though trunk-like, were small for his enormous body, and they were ill-suited for sand. He took at least two steps for one, and clouds of powdery sands sprayed from his track. He was no more than one hundred paces now from where Ninshi stood, stance loose, sword at ready, tiny against his dark immensity.

Miri blinked away tears. They had nearly escaped. The Beast would be upon Ninshi soon, and even she, for all her centuries of fighting, would be no more than a moment's pause for this mountain of a boar.

The Behemoth let out a great, bellowing cry, and the churning of his legs redoubled. He should have been to her already, but the sand was intractable. His enormous weight was poorly supported by such tiny feet, and each step thrust deeper into the sand. Now, only a few arm's lengths from where his tormentor stood, his progress halted. Once more he bellowed in rage, and once more he bellied, thrust and churned. But now to no avail; the burning land would let the Great Beast go no farther.

He chuffed, and then turned his head to the side to glare with one red eye at Ninshi. For a moment they stood facing each other, each with their own thoughts, ancient and deadly both in their own ways. Then Ninshi turned, and trudged her way slowly up the dune to join Miri at the top.

The Behemoth gave one more bellow of rage as they headed down the far side of the dune and away from it. For a great while they could hear his chuffs, and the gentle wind shifted now and again, bringing with it the sharp odor of the ancient beast. After a while, the chuffs stopped, or were lost in the distance. They continued on to the soft sound of their footfalls and the whisper of the sand as it filled their footprints behind them.

A. Kiwi Courters has fought and faced down a behemoth of her own. Survival is, after all, rather large on the scale of 'Important Things in Life.' That she's successfully done so, and in the meantime laid the foundation for a strong writing career, is testament to her determination. I think her battle must have been a lot like her story: methodical, reasoned, begun with hope and completed with passion. This is an adventure filled with thrills of the hunt and the rough edges of confronting one's fears, alone and before witnesses. Perhaps this tale is a bit more biographical in nature than most included in this anthology...

Stalker of the Blood-Red Sands

A Tale of the Deserts

**by A. Kiwi Courters
& cover art by Johnney Perkins**

ONE: Slaughter upon the Wastes

"Thirteen corpses—will it never end?" Psamti put both hands to his shaven head and fell to his knees in the red sand. "Surely, the usurper has sent a demon from hell!"

The party from Elephantine had finally come across the long-lost Peninsula caravan in the Horitea Wastes — one man at a time. Each had been torn asunder and left to bake beneath Re's merciless gaze many leagues from the frontier villages of Elephantine's control. The men looked at the most recent body in trepidation.

Duma, their future queen, knew she could show no hesitation. "Demons leave no spore, Psamti. These are animal attacks." Drawing the gleaming yard of *Apademak's Claw* from its scabbard, she strode to the top of the rocky rise. From here, the vast panorama of rust resembled a ruddy ocean, stony plateaus rising like islands from red waves of sand, a wavering mirage giving the scene the cast of liquid. Gritty, hot wind belayed the illusion. The top of this rise would have been a wise place for a wary guard to survey the shifting sands. Would have been, save the evidence of the fallen victim.

Seeing no wounds evident, Duma crouched down, sword at the ready. The victim wore little but strange armor: armlets of heavily worked gold, a cuirass of gold-plated bamboo scales, a kilt of orange and black striped hide, a belt of many leather strips, and boots of glossy red, the toes pointed. A short, angled sword hung from the complicated belts, and a head covering of bright fabrics laid several paces away. The body lay twisted upon its side, and flowing black hair covered the face.

With her left hand, Duma turned it over. The black hair fell away and the curve of the cuirass revealed a woman, her golden skin covered with scarlet dust. A gasp from her cracked lips made Duma start. "She's alive! Bring water!"

"She?" Psamti asked, even as he hurried up the rocky slope. Upon seeing the woman, he stopped in surprise. "A Marut with a caravan? This makes no sense."

Duma took the waterskin from him. She was from the south, new to these lands. "Who are Marut?"

"Elephant cavalry of the Harappa, holy warriors of that land," Psamti said, almost to himself.

Duma noticed an ivory elephant emblem on the breastplate. That other lands used elephants in combat amazed her. The animals of Elephantine — a herd of only a dozen — were a gift of her distant southern home, almost unheard of along the shores of the Great River. She had much to learn of her new home.

The Marut sputtered as the princess of Elephantine wet her parched mouth. "Slowly."

As Duma fed the Marut water, she gazed out across the wastes. A predator stalked the trade routes across the dunes from the Blood Sea; a beast with a taste for human flesh. Constant winds erased tracks with a subtle hiss of soft, dusty sand. Coming across the predator would surely be as much chance as skill.

The Marut's long lashes fluttered and Duma found herself looking into the woman's eyes. Lightning fast, the warrior's hand moved to her angled weapon. Duma caught the rising wrist before it freed the blade. Though thirst made the Marut weak, the princess could still feel a steely strength before the foreigner lost consciousness again.

The scouting party formed a travois from a sheet of linen, and gently lifted the Marut. As they returned to the hunters, various possession were discovered in the drifting dust of Horitea: a quiver of stout bronze bolts, a torn waterskin, a shield of wrinkled, gray tembo hide, javelins tipped with strange red quills, and most curiously, a bow transfixed on a carved wooden stock.

These they collected, Duma noting a place on the Marut's armor where each might be carried, freeing her hands.

"A survivor?" Udimo, heir-apparent to Elephantine's throne, leaned heavily on the haft of his spear. A grievous wound to his left shoulder had healed, but it pained Duma to see the withered arm below. Even after many months, her husband remained drained. Yet it was Udimo-Den's duty as prince to protect the trade of Elephantine.

Psamti nodded, presenting the transfixed bow. "A Marut, of all things."

"Here in the wastes?" Hopshef, captain of the palace guard, looked the woman over. Curious warriors of Elephantine left the shade of their shelters. "I've never known people from the Harappa to caravan."

Duma nodded at the collection of weapons. "Perhaps a hired guard?"

Udimo shook his head. "Marut are temple guards, sacred warriors. Let's return to camp. She's obviously suffering from exposure—perhaps the waters of the Great River will revive her."

As they broke down the shelters, Psamti approached Duma. "You have seen weird horrors in this world. Could this demon predator be the reason a Marut has come to the Horitea?"

"It is no great cat we're after," Duma mused. "A male simba, you say *lion,* at the end of his power, will attack men as easy prey. But the victims we found bear no bite wounds to the head and neck. This is the way simba kills a man. The caravan was butchered. This beast kills in a way I've never seen."

"Then perhaps the Marut did come in search of a demon." Psamti shuddered.

TWO: A Princess of Elephantine

Re gazed westward as the hunters made for the river after another long, hot day of unsuccessful hunting. Their sandaled feet kicked up a wake of dust. Thoughts of leaving the Wastes and reaching the Great River lent speed to their heels; soon they crossed from the rocky ground to the wide, flowing blue river nestled in the Red Desert. Tembo stood in the shallows, spraying each other with their trunks.

The river did not inundate the desert with life-giving black soil here in the wastes north of Elephantine's control. Patches of thorn forest inhabited by the Nyoka stood at the edge of sight. Duma saw her husband's eyes stray to that horizon, and her own went to the mark left upon his shoulder by one of the snake-men's spears. When Udimo's gaze returned to her, his drawn face collapsed in a smile. "Come, princess. Let us join the much wiser elephants."

Without removing her shift, Duma waded into the water, Udimo at her side. The cooling fluid sluiced over her legs, removing a patina of dust. One of the tembo saw them, and released a great spray of water.

"You are very helpful, Tiko," she addressed the tembo.

The elephant seemed to smile at her.

"Prince Udimo! The Marut has escaped!"

Udimo turned at the shout. "Escaped?"

Hurrying, the couple reached a lean-to near the shore. One of their warriors lay dead inside.

"Here!"

Udimo and Duma raced across the blasted sand toward a low plateau. The Marut stood against the rocky slope, her long, crooked sword and shield held high as the soldiers faced her at spearpoint. "Stand down!" Duma commanded, and the men carefully backed away.

"I am Duma. We mean you no harm."

"What does a Nehesi in the company of Elephantine?" the Marut demanded.

Duma bristled at the derogatory term for southerners. Udimo stepped forward. "She leads them as their future queen. Sheath your knife, Marut. Had we wanted your death, we would have left you in the wastelands."

"These men laid hands upon me! I am Marut, it is not allowed." Her black eyes flashed, knuckles white around the sword's hilt.

One of the soldiers protested, "With damp linens only—to revive her."

"On my orders," Duma said. "A thousand apologies. If men might not touch a Marut, would you accept my help?"

"I'll accept your death!" The Marut charged, bronze sword flashing in the sun.

Duma drew *Apademak's Claw*, the curve of its steel glimmering like lightning. The Elephantine princess was well-trained in arms, drilling since she could walk. But she quickly learned that the Marut's fighting style was something new. With arching blows, the Marut seemed intent on breaking bones or severing limbs with every move. When *Apadamak's Claw* slashed at her ankles, the Marut leaped high into the air. Instead of retreating, she kicked in a backward-flipping circle, nearly catching Duma with a curved toe. Stooping beneath the kick, the princess lunged and drove the point of her sword through the elephant hide shield. Gasping, the Marut fell back, leaving the shield impaled on Duma's blade.

With the sword encumbered, the foreign woman hacked at Duma's unguarded left in a two-handed, whirlwind attack. But Duma did not let the added burden slow her. Shield and all, she parried the short sword, then sent a fist crashing into the woman's gut. As the Marut tried to get her wind back, Duma freed her sword and tossed aside the shield. Even then the Marut fearlessly attacked, leaping, spinning, slashing.

As powerful as the roundhouse cuts were, they also foretold the Marut's moves. In a minute, Duma found her distance. By controlling the distance, she controlled the fight. For a time, there was no sound on the desert save the grunt of effort and the clang of weapons. Then Duma found the Marut's flaw. The foreigner would bend her knees slightly on every feint. Duma pretended to fall for it several times, waiting for the right moment. It soon came. At the start of the next false attack, the princess lunged. With an underhand twist, she disarmed the Marut. The point of *Apadamak's Claw* nicked the woman's throat — and held there.

Duma shouted, "I am Duma of Valley Kifaru, Princess of Elephantine! Submit!"

Fierce fire blazed in her eyes, but the princess could see the Marut was on the verge of exhaustion. Still, as a woman warrior, Duma felt a kinship and would not shame the Marut with her weakness. After several heartbeats, the Marut bowed her head.

"Leave us," Duma ordered.

It wasn't until the soldiers and their prince moved away that the Marut finally sagged to the ground. Duma crouched beside her. "How long were you in the wastes—?"

"Dharti," the woman supplied her name. "Six days. It was not until some legged snake punctured my waterskin that I succumbed."

Darkly, Duma mused, "The Nyoka enjoy the taste of human meat."

"This one enjoyed the taste of bronze well enough."

Duma helped the Marut up, leading her back to the shade of the lean-to. "Another beast stalks these wastes, perhaps more lethal than the Nyoka. We do not know its nature. It has killed all members of a caravan headed for Elephantine."

Dharti said nothing. In the shelter, her eyes fell on a sealed jar of beer.

"It is impossible to track when the winds move the sand," Duma continued. Casually, she took the beer jar, breaking its seal. The bitter liquid flowed down her throat.

Nodding at the jar, Dharti asked, "Is that beer?"

"Not recommended for someone in your state," Duma said. "In Valley Kifaru, we train with foreign weapons. But I've not seen any like those you carry."

Understanding crossed the Marut's face, though her eyes did not leave the jar. "Your warriors are legend. You've married Elephantine in alliance?"

"Elephantine and Valley Kifaru are much alike. The rest of the river-dwellers are a strange lot."

Duma handed over the jar, Dharti's eyes lighting up. "Ahh!"

Dharti handed the jar back. Duma sipped. "What is the twice-curved bow on the stock?"

"A crossbow. Very accurate." Dharti took the jar back. "It has all the power of a much larger bow, but far easier to carry into battle."

The Marut drank, passing the jar back. "And your armor is of gold." Duma drank, returning the beer.

"Ornamental," Dharti said. Alcohol on top of dehydration made her slur boastful words. "Marut fight with such skill that armor is not needed." Dharti raised the jar as if in salute, a half smile on her face.

"Why would a great warrior ride with a caravan from the Peninsula?" Duma grabbed the jar away, playfully.

But Dharti's face grew dark. "Men of their ilk took prohibited goods from the Harappa a year ago. I signed on with them as a guard to learn their route."

Duma passed the beer. "Stolen goods?"

"It is taboo to take the kit of the mantichor." Dharti took a deep draft.

The princess did not know the word. But she suspected what it might mean. "A man-eater."

"*The* man-eater, from the southern jungles. It lives only to devour men. And someone in this arid hell wanted them for pets."

THREE: *Music in the Night*

Moments later, with the Marut passed out, Duma exited the lean-to.

"What have you learned, Princess?" Udimo took her hand.

"She seeks the beast we do. Man-eaters called mantichor stolen from the Harappa." Duma looked up at her husband. "Do you know of this beast?"

"From trader tales," Udimo said. "Mantichor are like great cats, but with human faces and scorpion tails. The stuff of legend."

Duma smiled grimly. "She encountered a Nyoka in the wastes. No doubt a legendary beast in her country."

"How could a creature as large and ferocious reach the Great River without being reported?" Udimo folded his arms.

Looking back at the unconscious figure, she recalled Dharti's words. "She claimed someone wanted it as a pet."

"Kings of the north are fond of menageries; the more exotic the beast, the more desirable." In the west, Re closed his blazing eye. "We must learn more of the creature so we can best destroy it."

Across the river, Duma watched the Red Desert become bruised in shadow. "Let us set the watch. I should not want a cat with a scorpion tail to surprise us in our sleep."

"I will take first watch with Hopshef," Udimo said.

Duma put a hand on his scarred shoulder. "You will rest the entire night. For all your show of strength, you cannot fool your wife, my prince. If you overtax yourself, you may never recover the full use of your arm."

Seeing that argument was useless, Udimo nodded. As he sought his shelter, Duma found Hopshef and Psamti.

After dividing the night into three shifts, Duma said, "Wake the others at any sign of strangeness. We know nothing of this mantichor's ways, save that it will kill men without hesitation."

"Should we sight the animal, how do we dispatch it?" Hopshef asked.

Chuckling darkly, Psamti said: "Hopefully, at a great distance."

Night brought a chill to the dry air, and Duma brought her bedroll to Dharti's lean-to, partly to stave off the approach of the soldiers. And should the holy warrior wake, the princess might learn more of the mantichor.

Some time later, she started awake. No one stood at the mouth of the shelter to rouse her. After a moment, she realized it was the sound of tembo that woke her. With low trumpets and splashes, she heard them gain the river. Duma grabbed the quiver and bow leaning against the shelter linen and padded to the shore.

"What is it, Tiko?" she whispered to the animal. The tembo shied from her. Skittish elephants bode ill. Duma nocked an arrow.

Stalking around the silent camp, she peered hard into the gloom. Night winds blew through the rocks, whistling, chilling her to the bone. Moving toward an elevation overlooking the Great River, she sought the guards posted there.

"Manu…"

She stopped at the sound, knowing it was more than wind in the rocks. It sounded musical, almost like a flute, yet she recognized the name as that of one of her warriors.

"Manu…"

The voice lilted in the night air, soft and echoing in the frigid desert.

"Why have you left your post?" Duma demanded.

"Manu…"

It was the same, fluted tone, this time the word undeniable. No longer did Duma think it some trick of the stony formations altering the sound of the wind. Holding her breath, she listened.

Stealthily, she closed on the guard post, bare feet making no sound. Pulling the bowstring tighter, Duma began to ascend the plateau. The voice came from behind this rise, that much she could tell. If she could gain the top quickly, she would have the advantage.

A massive shadow she had mistaken for a boulder moved with sudden liquid grace, turning luminous eyes upon her. Simultaneously, the princess raised her bow and the huge shape leaped. Loosing her shaft, the princess dodged from the onrushing horror's path. It wasn't enough; even the glancing blow sent her rolling down the slope, over and over. After an eternity, Duma regained her feet, flesh scraped raw, head swimming from the impact of rocks. Still, she came up with a second arrow drawn. Above her, the black mass rumbled, storm-like, eyes like lightning. Again, Duma released her arrow, and a third.

Her quiver had nearly been emptied in the fall, but it didn't matter. The beast stalked toward her, shaking off her missiles. Arrogantly, slowly, it came. Finally, Duma's hand groped an empty quiver. The shadow's rumble changed, became an almost-purr. It crouched, gathering its legs beneath it. Then it relaxed, its lilting voice calling out.

"Dharti…"

It seemed to Duma that the oddly-toned voice of the monster called out to the Marut. Dharti appeared from the night, her eyes wide, her crossbow armed with a bolt. Saying nothing, she raised the weapon to her shoulder. With a reverberating *thunk,* she released the bolt.

The monster shuddered and an angry hiss cut through the night. One of the tembo at the river trumpeted in fear. Surprisingly, a similar sound echoed from the angry beast. Then the princess understood that the creature did not truly speak; it but mimicked their voices and other sounds of the night.

Dharti reloaded the crossbow, cranking back a scrolled lever and setting a bolt in the trough. The shadow beast fled with a defiant snarl and a leap that took it clear over the stony rise. The sound of a fired crossbow came to them, mockingly, on the breeze.

FOUR: *Or a Little Drunk*

They found the bodies in the light of false dawn; one of the watchmen was indeed named Manu. Armed guards had spent a sleepless night gazing into the darkness, listening to the haunting voice of the mantichor as it moved, unseen, through the desert night.

Dharti had found their supply of beer. She sat on a boulder as Re opened his eye in the east, enjoying her discovery. "It will not remain here. When we attacked, the mantichor stopped thinking of us as food."

"Then what *will* it do?" Udimo demanded.

Dharti tipped the jar up, emptying it. "Head south, looking for a mate. It is the season. Its home is the jungle; it knows not desert ways, so it will stay close to the river, following it upstream. Instinct will drive it, and it will kill as it goes."

"Elephantine lies upstream," Udimo said.

"Our villages lie but a day south of here. Elephantine soldiers could never arrive in time to aid them. We will have to destroy the man-eater before it reaches the farms."

"How do we kill it?" Udimo asked. He had found the bolts and arrows fired in the night, their bronze heads shattered against tough hide.

Dharti tossed the jar away and broke open another, drinking deeply of its contents. "I can only tell you how we kill it. The mantichor will not kill tembo," she gestured to the elephants in the river. "Though it is nearly as large as the tembo of the Harappa, the reason is a mystery.

"As fierce as it is, the mantichor is a careful hunter, hunting like a man. From its tail, it fires poisonous barbs at its prey, then devours it. Using its voice, it can lure prey to it."

"A beast that talks?" Psamti asked.

"In our land, we have many birds that can mimic speech. It is not an uncommon thing."

"We have birds like that, too," Psamti said.

Dharti shrugged, and took another drink. "It has teeth that can easily strip flesh from bone, but no snout, so it does not bite in attack. When a mantichor is seen near a village, Marut will hunt it from elephant-back, cornering it. Only the most holy of warriors such as I will face it on the ground, and that only with these." She slapped her palm against the quiver of bolts beside her. "Without these, only a very good shot into the eye or the mouth with normal weapons will penetrate."

Duma frowned. "You must be very brave to hunt such a monster."

"Or a little drunk." Dharti smiled. "Usually, to hunt a mantichor, all Marut will participate. We tip our javelins with the beast's spines, too; they will puncture its hide."

Dharti finished the second jar and tossed it after the first.

"How did you hope to kill the mantichor by yourself?" Duma asked.

"Oh, I didn't." Standing up, Dharti began undoing her complicated harness. "My task was to find the man responsible for taking the monster out of our land, and kill him."

Psamti murmured, "I couldn't prove it, but if what you say is true, about the mantichor heading south and killing along the way, I have no doubt who your man is."

"Srqt, the usurper." Duma said. "He has subjugated several small kingdoms by fear and by crime, but is no match for the military might of Elephantine. Instead of open warfare, he attempts assassinations on the royal family and plagues the capital with dark magics."

Udimo nodded. "This trickery could not be traced back to him, should he loose some foreign beast upon our soil. That is his method."

"Should I survive, I will pay a visit to this usurper." Dharti continued to shed her armor and weapons. In a moment, she stood naked in the sun. "Right now, I will take a bath." With a belch, she staggered off to the river.

Psamti watched her go, and quickly stood up. "I think I will see to it that she does not drown."

"I will, too," Hopshef jumped up.

Duma frowned. "Leave it. The tembo will see to her. Can you not see how frightened she is?"

Psamti shrugged. "I just thought she might want to make the most of her last days. The mantichor could take us at any time."

"I bet you say that to all the girls," Udimo said.

Duma gazed out across the bleak expanse. "We have similar ways of dealing with simba when they become man-eaters. If we hurry, we can arrive at the southernmost village before the mantichor."

"And then what? Pray to Re that our arrows find a vital spot?" Psamti stood, still watching the retreating Marut.

Duma stood. "If we make preparations, we can take all the need for prayers out of it."

FIVE: A Leader by Example

Camp was broken down, tents and supplies packed quickly. Tembo were harnessed with tandem saddles. Dharti, once again clothed, joined Duma on the back of Tiko.

"I like the great, flapping ears of your tembo," the Marut said, voice a little slurred. "But the Marut ride six or seven to a single beast."

Duma tapped Tiko on the head with the hooked crop, and the young male began to move. "We like to keep a light burden on the tembo."

"Why is that? The beasts are mighty—" She let out a whoop as the elephant splashed into the river, wading into the center. In a moment, his great feet churned beneath the water and the beast swam swiftly against the current.

"A lightly burdened tembo can outpace a ship," Duma said.

Dharti laughed, throwing back her head. "They seem to like it!"

"We must move faster than the mantichor."

The Marut's mirth died. "The mantichor is a jungle cat. How can you expect to beat it with the tembo?"

Tapping Tiko's head, Duma urged the beast to swim faster. "We have the river on our side. The mantichor will have to pass through the thorn forest — and the Nyoka."

They traveled the whole day, letting the elephants rest little. From the area where the thorn forest nearly reached the river, the hissing tongue of the Nyoka could be heard. Udimo kept spear in hand, for his life was nearly lost on similar rocky shores. None of the snake-men appeared, and Duma hoped the creatures were engaged with an even more evil beast.

They reached the village at the edge of the wastes, the northern extent of Elephantine's rule. In this season, the rocky landscape was empty, pale-colored rock formations surrounded by growing fields and encroaching sands. Keeping the crops watered was difficult work in the blast of Re's vision; only by muscle and will did the villagers stave off the Red Desert. Duma felt guilty asking them to do her bidding. But completing the task could well mean the lives of everyone in the village — and beyond.

The governor arrived from his great house to greet them, kneeling before the prince and princess of Elephantine. His well-pleated kilt and collar of gold spoke of the village's wealth.

"We need as many men as can be spared," Duma said. "And tools for digging."

Dharti gazed around the village of plastered huts and date palms. "And beer. We'll also need beer."

The soldiers led a troop of several dozen men nearly half the distance to the gray line of thorn forest. Once there, Duma ordered the men to pull the sparse desert scrub from the arid soil and dig.

"You hope to trap the mantichor in a pit?" Dharti mused. "It had better be very wide, and very steep, and very deep."

The villagers, used to working the soil with stone adzes and picks, quickly excavated a trench. The soldiers pitched in, hauling buckets of earth from the hole. Even Duma took a turn with a pick, feverishly hacking the soil loose. Seeing their future queen hard at work inspired the farmers to dig harder. Near dusk, the pit sank ten strides deep. Uprooted brush proved too little to hide the trap, and thatch was carried to the site.

Udimo crossed his arms, gazing at the darkening thorn forest. "How can you be certain the mantichor will come?"

"There is only one way to trap a big cat." Duma said as Re's fading vision filled the sky with color. "Bait."

Psamti walked to her. "I know you are brave, Princess, but I will not allow you. I may be a common soldier, but this I swear."

Hopshef smirked. "You will stand as bait for this monster?"

"I hoped someone braver might volunteer," he admitted. "But if that is what it takes."

"No." Dharti staggered forward. "The mantichor is my problem. My javelins are tipped with the beast's spines. My shield is of tembo hide. None of you has fought one before. But first, I would bathe."

Duma rolled her eyes, but before the Marut could expose herself again, a commotion sounded in the thorn forest. A rasping moan drifted from the gray line of trees, almost feline, but with more of a drone.

"The beast's natural cry," Dharti whispered.

Duma grabbed Psamti by the shoulders. "Take the villagers home and return with the elephants. Unless we are locked in combat, approach no further than those rocks." She pointed to a ragged formation behind them.

"If you fail me, I will surely die. As your princess, I order you to go. Even you, Den," Duma called her husband by his familiar name. "Would that you were fully healed, I'd trust you in my place."

Udimo crossed his arms. "There is no particular attribute that might make you better bait than I, Princess. You have, however, fought from elephant-back since you could walk, and you've destroyed man-eaters before."

Again, the low, mournful sound issued from the dry tangle of thorns. Duma looked on as villagers mumbled amongst themselves, straying toward home. "The heir apparent of Elephantine should not risk his life so."

Udimo kissed her. "Our land is still strange to you, our ways. You need to prove yourself to us, in your heart. But you cannot do all the fighting by yourself. I ask you to trust me."

For a time, she stood speechless. Finally, Duma nodded. "I will return with the tembo." She hurried toward the village, the soldiers turning to follow. It took all her will to keep from turning back.

SIX: *Naked Bait*

Astride Tiko, Duma scanned the darkening desert. A susurrus chorus of hissing screams rose from the thorn forest, and then died with the falling of night — the Nyoka became torpid with darkness. A silhouette among silhouettes, a shape crossed the sandy gap between the naked rock formations and the prickly woods.

"Hai!"

Duma nearly froze as her husband called out. On the dim dunes, the shadow figure froze for a heartbeat. Then, it began to stalk.

Dharti had stripped herself bare, regardless that the Great River was out of sight, and did a slow dance around the prepared lion trap. Had the mantichor not imperiled the night, Duma would have ridden over and slapped the Marut for behaving so in front of Udimo. Instead, she kept one hand on the riding crop, one on the pommel, and waited.

In the tiniest flicker of a campfire, Udimo turned his back to the approaching danger (and the dancing Marut) so to invite the creature's pounce. Dharti pranced about, oblivious to all eyes on her, save the predator crossing the sands.

The soldiers of Elephantine gave a low cry when Dharti fell to the ground. Duma knew it was not out of intoxication. She also realized the warriors were more closely watching the Marut than the mantichor. She thought them unprepared, but bows creaked with stringing at her insistent gestures toward the marauding creature.

The mantichor loped forward, sensing an easy kill. When it came within pouncing distance, the Marut suddenly rolled over, crossbow in hand. A shuddering report followed, and the monster cried out in anger. It sidled forward, crouching low for a pounce. But it placed its forelimbs over the pit's concealed edge, sliding in with a growling cry.

"Go! Go!" Duma urged Tiko forward with a sharp tap on the head.

Udimo kicked the fire, sending blazing logs into a prepared nest of tinder. The tembo's charge reached the pit just as the ring of flames surrounded it. But from the high vantage of the elephants' backs, they easily shot down at their quarry.

After letting fly, Duma was shocked at the creature's appearance. Covered in red fur, three quarters the size of a tembo, the mantichor snarled up at them with an almost human face. Claws dug at the soil, but the beast found no purchase. Nocking arrows, the warriors sent a hailstorm into the pit. Stone and bronze tips glanced off the rubicund fur.

"Aim for the eyes!" Duma commanded. The mantichor roared, opening a strangely hinged mouth the width of its head. It seemed a thousand sharp teeth resided within. The princess took her shot, aiming to fire straight down its gullet.

But the mantichor turned its vast, ruddy face, the arrow glancing off its skull.

"Princess! The fire!"

Duma turned in her saddle to see that the hastily built fire circle had died along one edge. The mantichor saw it as well. With an impossible leap, it cleared the pit. A tembo reared, throwing its rider.

Duma freed *Apademak's Claw* while guiding Tiko into battle. Frightened trumpeting and the panicked cries of the soldiers sounded as the mantichor turned to face its foes. A heavy, curved tail extended to its full length, then snapped forward.

Duma realized what it meant just in time. Her sword swept the rain of spines away. Others screamed, succumbing. Near her, a tembo turned, its hide stuck with slender red barbs, and slammed into the elephant behind. Riders fell, trampled beneath the animals' stampede. Duma hurried Tiko from the onslaught. She saw one bequilled tembo drop into the pit. Screams from the bottom chilled her bones.

But she could not turn from the fight. Crop in her left, sword in her right, she spurred Tiko to charge the spitting mantichor. At the elephant's closing, the monster reared up, and up and up, balancing on its heavy tail. Sheathing the sword, Duma grabbed the bow from the saddle horn, letting arrows fly toward the exposed underside.

Her missiles had little effect, but in a moment, Tiko plowed his heavy shoulder into the mantichor's flank, toppling the creature. Crushing impact threw Duma from the saddle, but she rolled gracefully down the tembo's back as one who grew up playing with the war beasts. Landing on her feet, she drew her sword.

Half-stunned, the mantichor pawed the sand, sending up clouds of dust. Duma darted in and thrust at a huge green eye. The creature flinched and sparks flew as the blade slid across the flat, almost human face. Rolling to its feet, it roared, its open mouth revealing too many teeth and sending its fetid breath into her face. Duma refused to think and simply reacted. She lunged, sinking the point of *Apadamak's Claw* into the mantichor's soft upper palate. It screamed and shook its head; then lashed out and swept her aside with scaled talons. She lost her grip on the sword and tumbled through the dust.

The princess staggered to her feet to see the mantichor clawing at the blade lodged within its mouth. She turned to find a weapon and saw Dharti appear, naked save for her boots and weapons. The holy warrior knelt on the dune and propped her crossbow atop her shield and aimed at the beast. When its open maw turned toward her, she fired.

The bolt sailed true. "Take a javelin," Dharti shouted, not looking up from reloading her weapon.

Duma slipped one from the sling across the Marut's back. Doubting the slim red tip would penetrate, she flung it with all her might. To her surprise, the weapon sank deep into the horror's neck.

The mantichor screamed and pawed the sword free in raging frenzy. Blood drooled over its distended gums and madness gleamed in its eyes. The man-eater retreated, keeping the warriors before it.

Dharti shouted, leaping to her feet. "We have it!"

"Dharti, wait!"

Heedless of Duma's warning, the Marut sprinted forward, crossbow leveled. A bolt sprang from the weapon and buried itself in the mantichor's eye even as Dharti pulled a javelin from her quiver and ran on. The enraged monster howled and lurched forward. Javelin and talons met with a terrible, meaty thump. Dharti landed several paces away in the sand and lay still.

The maddened beast, blood seeping from its many wounds — the latest from the javelin hanging from its chest — turned on Duma. She had nothing to fend it off — *Apademak's Claw* lay too far distant, as did the weapons on Dharti's body. Despite its limping, the thing closed on her. Duma knew she could not outrun the beast, even though it was slowed by its many wounds. She prepared to meet her fate instead. "Auset," she beseeched the goddess, "welcome your servant!"

An instant before death struck, a second beast charged into the fray. Tiko crashed into the injured monster, knocking it back. With a snarl, the mantichor swiped at the tembo, then raced away into the darkness.

SEVEN: Secrets from Harappa

Duma sat on the edge of the pit, elbows on her knees, head in her hands. Only two elephants had not run off, and only seven men remained alive, three of those seriously injured. They buried Dharti deep in the sand alongside the others. Her belongings they kept, to be sent back to the Harappa.

Psamti sat beside her. "She was strong and brave. Plus, she was frequently drunk and naked—qualities I admire."

But the soldier's levity did not raise her spirits.

"We must send for troops," Hopshef said.

Udimo shook his head. "It would take days for them to arrive. We must track it down and kill it."

Hopshef's face was grim. "But how, my prince?"

Udimo picked up one of Dharti's javelins. "How can such a weapon penetrate the mantichor's hide when bronze and steel cannot? And why does it shy from the elephants when it could easily kill them?"

"Elephants are virtuous beasts. The mantichor is a demon from hell." Psamti shrugged.

Udimo began to pace. "What does this javelin have in common with an elephant?"

Duma stared down at the body of the tembo. They'd had to kill it as the fall had broken its legs.

Udimo returned with a spine the mantichor had flung and held both spine and javelin up for all to see. They looked nearly identical, save for the ornate carving on the weapon's slender tip. "If we only had enough of these, we could make arrows and spears, hunt it down before it kills again."

Hopshef stared down at the dead tembo. "Shall I take the tusks before the villagers arrive to bury this animal?"

"It fought well. Let it be buried with its natural weapons," Udimo said. Duma looked up at him, an idea growing in her mind. "May I see the javelin?"

Udimo handed it to her, watching her expectantly. The princess took the utility knife from her girdle, prodding and cutting the point. Tossing it aside, she took the mantichor spine, whittling a bit of the red material away.

"Despite the color, do you know what this is?"

Understanding illuminated Udimo's face. "Ivory."

The four of them gazed down at the dead elephant.

It took several feverish hours of work, but soon four great spearheads were carved from the tembo's tusks and mounted on heavy hafts. Hefting a weapon, Udimo smiled grimly. "It will not take the attention of a god for such a weapon to prevail."

As a member of Valley Kifaru's royalty, Duma was fully trained in cavalry tradition. The remaining two elephants were saddled with mighty rigs hastily assembled from salvaged wood, harness and hide. It would take two riders riding in tandem upon a tembo's back to control the oversized weapons. "I only wish Dharti were alive to see this," Duma said as she clambered up Tiko's front leg.

"Princess, a gift." Psamti handed up a quiver of five arrows. Duma pulled an arrow free and studied the broad flake of carved ivory at its tip. She smiled at her sworn protector. "Mount your tembo, soldier."

"Yes, Princess." He turned and she noted that his own quiver practically burst with arrows. Duma smiled to herself. As devoted to her safety as Psamti was, he was not the bravest of men.

EIGHT: *The Bravest of Warriors*

Blood made tracking the manticor easy. That and the gentle winds that had not hidden all of the beasts tracks yet. The deep red color of the monster should have made it stand out against the bright sand and rocks, yet they had not sighted the creature by sunset.

Psamti gazed at the failing vision of Re. "It wanders in circles. Perhaps the manticor is dying."

"If so," Hopshef said in the saddle behind Psamti, "its continuous gait is a fabulous ruse."

They slowly circled a broad spine of blue and green stone, its shadow undulating across the dunes. "It moves in circles, like a hare," Udimo said from the saddle behind her. "The pain must be driving it so."

Duma brought her elephant to a halt beside the slope of stone. "Unless…"

She leaned forward and whispered in the tembo's ear. It knelt, and she dropped to the ground. After a heartbeat's examination, she jumped to her feet. "String your bows! There are two sets of—"

A roar came from behind them. Spears unready, bows unstrung, they were not prepared for the manticor's charge. Tiko, without a master in the lead saddle, ran, taking Udimo — and Duma's bow — with him.

Hopshef and Psamti struggled to turn their tembo. Psamti strung his bow and loosed an arrow. It hit its target in the shoulder and drew the man-eater's attention. The beast bellowed and the elephant turned to face its challenger. To Duma's horror, rather than charge, the manticor extended its spined tail at the totally exposed men.

"Tembo!" Duma shouted. "*Juu!*"

Heeding her command, the well-trained animal reared on its hind legs, its forelegs pawing the air. The manticor snapped its tail and the spines bounced harmlessly off the undercarriage of the rigged war harness.

"The spear! Assemble the spear!" she ordered. Elephantine's soldiers rarely used elephants in battle; their lack of coordination was obvious. They needed more time.

She drew her sword and hastened into the fray. The manticor swung its head in her direction and charged. Before it reached her, several fletched shafts seemed to spring from its hide. The horror slowed its assault and clawed at its latest wounds. Glancing over her shoulder, she saw Udimo guiding Tiko back into the fight.

Duma found two of the monster's spent spines lying among the rocks, oozing a foul oil. She sheathed her sword and snatched them from the dirt. The princess quickly mounted the stone rise and raced up the slope. From the higher ground, she saw the soldiers still readying the big spear. And still too slowly. The mantichor vented its rage at losing sight of her in perfect mimicry of human cries of frustration — then turned its attention toward the men. Duma moved along the height above the creature's back, gripping a spine in each hand like a brace of daggers. Psamti and Hopshef struggled to set the spear end of the haft into the butt. They didn't see the approaching beast. They did not see it crouching, did not see it prepare to pounce.

There was no more time for thought. Duma leaped, landing on the monster's neck, and jammed both spines into the heaving red flesh.

The living mountain rose beneath her, twisting and spinning, the humanlike face glaring at the princess, its razor teeth snapping just short of each hand. Duma clamped her legs tight around the bulging neck and clung to the spines with a death grip — but she expected to be thrown in moments. Thrown and then slashed apart by talons. Instead, the mantichor rolled into the side of the ridge. It slammed into the rock wall, scraping her along the jagged edges. Crushing pressure took her breath; rough stone took her skin. Her vision dimmed, and her grip failed.

She fell beneath the beast.

Duma lay watching her doom descend upon crimson talons. Something suddenly smashed into the great beast's side and flung it against the rock wall.

The mantichor screamed and Duma crawled away from its kicking hind legs. Shaking her head, she sat up. Psamti and Hopshef had finally finished the spear. The mantichor lay spitted against the ridge, its warm blood flowing across the rock face and soaking into the sand. A score of arrows jutted from its side, slowly rising and falling with its heaving breaths; stilling as it died.

Duma felt like the monster looked.

Udimo arrived at her side. "Foolish girl!"

"I had to distract it. I knew you would win."

Sitting beside her, he ran his hand down her cheek. "The usurper's tricks are getting better. We all nearly died—and how many more if we had failed?"

Vision still swimming with black dots, Duma bared her teeth. "For Dharti, for the soldiers and the tembo—for all who died, I will unseat Srqt. So swears the princess of Elephantine."

Mysterious Jungles

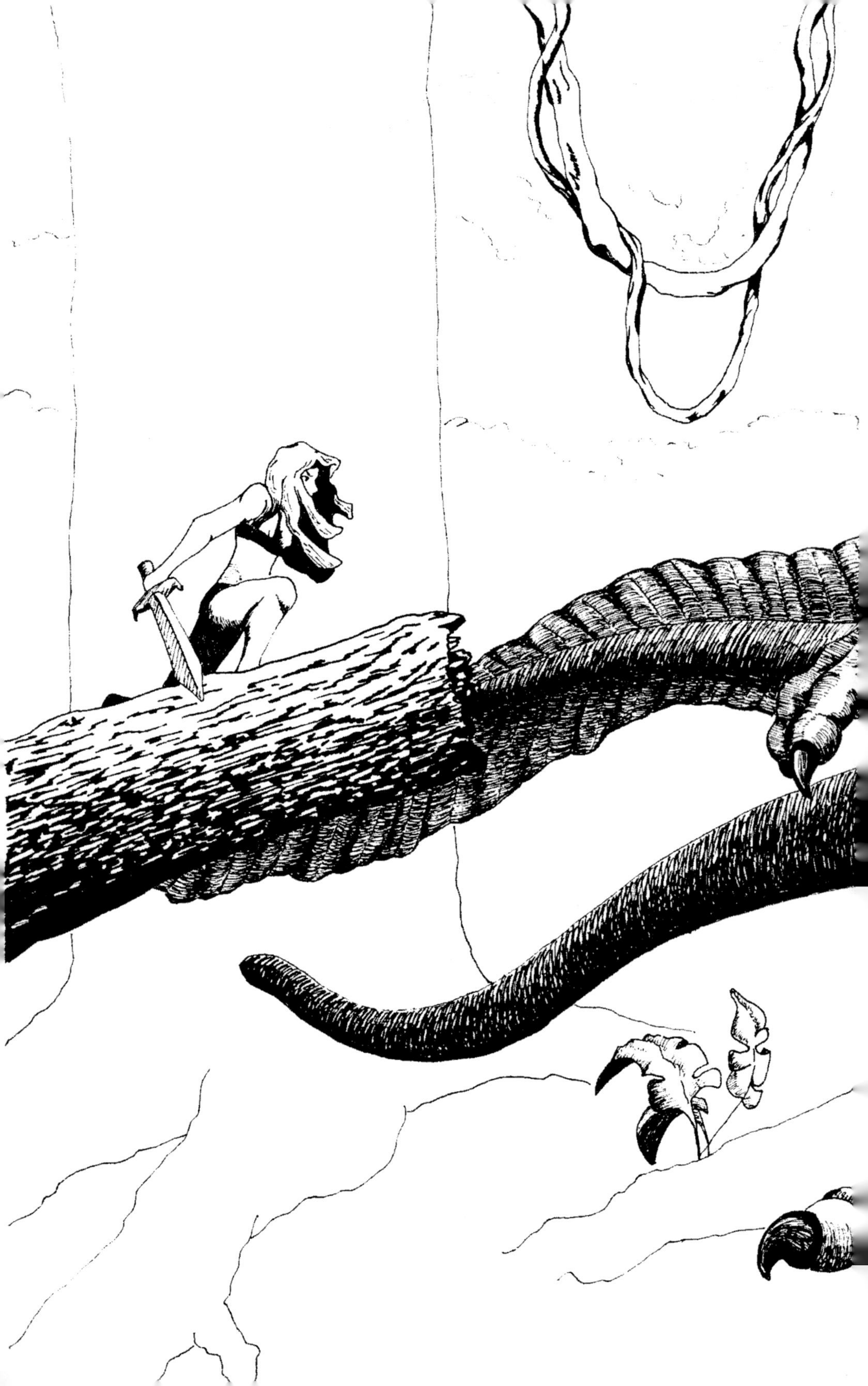

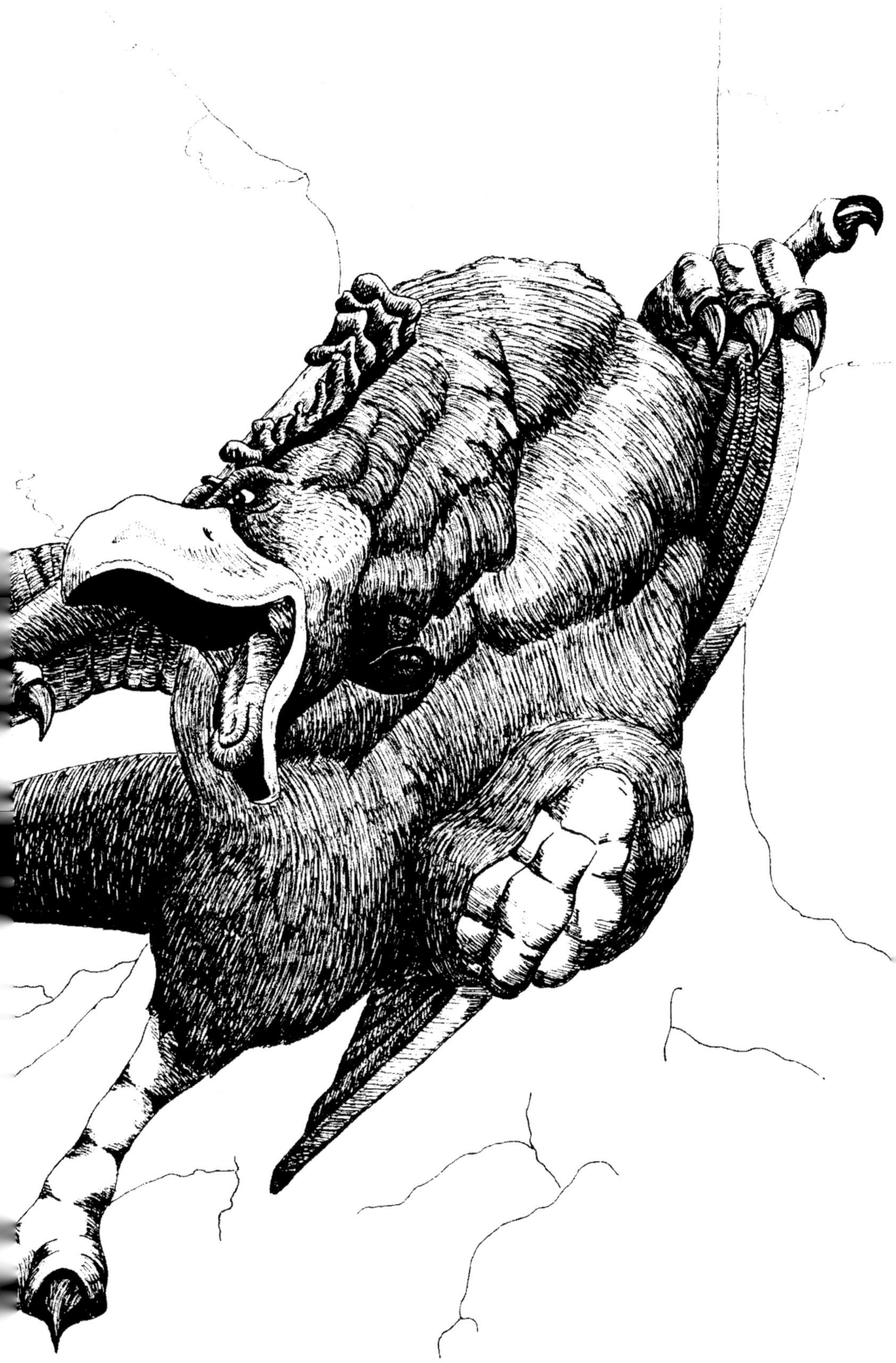

Kate Martin is a substitute teacher by day, a dance teacher by night, and a writer every minute in between. Growing up on the side of a Connecticut mountain in the middle of nowhere wasn't much good for afterschool shenanigans with friends, but it was spectacular for building an over-active imagination. Since she has been plotting and storytelling even before she knew how to put words on a page, she is now the proud host of dozens of characters. Her education includes a B.A. in Elementary Education with a minor in Psychology, used, of course, to keep the voices in her head at bay. In the fall of 2005 she attended the Viable Paradise Writers' Workshop and then moved on to get her Masters in Writing Popular Fiction from Seton Hill University. You can visit her website at http://kate-martin.com to find out more about Kate's writing life. The behemoth in the following tale is one of the most ferocious present in the anthology. Yet there is no denying it must be faced, for in the pursuit of truth, in the search for what is right, a willingness to sacrifice all is often necessary.

Poisonous Redemption

A Tale of Rica

by Kate Martin
& illustration by John Whitman

Razor sharp teeth are not the easiest thing to avoid. Especially when pressed against exposed and vulnerable skin. Saliva dripped down each elongated tooth, oozing onto Rica's arms, thick and warm. She had to remind herself over and over again not to move, not to flinch. Innate instincts made every fiber of her body scream to flee, to fight.

But this wasn't her enemy. This was her friend.

The point of one canine nicked the inside of her forearm. She jerked against her restraints involuntarily.

"Ow! Damnit, Weylin, be careful!"

His teeth bit closer, and finally the rope around her wrist came free. Rica quickly reached across and undid the sloppy knot around her other arm while Weylin worked on her ankles. He managed to only puncture her skin one more time.

She rubbed at her sore appendages before wiping the sweat from her face. The humidity was unbearable; not yet midday, and it would only get worse. Dawn, apparently, was the perfect time for sacrificial offerings.

Though Rica was fairly sure it didn't count when the offering was an abducted traveler and not one of your own. The townspeople who had ambushed her were in for a world of trouble. Either from the unappeased creature, or from Rica.

If they were lucky the creature would kill Rica first and they would be spared her wrath.

But really, their immature attempt to sacrifice her instead of tying one of their own daughters to this gnarly and ancient tree was nothing more than a small hindrance in her overall scheme.

She had come hunting what they planned on feeding her to.

Weylin whined, impatient. Rica still thought the sound seemed unnatural coming from the giant grey wolf. His broad shoulders stood as high as hers, and every muscle beneath the thick fur stretched and flexed with each tiny movement. A creature as physically powerful as that should never be caught whining.

Rica cracked her back to ease the pain then lifted a hand to shade her eyes from the bright, but rare, rays of sunlight that poured in through the canopy of the forest. The sky above was clear blue.

What she wouldn't have given for rain.

"Where did you stash my things?"

Weylin jerked his massive head to the left and Rica spied an opening in the foliage. They knew each other well, having done this together countless times. They took turns, one remaining human while the other shifted. Rarely did they occupy the same shape at the same time. She could barely remember the last time her human eyes had looked upon his for longer than a few moments. Weylin had shifted three days ago. Tonight he would change back and it would be her turn.

They had until then to kill the beast she knew lurked in the dappled shadows, or she would lose her chance for retribution.

Weylin had dragged her sword and bow into the jungle when the villagers had surprised her and manhandled her into the jungle. Had there been any danger he would have intervened, but otherwise they couldn't be allowed to see him. Shape-shifting was a forbidden evil in these parts. Regardless of the good it could do them against man-eating, poisonous monsters. Rica retrieved her blade and strapped her bow to her back, securing the quiver last.

She took one last look around. The clearing was small, barely more than twenty paces in each direction, but it served as a good focal point nonetheless. The villagers had tied her to the tree facing the north, so north they would go.

Weylin pressed against her side. His body heat was nothing compared to the air around them. They were used to a colder climate. Home seemed impossibly far away. Rica hadn't seen the pure white landscape in nearly five years. Not since that fateful day when she had returned from hunting to find the front room of the small log cabin covered in her sister's blood and her nephew's cradle empty. She remembered running with every bit of strength she had to reach the town square in time. But she was too late. Immy hung from the gallows, pale and dead. That day had led her to this jungle.

Weaving her fingers into Weylin's soft fur Rica took a deep breath then forged ahead.

This jungle was the largest in all the five empires, spreading out over the borders of two. They had been traveling through it for nearly a month and had barely penetrated its true depths. All the same, Rica felt fairly confident that she had learned at least the basics of its defenses and dangers.

Snakes disguised themselves among the branches of nearly every tree. Some were no bigger than her forearm, while others could swallow her whole and still have room for more. The tiny red snakes that hid in the fallen and decaying leaves on the ground were by far the most bothersome. They latched onto the ankle with their sharp and poison-less fangs before curling their bodies around the leg and going along for the ride. They couldn't kill, but they were annoying. In most cases, Rica kicked them off and Weylin ate them.

The smaller mammals, rodents and the like, gave them a wide berth. Giant wolves were good for warding off pests. The larger animals, mostly big spotted cats, followed at a distance, curious. They would attack if they got the chance, or feast themselves on the prey that, in their concern with avoiding Weylin, would foolishly not notice the secondary predators.

Oddly enough, what posed the greatest danger in this gods-forsaken jungle were the trees. Vines clung to their trunks and branches, choking the ancient plants into submission. They were no longer anything more than grounding points for parasites and poisoners. The vines had a life of their own, reaching out in unsuspecting moments and brushing against Rica's exposed skin. Since coming here she had been the victim of numerous rashes and burns. More than once, she had considered changing shape even when it wasn't her turn. Fur made an excellent barrier. But the rashes weren't even the worst of it.

Some of the vines bit. And those were poisonous.

It was for those flesh-eating plants that she kept the sharpest eye out as they crept into the jungle. The leaves of the trees pressed close, and the vines slithered up and down their perches like snakes. She had never thought it possible, but she couldn't wait to return home.

Unfortunately, she couldn't go home without proof. One step over the border without tangible proof that she was who everyone claimed her to be and she would have no hope of rescuing Immy's son and dethroning the tyrant who had taken him. She and Weylin had fled the moment they learned the reason for Immy's death. The king had discovered that the youngest daughter of the former rulers had survived his attack a decade earlier. A link to the legitimate royal bloodline meant power for those who opposed him. Power and a right to the throne.

Rica had long been a part of the resistance. The man and woman she called Father and Mother had allowed her to train from a young age. Rica had no illusions of them being her real parents; Immy was a mere month younger. Rica's true family had been killed in the takeover. A reoccurring nightmare allowed her to relive that over and over again. The details were fuzzy though, save for one. A giant black wolf, bursting through the flames that surrounded her hiding place. Each time, the creature snatched her up with such gentleness and carried her through the smoke and debris to safety. That image of her savior had been the reason Rica had insisted on learning to shift shape. That was how she had met Weylin and his father. And it was that ability that had allowed her to flee their homeland without being seen. Immy hadn't been the one they wanted. Rica was the supposed heir.

Weylin left her side, searching further west. Rica knew he wouldn't get far enough to lose her scent, but in human form she quickly lost his. Not that it much mattered. Once they found the creature, it would be all up to her anyway. Teeth and paws wouldn't stand a chance. Hands and weapons would have to save them both.

Insects chirped and sang from every corner of the jungle. She couldn't stand it. Home didn't have such things. Too cold. Rica wiped the sweat from her face yet again, then side-stepped the angry hiss of a particularly large snake. Its head hung in her path from the nearest tree, almost the size of her fist. Not a threat, but a pest. In her haste she bumped the blossoms of another tree's vine. The skin on the back of her shoulder burned. She jerked away and swung her sword at the plant just for good measure. The bright pink flower shuddered and hit the ground with an audible thud. Much too heavy for any normal flower. Curious, she stuck the tip of her sword into its fat leaves. Purple blood oozed out bringing with it a foul stench that caused her throat to constrict. She clamped her hand over her mouth and moved away carefully, but quickly.

The heat in the air felt so heavy it made her muscles ache. It also made her tired and darkened her mood. She cut down another vine that threatened to bite into her arm, and flicked away a troublesome red snake from her ankle. The creature couldn't be far. If the villagers had foreseen the need to appease its appetite then it must have been some time since the last time it had attacked. Pressing close to one blessedly vine-free trunk, she took the opportunity to breathe deep and recalled what the villagers had told her the previous night over a friendly meal; before they had seen fit to waylay and kidnap her.

It had to be what she sought. No other creature could possibly even remotely resemble this monster. The villagers had described a long scaled tail, flicking in and out of the trees, and a terrible cry like that of a dying chicken in the jaws of a dragon. Oversized feathers had been found at their sacrificial sites.

Rica pushed away from the tree and crept forward, watching everything around her as she had been trained to do. A shadow in the distance swung between two prominent trees. Rica's breath halted, the memory of the flow of her sister's skirt as she hung in the town square returning unbidden. The shadow fluttered, taunting her, then vanished with the dappled rays of sunshine that floated down between the leaves. Ghosts were said to haunt the living, but if what she had seen was a ghost, then Immy's spirit had followed her far and long.

And then Rica saw it. Her first sign. Her heart jumped in her chest and she felt a childish smile creep across her face. She hopped over a fallen tree and dropped to her knees in the decaying debris that littered the jungle floor.

They were so obvious, so blatantly visible. Footprints. She stretched her hand out above each, not touching, just gauging. The prints were easily three times the size of her hand and closely resembled the dragon prints she had tracked as a child. Only these showed a different weight distribution. Instead of four legs, this creature walked on two.

Two dragon-like legs, and she knew what they would carry. A dragon's body and tail, with the chest and head of a giant rooster. The cockatrice. Ugliest creature ever to be created under the gods' supervision. And the one thing that could deliver her birthright and Immy's justice.

More prints followed, continuing north. She followed them like a path to the holy land.

The vines seemed to seek her out as she passed, slithering to the lowest branches and extending their sticky and thorny tendrils into her set course. She cut them all down. Her legs screamed with effort as she ran through the thick air, skipping over the prints in the ground and crushing instead every annoying singing bug she saw.

Ahead, brush and trees rustled, and a deep breath rumbled. None of the large cats had dared to follow, and they knew how to be silent. Rica pulled to a stop, hopping onto a couple of trees that had fallen together. The snake that inhabited them hissed and struck at her. She ran her sword through its head and watched the venom and blood leak from its mouth. No time for petty creatures. Immy's son waited.

Checking multiple times, she cleared the lowest branch of the nearest living tree of vines and snakes, then climbed onto it. Perched safely within its benign leaves, she pulled them aside and peered into the jungle beyond.

It took a moment before the creature moved into sight. A wing first, clawed at the end with skin drawn tight like on those of a bat. Then the beak; crudely orange and lined with what Rica knew to be deadly, needle-like teeth. If the ancient accounts were right, the teeth were barbed like quills, designed to rend further damage when pulled free. It wouldn't matter in any case. If the monster got its jaws on her, it was all over. Its saliva was poisonous. So was its blood. If it entered her bloodstream, she had no hope.

Its feet and legs were the size of a male dragon, all muscle and lined in grey scales. The tail swung around behind it, curling and licking the air like a snake's tongue. She didn't dare try to get a good look at the head. One wrong move and she was dead. Or stone, more accurately. Eye-contact had to be avoided at all costs. No one in the north had encountered one of these things in over three hundred years, so the stories could all be nonsense, but Rica wasn't willing to take that chance. If the bards wanted to spin tales of stony-stares, she would listen. Someone else could test the truth of those legends.

Whatever the facts, she only cared about one. She had been right. Somehow, a cockatrice had found its way into this jungle. And somehow, she would kill it.

She had to. Despite the poison, and despite the possibly stony-stare.

The cockatrice pawed and paced amongst the trees. Rica watched, judging its competence and balance. This was a desert creature. Why it had come to the jungle, she had no idea, but its body hadn't been built for negotiating trees and debris. Hopefully that gave her an advantage.

She couldn't hear Weylin in the woods, but that didn't mean he wasn't there. He could hear her, smell her; she knew that. If something went terribly wrong, he would make himself known. Balancing on her perch carefully, she set her sword across her knees and drew her bow. Sighting along the arrow, she aimed at the feathery neck. The cockatrice pushed leaves and sticks aside with its beak, searching for insects, grubs and probably small mammals to eat.

She loosed her arrow.

The *thunk* of its impact was low and muffled by the feathers. The scream of the creature shook the jungle. The tree Rica hid in trembled and jerked, tossing her from the relative safety of its branches. She hit the ground and covered her ears to protect them from the terrible sound that echoed far and wide. She could feel the vibrations in her bones, in her organs. She wished for death; then remembered who she was and what she was there to do. Utilizing every bit of concentration she had, she wrenched her hands from her ears, took up her sword and pushed herself to her feet.

The cockatrice hollered once more, sending her stumbling, then shook its massive head in displeasure and quieted. The arrow protruded from its neck, the white feathers of the weapon contrasting sharply with the black feathers that coated the top-most portion of its body. Dark blood, almost black, oozed out over both. Rica's hope of killing it without getting too close died. Of course, if it had been that easy the pathetic villagers would have done it themselves.

She hoped Weylin remembered what she had told him to do in the event of her death. She did not want to be buried here in this hell of a jungle. But death wouldn't have her easily. For the sake of her stolen nephew, she had to get home. She could not allow him to be raised in loyalty to the man who had slaughtered his mother.

Carefully, Rica set her sword between her knees, hilt up and ready, and drew another arrow. She had the bowstring drawn back to her mouth when she felt an odd slithering sensation on the back of her leg.

The arrow flew wide as Rica grabbed for her sword and spun quickly, swiping at the snake with her blade. It hissed and stood — if snakes could be considered able to stand — tall, its head even with hers. A red tongue flicked out tasting the air, tasting her. Sounds of struggle and irritation rustled and squawked behind her, but she didn't dare move to look. The hood of the snake flared, showing off bright red and purple swirling patterns meant to intimidate and warn. The snake hissed again, and Rica could see the venom dripping from its curving fangs. Its body drew back.

Rica struck.

The head of the snake spun through the air, flinging blood across her face.

The swaying body flopped heavily forward and forced her to jump aside. The snake had been easily the length of three full grown men. It would have swallowed her whole and felt empty. The pounding of her pulse filled her ears. Not a good sign: the snake wasn't the worst thing she would face. She breathed deeply and recentered herself. Her hearing returned.

A squawk rumbled to her left, and hot breath splashed against the back of her neck.

The snake had distracted her too long.

She reversed the grip on her sword and thrust upward behind her, blind to her target. Her blade bit deep. The screech of the cockatrice sent the entire jungle into a vibrating frenzy. Its right wing tore as Rica twisted around, splitting against her blade like a thick hide. Her arms shook with the effort. One long clawed finger came away with her sword when she finally pulled free.

Hopping away, she kept clear of the creature as it writhed in pain and anger. Its tail swung in every direction, taking down branches and sending a few tree snakes flying through the air. Rica ducked behind the far side of a tree and prayed to her gods that the vines and their accomplices would leave her alone just this one time. Dark blood dripped off the tip of her sword and where it hit the jungle floor, the ground burned.

She would have to get this over with quickly.

Circling around the tree, Rica attacked from the opposite side. She saw her second arrow lodged at the base of the tail; no blood trailed from the wound. From the looks of things, it hadn't done much more than cause an annoying itch. She charged and brought her sword down in a mighty two-handed blow directly where feathers met scales.

Black feathers filled the air along with another horrible, eardrum-splitting cry. Rica hopped away from the blood spatter smoldering on the ground, and gagged on the acrid smell that sliced down her throat. She felt the steel of her sword becoming hot; saw steam rising from the blade.

Rica swung again.

And missed.

The thick, massive tail struck her full force. The impact knocked the air from her lungs, left her pained and choking, and swept her from the ground. Her throat burned as she tried desperately to remember how to breathe. Rica hit a tree hard, heard it groan in protest. She gasped and sweet air finally flooded her lungs. Her fingers strained against the hilt of her sword, gripped so tightly that she hadn't lost it in her induced stupor.

Then the tail came back; not to strike, but to grab. The tip flicked, then coiled around her, starting at her waist and working its way up to her neck. Rica kicked and struggled, but only managed to keep one arm free. She was angry now. She had been wrong about the cockatrice.

Not a dragon's tail. A snake's.

She hated snakes.

The tail tightened, squeezing the air from her lungs once again. She breathed shallow and slow, trying to remain calm while the tip of the tail caressed her neck. Her right arm ached, caught between coils and still desperately clinging to her now only weapon. The cockatrice turned toward her.

Rica forced herself to look down. She kept her stare below the beak, fighting the almost irresistible urge to gaze into its eyes. Being turned to stone would not get her back home.

The reptilian-bird snapped its beak, squawking like the chickens Immy had kept out behind the house. The tongue inside was thick and black behind bright and brilliant white teeth, just like the winter snows at home. It bobbed its head and the grip of its tail tightened, lifting her from the ground. The cockatrice lowered its head, trying to dip beneath her guard.

Trying to look her in the eye. She had underestimated it. Nothing she had ever read indicated they possessed a high intelligence.

Her free arm was becoming numb, a vague tingling replacing all other sensation. Much longer, and she wouldn't be able to hold onto her sword. The cockatrice steadily raised her feet off the ground; she could see just above its beak now, and the thing kept lifting her higher. She would end up accidentally losing herself in its gaze if this continued.

Rica closed her eyes.

Keeping a mental picture of the creature in her mind, she drew her sword arm back as best she could, turned her sword — then thrust forward with every bit of strength she could summon.

The jungle erupted in another world-shattering scream that would have sent her reeling back — if not for the cockatrice's tail wrapped around her.

The tail constricted violently, and Rica heard something inside herself crack. Then she was somersaulting through the steaming air. She crashed head-on into the thick branches that barred her path. She tumbled through leaves and stinging vines until she finally struck the ground.

Cautiously, Rica pushed herself up. Her ribs hurt like all the three hells — making breathing an agonizing ordeal. Warmth flowed from her left ear. She touched it, and her hand came away bloody. The cockatrice had ceased the worst of its screaming, but its continued squawks sounded muffled to her. She glanced at her foe and saw her sword embedded sideways in its chest.

Small favors from the gods.

Its head snapped in her direction.

Rica averted her gaze.

It charged.

She had no weapon.

The cockatrice's wide feet carried it clumsily across the jungle floor, its wide body bouncing between trees and rending their branches. A line of trees grew at Rica's back, preventing any quick refuge. She reached up and grabbed a branch, pulling herself to her feet. Her ribs flared with pain. The branch hissed.

The cockatrice squawked, showing no sign of slowing down. Rica yanked the hissing branch down from the tree and quickly adjusted her grip so that she held the snake just behind its head and at arm's length, keeping safely out of reach of its fangs. She stood there, snake snapping, cockatrice charging.

She had no idea what she planned on doing next.

A rustle and growl came from the brush, and Weylin sprang from the darkness of the jungle. Rica panicked.

They had agreed that he would not attack. The only weapons he had were teeth and claws, and the cockatrice's blood was poisonous. He was not supposed to risk contact; not supposed to sacrifice himself.

Rica could do nothing to stop him.

Weylin collided with the cockatrice, his powerful shoulders slamming into the long feathered neck. The two of them crashed full force into one of the ancient trees beside her. The trunk shuddered, then fell.

Rica screamed, and started to drop her arms.

The snake pinned in her hand hissed and snapped. She quickly held it out at arm's length again, afraid to release it lest it come straight at her for revenge.

Weylin whined and shook, and staggered to his four feet. Rica didn't see any sign of burns; perhaps he had managed to avoid the blood that coated the side of the creature.

The cockatrice screeched and jumped to its feet; the force of its weight shook the jungle. Weylin lost his balance and went down. The snake struggled to break Rica's grip. The cockatrice whipped its head toward her. She snapped her eyes shut.

The snake stopped whipping and jerking. Its warm skin turned cool and hard. Rica cracked one eye open.

She no longer held living flesh and blood. Cold, unyielding stone filled her hands. Her fingers convulsed and she dropped the snake like it was the plague. The stony-stare was more than myth.

Her first instinct was to turn and run. Her pride, however, wouldn't let her. Neither would her vendetta. She needed the death of this monster.

Another hideous squawk rang through the trees. Rica trained her eyes on where her sword still protruded from the monster's bloodied chest, still useless to her. The cockatrice flapped its one whole wing, and came at her again.

Rica sprang to her feet, ignoring the pain in her chest and ribs, and ran. She could hear it gaining on her even as she dodged the trees and branches. This native desert creature had clearly been here long enough to adapt. Rica was smaller; she should have had the advantage.

She jumped over another fallen tree and her feet skidded out from under her when she landed on dried leaves. She lost her balance and she flailed backward.

But she didn't hit the ground. Something hard caught the middle of her back and flung her forward. She grabbed at the nearest tree and used it to turn herself around.

And came face-to-beak with the cockatrice.

Needle-like teeth greeted her as the creature opened its bright orange beak, inches from her head. The clawed hand at the tip of its only functioning wing slammed against her chest and pinned her to the trunk of the tree now at her back. Pain from her already aching ribs flared through her body. The beak — large enough to swallow her head — stretched wider with each breath.

Her gaze fell upon the sword still buried in the creature's flesh, just out of reach.

Rica lunged forward with all her strength — the sharp edges of the beak scraping her cheek — and wrapped both hands around the hilt of her sword. She drove her body weight to the left, then up.

The blade slid in to the guard. The tearing sound as she forced the blade upward through the feathered flesh of the neck was wet and jagged. The scream of the cockatrice was even worse.

The smell of the acidic blood was worse yet. It burned Rica's nose and made her gag, but she held tight. She dared not let go. She wrenched her sword free and thrust it again into the scaled chest without hesitation.

The cockatrice thrashed, jerking its shredded neck side to side, raining dark blood upon everything. Rica leaned into her attack, forcing the blade deeper. Blood ran over the guard, over the hilt, and toward her hands.

She refused to let go.

Rica tensed as the blood neared her skin, anticipating its corrosive bite. She cringed as it oozed over her skin. Hot — yet no different than if she had spilled warmed mare's milk upon herself. She relaxed, surprised. Then screamed at the sudden pain of blazing heat that rushed over her skin. The muscles of her hands seized around the weapon — she could not have let go if she had wished to. She would not; not until the beast was dead.

She closed her eyes, afraid to watch what happened to her flesh. But she could still smell, and her corroding skin stank of sulfur and charcoal. Her wrists felt the ebb of hot blood next, then the sensation traveled down her arms to her bent elbows, where it dripped and splattered against her legs. Her pants were no sort of protection; her thighs soon burned as hot as her arms. Her throat was raw from screaming, and tears flowed down her face.

The cockatrice jerked, went rigid — and fell. Its collapse dragged Rica down, her fingers still locked on the sword still caught within its armor-like scales. She tried to let go.

And screamed.

Her fingers sloughed from the hilt of the sword, leaving a string of her melted self behind. Black blood coated her arms from her wrists to her elbows. Black smoke billowed from them; more rose from her legs. She could feel her skin burning and flaking away. She could see it. She scrambled backward and tripped, landing on the jungle floor, still screaming, but unable to look away from the ruin that was becoming her arms.

She had no hope now. Her victory over the cockatrice — this — should have proved her birthright. But not if she burned like this; not if her flesh melted away.

As if her thoughts had set something free, Rica felt a new sensation creep along her arms. An icy touch, just beneath the burning heat of the blood, began to wind its way across her limbs. White smoke mingled with the black, swirling in and out until the light color outweighed the dark. The burning receded, quelled by the ice that welled up from inside her. The black blood turned to mist and floated away.

Rica stared at her arms in disbelief. She had seen her skin blacken and flake away. Yet she was whole.

A cold sweat, not triggered by the unbearable heat of the jungle, broke out over her entire body.

She was who they said she was. She finally had proof.

So much for unfounded nightmares.

"Are you about to throw up?"

The unexpected sound of his voice made Rica jump. She caught herself with one blissfully whole hand before looking up at Weylin's human face. She took a deep breath so she could speak. "I didn't hear you change."

"You were too busy screaming."

"I had good reason." She examined her arms one more time, touching them in turns, not believing the smooth and unmarred skin she encountered.

Weylin knelt beside her. "I take it we can go home now?"

Home. Truthfully, she hadn't ever expected to see it again. The cockatrice lay dead on the ground a mere six paces away. She needed its blood. But smoke rose from all around it, and the ground had been eaten away. She knew without looking that nothing remained. The monster's neck had been torn wide open, and the whole in its chest was large enough to fit a small child through. She had bled it dry, and had eliminated her only chance of redemption.

Home wouldn't have her. Immy's son would remain in the clutches of a tyrant who thought the boy possessed a power he did not have.

"There's no blood," she said. "I can't prove anything without the blood. And even if there were, nothing we brought with us would have been strong enough to withstand the potency." They had hidden their belongings just outside the village, but the cases of waterskins and pottery — even the steel — would not have been enough. She gestured dejectedly at the remains of her sword. It had as many holes in it as the cheese Immy had made. "We need a new sword."

Weylin grunted and set his chin on his hand. Rica used the brief moment to make sure he wasn't injured. His suntanned skin looked unmarred, and no bones appeared to be broken. He was in better shape than she was. Aside from her arms, which had healed themselves with remarkable skill, she felt like the cockatrice looked: dead. Her broken ribs made each breath painful and her head swam with the effort.

Weylin stood and offered her his hands. "I think I have a solution."

"And what would that be?" She took his offered assistance and got to her feet. A nice long sleep in a soft bed sounded good. Too bad the closest village had tried to kill her.

"She was leading you away from something."

"She?"

"Yes. Can you walk?"

Even if she couldn't, she wouldn't have admitted it. "Of course."

"Then follow me." He turned and headed back the way they had originally come, before the cockatrice had thrown her, chased her, tried to eat her. But he didn't release her hand; he knew she was close to keeling over.

A thousand painful steps later, he stopped and pulled aside a collection of fallen branches. "I sniffed this out while you were irritating her with arrows."

Rica ignored his jibe and stepped up to see what lay hidden beyond.

A pile of sticks and leaves reaching the height of her hips sat surrounded by the carcasses of small mammals and birds. At the center lay a brilliant white egg.

A solution indeed.

For a moment she thought she might cry.

An egg would be easy to get back, as long as they kept it warm. If it hatched along the way the creature would be small enough to lock within a cage for safekeeping. By the time they reached their homeland they would have a cockatrice of manageable size that could be pricked and bled for the purposes of revealing her birthright. She wouldn't have to bathe in the blood like she had this time.

They could go home.

Justice could finally be hers and her family avenged.

Bruce Durham has appeared in publications such as Paradox, Flashing Swords, Abandoned Tales *and the* Return of the Sword *anthology. He administers the community forums for the official website of Conan Properties Inc., and moderates the Fiction Forums for Paradox Interactive Games. His short stories 'The Marsh God' and 'Homecoming' won back-to-back Preditors & Editors Readers polls for Best SF&F in 2005/2006 respectively. His story 'Valley of Bones,' in* Return of the Sword, *finished 7th in the 2008 Preditors & Editors Readers poll in the Best SF&F category. Visit his website at www.brucedurham.ca for story excerpts and other cool stuff. Bruce pens soldiers as if he sat in a barracks among them 24/7. Mortlock's observations — and actions — are spot-on soldiery-sage; the words and deeds of the worldly-cognizant and risk-inoculated. This is entertaining and appropriate in this tale of other-worldly creatures which enjoy toying with humanity.*

Yaggoth-Voor

A Tale of Mortlock the Footman

by Bruce Durham

It was the lookout who spotted the wreck and shouted a warning.

"Damn," I explained as a pair of dice bounced wildly from my hand, tumbling and rattling across the wooden deck before coming to rest. A one and a three. "Damn," I explained again, reaching for a re-roll.

"What are you doing, Mortlock?" Creeson inquired, glaring at me with small, close-set eyes. With a small, battered nose, his face resembled a slab of meat ground by a boot. His scarred hand shot out to intercept mine.

"Stupid lookout spoilt my throw," I mumbled, dodging.

Creeson cupped his hand protectively over the dice. Gyvens and Tek, rounding out our foursome, fixed me with their best *nice try* look.

We sat cross-legged on the deck of the *Fat Lyla*, a pile of coins stacked before us. *Fat Lyla* was a merchant transport that Sergeant Clantalion had requisitioned for our trip home. Until recently we had campaigned with the Duke of Qialtl against the Tyrant of Sholdathos. Qialtl was a city-state located in the country of Meizak, and had ties to my homeland of Coranthe. Apparently the Ducal line was descended from a certain Dalacroy Kildonan, who, the story goes, helped his girlfriend overthrow the bad men who had captured her city and sent her into exile. It was obvious she was grateful. She married the guy and begat a family tree. Of course, this all happened hundreds of years ago. As it was, Kildonan originally hailed from Coranthe, hence the close ties.

So, for a while I had played mercenary, hoisting my pike in a land of feuding city-states where enemies one day became friends the next. That aside, it was good pay with a sizable bonus. And we won, which was a plus. No doubt my wife would walk with pride and brag to her friends while making plans to spend my gold. The kids would shrug and play in the dirt.

Of course, all of this meant little to Creeson. He continued to cover the bones.

"What?" I asked, distracted as several men hurried past. Their shouts attracted another group. Curious now, I watched them gather along the rail, joining those green-faced usual suspects who offered libations to the gods of seasickness. I threw my arms in the air. "Fine. I'm tired of this anyway. No competition." I collected my coins, including my ante.

"Hey," chimed all three.

"What?" I stood, my knees popping. "I want to see what's happening." At the rail I pushed between two pikemen. They scowled, but held their tongue on recognition. Some years back I had gained a reputation after the Battle of the Bones, and was viewed as something of a hero. Not only had I saved the King's life, my wounds were treated by his personal physician. Afterward I was paraded before the nobles and presented with a cash award. The King even shared a private joke with me. Heady stuff. Suffice to say, I wasn't ashamed to exploit my ties with the big guy.

Ignoring the scowls, I shaded my eyes. The lookout was right. In the distance floated the remains of a ship. They were meager, little more than splintered wood, a rudder, barrels bobbing gently in the turquoise water, split oars, a broken mast partially covered with torn sail and frayed rigging.

"What caused that?" a pikeman asked.

I looked at the sky. It was clear and blue, a faint dusting of clouds gathered along the horizon. A few gulls circled overhead. As no one answered, I cleared my throat. "Wasn't a storm. Maybe a reef. Judging by the wreckage, I'd say whatever happened, happened recently."

"How would you know?"

"The debris is cluttered. Very little drifting."

The pikeman nodded sagely.

The lookout shouted again, "Survivors!"

I scanned the wreckage, but try as I might, didn't see them. Like my body, my eyes were not as sharp as they once were.

A voice cried triumphantly, "There! Beyond the mast."

I squinted, barely making out two figures lying prone on a half-submerged panel of wood.

"Man the oars, bring 'er about." Striding the deck like a pumped up admiral, the ship's captain was short and bellicose, had small ears and a large nose. He went by the name of Amery. Properly cajoled, the crew responded, and groaning in protest, the transport shifted course to inch through the wreckage until slipping beside the shattered section of hull.

The survivors were a man and child. The man was definitely the worse for wear. His right arm and leg were clearly broken, and a wicked gash ran the length of his hip. The child couldn't have seen more than eight years, about the age of my daughter. Her naked body had severe bruising on back and legs, a sight that brought a scowl to my lips. I turned away. Nothing more to see, nothing I could do.

Creeson hadn't moved from his seated position. He watched me with a look that was both accusatory and inquisitive. I sat nonchalantly, kept my face impassive. I knew he was dying to hear the details. I ignored him and inspected my fingernails.

Finally he snapped, "What was that about?"

I shrugged. "Nothing much. A couple of survivors. Man and child."

His eyes lit up. "A girl?"

"Couldn't tell. Much too young for you, anyway. The guy's more your age. A little beat up, but shouldn't bother a stud like you."

Creeson bared his teeth and gave me the universal sign. I returned it. Creeson was an ass, but he was a useful ass, especially when it came to dicing away his money.

Gyvens and Tek sat. Gyvens was gangly, all arms and legs. Tek was tall and thin. Men swore he could hide behind his pike.

I grabbed the bones and dropped a coin in the ante.

Gyvens swallowed; his pronounced Adam's apple bobbed with the motion. "The guy was in bad shape, eh Tek? Arm and leg busted, side torn wide open. Amazing he lived."

I paused mid-shake. "He did?"

Tek shook his head. "Did. Died soon's after they gots him aboard. Tried to speak, but no one gots a word. Gots real agitated before he went, though."

Gyvens nodded. "Sounded scared, eh?"

Creeson watched my hands. "And the child?"

"Girl," Tek stated. "Alive, too. Awake, but…"

"She's touched," Gyvens cut in. "Stares at the deck."

"The crew is nones too happy," Tek added. "They wants to throw her back. 'Cept Sarge won'ts allow it."

Inwardly I smiled. Contrary to his gruff exterior, Sarge was a good man. Suddenly I thought of my daughter, Katlyn. *So young and playful.* I scowled at the idea that anyone would dare leave a child to the mercy of the sea. Forcefully I released the dice. They scattered across the deck. Five and six. About time. I snapped, "Sailors are superstitious. Say it's bad luck having a female on board."

"To shore! To shore!" The lookout again, his voice high pitched and panicked.

"What now?" I mumbled.

Men rushed past us again to gather along the portside rail, scattering our pot across the deck. My curse was lost in the general chaos and shouts of alarm. I gathered what coins I could before pushing my way to the handrail.

I stared. My mouth dropped. Weak eyes or not, I had no trouble with this.

A creature unlike anything I had seen in my painfully long life stood at the edge of the thick jungle. It almost reached the upper limbs of the ancient trees, rocking gently on two long, sinuous legs. Its torso was a thick cylinder of pink, mottled flesh, its arms two appendages ending in fingerless, diamond-shaped clubs. A surrounding carapace spanned its sloping shoulders, hiding whatever served it for a head deep within its shadow.

The outcry from the men trailed away and we faced off, man and creature, waiting tensely in one of those awkward moments of indecision.

It slithered into the water toward us.

Captain Amery exploded into action. Crewmen scattered among the rigging or ran out the oars.

I watched from the rail. The thing had submerged, its foaming wake coming straight toward us. "Not enough time," I mumbled. "Not enough time."

I jumped at the loud clatter of metal striking wood, followed by Sergeant Clantalion's booming voice. "Defend yourselves." I turned. A pile of swords lay beside the open cargo hatch.

Gyvens brushed past.

"Bring me a blade, will you?" I shouted. There was no sense entering the mess of people descending on the weapons.

I waited pensively until Gyvens slipped away from the crowd with a pair of blades. He triumphantly presented both, like a child showing off new toys. "Which one do you want?"

I bit off a retort and snatched one, just as the transport tilted violently, its port side tipping seaward. Timbers groaned in protest, a boom swung wildly. I staggered and struck the rail, desperately slipping my arm through a slat. I grunted as my arm took the weight of my body. I was lucky. The less fortunate went overboard, their cries cut short as they plunged into the sea. The ship reversed direction and slanted dramatically to starboard. My feet left the deck. For a moment I dangled midair before hitting the planks hard. The sword slipped from my hand and clattered toward the starboard rail. I followed it unceremoniously, sliding along the wood, grabbing at anything remotely secure. All I managed were splinters. I hit the rail as the boat shifted again, fell back on my ass and rolled. My body would pay for this later.

The shift was not as dramatic this time, and the boat soon came to rest, gently rocking from side to side.

Someone yelled, "What in the Three Hells just happened?"

"It tried to sink us!"

A third voice, Gyvens I think, said, "It's given up."

A long, smooth, fleshy tentacle erupted from the water to hover above us, its wedge-shaped club flexing slowly, deliberately.

I shot Gyvens a withering glare as men scattered. The appendage swept the deck, snatching a crewman about the waist and hoisting him high. A series of sharp cracks ended his scream of terror. The massive club uncurled and the sailor struck the deck like a sack of flour.

It was then I saw the girl, propped against the mast, her eyes fixed on a dangerously close limb. It missed her by inches. A blade rattled near my boot. I snatched it up and raced over, planting myself before her.

~ Yaggoth-Voor ~

The ponderous tentacle swept past and I swung hard, cutting deep into the fleshy appendage. Bright red blood jetted from the gaping wound, soaking me from head to foot. Desperately I wiped at my eyes, blinded by the spray. A hand gripped my shoulder and pulled me back. I slipped on the blood-drenched deck and fell hard on my ass. I wiped, blinked, wiped again. My vision cleared.

Over half a dozen men had jumped in, attacking the tentacle with fervor. Deciding it acceptable to share the glory, I knelt beside the girl, determined to shelter her from the surrounding chaos.

Three additional men died before our blades convinced the thing that enough was enough. The damaged tentacle slipped beneath the water. The men rushed to the rail, all pumped with victory.

"It's heading to land."

"See the blood trail? We got it good."

"Must have been what sunk the boat."

"There's a path in the jungle. See it?"

"It looks well used."

"And there it goes."

"Last we've seen of that."

"You hope."

I unfolded from my kneeling position to sit beside the girl. Like me, she was coated in blood, though her look remained distant, fixed on gods knew what. I frowned. I had seen that look before on the mind-addled. Tentatively I wiped blood from her face, creating bands of red and pink.

A figure loomed above us. It was Sergeant Clantalion, large hands planted firmly on hips, dark eyes flitting from girl to me and back. "You look like crap, Mortlock," he said in his gravelly voice.

"Thanks, Sarge. You have a cloth?"

"Do I look like someone who carries cloth? Best take a jump in the sea."

"I can't swim."

Clantalion's lined face softened and he chuckled, a sound like dry leaves. "Neither can I. Don't worry; it's shallow where we're headed."

"Oh?"

"We have to beach. *Fat Lyla's* leaking below deck."

Great. Just great. "And what about that thing?" I pointed landward for emphasis. Thick red dripped from my hand and arm. I frowned. "That's a lot of blood, isn't it?"

Clantalion smiled; a rare sight. "Should see you from my end." His face hardened. "If it can bleed, it can die. It won't bother us again."

The girl fixed the sergeant with her vacant look.

Clantalion turned on his heel.

The jungle was a wall of heavily knotted trees with thick limbs, broad leaves and dangling vines. Its encroachment on the shoreline provided precious little beach.

Insects swarmed among the dense undergrowth, taking delight in the arrival of warm flesh. They really liked Creeson. Fortunately, Captain Amery was a veteran of the southern climes and ordered the construction of a dozen campfires. Soon a cloud of thick smoke, courtesy of the green tinder gathered from the lip of the jungle, forced the bugs back to a respectful distance.

With that settled, Captain Amery wasted little time setting his crew to work repairing the hull. Meanwhile, Sergeant Clantalion had our men break out their weapons and take defensive positions along the narrow beach.

Except for me. I stood knee deep in salt water, scrubbing the blood from my flesh with a rough cloth. The girl sat close by, near the shore's edge, knees drawn to chin, staring out to sea. I had scrubbed her first and dressed her in a spare shirt. The garment engulfed her small body. Once cleaned, I was surprised at how closely she resembled my daughter. *Same long dark hair, little dimples at the corners of her lips, pert, freckled nose.* Only her eyes were different. Instead of lively, these were blank.

Gyvens walked up, sparing the child a quick glance. "That pasty body of yours scares the fishes, Mortlock."

I ignored the jibe. *Why give him the satisfaction of a response?* I inspected my body. No more blood. I frowned. I *was* pasty. I stepped to shore and reached for my pants.

Gyvens glanced again at the girl. "Funny how different she looks after a good wash. She said anything yet?"

I shook my head and lifted a leg to pull on a boot. I placed a hand on Gyven's shoulder for balance.

"The crewmen are grumbling."

I shifted hands to put on the other boot. "Why?"

"The girl again. They insist she's bad luck."

I reached for my shirt. "Didn't we have this conversation?"

He nodded.

I picked up my leather cuirass. "We all have our superstitions. For example, you kiss your pike before battle."

Gyvens helped with the straps and buckles. "You noticed?"

"Hard not to. A word of advice, don't give it tongue."

He laughed weakly. "Caster, *Fat Lyla's* first mate, told me a tale about Yaggoth-Voor."

"Yaggoth-what?"

"Yaggoth-Voor. Says it's a legend popular with the city-states in northern

Meizak. He thinks that's what attacked us."

I rolled my eyes. "Legends aren't real. That's why they're legends." Taking my baldric, I left the gangly pikeman to join Sergeant Clantalion. "Where do you want me, Sarge?"

Clantalion peered beyond me and down. His heavy eyebrows drew together. "I think she likes you."

"What?" I turned. The girl had followed, standing passively within reach. She looked ridiculous in my shirt. The garment reached her knees, the sleeves passing well below the hands. "I'm beginning to side with the sailors, Sarge. She's addled. Can we keep her on board?"

The child bolted past. Clantalion and I stood slack-jawed as she darted along the beach, her bare feet kicking sand.

"Was it something I said?" I mumbled.

Clantalion cursed. "Probably. Go get her. Addled or not, no child dies under my command."

I eyeballed the sergeant. There was that soft spot again.

His brow furrowed and he snarled, "Move it."

So much for the soft spot. Slipping the baldric over my shoulder, I turned and whistled. Heads popped up. "Creeson, Tek, Gyvens, on me."

"This better be good, Mortlock," Creeson snapped. He slapped at a bug for emphasis, a mosquito the size of a gold coin.

I pointed at the receding figure of the girl.

Gyvens moaned. "Ah shit. Can't we just let her go?"

"Afraid not." I saw Tek shift nervously, sword tight in his hand; knew he wished he was elsewhere. *A sentiment no doubt shared by many of us.* I touched the hilt of my own sword, wondering if blades were enough. I decided they weren't. "Creeson, Gyvens, grab pikes." Fortunately Sergeant Clantalion had the foresight to retrieve the pikes stored in the ship's hold.

"Why?" Creeson asked.

"Should be useful if that thing's still out there."

The men looked to Clantalion, who nodded agreement. I frowned, thrilled that I inspired such devoted, unquestioned leadership. Wordlessly, they went to a stack of weapons and returned, each carrying a long, steel-tipped pole.

Gyvens sighed, "What I wouldn't give for a musket."

"You'd only shoot yourself. Ready?"

Creeson snarled, "Let's get on with it." He slapped at a bug. "Before I'm eaten alive."

We hurried along the shoreline, quickly gaining on the child. We were not fast enough. She reached the path the creature had retreated through and entered. We arrived moments later, pausing to exchange nervous glances. The passage was well-worn.

Creeson smacked his arm with a free hand. "Damn!" He glared at me. "Who goes first?"

I guess that would be me. I took a tentative step forward.

"Did you hear that?" Gyvens asked.

I stopped. "Hear what?"

"Nothing."

"Nothing? Idiot. Why—"

"That's what I mean. I've heard nothing since we landed. No animals, birds, lizards. Nothing, 'cept these blasted insects."

Thing about Gyvens, he could really put a fellow at ease. I chewed it over. He had a point. But orders were orders, and the kid was just ahead. "That's not our concern."

"Shouldn't it be?"

"Shut up, Gyvens. Let's move. We're wasting time."

We entered the jungle. I led with sword drawn, Creeson and Gyvens followed, Tek taking the rear.

The trees stood thick and tall, ancient behemoths stretching toward the sky. The jungle floor was carpeted with spongy green moss, tangled vines, patches of wildly colored flowers and exposed, gnarled roots. Overhead the canopy of branches and leaves blocked the sun, casting us in deep shadow. The heat quickly grew oppressive.

"This place stinks," Gyvens said.

"Damn," Creeson whispered harshly.

I glanced over my shoulder, gave them both my best *shut up will you* look.

"No insects," Creeson explained.

I pondered that. *He was right.* It did nothing for my unease. *Where was the girl, anyway?* I swallowed and continued. Two dozen steps and the shadows lightened. I increased my pace. Another dozen steps and I saw sunlight through the foliage. *Had we passed through the jungle so soon?* I aimed for the light, rounded what had to be the largest tree in the world, and stopped.

Creeson joined me, whistled in surprise. "Something that size just has to have treasure."

Several hundred feet distant lay the ruins of an ancient city. Once home to majestic buildings, temples, palaces and spires, it was now little more than a collection of shells, crumbled stone and jagged brick coated with slick moss, creeping vines and patchy undergrowth. Still, it was magnificent.

Though distracted with slack-jawed wonderment, I remembered why I was here. I spotted the child, seated a mere stone's throw away in the middle of a granite roadway that led straight into the city. I stormed toward her, my boots echoing on the ancient slabs. She paid no notice.

Creeson caught up. "What about the treasure? Can we look around?"

"No. We take the girl and tell Sarge. Let him decide."

Creeson crossed his arms; his pushed-in face a mask of defiance. Whatever retort lay on his lips was silenced by a loud wail. We froze. It had come from the ruins. The creature.

Why me? "Keep sharp," I commanded. I ran over, placed my hand on the girl's chin and tilted her head. She wore the same blank expression. The thing wailed again. I looked up, and my flesh crawled as it rose from behind the jagged shell of a building, one tendril coiling open and close, the other hanging loose, badly damaged from our earlier encounter. It wailed again and slithered over the crumbling brickwork toward us.

Sheathing my sword, I swept up the girl. At first she was dead weight, but then she wrapped her thin, bruised arms around my neck. I turned and shouted, "Back to the ship" — but Gyvens, Creeson and Tek were well ahead of me. *Cowards!* I hurried after, hoping they had the presence of mind to alert Clantalion.

I entered the jungle running, praying no vine or root would trip me up. I didn't dare look back, though a quick glance at the child saw her peering beyond my shoulder, head tilted high. I increased my speed, heard the sharp crack of limbs snapping. It wailed, and I stumbled, barely kept my footing. For a moment I thought of self-preservation, of dropping the girl and leaving her to her fate. But I couldn't. She looked like my daughter. I just couldn't. I ran.

I reached the beach. Panting heavily, I cut right and bolted for the camp. With relief I saw Sergeant Clantalion leading his men and the sailors toward me. The sergeant motioned violently to his right. Motioned violently again. I darted to my left. A fleshy tentacle slammed the shore, missing me by inches. I stumbled into the water, its sudden drag throwing me off balance. Two awkward steps and I slipped and fell on a carpet of pebbles. Try as I might, I couldn't twist my body to protect the girl. She hit hard, me on top.

Quickly I rolled on my back and heaved her over so she wouldn't drown. She was limp, unconscious from the impact. That last effort had done it. I sagged. I had nothing left. I covered her in a feeble attempt to protect us from our final moments of horror and closed my eyes.

Nothing happened. Footsteps pounded past. Voices shouted. I heard the wet sound of metal piercing flesh, heard the swish of slashing limbs. The creature wailed; a high pitched tone. *Was that agony?* I opened my eyes.

Sergeant Clantalion stood before me, facing the beast, halberd in hand. Gyvens anchored one side and Creeson held the other. Before them was a ring of ten pikemen. Together they held guard as the sailors and balance of our men surrounded the thing and hacked it with every weapon at their disposal.

It fought desperately, its mangled tentacles knocking men aside, snatching them in a constrictive embrace, or crushing their screaming bodies under thick, sinuous legs.

The sand became thick with blood as blades and pikes opened deep wounds and carved out chunks of flesh. Gradually its furious attack weakened before slowly, ponderously, it collapsed. The fleshy torso struck the water with a resounding splash, submerging the thing from mottled trunk to bony carapace. Its snake-like legs writhed violently, carving deep grooves across the sand until they convulsed, twitched and stopped. The men continued to hack at the still body.

"Put up your weapons." Sergeant Clantalion had seen enough. He glared at the sailors who ignored him. "I said put up your weapons. Now."

Slowly the sailors backed away. Instinctively they gathered into a knot separate from our men. I couldn't help but notice the dark glances passed my way.

Grounding his halberd, Clantalion offered me his hand. I took his wrist and let him pull me to my feet. My legs were rubber and my breathing ragged. I mumbled thanks. It was all I could muster. The sergeant pointedly ignored my condition and looked at the girl. She was still fast in my grip.

I stepped from the water to the narrow beach and knelt, gently releasing her. A quick inspection revealed a nasty bump on her forehead. I cleared a strand of hair from her face. Her eyes fluttered open and slowly she sat, facing the creature. I watched for any sign of reaction. Nothing. Her look remained vacant. Sighing, I saw Gyvens and shook my head. *Perhaps a magic-user would be her best hope. They would have insight into a condition like hers.* Touching her shoulder, I said, "I have a daughter near your age, you know. Would you like to meet her?"

Gyvens gave me a strange look. "You are not really thinking of taking her home, are you? What would Helyna say?"

"A lot at first, no doubt." I helped the child to her feet. "What can I say? I've grown attached to her talkative ways."

"Well don't grow too attached, dad," Creeson snarled. "We may have a problem."

The crowd of sailors approached, each brandishing a bloody weapon. From their surly looks their intent was far from peaceful.

My hand drifted to the hilt of my blade. I was really growing tired of this. Clantalion grunted and stepped before the sailors, halberd propped lazily against his shoulder. "Well?"

Good old Sarge. Straight to the point.

A sailor stepped forward, chest outthrust, no doubt full of piss and bravado after the kill. "The girl. She's bad luck. Been nuthin' but bad luck since we found her. Wrecked the first ship, almost wrecked ours. Brought the thing that killed many of our mates." He jerked a thick thumb at the creature, its carcass already attracting an army of squawking scavenger birds. The sailor swept his hand toward the bodies strewn on the ground. "And yours too. She's bad luck I say. The gods are angry. She must die." The crew mumbled agreement.

"That so?" Sergeant Clantalion snapped his fingers. The air filled with the metallic rasp of drawn steel. His voice became gravel, a tone we knew well from past experience. "Superstitious crap. Lay down your weapons and return to the ship. Continue this nonsense and you'll feed the crabs. Every last one of you."

I stood and strode over to stand with Clantalion, drawing my blade. I pointed it at the spokesman. "And you will be first."

The sailor glanced back at his companions. They indicated no willingness to stand down. Apparently superstition clouded judgment. He ignored my blade and sneered. "The brat's keeper. Perhaps you should join her."

"Perhaps," I said. A swift lunge and my blade pierced his heart. I stood back as the man's eyes widened before he collapsed. "But not today." I held my blade out again, feeling no remorse. The child was mine to protect. "Next?"

Captain Amery rushed up, shouting at his men to put up their weapons. It was hard to tell from his dark eyes and impassive face if he had been part of the insurrection. If he was, he now knew it would end badly. Briefly he appraised the dead sailor before taking the sergeant aside. They conversed quietly for several moments before Amery approached his men. "Back to the ship and back to work. Now."

Slowly the crew obeyed, grumbling and cursing. No few cast dark looks toward the girl and me. I was surprised to find her looking back. *Did she understand what had happened, after all?*

Captain Amery swung on Clantalion. If there was any anger or resentment, he hid it well. In an eager voice he asked, "So, what's this I hear about treasure?"

The sun had set shortly after the events on the beach. Exhausted, I fell asleep beside a smoldering fire, waking at dawn to find the child by my side, sitting in her familiar pose, knees to chin. I ventured some small talk to see if anything had changed. It hadn't.

Gyvens sat on my other side; pike in hand, head down in repose, gently snoring. He had covered my turn at guard duty, protecting the girl and myself from the vindictive crew. I guess I owed him.

As for the crew, they had worked into the evening and through the night, and by early morning *Fat Lyla* was ready to sail. At first I had put their motivation down to fear, but subsequently discovered Amery had used the rumor of riches as bait. Their reward for a job well done was a treasure hunt.

Leaving Gyvens to sleep, I searched out Sergeant Clantalion to tell him I wasn't sure if these riches existed. The idea had derived from an innocent assumption made by Creeson. The good sergeant shrugged, suggesting the diversion would keep the crew's mind off of thoughts of retaliation. I couldn't fault his logic.

When we exited the jungle later in the morning we found the sailors scrambling over the ruins like ants on a honey cake. Those of our men caught up in the gossip of treasure watched with jealously. Sarge had prohibited them from hunting. They grumbled, but discipline won through. Even so, I was certain Clantalion would demand a share of any spoils as payment for protection provided from potential danger, even if that potential danger was a pink carcass lying on the beach. So we waited, passing caustic comments as we watched the sailors slip along the slick moss, or tumble from sagging vines as they struggled to reach inaccessible terraces and dark, recessed apartments.

Morning dragged.

At the edge of the road I found a piece of worn stone useable as a seat. Growing hungry, I rooted through my sack for two strips of salted meat and offered one to the child.

She sat in her usual position. I suppose, in her skewed mental state, she understood I was her protector. It was flattering in a way, though I would have preferred words of thanks in lieu of endless staring. As expected, my offer went unnoticed. I passed the food off to Gyvens.

A faint, piercing shout caught my attention mid-bite. It had come from deep within the city ruins.

Gyvens sighed. He had really wanted to hunt for treasure, wanted to find some shiny bauble for his girl back home. I'd seen his girl back home. An oat bag would have sufficed. "Must have found something," he mumbled. "Lucky bastards."

The shout became a series of calls, each one closer as the sailors responded with concern. A final query echoed into silence, and then someone screamed. It was high pitched and wild. The follow-up scream ended abruptly.

We didn't need Sergeant Clantalion to get us on our feet, reaching for our weapons.

He was there anyway. "Form a line. Pikes in front. Swords to the rear. Quickly now."

I still had my sword, so I placed myself on the right flank of the third line, nearest the child. She worried me. She had reacted when the first screams sounded from deep within the ruins, her head turning sharply in that direction.

Clantalion quickly walked the breadth of the front line, his eyes dark, his face grim. He stopped beside me. His voice was a harsh whisper. I detected a touch of apprehension. "Twenty-eight men, Mortlock. Twenty pikes and eight swords. I have no idea what's happening in there. Do you?"

I was surprised he actually took the time for my opinion. I shrugged, which probably meant he'd never ask again. I took a stab anyway. "Maybe that thing on the beach has a brother."

He looked at me, his lips a thin line. "My thought exactly."

Those sailors nearest the edge of the city resumed calling out to those shipmates who had ventured deep into the ruins. Names echoed back and forth in response. Some names were repeated, but only to silence.

Then we heard the wail. It was ear-shattering, a deep bass that shook the ground and caused my bones to vibrate. The sound died off. I exchanged looks with Clantalion and mumbled, "I don't like this."

A building exploded in the far distance, a loud, sharp crack that sent a cloud of dust and debris high into the cloudless sky. It had been one of the larger ruins, perhaps a palace, or a temple to some forgotten god. I watched the

~ Yaggoth-Voor ~

fragments soar through the air, and felt my belly tighten as they grew in size. I glanced at the girl, standing by the stone seat. I motioned for her to get down. A wasted gesture. She wasn't looking.

A piece of column struck not fifty paces from our line, its impact erupting into a smaller shower of dust and debris. That was the start. Larger pieces of marble and stone crashed into the ruins, smashing old brick walls and collapsing decayed buildings. Some impacted on the road, splintering the ancient granite blocks. Yet more toppled trees in the surrounding jungle — a veritable rain of death.

I watched a sailor crushed to pulp by a massive block, the force of impact burying half its size into the earth. Two of our pikemen had their heads split like over-ripe fruit by smaller fragments. A jagged piece crashed scant feet behind me, the explosion of particles bouncing off the armor on my back. I glanced at the girl. She was unharmed.

The deadly rain subsided and the two dead were pulled aside. We resumed our places in line, wondering aloud at the cause of the explosion. We didn't have to wonder long.

The ground shook as the wail sounded again. There was a smaller explosion in the distance. *A building collapsing?* It was followed by a deep rumble, and then another explosion.

Then I saw it, and knew we were dead.

The thing rose slowly from within the far reaches of the ancient city, like it had crawled from some deep pit. It was massive, godlike, dwarfing the tallest spire.

I looked to Sergeant Clantalion. "That's no brother." I'm not sure he heard me. My mouth felt like dry parchment.

His face was pale, and for the first time I saw a hint of fear. "The other was a child compared to this."

"It's coming," Gyvens squeaked.

He was right. The fleshy, snake-like legs slowly undulated, carrying it through the ancient city, collapsing buildings with the ease of a child destroying sand forts. The sinuous arms swept the ground, smashing buildings and toppling towers. And as it neared the outskirts I saw a red smear coating each of the diamond-shaped clubs that were its hands.

With a chill I realized it was not some aimless creature. It was intelligent, it was furious, and it sought revenge. It searched out the crewmen, crushing them beneath the weight of its immense legs, or picking them from buildings and squeezing their screaming bodies to pulp.

Creeson stood in line directly before me, his pike wobbling in shaky hands. He dropped the weapon and spun to face me, his eyes wild. "We can't fight that." His look shifted to Clantalion. "Sarge, we can't fight it!" He bolted, starting a flood that included more than half the men.

Clantalion watched helplessly. "Nothing we can do here, Mortlock. We'll hide in the jungle until it returns to whatever pit it crawled from."

243

He didn't have to tell me twice. I sheathed my sword and rushed to the girl. Not surprisingly she ignored me, her blank eyes fixed on the behemoth. I scooped her unceremoniously into my arms and ran as fast as I could.

Twice now. This is becoming habit.

The thing wailed. The ground shook.

The girl was not light, and though the path from ruins to beach was short, my lungs were soon on fire. I paused a moment, sucking in deep breaths of air, each stabbing me like a hot poker.

From behind came the sound of splintering wood, the sharp crack of thick trunks split like so much kindling. The sun disappeared and I fell into shadow. The hairs on my neck stood. I looked back, and up.

The thing loomed over me, rocking ponderously on its snake-like legs. I am an ant to a giant, an insignificant piece of dirt. If only it were true.

It saw me.

Slowly the torso bent, and the gigantic carapace topping its sinuous shoulders came near. As it did, encroaching light revealed the darkness held deep within the protective casing.

I saw, and shivered. Nestled within the bone carapace was a human head. No larger than mine, the skin was smooth and hairless. The eyes were cold, black orbs, the mouth a circular pit of razor-sharp teeth that resembled the sucker of an octopus' tentacle. A tongue slithered from that mouth, a tubular slug-like thing.

I whimpered, and shielded the girl.

But it ignored us. Instead, the foul head turned, and the gigantic body shifted to inspect the smaller version of itself on the beach. One enormous tendril descended to touch the carcass. It nudged it, pushed it, flipped it over, and reared back and wailed — an inhuman cry of anguish.

The raw force of the sound staggered me. Desperately I turned to flee, but as luck would have it, the girl picked this moment to show life. She struggled, pushing against my grip. I shouted at her to calm down. She didn't, so I clutched her tighter and ran.

I almost reached the ship, making more distance than I ever expected. It was a small, wasted comfort. To the side I spotted Gyvens crouched near the jungle's edge, waving furiously. He looked up, his face draining of color, and faded into the dense foliage.

A giant tentacle struck the ground mere feet before me. The resounding thump blasted a shower of sand high into the air, raining hard over our bodies.

Trapped.

Resigned to my fate, I turned to face it. The carapace with its hideously human head approached, the dead eyes locked on mine, its round, sucker-like mouth with the razor teeth and slug-like tongue working silently.

Somewhere inside me I found a spark of anger, and I fumbled with my sword. I prayed for at least one strike before death.

The girl chose that moment to push out of my grip and step away. Weakly

~ Yaggoth-Voor ~

I reached out in a vain attempt to put her behind me, but she eluded my grasp. I looked at her, confused. *What was she thinking?*

The thing paused to watch, and if I had my wits I would have said it did so with curiosity. But my wits deserted me, my confusion became anger, and I screamed, "All right! Let's have at it!"

The child ignored my outburst and faced the creature. And then faced me. A finger went to her lips and she shook her head. And she did something totally unexpected. She smiled.

Slowly her body transformed. It was subtle at first. The fingers fused and the hands flattened, the toes melted into her feet and merged with her legs. She grew in stature, splitting the oversized shirt she had worn since her rescue. The limbs lost their skeletal structure, becoming smooth and boneless. A carapace emerged from the sloping shoulders, curving into a protective semi-circle. The mouth distorted into an oval and her teeth sharpened into dagger-like points. The change ended when she reached the size of the creature lying dead on the beach. Even so, she was dwarfed by the parent behind her.

A tendril reached for my head. I closed my eyes. I understood now we were responsible for the death of her kind, and revenge was her right. I would not attack her. The appendage touched my shoulder, surprisingly gentle. It moved from my shoulder to caress my cheek. I dared open my eyes and met hers. They sparkled with life.

She turned to her parent, her tentacles uncoiling to slip around a gigantic arm. The parent rose to its full, colossal height and swung about to slither along the shoreline. It paused to retrieve the body before entering the jungle.

I let out my breath and sat for long moments. Distantly I heard the rustle of undergrowth and the sound of men as they cautiously approached.

Gyvens was first by my side. "What just happened?"

I shrugged. What could I say? The child who resembled my daughter was a monster, and for some reason had assumed her form to use me?

Sergeant Clantalion knelt and offered a skin of water. "I don't know what gods you pray to, son, but I think we owe them."

I took the skin and swallowed deep, and as I had no desire to discuss what just happened, asked, "How many survived?"

"Too few. Thirteen. All soldiers. No sailors I know of."

"Thirteen? No sailors? Funny that. Sailors wanted the child dead."

"That so. Lucky for us you protected her, then. I guess she felt she owed you."

"Some protector." I looked at the turquoise sea and shook my head. "Some child."

Gyvens mumbled, "Yaggoth-Voor."

"What?"

"Yaggoth-Voor. The first mate told me the story, the one you didn't have time for. It goes that Yaggoth-Voor was one of the first gods. He had two children. Kag-Zoroth and Zog-Arak. A boy and girl, or girl and boy. Can't remember which was which."

"Does it matter?" Clantalion asked.

"I suppose not. The story went they took turns posing as stranded children, luring ships to shore. Once lured, the other attacked. Their idea of playtime, I guess."

"Something must have gone wrong, then." Creeson had joined us while Gyvens spoke. "She was very much human on the wreck."

Gyvens shrugged. "Maybe she, it, was knocked unconscious before changing."

I thought on it. She could change form; could she read my thoughts as well? Had she somehow plucked my daughter's image from my mind? I suppose I'll never know. I said, "Her transformation was slow. She would have been vulnerable, and she was never out of my sight. Yeah, she may have been injured."

Creeson grinned. "So they were gods, were they? And we killed one. The ladies back home will love that!"

Sergeant Clantalion grunted and stood. "Gods or not, we have a bigger problem."

"What's that," I asked.

"Can anyone sail?"

Jason E. Thummel and family live in a log cabin in the woodlands of southern Indiana. When not working, tending to a slew of domesticated animals, and spending time with his wife and son, he valiantly struggles to preserve his homestead against the ravages of the elements and to keep the feral woodland creatures at bay. Some of his other stories either appear or are forthcoming in Black Gate, The Town Drunk, Flashing Swords, The Lorelei Signal, *the anthologies* Magic and Mechanica, The Infinity Swords, *and a yet-to-be-named Norse-themed anthology forthcoming from Morrigan Books. Revenge is best delivered in a hot passion…after being coldly determined. Yet it is costly in its delivery, to self as much as foe. Perhaps more so. Unless…unless there is something to redeem; someone to save our hero.*

Runner of the Hidden Ways

A Tale of the Jungles

by Jason E. Thummel

Silence. Not even the fall of a single dew drop disturbed the ominous slumber. Thick vines twined their way from out of the choking undergrowth to quietly stalk and strangle the tall, sinuous trees whose canopy blanketed the sky and cast the world below into a constant, green-hued twilight. And through that deep quiet came a whisper, like a gentle caress of wind winding its way down unseen trails in the growth.

Ikuru felt power surge through him, coursing beneath his skin, lending strength to muscle, sinew and bone as the jaguar tattoo transformed him into something other than himself. His blood pounded with the power of the Runner, and the jungle's unnatural stillness spoke to him of horror. He plunged farther ahead into that absence of sound, of life, following its tale toward the acrid scent of fire and death that clung to the stagnant air; ever away from his painful past and deeper into lands unknown.

He soon found this story's sad beginning. The huts were smoldering skeletons, cradles of soot and ash that still embraced the bodies of the villagers who had once lived here. The terrifying scene reminded Ikuru of his own village, a season ago, when the skinless men and their cruel priests had brought the road of death to scar the Mother jungle.

They had spoken to the king with lies of undreamt wealth, had exchanged gifts and accepted hospitality. Then came the great treachery, and in the course of one night their superior numbers overwhelmed and massacred all of the soldiers and any who they thought might offer resistance. Even the totemic powers of the King's personal guard, the most powerfully tattooed and feared of all the warriors, fell in the tide of slaughter. In one night the kingdom, and a people, ceased to be.

The deceivers then chained the survivors to strange machines and marched them toward the distant holy mountain of the Feet of the Old God. Always down the ever-growing road toward the mountain, but never back. And those who could not keep the pace, those too old, or too young…

Ikuru cursed the skinless men. It was not enough to capture and enslave. Their appetite for brutality and destruction grew with every passing day until now they no longer took prisoners for their labor or lust, but destroyed villages whole, sparing no one.

He did not know the dead's burial customs — the familiar lands and people of Ikuru's memory lay weeks behind him — but he would not leave them unsung. So using his own funerary rites, he rubbed soot upon his bare arms, legs and chest, and sang them to their place in the Dream. Tears flowed, eroding the grime on his face and dripping unashamedly to the earth as new sorrows were woven into old. *From the Mother, to the Mother, so must all be.*

Soon it would be the skinless that soaked the Mother with their blood and fed the soil with their flesh, and they would have no song. He would see to it.

Ikuru concluded the dirge and wiped his eyes. He would not take the sorrow with him, only the memory of their suffering and the rage it provoked. The water he had shed would be left with the village to soak into the soil, seeds of mourning to honor and comfort the dead along their way.

Ikuru called the power. The shaman's tattoo crawled beneath his skin as it stirred. He relaxed his eyes and a path opened before him, yielding to his training and the magic inked into his flesh. Although he no longer ferried the messages of his King from village to village, he was once again as he had been, a Runner of the Hidden Ways.

But there were no more proclamations. No more royal decrees. Like his pride and his joy of life, his purpose had been destroyed when the kingdom fell, when his village and his family had been murdered; to be replaced by a cold, dark, emptiness. Now he brought only the swift message of death to the skinless men, gliding along their ever-growing road like a viper.

He gazed down along the trail of the opened Way and felt the muscles of his legs ripple and coil—

The familiar, fetid stench of a waluti chilled him and he paused, listening. They were the solitary scouts and butchers of the skinless, and though they came from the priest's homeland and were not native to the jungle, they moved stealthily and easily through its growth.

Bred and beaten to obedience, they were beasts of war, good for tracking, killing and nothing else. Their capacity for violence was honed to such a singularity of purpose that a chance encounter between two, in the absence of their master priests, would quickly become a fight to the death. As a consequence they were few, and widely dispersed. It was no coincidence to find one here. It was likely the very one that had destroyed the village, returning for some unknown reason.

Or had it smelled him?

Regardless, if it roamed the jungle the priests would have dressed the beast for war and slaughter and that would keep it from moving silently or climbing and attacking from the trees.

Ikuru slipped his blowgun free from the belt that was his only garment and loaded a poisoned dart. It would kill a man easily. But the waluti, gorilla-like but much larger, stronger, with a high conical forehead and boarish eyes, was not a man. He had seen a waluti hit with several darts go about its gruesome and brutal business, seemingly unfazed.

Ikuru eased back toward the lush growth at the village's perimeter, quietly slipped his hatchet free, and carefully squatted into the cover of a large fern bed. He heard a distant rustle of disturbed leaves and the gentle friction of fronds rubbing. A deep sniff and low grunt sounded, their origin quickly swallowed by the dense vegetation. And then all was deathly silent.

Ikuru inhaled and raised the blowgun to his lips.

The jungle exploded. Undergrowth bent and broke in a deafening chorus as the waluti surged from the other side of the clearing and charged directly at Ikuru.

His dart struck the beast in its unprotected neck but it did not break stride, its huge, armored arms tearing up turf as it loped on calloused knuckles across the ruined village, heedless of smoldering embers and searing ash. Cruel crimson eyes glared with an almost human intelligence, an intellect that had been warped to serve the sadistic whims of its priestly masters. He knew then that he could not defeat it and turned to follow his path through the Mother. She would guide him, and he would outrun and lose the waluti.

The Mother opened her secret ways to him. The path pulled faster and faster and the fatigue he felt drained from him. The sounds of clumsy pursuit were already beginning to fade. *Who could catch the jaguar that knew the secret ways?* And that was when Ikuru saw the little girl.

She was naked and filthy, caked in mud and sweat and the smell of the skinless men. Her wrists were raw where bindings had held her, and her right ankle was swollen where rope had rubbed through the skin to let the infection in. Her eyes were fevered and distant, but they opened in panic as he ran toward her. She turned to run and fell as her bad leg collapsed beneath her tiny frame.

"Girl, what are you doing?" Ikuru whispered, kneeling beside her.

"Home," she said and pointed back toward the village. "Please, just let me go home."

The warning calls of terrified birds shattered the stillness as the waluti closed the distance. Ikuru could not carry her and run as the jaguar both — but to leave the girl meant her certain death.

"I will run as a man, then," he said. Replacing his hatchet and blowgun, he scooped her into his arms. And ran.

Lungs and legs trembled and burned. Roots and groundcover tangled his feet and threatened to trip him. The girl's unaccustomed weight slowed each faltering step while thorn and vine dragged painfully against his skin, holding him back. Monkeys and birds called from above, seeming to mock his feeble efforts. Ikuru's face was a mask of agony as he stumbled into the frigid flow of a small stream and placed the girl on the far side. And all the while the waluti gained.

He could not outrun it. A waluti could run this pace all day and Ikuru was tired. His body had been pushed beyond its limits, beyond even its ability to survive calling the jaguar now. Not that he would run. No, the only thing he could do would be to try to stop it.

Perhaps, if the girl had been in better health, she could have run while he fought; could possibly have put enough distance between herself and the beast to improve her chances. He watched her limp into the cover of the fragrant flowers and ferns that grew on the stream's edge and knew otherwise. *No. There will be no more running.*

How many skinless have I killed since the kingdom fell, twenty, thirty? Individual men on sentry duty or relieving themselves in the night; small groups traveling together up the hated road. He could never kill enough of them. But here, at last, was his chance to make a difference.

Ikuru readied his blowgun and hatchet and thought again of his own village and family. It seemed so long ago. If only he had been there when the priests had spread their lies, shackled the able-bodied, and loosed the waluti on those that remained. If only his duty had not taken him so far away. At least then he would have been with his kin, would be with them now in the Dream.

He breathed deeply of the humid air and let the thoughts fade as mist from his mind, let the fatigue and weight of his inner emptiness fade, back to the Mother. Instead he conjured the faces of the burned and the dead; the cruel smiles of the skinless men and the evil priests as they laughed and beat their captives; the ravening road as it ate its way through the Mother toward the distant holy mountain. Each image became a beacon of vibrant and consuming anger, smoldering and building until it grew to an uncontrollable crimson rage, calling Ikuru to unleash his wrath.

Let the beast come! The girl will live, the waluti will die.

It was not long in coming.

The great beast tore from cover on its elongated arms. Ferociously ripping and shredding plants, it stomped and pounded its massive fists against its armored chest in a terrifying display. The wide, thin-lipped mouth split with a feral scream, showering Ikuru with the warmth of the waluti's foul spittle and showing its grotesque, ornamentally gilded fangs.

Ikuru shot the poison dart from his blowgun and quickly discarded the weapon. He would not have a chance to use it again.

The beast paused and plucked the dart from its neck, casting the tiny nuisance aside, then let loose another tremendous roar. Ikuru screamed back his own blood-curdling challenge and felt surprise as the jaguar's power stirred within.

The waluti's arm lashed out like a whip. Ikuru launched himself away and his side caught fire as one of the sharpened metal blades that adorned the beast's thumbs gently slid along his ribs. But the pain was forgotten in a euphoric surge of adrenaline as the power grew, and with each passing moment his movements became increasingly faster while the movements of the waluti turned awkward and slow.

He rolled under another heavy blow and the backswing of his hatchet found the back of one of the beast's short legs, cutting sinew and muscle. The waluti staggered but kept itself upright by using an arm to support the weight of that side. The cut leg dragged limp and useless beneath.

Ikuru pressed his advantage, dancing in and circling, forcing the lumbering beast to continuously turn toward the injured side, even as his hatchet flicked quickly and repeatedly like a serpent's tongue. They were small cuts but they bled, and they were many; the waluti weakened.

Beneath its armor, the waluti's massive chest heaved in labored breath. The arm supporting the useless leg shook and faltered. Ikuru jumped in and leapt upon the beast's back, grabbing hold of its armored collar to pull himself up and astride the monster. And then his hatchet rose and fell, raining a barrage of savage blows against its neck even as it crumpled to the trampled ground beneath it.

Ikuru staggered from the dying beast and collapsed near the stream. He rolled to his back, closed his eyes, and listened to the voice of his Mother. Tree frogs started to sing and birds to call each other through the veil of leaves and vines.

Is this my song, then? Will this sing me to my own place in the Dream?

Cool water caressed his feverish lips and slid into his mouth. Ikuru swallowed and coughed. He opened his eyes. The girl knelt beside him, and her cupped hands held more water which he gratefully accepted. The distant thrashing of the beast had stilled.

"You should go," Ikuru said. "Get far from here before the skinless men come."

"We must save the god," the girl said.

"What?" Her accent was strange but the language was understandable.

"The road is there," she pointed downstream. "Not far. We must go to the holy mountain and save Chumatembe, the New God."

The road? Surely the holy mountain she spoke of was the Feet of the Old God. They had run much farther than he had thought; much farther and closer to the mountain than he had ever been.

Ikuru propped himself on an elbow to rise but a wave of vertigo sent him crashing back to the earth. He was still bleeding and soon would lose too much blood to do anything but die.

"New God?" he asked.

"Yes. Chumatembe, born of the Old God, who came from the fiery cave in the side of the mountain. Chumatembe, who spoke to the Elder and gave him power and knowledge to lead our people."

"I still don't understand," Ikuru said.

The girl rolled her eyes at him and sighed in exasperation. It reminded him of his sister, when they had played as children, and the fondness of her memory gave him strength.

"Warrior ants," Ikuru said. "I need warrior ants. You know them? Good. Bring me twenty or so, alive, wrapped in a leaf to protect you. Bring them quick if you can find them, and then we will go to save the god."

"But they pinch. They are dangerous."

"I know," he tried to smile through waves of nausea. "So be careful."

Whether he passed in and out of consciousness or simply rested he did not know; it seemed only moments before the girl returned with what he had asked. Carefully he reached into the leaf pouch and plucked out an ant, its violently twisting body the size of his thumb. Ikuru pinched his cut together and pressed the ant hard against it. The mandibles closed as the aggressive ant bit through the flaps of flesh, pinning them together, and Ikuru used his nails to pinch off the ant's head so that the jaws would remain closed. Ant by ant he slowly stitched his wound.

The stench of the camp, with its filth and cruelty, filled the surrounding jungle with despair. Carefully concealed, Ikuru watched from a safe distance as the skinless men drove both villagers and their own kind alike with the rhythmic lash of their hungry whips, down into caves they had made in the mountain. To what purpose, Ikuru did not know. But slaves brought sleds of rock from out of the holy mountain, and the priests were excited by what they saw.

The Old God seemed content with the ravages of their picks and shovels and did not stir. There would be no help there. It did not surprise Ikuru, for the god had given up caring for the Mother and her people long ago, and though he had rumbled in anger from time to time, he had not moved since their ancient parting.

Ikuru found his eyes drawn again to the prisoner he had promised to save: Chumatembe, the New God of the girl's people. He had neither seen nor heard of such a formidable beast. Its body was that of an elephant, only three times the size, and the thick hide was armored with heavy scales of mottled green and brown that mimicked the jungle beyond. On each side of its shortened trunk, deadly yellowed tusks curved skyward to end in sharp, killing, tips. Its eyes burned with intelligence and hatred.

A true god or not, how they could possibly have captured so strong and fearsome a creature, he couldn't say. But now chains kept its head immovable, attached to a series of leg-irons that limited its pace to a mere crawl as it pulled a heavy-timbered wagon filled with mined stone. Sitting high on its back, jabbing a sharpened stick into its neck, sat the priest who the girl, Ashti, had said held the key to those chains. The New God could not run. It could not fight.

"But soon you will," promised Ikuru, slipping deeper into the jungle to await the night.

It was moonless. Large bats sliced through the dark overhead, attracted by insects and the guttering fires in the clearing below. Curious creatures kept to the jungle but crept to the edges of the flickering light, watching through large, black, nocturnal eyes. Ikuru squatted among them.

Ashti and he had moved frequently throughout the day to avoid detection. Ikuru had hoped to discover lamoto bark or barida root during their travels. Either would ease her pain and fever, but he had found none and by evening her fever had worsened. She needed a healer. But whenever he told her this, she demanded that he free the god as he had promised. So he found as safe a place as he could, told Ashti that he would return, and left her. If he was not back by morning, she was to leave immediately, though she would have to make her own way.

Ikuru was worried. It had been a long time since he had been worried, and other confusing emotions he'd thought long forgotten swam in its wake. He thought about his family and his regrets at having been away from them for such long periods. He had always thought that there would be time — later. His duty to his king and the lure of the jaguar — of its raw power, of the Hidden Ways — had always called him away. Now there was no time. Those chances were gone.

He angrily jerked his thoughts away from the past. *Focus. What is the point of this pity and blame? It is nothing but distraction, and it will get both of us killed.* He stoked his anger and built it, putting all the other memories and emotions out of his mind. He would have need of that rage soon enough.

Ikuru's dark skin and hair would make him difficult to pluck from the shadows for all but the most keen-eyed sentry, but he had still covered himself with mud to better mask his scent and the glistening sheen of sweat on his skin. He had seen no waluti near the camp, but he could not chance one, unseen, catching his smell. It was apparent from the relaxed manner of the sentry before him, however, that so far he was undetected.

Ikuru sprang upon the man, clamped a strong hand over his mouth and wrenched back hard. The blade of his hatchet cut deeply into the man's neck, and Ikuru held him tightly until the guard ceased to struggle and became limp. He eased the body down into shadow, removed the man's two leaf-bladed daggers, and tucked them into his belt. He would have to be quick, now, before the body was discovered.

The hut of the priest that held the key to the New God's freedom was near. With any luck, he would be asleep; an easy kill. Once he had the key, it was twenty paces past the hut to where the god was chained between two large trees. Before the last of the light had faded, Ikuru had noted that there were no sentries posted near the creature. Clearly they feared to be any nearer to it than they had to be.

There was a chorus of loud shouts from the other end of camp, an excited babbling in a language Ikuru could not understand. He threw himself beneath a small wagon. His eyes scanned his surroundings frantically, searching the twisting shadows, looking for the first threat. But he had not been discovered, as he had feared. Instead, in the dimly lit distance, he saw a knot of skinless men shoving someone before it. Ashti.

Oh Great Mother, what I have done? I should never have left her. How could I have left her?

Fear and doubt crept into his mind. He felt a sudden sickness in his stomach and fought the urge to vomit. He did not need to speak their language to understand what they intended.

This cannot happen. I will not let it.

The hut flap was thrown back and the pale, bloated priest stepped out, hastily tying a robe about his nakedness. He held a bared blade in his hand, as if fearing treachery, but when he saw the girl pushed to the ground, the priest smiled and relaxed his guard. The key dangled about his neck on a leather thong. Ikuru pounced.

The priest heard the charge and turned. Faster than he looked, he managed to deflect Ikuru's hatchet with his blade. Ikuru rolled under the powerful swipe of the priest's counter-attack, but the blade caught his hatchet and pulled it from his grip. In the distance the skinless men looked momentarily confused, the girl at their feet all but forgotten.

Good, Ikuru thought. But soon they would get over their shock, and by then he had best have the key in hand. He pulled the daggers and circled.

The priest swung again and Ikuru caught the downward blow between crossed knives, the impact numbing his arms. His foot lashed out and kicked hard into the priest's rotund stomach and the man staggered back, off balance. Ikuru dove forward and opened the priest's belly. The other knife slashed indiscriminately at the man's throat, cutting flesh and thong. Ikuru grasped the key and pulled it free from the fountaining gore.

Sounds of trampling feet approached and Ikuru regained his hatchet and hurled it into the oncoming rush of men. There was a scream as it struck and a moment of confused shuffling as the men fought each other to get away from the next deadly throw. It would be only moments before they realized there would not be another. He turned his back to them and ran to Chumatembe.

Unknown power flared through Ikuru, nearly overwhelming him in its ferocity. He staggered beneath the sudden onslaught. Reserves of power he had never sought — never known — drove through his mounting exhaustion, searing a path along the mystic patterns inked upon his flesh. Unrelenting waves of energy hammered him at every step, burning in intensity, fueled by supernatural power only a god could possess. *A god?* Ikuru persisted against the pain, against the ravening fire coursing through his tattoo — and stood beside the chained deity.

The well-oiled locks turned easily, and the chains slackened and fell away. One massive, obsidian eye turned to regard Ikuru as Chumatembe held him in its wild, horrifying gaze. Power recognized power — and Ikuru saw within the infinite, black depths a terrifying vengeance and madness. He quickly looked away lest the untamed consumed the tamed.

Ikuru saw Ashti in the distance. She had pulled herself from the ground and knelt, looking weak and confused. Her hand reached out to him as she saw him, and he ran toward her. A guard brandishing a club did so as well.

Ikuru's sprint became a dive and his shoulder slammed into the man. The impact drove them both to the ground in a tangle of limbs and flesh. For a moment it appeared that they lay frozen and unmoving as each infinitesimal gain was contested with hard, unrelenting muscle. Both knew there could be only one outcome, and its finality drove them to their limits. But the guard could not match the strength of the empowered Runner, and Ikuru broke the hold.

The guard punched heavily into Ikuru's side. An explosion of pain ripped through his body and warm blood seeped from his wound. With his free hand, Ikuru speared his thumb into the other's eye; the force of his blow knocked the screaming guard back and drove him to the hard-packed earth.

Ikuru quickly rolled beside the man, trapping a flailing arm beneath his body, and delivered several crushing blows on the guard's exposed throat with his elbow. In that instant it was over.

Behind, Chumatembe turned to face the camp and trumpeted a deafening call. The surrounding jungle answered, erupting into animal cries of panic and alarm. The crashing of brush and leaves rippled outward from the epicenter as animals fled the danger.

The mammoth creature shook its awesome head, flailing the loose chains that dangled from it, and roared again, slamming aside wagons and huts, flinging skinless men caught in its path as a man might flick a fly. Its heavy tread shook the ground as it set about destroying everything in its path, and the screams of dying men marked its progress.

Ikuru saw slaves pouring out of the caves in the mountain like ants from a disturbed hill: some fled while others armed themselves with whatever was at hand. Those guards who had not already abandoned their posts were quickly overwhelmed by the mob's fury, either trampled beneath hundreds of calloused feet or cut down by a storm of splintered wood and sharpened steel. A chant sprang up, a single word repeated again and again throughout the churning morass of brutal, raging bloodlust; accompanying the screams and shouts, chaos and death; riding the fire spreading along the huts and painting the sky in savage red and orange: Chumatembe.

Some of the priests and skinless men had escaped into the darkness, into the jungle and down the road. A few might even survive. *It matters little.* Let the priests return to the holy mountain if they dared. The New God would be there to greet them with bloodied tusks, trampling feet, and death. Their tyranny had been broken, and as word spread through the jungle, others would rise up and find their strength. The jungle would be ready should the skinless men return.

Ikuru hefted the girl and disappeared through the chaos into the Mother. No one sought to intervene. Swift feet carried them ever deeper and faster, past the mountain and far from the raging inferno behind, toward unknown lands and unknown people. There would be villages where the stream met the river, and they would have medicine and healers. He would run for as long and as far as he had to, pay whatever price was asked, and he would spread the message of Chumatembe's triumph over evil. Ashti had given him a purpose beyond killing, vengeance and death. Ikuru was once again proud, a true Runner of the Hidden Ways, possessed of the power of the jaguar. He would not let her die.

Brian Ruckley was born and brought up in Edinburgh, Scotland, and now lives there once again after spending a decade or so in London. He caught the reading and writing bug at a very early age, and sold a couple of short stories to UK fiction magazines in the 1990s, but only started to take the idea of writing a novel seriously around the dawn of the 21st century. That first novel turned out to be a fantasy trilogy, with the overall title of 'The Godless World.' The first book — Winterbirth *— was published in 2006; the final title —* Fall of Thanes *— just this month. For lots more information on Brian and his work, check out his website at, www.brianruckley.com. As for this tale? Learn that, despite having all the potential in the world, being in the right place at the right time — or not — really can make all the difference. For when messing around where you are not wanted, know your enemy...or ensure that you have a bigger support group.*

Beyond the Reach of His Gods

A Tale of Rhuan the Exile

by Brian Ruckley
& cover art by Johnney Perkins

An unseen log boomed against *Wolfrun*'s hull. In the last few days, Rhuan of the Grey Hall had taken to posting a lookout on the prow, to ward against just such events. This great, fat monstrosity of a river seemed at times to carry almost as much debris as it did water. Some of that flotsam weighed enough to punch a hole clean through the planking: mighty timbers, even whole trees; once, a clump of them that drifted on the current, riding upright on their raft of sodden earth and entangled roots. Their uppermost, trembling branches had reached almost as high as the masthead, and a lizard as long as a man's arm perched amongst the boughs like the captain of that mad vessel. Such a sight would be unthinkable in Rhuan's cold homeland, but these foul and fetid territories held much that ought to have been impossible.

An arrow clattered against the barrel next to Rhuan and fell beside him. Here was the reason why no watchman could now ride the wolf-headed prow, and why Rhuan himself hunched behind the gunwale of his longship: arrows too feeble to punch through anything but the thinnest hide, yet capable of killing a man if they so much as scratched exposed skin. The savages who loosed them set some dark, tarry matter about the points, and it gave any wounds they delivered a vile potency. Rhuan had already watched two of his men die agonizing, fevered deaths. One, whose hand had been transfixed by such an arrow, had lived long enough to see his arm turning black, stinking of rot, drawing attentive hosts of the flies that infested these jungles. They had cut it off and cast it overboard, and sealed the stump with fire, but still he had died. It was a cruel end. Crueler still for coming in exile, in a place so sodden, so bloated with water, that no funeral pyre could be built to ease his soul's onward journey. A place beyond the reach of the gods of their homeland. Beyond the reach, surely, of any god save a mad one.

Rhuan ventured a brief glance over the shields hung in protective rank along the side of the ship. There was, as ever, nothing to see save the wall of riotous vegetation. Trees and bushes of every ilk choked the bank of the river. They trailed their garlands of vines into the brown water, built turrets and parapets from their festoons of dark, glossy leaves. And hid, amidst their horrible vigor, the enemy Rhuan sought. Another arrow came arcing out toward *Wolfrun*, struck its shielded flank and fell back into the turbid river.

Rhuan glared at the small, brown-skinned man crouched close by: their guide, though since he spoke no tongue save his own his guidance amounted to little more than nodding and gesturing. His name, as best Rhuan had been able to determine, was something like Ahenotoc. At this moment, he appeared entirely untroubled by either Rhuan's anger or the desultory volleys of arrows from which they sheltered. He smiled, his teeth bright. Rhuan growled in irritation.

"Faster!" he shouted down the length of the ship.

The oarsmen redoubled their efforts. They were bare-chested, every one, and their reddened, peeling backs shone with sweat as their muscles flexed. Not the beads or trickles of sweat that might adorn the brow of a farmer laboring in his field in a northern summer. No: so thick and sluggish was the air in this pestilential land, so oppressive the remorseless heat, that sweat came forth in torrents. Men wore it like a second skin.

Rhuan felt the ship respond to the increased beat of the oars. It surged on upstream, slicing through the opposing flow. Birds — as abundantly colored as the most garish of flowers — went squawking overhead. As their harsh voices faded, Rhuan realized that in their wake they left no sound save that of the grinding oars, and the gasping breaths of the men who worked them. No more arrows rattled against wood.

He straightened cautiously. Nothing. Just the faceless, formless jungle staring back at him. As before, the unseen savages had no desire for pursuit. They merely sought to kill those who happened to come within their reach. An idle kind of bloodlust drove them.

"What is he saying?" Rhuan muttered.

Garnok grimaced. "I am not sure, lord."

The priest frowned as he tried to follow Ahenotoc's fluid hand movements. "Possibly that we draw near to our destination?" he suggested doubtfully.

Ahenotoc grinned, pointing upriver, jabbing three fingers at Rhuan. Nodding with raised eyebrows. Rhuan leaned out over the gunwale and stared ahead. The broad river wound its bloated way into the distance, running between the endless green battlements of the jungle.

"I see nothing," he muttered. "You are no longer of any use to me as a priest, Garnok. If you could make sense of this man's…waving about, as you said you might, that would be at least some small compensation."

"Not by my choice did we journey beyond the bounds of the known world," said Garnok at once. "I spoke with the Gods on your behalf—brought forth favorable winds, and summoned birds to guide us—while we were still within earshot of their Stone Thrones. But there is no mortal voice could carry over such distances as we have traversed, and if there are other gods who inhabit these noxious climes, I know not the language in which to beseech their aid, nor the rituals to foster their goodwill. None of us does."

Rhuan made no reply to that. Though Garnok's argumentative manner was troubling, he was far from the only one becoming restive. Every one of these men had willingly followed Rhuan into exile after his father's execution, but he was not so foolish as to assume that their undoubted loyalty to him was the sole star by which they steered. Many had faced the same choice he had: exile or a hard death on the Blood Wheel. All had hoped that he would lead them to adventure, and glory, and plunder; discover for them fresh lands to raid, perhaps even rule.

Now, he knew, they began to doubt him. He had led them further than any of their people had ever gone. In half a year of relentless journeying, driven by angers and hungers he barely understood himself, he had surpassed the deeds of their greatest song-remembered heroes and outshone the most legendary of seafarers. Following the faintest of rumors — mere whispers of distant territories awash with gold — he had brought them to these unknown, undreamed of, shores. Where there was, as yet, little sign of gold. Fevers and sweat; sores and sunstroke. Swarms of blood-hungry insects, and a trackless wasteland of impenetrable jungle. Death, for some. But not gold. Not yet.

Ahenotoc gave an excited cry, and shook his outstretched hand.

Rhuan saw, as a long bend of the river slowly opened itself out ahead of them, a break in the monotonous, implacable jungle. A vast clearing spread back from the riverside. And there were, he could tell even at this distance, even as he blinked to clear the sweat that ran into his eyes, buildings there. His spirits soared at the sight. Perhaps now he could deliver to his followers the harvest their efforts deserved. Perhaps now he could claim for himself some of the riches and the glory he would need, if ever he was to return to the land of his birthplace and visit vengeance upon those who had slain his father and cast him out.

"All your strength!" he cried to the crew. "A few strokes more, and you can set aside those oars and take swords in your hands instead."

A ragged cheer, blunted by the exhaustion of those who raised it, met his words. The air here was so lethargic and heavy that there was seldom even a breath of wind; when it did stir itself it came with torrential rain and lightning that shook the sky. *Wolfrun*'s sail had slumbered, useless, for days; there had been no respite for the oarsmen.

"A crowd gathers," said Garnok.

There were indeed figures assembling along the riverside. They milled about, and though no sound carried down to the approaching ship, Rhuan thought he detected in their chaotic movement the signs of fear, perhaps even panic. All the better.

Those figures massed at the head of a shallow, shelving beach of sand. Several of the carved, hollowed-out logs these people used as boats were drawn up on it.

"Take us straight in," Rhuan called to Panur the helmsman. "Run up onto that strand."

Panur nodded firmly, his loose blond hair brushing at his shoulders. Rhuan stared out past the wolfish prow, counting. A hundred or more men and women were gathered there now, and he could see many others beyond them, running this way and that. He would have no more than thirty men at his back when he sprang ashore. It would be more than enough. Even as he watched, the crowd began to scatter. The people — most of them, at least — were slipping away into the surrounding forest.

Rhuan smiled. This was going to be even easier than he had imagined.

The first village they found, along the coast of this wild land, had been a disappointment: nothing more than a handful of rickety huts, clustered on the shore at one of the few points where the exuberant jungle did not overspill the land and merge itself with the sea in a forbidding tangle of looping stems and spines. They had driven the inhabitants off without difficulty, and torn most of the hovels apart in their determined search, but were rewarded with nothing of worth.

The second village, at the mouth of this very river, had appeared no more promising at first. Its inhabitants, though, had not fled. Perhaps forewarned, they abased themselves before Rhuan and his men, and produced gifts. Tribute, if such meager fare could be dignified with such a title. Wooden ornaments and seashells; bowls of strange-looking fruit and fishing spears tipped with bone. The people themselves offered no more promising an appearance. Most were all but naked, wearing the simplest and slightest of hide rags. Rhuan had felt a terrible, disappointed rage coming upon him then, but it had been stilled by a soft yellow glimmer amongst the polished wooden trinkets: a single, simple bead of gold.

Seeing his interest, the villagers had become excited. One — Ahenotoc — had come forward, and let fly an enthusiastic but incomprehensible stream of words. Again and again he had pointed first at the tiny ball of gold cupped in

Rhuan's palm, and then upriver. His meaning, his implied promise, had been clear.

As they surged toward the riverbank Rhuan reached for his patron God, Wen Iron-Arm. He did it out of habit. It had been many, many days since any such call had found an answer. There was but a trembling in his chest at the reaching; a tingling in the skin of his arms and down his spine. Not the burning fury and might that he could have called upon in his homeland. Here, his God could not hear him.

Some of his warriors were already on their feet, pulling on jerkins and mail shirts, settling shields upon their arms. Panur was shouting fierce encouragement to those who had not yet stowed their oars.

"Are we not the mightiest of races?" cried Rhuan, holding his sword and shield aloft.

The confirmatory roar was heartfelt.

"Are our blades not the sharpest, our gods not the fiercest?"

Still louder, his men bellowed out their agreement.

"Then let us prove it now," Rhuan shouted even as the keel ground into the sand and *Wolfrun* shivered to a halt.

He spun about and vaulted blindly over the gunwale, plummeting down into ankle-deep water. His knees buckled, but he drove himself upright and went pounding up the beach. He could hear the rest of them pouring after him, splashing ashore as he had done, rending the air with their wild war cries.

Rhuan ran into the clearing. The bare earth sent the sun's noonday heat beating back at him. A dozen or more long timber huts — only a little less massive than the meet-halls of the glacier-clad north — were scattered about the clearing. And there was stonework: two low, step-sided mounds, like crude imitations of some rocky hill. Between them towered a tree that was not a tree. A single perfectly straight trunk thrust up from the earth, climbing to the height of eight or more men. It carried no limbs, though so great was its girth it must once have supported mighty boughs. Its surface bore a strange decoration. At its base, the image of a man had been cut into the wood, and a huge carved snake rose from him, spiraling up about the gigantic column.

Rhuan slowed, his gaze following the coiling ascent of that snake. Only a flicker of movement glimpsed from the corner of his eye saved him as a flimsy arrow came skimming in at his chest. He jerked his shield up to send the shaft tumbling away, and veered toward its source. Close to a dozen men awaited him, and he rushed gladly into their midst.

They were not dressed as Ahenotoc's impoverished people had been, these dark-skinned warriors. Shells of hardened hide encased their chests, skirts of plated horn or shell hung from their hips. They held spears, and great clubs set with blades of bone.

Rhuan flung himself at them, howling wordless fury, spittle and sweat spraying indistinguishably from his lips. He saw their fear of him in their eyes. His shield shook at a blow from one of those cudgels; a thrusting spear grazed harmlessly along his flank. He permitted them nothing more than that.

A low, stooping slash and he cut the legs from under one man. A jab with his shield and he broke another's nose, split his cheek with its iron boss. One long, stretching lunge and the point of his sword cracked through feeble hide armor and sunk into the belly beneath.

Others were at his side, axes rising and falling, blades sweeping back and forth. Their opponents soon fled, sprinting for the safety of the mute jungle that crowded in around the clearing. All danger did not depart with them, though.

The man next to Rhuan — Olf, with whom he had hunted and fished as a child — gave a startled yelp and looked down at the thin arrow that had found its way through a gap between tunic and belt. He pulled it from his flesh and looked in blank gloom at the thick, foul concoction that crusted its tip. He held it out to Rhuan, who grimaced in sympathy.

"Get back to the ship," he said quietly, and went in search of more battles.

He found them, amongst the huts and the halls, and visited slaughter upon all those who would oppose him, fired now with a cold rage at the ugly death he so clearly saw lying in wait for Olf. Blood ran into the dusty earth, and vanished there, as if sucked deeper by hungry spirits. Sweat crawled over Rhuan's skin and soaked his shirt. Soon enough, there was no one left to fight. Those who were not dead had vanished into the green ocean of trees.

Two of Rhuan's men had fallen. One lay on his back almost in the center of the clearing. The side of his head had been battered in by one of those ferocious, toothed clubs. Flies were already darting about the wound. Rhuan watched the other die. The man was sitting against the wall of a longhouse. His neck was run through by a thin spear. Blood and saliva bubbled in his mouth as he faltered.

"Search, then" Rhuan muttered darkly to the survivors who gathered about him. "Find what we came for."

The place yielded its secrets reluctantly, but yield them it did. From hollow wooden tubes stacked beside hammocks spilled granules of raw, unworked gold. From about the necks of a few dead men came golden pendants. Hanging from the struts of the roofs were strange, bloated idols with golden eyes. It could not be accounted profuse riches, but it was something.

Rhuan looked for Ahenotoc. If anyone would know what else might wait to be found, it would be the man who had brought them here in the first place.

"Where is he?" he demanded of Garnok.

The priest nodded up toward one of the strange stone-built platforms in the heart of the village. Rhuan lifted his eyes, and saw Ahenotoc crouched there, at the very summit. He shouted, but the villager did not seem to hear him.

Rhuan climbed the crude stone steps, feeling the sweat tracing a score of different paths down his back. The sun's assault grew yet more brutal as he ascended. He had never dreamed the sky could harbor such a ferocious fire. The stench warned him of what he would find before he reached the top. He knew this compound of odors all too well: opened bowels; dried blood; exposed flesh.

Ahenotoc bent over the corpse of a young man dressed just as he was, with skin of just the same hue. The dead man was split open, from throat to groin. His ribs had been broken back to make of his chest an upturned, splayed hand of bony fingers. His entrails had been unwound and draped over his shoulders and thighs.

Rhuan grimaced and clamped a hand over his mouth and nose. Ahenotoc rocked slowly back and forth. It looked like mourning. There were more bodies — three of them — arrayed atop this stone hillock, blackening and rotting in the heat, attended by murmuring clouds of flies. All of them appeared to be of Ahenotoc's people. All had been treated in the same cruel fashion.

Rhuan understood at once, and cursed himself for under-estimating the small, almost delicate, man.

"We are your vengeance, then?" he growled. "It was not gold at all that you brought us here for."

Shouts from down below distracted him. He saw warriors pointing toward the fringes of the jungle. There were shapes moving there, in the gloomy shade; half-hidden, and difficult to distinguish, but clearly human. And clearly multitudinous. The edge of the forest teemed with people, more of them with every passing heartbeat. Scores, hundreds perhaps. Skulking there, mustering their courage. Readying themselves. Ahenotoc was, perhaps, not the only one he had misjudged.

"Enough," he snapped, and roughly pulled Ahenotoc to his feet. He pushed the man before him down the crude stairway. He strode back toward the river, shouting as he went.

"To *Wolfrun*! All of you, leave what you can't carry. Our time's done!"

Panur knew his business well. He already had *Wolfrun* back from the beach, rocking in the shallows a dozen paces offshore, with knotted ropes hung over the side. The men went splashing out and swarmed back aboard with all the ease of seasoned raiders.

Rhuan was the last of them. He watched as Ahenotoc clambered nimbly up and out of sight, then turned, knee-deep in the river's cooling waters, and looked back at the gigantic, unsettling pillar of carved wood that dominated the clearing. He could see people moving about it once again. Too late, he thought. Only by moments, but too late to claim any more of us. He allowed himself a moment of satisfaction, watching that scene, listening to the clatter of oars being readied, and to the sound of gentle waves slapping against *Wolfrun*'s hull. Then he reached for a rope and hauled himself up.

Olf was laid out on the boards, groaning as the poison wormed its way into the depths of his body. Rhuan averted his eyes, for fear of the weakening grief the sight might bring him.

Long, hard sweeps of the oars carried them out and across the current. The weight of the river's endless waters was with them now, and it turned the prow quickly downstream. Rhuan stood at Panur's side as the helmsman set himself to the task of holding a straight course.

"To the sea," Rhuan murmured. The sea, where they belonged. Where the air might have some life to it, and the world would widen itself beyond the constricting banks of this loathsome waterway.

He looked back, and saw a great crowd already drawn up along the edge of the clearing, watching them depart. He held his sword high, to give those observers something to remember him by. They would tell tales, no doubt, in years to come, of the pale—

He frowned in puzzlement as a figure came out from amongst the faceless throng: a man, clad in a long gown or cloak, wearing an absurd, eruptive headdress of vibrantly colored feathers. A youth followed this newcomer down to the water's edge and lay at his feet. The feathered man raised a knife, as if in answer to Rhuan's own gesture. Or mockery of it, perhaps.

"Garnok," Rhuan called, without looking away from the strange scene.

The figures were dwindling into the distance as the ship rushed on down the river, but still Rhuan could see the sun's fire glint for a moment along the black blade of the knife. And then it plunged down into the chest of the youth, and the priest — for surely that must be what he was — sawed vigorously at the flesh and bones of his victim. Who did not struggle, Rhuan saw; who did not cry out at his own horrific destruction.

"What is it?" Garnok asked.

"A sacrifice?" Rhuan said, pointing with his sword.

Garnok grunted. "Too late for them to beg their gods for aid."

The executioner stood erect once more, and now he held aloft not his knife but some smaller object. Gore trailed down his arm. Dark stains covered his gown.

"He cut the heart from one of his own," Rhuan murmured in surprise. "Such savagery."

"We'll be out of sight soon," Garnok said. "Put them from your mind. They cannot reach us now."

"You hope. I fear there is more to these people than we imagined."

The feather-headed priest flicked out his arm and cast his bloody prize into the river. They were too far off for Rhuan to see the splash of its disappearance into the brown water. He saw clearly enough what followed upon it, though, even at this distance: a foaming and boiling, spreading suddenly over the river's surface, writhing out from the bank toward the very center of the channel; a buckling of the water, drawing itself up into white-flecked humps; liquid convulsions spreading not in any natural pattern, but in a long, curving and re-curving line that wound its way downstream. As if reaching out for the ship.

Then they were around a bend and could see nothing more. *Wolfrun* was alone with the huge, silt-laden river, and with the disorderly armies of trees that jostled all along the banks. There was no sound save the rhythmic working of the oars, and Olf's pained curses through clenched teeth. No sensation but the familiar movement of his ship beneath Rhuan's feet, and the smothering weight of the sun's heat on his scalp, his back. He sheathed his sword.

"Keep to the center of the channel," he told Panur, and turned reluctantly to confront Olf's fate.

Instead, it was Ahenotoc that caught his eye. The little man knelt at the very edge of the deck, leaning over the shields, staring fixedly back up the line of their wake. Fixedly, and fearfully. Rhuan followed Ahenotoc's gaze, but saw nothing save the track of fading eddies left by the oars, the separating, sinking waves that marked their progress.

"He knows something we do not," he muttered to Garnok.

But the priest did not reply. He frowned, wincing. He shook his head once, sharply. Drops of sweat fell from the matted strands of his hair.

"Something is coming," he whispered.

And come it did. A great, bulbous bow wave rounded the bend in the river behind them. Some mighty hidden force piled up the water as it powered through it, and then spilled it back into a churning maelstrom that encompassed the entire breadth of the channel. Flocks of birds burst from the riverside canopy, climbing in raucous, gaudy panic and speeding away over the roof of the forest.

Rhuan watched in mounting horror as the river rose behind them. The wave thickened and swelled as it drew near, building itself up into a wall of dark water that rushed toward their stern. Rhuan could hear it now, could hear the seething deep in the body of the river, the rumble of its immense disturbance.

He opened his mouth to cry out a warning, but the alarm went unuttered. Quite suddenly, the river calmed. Its waters slumped back, and that great threatening wave became dying ripples.

"It's gone," he said in bewilderment.

"No," hissed Garnok, his voice a taut cord of strain. "Only deeper".

A boom, shaking the bones of the ship. A splintering chorus of shattering oars. A violent lurching sideways of the deck, as the entire vessel was flung across the current. Spray and fragments of wood stung Rhuan's face. He staggered, and had to seize Panur's arm to steady himself. Startled cries filled the air. A loose barrel went tumbling across Rhuan's field of vision. He saw it strike Garnok and send him reeling. Ahenotoc reached out a single, futile arm to try to save the priest, but too late. Garnok pitched silently over the stern.

Rhuan rushed to the gunwale and leaned out, searching the murky, roiling waters. He glimpsed Garnok's head and shoulder as he rolled, and sank, and bobbed to the surface once more.

"Turn us about!" Rhuan shouted, but it was hopeless. A swift glance down the vessel's flank revealed only the stumps of oars. Their blades had been sheared away, leaving only blunt and split stubs that flailed impotently at the water. Already, his proud ship was turning, drifting broadside to the river's flow.

He looked back in time to see Garnok taken. A huge fat, blunt head, wider than Rhuan was tall, rose to the surface, engulfed the torpid form of the priest and bore it down into oblivion. Like the fist-tipped arm of some titanic riverine giant, a sleek and darkly gleaming body, all dull browns and greens, flowed after that head, a body that seemed to be a single mass of muscle cloaked in mottled scales. Its girth matched that of the whales Rhuan's people hunted in the summer. A gargantuan monstrosity, this. Impossible. The waters closed, and hid the beast from him.

"Serpent!" Rhuan cried as he whirled away. "Make for the shore."

But he could see Panur's helplessness writ clear upon the helmsman's face. He hauled mightily at his steer board without effect. The ship wallowed and rolled. Rhuan could feel its struggle, its wounds, through his feet and in the shape of its faltering. The hull was breached, somewhere; the planking split. He could feel, with every long-honed instinct, the weight of the water slowly gathering in its shallow belly.

The men who had lost their oars were getting to their feet, reaching for swords, axes, shields. None had seen what Rhuan had, he guessed. They did not know what they faced, and how overmatched their weaponry was likely to prove.

The ship shook. The mast trembled, describing a widening circle. A rasping, grating groan ran through every timber as something massive scraped itself under the keel. Rhuan heard the first stirring of fear in the voices of his brave warriors as they looked this way and that. Some were trying to move oars across to replace those destroyed, but it was too late.

The river shrugged, and *Wolfrun* rose. Men sprawled and slipped. The stern bucked, throwing Rhuan to his knees. The mast creaked. Then the ship slapped back down and muddy waves broke over its sides. Rhuan struggled to his feet, water sloshing about his boots and soaking his leggings.

And suddenly the giant, malignant head rose upon the tower of its neck, the river falling away from its scaled body. It rose between Rhuan and the sun, and it cast its shadow upon him and it felt chill and heavy, as if he had fallen into the shade of some ice-bound mountain. He saw a spear lance up and rebound impotently from the glistening scales. And still the serpent reared higher and higher from the water, no end to it. A tongue, fat and forked, writhed out from its lipless mouth. The beast lifted its head until it over-topped *Wolfrun*'s mast, and it stared down upon the ship and its scrambling, shouting crew with eyes like worn red jewels. Then all its weight came crashing down.

Rhuan was thrown into the air, and he tumbled through a cacophony. The cracking of failing timbers. The howls of men, colored by rage or terror or pain. The river twisting and tearing itself into a storm of foam. As he fell, he caught glimpses of the world: the green mass of the jungle; the brown river strewn with broken wood, and a body floating face down; the serpent's huge flank rippling as it tightened itself about *Wolfrun*.

He hit the water, and went under. There, in the roaring, crushing darkness, the sounds were deeper, and they rang in his breastbone and his skull. He could hear his ship dying, and its death throes were like the slow rumble of snow down a mountainside. The river took him in its irresistible grasp and swept him along. Invisible objects battered against his legs: rocks or men or debris, he could not tell. He blinked, and felt the grit of the river searing his eyes. There was, though, a hint of pale light, distant and frail but real.

Rhuan hauled himself to the surface, and found himself facing the riverside, staring at a jumble of rocks and dead wood overhung by a chaos of vegetation. He turned in the water, and bore witness to *Wolfrun*'s end. The serpent had thrown its vast coils around the ship's midriff, once, twice, thrice. From that immense embrace, there could be no escape. As Rhuan watched, drifting numbly away downstream, *Wolfrun*'s back broke with a hollow crash, and her prow and stern folded up toward one another. The mast was smashed against the serpent's back and snapped like so much kindling. Men spilled from the shattered vessel, plunging into the river.

Even as its body sank slowly down, taking the carcass of the ship to its dark grave, the monster's head scythed back and forth over the river's surface. It bludgeoned men and crushed them in its jaws and dragged them under. Flailing figures dotted the river across its whole turbulent width. Many of them could not swim, Rhuan knew. Many others had been wearing mail, or had gold about their necks and stuffed inside their shirts, and would live only if they could free themselves of it. Some were in the very middle of the channel, where the mindless grip of its current was most ferocious; they went racing away beneath the sun's impassive, brutal glare, arms clawing at the air, cries fading quickly. The river took its share of the serpent's bounty.

Amidst the slaughter, in a last great foamy gurgle, the carved wolf's head of the prow was the last of the ship to disappear. It slipped slowly, almost solemnly out of sight, and *Wolfrun* was gone. Rhuan rolled grimly onto his front and swam for the shore. He had given up wearing his mail vest just two days ago: it was too burdensome to bear in this heat, and it had been rubbing sores into his shoulders. Still, the river wanted him. It pulled at him, and his sword was heavy at his hip. He might have succumbed, had not a long branch suddenly been extended and pushed into his hand. Gasping, Rhuan allowed himself to be dragged out onto the rocks, and looked blearily up into Ahenotoc's narrow, thoughtful eyes.

Ahenotoc led him into a gloomy, frightful world; from the light and heat of the river to a suffocating and dank domain. The trees pressed so close together, in such profusion of form and size, that all beneath them was shadow and they had smothered the ground with their decaying leaves. The air was so burdened with moisture that it felt heavy in Rhuan's lungs.

The awful sounds coming from the river faded slowly behind them. Rhuan felt a dull shame at his impotence in the face of such destruction, and a part of him would gladly have thrown himself back into those churning waters, to die with his men and with his ship. But Ahenotoc pulled him insistently along with little tugs at his sleeve and nagging mutters. An urgency possessed the man that Rhuan did not entirely understand.

No forest in his own lands could have prepared him for the overpowering abundance of this jungle. The tallest of the trees soared out of sight, merging themselves into the endless, many-layered roof of leaves. Vines and creepers and ferns dripped and tumbled from the trunks and branches. Great curving fronds tore at him with hooks as he stumbled along. And the noise: a throbbing, whining drone of sound came from every direction at once; innumerable insect voices blended into the single monotonous song of the forest itself. He felt a soft impact on his shoulder, and found a huge beetle clinging to him, its carapace spined and twisted like something a delirious child might shape from a memory of fever. He hissed in alarm and knocked it away.

Never had Rhuan known any place so remorselessly hostile and unsuited to human life. He could see no trail. He blundered into patches of vicious thorn, slipped on mossy rocks, started away from fleeting movements glimpsed and then gone before they could be given meaning. None of this troubled Ahenotoc, who drifted easily and silently through the madness, barefooted and near naked, yet unscathed by any of the countless insults the jungle offered.

They climbed a long and shallow slope. Rhuan heard some animal crashing away through the treetops over their heads; he peered uneasily upwards, but saw nothing save a shower of tumbling leaves. His legs grew heavy. His thighs and knees ached. He grew angry — at Ahenotoc, at fate, at the intractable jungle and its utter indifference to his desires and ambitions — and slumped heavily down on the sloping root of a huge tree.

Ahenotoc, a little way ahead, turned and shook his head.

"I cannot walk forever," Rhuan said. "My ship, my men—all gone. Leave me to mourn them. Leave me to my sorrows."

He fell silent, staring with furrowed brow at the forest floor around his boots. It had come alive. Dozens — scores — of tiny black worms looped their way over the fallen leaves, closing from every direction upon his feet. He rose hurriedly and took a few steps sideways, not knowing what new horror this was and not wanting to know.

"A man cannot even rest for a moment in this forsaken wilderness," he muttered.

Ahenotoc beckoned him onward. He looked worried.

"Leave me be," Rhuan snapped, "lest I decide to avenge myself upon you for what your cunning has wrought."

He found his bitter rage difficult to sustain, though. Ahenotoc had, after all, hauled him from the maw of the hungry river. And Rhuan knew he must bear his own heavy share of the blame for what had happened. His will had been what carried *Wolfrun* halfway across the world, to lands that would best have been left unknown. His promises of gold had sustained his men, and goaded them into this doomed adventure. His pride had left him fatally unwary of meddling in the contests of people whose wiles, and whose gods, so exceeded his expectations.

Ahenotoc cupped a hand to his ear and leaned back the way they had come. Rhuan frowned at this exaggerated mime.

"What?"

Ahenotoc repeated the gesture, leaning still more steeply downhill, spreading the fingers of his hand at his ear.

Rhuan listened, and soon enough he heard it too. A sound of vast violence, rendered indistinct by distance but retaining its horrible threat. Trees crashing, shaking, grinding against one another. The earth groaning as its fabric was twisted and torn. Stone and soil and timber all protesting at once, as they were reshaped, brushed aside, crushed.

"It is not done?" Rhuan said in disbelief. He looked at Ahenotoc, wide-eyed. "I thought it a beast of the river, a beast of the water."

But no, he realized. Of course not. It was a God not of the river, but of the jungle, whole and entire. Here, where water, sky, earth, all the elements were so cruelly transformed and intermingled, such a monster would acknowledge no boundaries. There would be no frontiers it would not cross.

"It comes for us, then?" Rhuan asked.

Ahenotoc beckoned him onward.

Darkness fell like the descent of nightmare. The jungle became a hallucinatory welter of veering moon shadows, unexplained sounds, unseen logs and vines and holes. Rhuan's skin became a muddle of lacerations and bruises. He struggled on, following Ahenotoc's soft guiding whistles, only because always at his back, always drawing incrementally nearer, grew the mounting thunder of the serpent's catastrophic passage.

That grim tumult came to dominate Rhuan's senses and his thoughts. He imagined it to be the baying of an army of hounds, upon the trail of a stag. He heard, in the rending apart of the jungle, his own inevitable doom closing upon him. He could envisage the cloud of debris through which the huge serpent writhed in its pursuit; a formless, sharp fog of tumbling leaves, splinters, shredded bark.

He blundered clumsily into Ahenotoc's back, and was wrenched from his bleak reverie. The villager set a hand on his shoulder and gently but firmly turned him about. And Rhuan found himself looking down upon a scene of strange, silvery beauty.

A giant of the forest, a tree so mighty it beggared the imagination, had fallen, toppling back down the slope. It had come to rest some way short of the ground, caught precariously on the lower boughs of the one tree sturdy enough to withstand its fall; but still it had torn open a huge rent in the canopy. Through this window, Rhuan now gazed out. At a sky strewn with such a thick dusting of stars it seemed to glow. At a moon so full and bright it painted the rolling, unbounded sea of the treetops with a silver sheen. At an immensity of space, and of life, that he would not have guessed the world contained.

And at the serpent's track, a wound scored across that immensity. It looked as if some giant's — or god's — hand had reached down from above and gouged a fingernail across the surface of the world, cutting a weaving path through the jungle. It might have been the curving channel of a dark river, working its way toward them — but for the advancing head of that river, before which the trees rocked and quaked and broke.

Rhuan felt Ahenotoc's touch on his arm. The villager, absurdly, stood smiling in the moonlight. He pointed at the sword sheathed on Rhuan's belt.

"What? You want this?" Rhuan shook his head.

Ahenotoc pointed again. Rhuan laughed.

"You can't part a man from his sword just by the asking, not even if—" The words suddenly felt foolish on his lips. He bit them back. He was, he thought with all the cold clarity of the defeated, a dead man without Ahenotoc's aid. Without his guidance. Lost, and alone, in a place he did not understand; hunted by a monstrosity his mind could barely grasp. The clamor of the behemoth's approach was there, at his back, coming closer.

Reluctantly, Rhuan freed his sword and extended its hilt toward Ahenotoc.

In an instant, the little man sprang onto the fallen tree and danced his light-footed way up its angled bole. Rhuan's beloved blade flashed, catching the fire of the moonlight. All confidence and lithe agility, Ahenotoc swung around outstretched branches and shrugged off the attentions of the tangled creepers that had been dragged down in the tree's death throes. Rhuan craned his neck back to keep him in sight.

"We've no time for this," he said. He could hear the serpent, drawing ever nearer; could hear the havoc of its ominous movement.

Ahenotoc flailed inexpertly at a long, straight spar projecting from the side of trunk. Rhuan winced at the sound of his sword's keen edge being so abused. He bore it for a moment or two, but then could suffer it no longer. Even as he drew breath to protest, the branch gave way. Ahenotoc examined it appraisingly and then dropped it down to Rhuan.

It was old, hard wood, long ago stripped of its bark; longer than Rhuan was tall, just thin enough for him to encompass with his hand. Ahenotoc had broken it off in such a way as to leave a crude but sharp point. Rhuan regarded it skeptically. Ahenotoc gave a low whistle to draw Rhuan's attention upward once more, then made enthusiastic stabbing motions and pointed at his own neck, behind the hinge of his jaw.

Before Rhuan could respond, the villager was off again, clambering still further up the ramp of the toppled tree. Rhuan lost sight of him, and found him again only when he came to a halt, perched amongst the interlocking branches that had arrested the great tree's fall, and held it suspended. Ahenotoc leaned and twisted this way and that, examining the knot of timber with evident care and suspicion. Shortly, he began to cut. The sword sent chips of wood tumbling down toward Rhuan. He soon understood Ahenotoc's intent. He found himself less alarmed by it than he should have been. It stank of madness, but madness seemed the most fitting of odors on this night, in this place.

Rhuan of the Grey Hall waited patiently for the beast to come to him. The jungle sang its droning song all around. He watched the tiny blood-hungry worms making their hunch-backed way toward him across the moon-lit leaf litter. Most, he flicked away before they could fasten themselves to his flesh. One or two escaped his attentions until they had taken hold on his hand or neck; those, he crushed between finger and thumb, making a smear from their soft bodies and the blood they had sucked from him.

The storm drew near: a brittle, rising thunder of destruction. He reached with his heart for Wen Iron-Arm, but there was, of course, no answer. He had no god of his own to set against that which approached. In truth, he was not certain it would have made any difference, even if his body had been flooded with borrowed divine might. He doubted now, as he never had before, whether his gods were truly the fiercest of them all. This wild land he had discovered bred deities in its own image, and there was surely no place fiercer than this.

The jungle before him shook. The host of shadows shifted and coalesced. The trees shivered, from their mighty roots to the highest tips of their vaulting crowns. The insects fell silent. The serpent's blunt boulder of a head pushed its way out from the gloom. Rhuan could smell it: mud and water and weed and earth. Its split tongue curled and trembled. Its lidless red eyes glinted with motes of the moon's light.

Rhuan stood before it, spread his arms wide, and roared his challenge. He shook his makeshift spear in defiance. It came at him, a vast eruptive writhing that battered trees aside and ground rocks beneath it; a surging of darkness as if the whole jungle had come to furious life. He ran.

He sprinted beneath the huge mass of the half-fallen tree, and turned beyond it. The monster was there, on his heels, its jaws gaping as it thrust itself through the opening in his wake. He saw curved teeth like scythes; he saw scales the size of shields. He smelled its corrupt breath, all rot and doom. He met its implacable animal gaze. He heard, above the crash of the serpent's advance, a flurry of blows overhead: Ahenotoc, hacking away at the last tenuous attachments by which he had left the great dead tree supported.

Rhuan threw himself aside as those jaws reached for him. The great snake gathered itself for another blow, and in doing so it jarred its broad back against the slanting tree trunk. With a last harsh crack of sword against wood, a branch gave way, and the world convulsed around Rhuan. A deafening groan, as of a glacier rumbling its way over rocks; a tremor rocking the earth upon which he lay; a blasted exhalation from that vile serpentine gullet.

He scrambled to his feet to find the giant beast pinned to the ground. The tree had fallen square across its neck and punched the jagged stumps of branches through even its armored hide. But this god had might yet flowing through its huge form. Rhuan saw its body rising in a huge arch, hunching up against the star-flecked sky, climbing higher and higher. It strained against the trap that had closed about it, and the forest shuddered. Some of the boughs that impaled it broke. The gigantic tree trunk itself shifted, began to turn.

Ahenotoc dropped from above. He fell recklessly, carelessly, and hit the back of the serpent's head with a dull thud. It spasmed at the impact, and smashed him aside like a bull flicking away some irritant fly. But he left the sword planted behind its skull.

Rhuan darted in, seeking the place he had been told to seek: the underside of the jaw, in behind the bone. The serpent twisted itself toward him, its scales scraping over one another, the dark patterns of its hide shifting and warping, its body a bending wall, closing on him, overshadowing him. When he thrust with his crude spear, it glanced off the plated mass. Still the beast remained pinned, and hampered. It bent its head away from him, shaping its body for another titanic effort against its restraints, and as its neck curved, its scales splayed a fraction. Rhuan stabbed into the sliver of a gap that opened before him, and drove the spear in as deep and hard as his weary muscles would allow.

The great head snapped back toward him and knocked him from his feet. The spear came free as he fell back, and after it spewed a flood of steaming ichor. The noisome fluid splashed around him, and across his scrambling legs. It pulsed out in viscous strands, thickening as it came, congealing upon the forest floor in a dark, spreading slick.

Such convulsions shook the serpent then that it carved gullies into the earth, and drove up the leaf litter into great drifts and piles. It threw the fallen tree from its back. Its huge undulating form thrashed at the very canopy of the jungle. Debris rained down around Rhuan and he curled into a ball, hands clasped over his head. The ground beneath him bucked and hammered at him, ringing like the most dolorous of bells as the dying giant beat against it.

In time, there was a gentler rain, of soft leaves, and stillness. Rhuan lay for a moment, listening to the rattle of his own heart, and then unfolded himself. He rose on unsteady legs, scraping dirt and dust and gore from his chest and knees. The stench of the serpent's blood was sickening, almost choking.

It had opened a still wider clearing about itself in its struggles, and lay now, along its whole unmoving length, in moonlight. Rhuan looked upon it in awe. Four longships, five perhaps, could have been laid alongside it without matching it. Its eye, quite lightless, like an ochre stone, was twice the size of his fist.

Ahenotoc suddenly appeared atop the immense corpse. He grinned — a flash of white in the dark — though Rhuan saw that one arm hung limp and a bloody welt marred his flank. Ahenotoc hauled at the sword still lodged where he had driven it, and when at last he managed to drag it free, he dropped it down to Rhuan with an exclamation of what sounded like simple joy.

Rhuan took the sword up and looked ruefully at its notched and battered blade.

Ahenotoc thumped to the ground beside him, less graceful now, less sure of his balance. But still smiling. He patted Rhuan on the arm and said something brief and mirthful, nodding into the distance. Rhuan shrugged his incomprehension. The villager laughed again, and walked away. Without looking back, he extended his good arm and beckoned Rhuan after him as he sank into the gloom of the jungle.

Rhuan reached out once more, extended a final forlorn invitation to his god Wen of the frost-gilded north, to share in this moment of triumph; to look out through Rhuan's merely human eyes and mark the glory of victory and of death once more evaded. Nothing. Nothing, save perhaps the faintest hint of winter's metallic scent, and the fleeting prickle of an icy chill across his face.

But those sensations were memory, not presence. Rhuan was exiled from far more than just his home and hearth. There was no god here save the great, dead serpentine monstrosity laid out across the slope. And its ruin had been wrought not by divine might, but by entirely mortal wit and courage. Those were the powers to which Rhuan must give his humble adherence now. Whether they resided within in him or elsewhere.

He sighed and sheathed his sword. He gave a last, lingering look at the fallen behemoth, then followed after Ahenotoc. Already, he could already hear the villager's light, fluting whistles calling him into the deep forest.

"Lead on, then," Rhuan said. "Lead on. Show me the way."

Ageless

Mountains

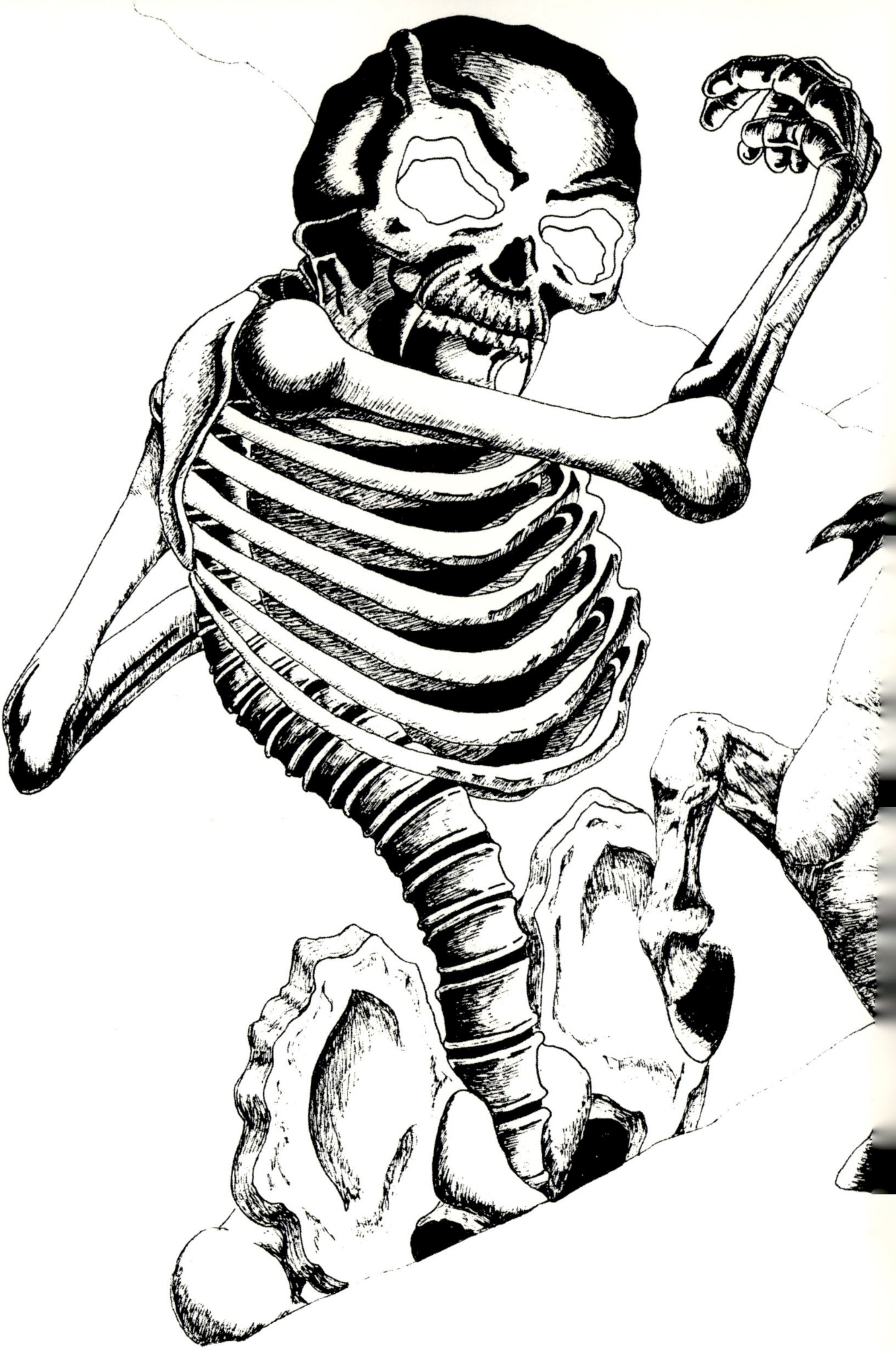

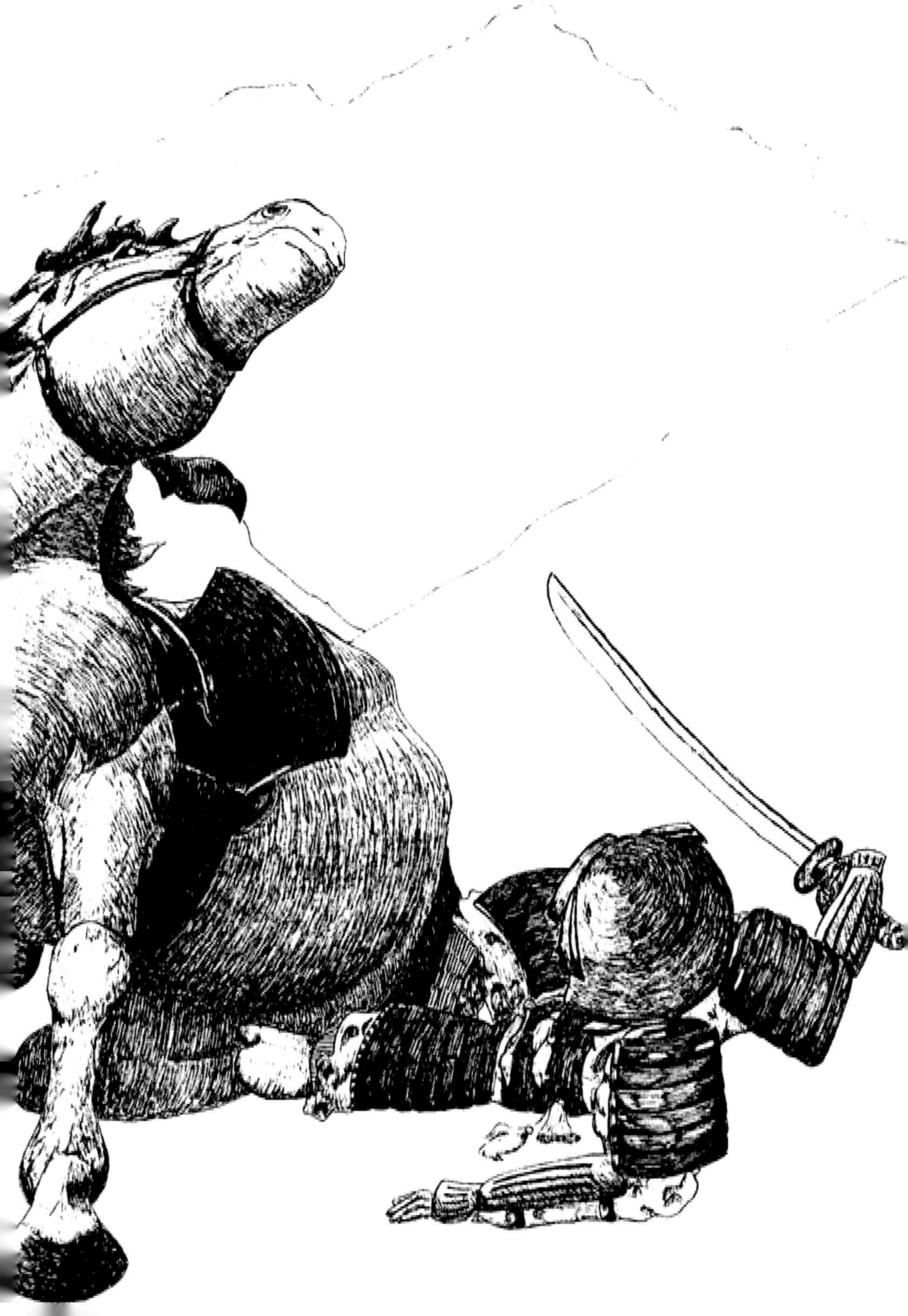

Lurking in the barren wastes of Arizona, C. L. Werner is the author of twelve novels set in the Old World of Warhammer™ and head background writer for Darkson Designs' AE-WWII, a pulp sci-fi setting of alternate history. An avid reader of adventure, mystery, horror, fantasy and military history, he cites H. P. Lovecraft, Walter B. Gibson, Sax Rohmer, Charles Whiting and Robert E. Howard as the chief influences on his work. In his free time, he enjoys watching Godzilla movies and plotting the downfall of humanity. Visit The Black Library for some of his books, or his in-progress website Vermintime at www.vermintime.com, for more information. What follows is his visualization of the type of Japanese heroic character Howard might have created. Shintaro Oba possesses an allegiance that knows no bounds; an allegiance that goes beyond the boundaries of this world and defies the assaults of all foes no matter their size. Such integrity is a rare thing — so rare, that it generates other rare acts.

The Rotten Bones Rattle

A Tale of Shintaro Oba

**by C.L. Werner
& illustration by John Whitman**

Cold as the wintry breath of the northern sea, thick as strands of gossamer, grey fog rolled down the wooded slopes, shrouding all in its spectral mantle. Trees, thin as rails and crooked as the fingers of a crone, leered from the misty shadows. Jagged slivers of shale jutted up from the desiccated ground like daggers of stone, their crumbling surfaces pitted by the elements and hoary with age. Thorny brambles squatted in the blinding murk, their spindly roots enjoying only the most fragile purchase in the rocky soil, their scrawny branches splayed like the claws of jungle beasts, waiting for whatever hapless prey might stumble into their coils.

A lone figure picked his way through the forsaken landscape, stalking past the thorn-ridden bushes and sickly trees. Fog swirled about the traveler as his dark shape drifted through the trees. His was an imposing visage; a tall man of pantherish build, his body encased in thick scales and plates of iron, overlapping to form a skin of metal that covered him from crown to shin. Beneath the bright red sash that girded his waist, two swords were thrust. The hilt of the smaller sword, a fang-like *wakizashi*, was brilliant even in the gloomy fog, a sea of small sapphires upon which tiny ships of gold rode an endless tide. The slender *uchigatana* was shabby beside its opulent companion, its sheath of sandal-wood marked only with fading paint, its hilt fashioned from a worn knob of bone.

The samurai's careful passage through the fog-draped trees came to a sudden halt. His hand fell to the horn hilt of his uchigatana, fingers closing about the worn bone with practiced familiarity. His keen eyes stared long at the grey veil, as though the mind behind them could force the misty shadows to surrender its secrets. Slowly, with creeping step, the warrior moved forward again. A flicker of satisfaction showed on his face as an orange glow appeared behind the fog, the faintest suggestion of flickering light somewhere ahead of him in the murk. He stood once again in silence, training his senses on the hidden light, peeling his ears for the faintest sound.

For many minutes he stood and listened, listened to the muted sounds of coarse laughter and harsh voices. After a time, a flicker of smile reappeared on the samurai's face and he made his way forward once more. Now his steps were casual, his poise one of confidence and unconcern. Only the fingers still wrapped about the hilt of his sword told of the wariness that yet ruled the warrior's mind.

By degrees, the orange glow revealed itself as a campfire. Scattered about it were five men and a woman. The men were scarred and ragged, their lamellar armor stained by both hardship and neglect, their swords a motley collection of katana and heavy tachi. The faces of the men were as motley as their weapons, unkempt and cruel. They betrayed too mongrel a collection of feature and tone to belong to any proper daimyo's retinue. As he emerged from the fog and strode into their midst, their reaction to the stranger was sloppy and disorganized, far from the drill and discipline of bushido.

The samurai ignored the cursing warriors as they stumbled to their feet, discarded bottles of saki to fumble at the weapons strewn beside them on the ground. He swept his gaze across the little camp, noting the bundles of supplies, the bed rolls and woolen tents.

The samurai crouched down beside the campfire, seeming to focus his attention on the iron pot boiling above the flame.

"Black Gods of Vuthoom's Abyss!" swore one of the warriors, a short man with pronounced paunch and flabby cheeks. He drew his sword, threatening the stranger with the edge of his tachi.

"If I meant you ill," the stranger said, his voice without emotion, his eyes never leaving the boiling pot, "I should have killed three of you before ever you saw me come in from the fog."

"Listen to the pig boast!" snorted a second warrior, his long face split by the grey streak of an ugly smite.

"He wouldn't be in any condition to boast if you scum were keeping watch!" roared a third, his pock-marked features as sharp as the face of a rat. "We are lucky half of Torohata's army didn't roll into camp!"

"They still might," the stranger at the fire said, lifting a clay bowl from the ground and dipping it into the pot.

"Nethers of the Snake God!" hissed a fourth warrior, a tall man with a battered helm strapped about his small head. He spun about, glaring at his fellows. "Jiro! Ogata! See if there are more where this pig came from!" He turned back to the samurai, baring his teeth in an ugly snarl. "You had best tell us where your friends are. You won't collect any gold from Torohata if you are dead!"

"I should not think he is one of Torohata's men." The statement came from the fifth warrior. Unlike the others, he had not leapt to his feet when the samurai entered their camp. He continued to lounge on his belly, resting on a nest of blankets while a woman kneaded the muscles of his naked back with her slender hands. The samurai had noticed the man in his quick inspection of the camp. There was a stamp of cruelty and evil about him far beyond the simple stupid brutality of his comrades. The fact that he remained indolent while the others swaggered and threatened spoke of a calculating and analytical mind that chose its battles with only the greatest care.

The other warriors did not relax their guard, keeping their blades turned upon the man by the fire, but the words of their comrade had thrown some confusion into their minds. "Why do you say that, Hanzo?" demanded the rat-faced Ogata.

Hanzo lifted himself onto his elbows, a snide smile on his cruel face. He brushed aside the slim hands of the girl tending him, shoving her away. He fixed his menacing eyes on the crouching samurai. He waited for the stranger to return his notice, but the samurai seemed entirely focused upon the noodles he slurped from his bowl. Irritated by the stranger's refusal to respond, Hanzo pointed at the man's armour.

"The scroll-work on his *gusoko*," Hanzo said. "That is the work of the Sekigahara clan. The sword he carries is called *Koumakiri* — the demon blade of Sekigahara. Even Mako Torohata would not hire ronin from a clan with a curse upon it!"

"I am no ronin," remarked the samurai in a low voice, though keeping his eyes still upon the fire. "Unlike some I might name."

The five warriors bristled at the scornful note in the samurai's tone. "We serve the lord Takegashi Shiro as well as any born into his clan!" snarled the short ronin.

"And for better money than some house-kept paper-tiger," sneered Ogata.

"A samurai understands that honor is a nobler coin than gold," the samurai said. "Tell me how much honor you have found wandering from one master to another."

"Who do you call master?" challenged Hanzo, sliding forward on his blanket. "The Sekigahara clan is no more; its line has been scoured from the kingdoms of Mu-Thulan that its curse might die with it."

The samurai turned, facing Hanzo for the first time. He straightened his back, lifting his head, presenting himself as though within the great hall of a daimyo. "I am Shintaro Oba and I serve Lord Sekigahara Katakura."

"Katakura is dead!" scoffed Hanzo. "His head hangs from the shogun's palace in Iwaza and his bones feed the crows! Samurai! Hah! You are nothing more than ronin, like the rest of us!"

Oba did not rise to Hanzo's baiting, but turned and began to eat once more.

"Say!" exclaimed the rat-faced Ogata. "If you are ronin, perhaps you could use work?" He crouched down beside the samurai, leering at him from above the boiling pot. "They say the Sekigahara clan was all master swordsmen, even before your lord sold his soul to demons." Ogata laughed. "You must be one of the best of your clan to have fought your way out of your lord's castle when Shogun Yoshinaga laid siege upon it! I am sure Lord Shiro could use a man like you and he pays well."

"I have heard much of this Takegashi in my travels, and even more of his enemy Torohata," Oba answered. "A worse pair of villains this side of hell would be hard to find outside of the shogun's palace."

The words caused the ronin to back away, his sword once again leveled menacingly at Oba. The other mercenaries began to circle around the crouching samurai while the lounging Hanzo furtively slid his hands into the folds of cloth underneath him.

"You refuse!" Ogata snapped. "You think perhaps Torohata will give you a better deal!"

Before Ogata could continue his tirade, his head leapt from his shoulders and crashed into the pot amid a sizzle of boiling broth. In one fluid motion, Oba had risen from beside the fire, drawn his sword and decapitated the raging mercenary.

The lightning-fast blur of violence and the death of their comrade had not registered in the minds of the other ronin before Oba's body was in motion once more. Spinning about, he slashed the edge of his uchigatana through the belly of the scar-faced ronin, slicing through armor and flesh as though it were butter. The ronin's body folded in upon itself, cut through nearly to its spin.

The others reacted now. The small, fat mercenary chopped at Oba with his tachi, but the heavy cavalry sword only cut empty air as the samurai twisted from its path. His own sword caught the ronin at the elbow, sending both arm and the blade it held flopping to the earth. A second stroke opened the wailing man from shoulder to groin and he collapsed in a gory heap.

The ronin with the helm came at Oba while he cut down the short mercenary. Snarling like a beast, the man brought his katana flashing at the samurai's neck, thinking to decapitate his enemy as he had done to Ogata. Oba ducked beneath the stroke, kicking out with his steel-toed boot and smashing the ronin's leg just above the knee. The mercenary gasped in pain. He had continued to wear his kabuto, but for the sake of comfort he had removed the awkward *haidate* skirt that should have protected his thighs and upper legs. Now he staggered from the bruising impact against his unguarded flesh.

Oba pounced upon the surprised ronin like a tiger upon a lamb. His uchigatana was a blinding flash of steel as it swept through the ronin's breast, the razor-like edge chewing through his armor and ravaging the body within. The stricken man swayed drunkenly, then crumpled onto his knees before sprawling face-first against the rocky ground.

Oba did not watch his enemy fall, however. Certain of the mortal wound he had delivered, he was already spinning about to meet a new enemy. He had not forgotten the lounging Hanzo and his so careful motions of his hands.

The samurai was surprised to find Hanzo staring up at the sky, his throat slit from ear to ear, his feet still drumming upon the ground as life fled his carcass. Close to his now lifeless hand was a hollow tube of bamboo and a long copper needle tipped in noxious green paste.

Oba studied his dead enemy for only a second, then lifted his eyes to the man's slayer. He had almost dismissed the woman from his thoughts. By her cheap dress and servile manner, he had taken her to be a comfort girl provided by Takegashi for the sentries. Now he stared in disbelief at the woman he had so casually forgotten.

She was of striking beauty, a quality that had lent itself to her performance. Now, however, with her docile mien discarded like the old skin of a snake, Oba could see the coiled strength in her shapely limbs, the sharp cunning beneath her pretty face. Hers was the terrible strength of the fox and the minx, to hide her lethal menace within grace and delicacy. The effect was only slightly ruined by the blood dripping from the knife in her hand and the hideously pleased gleam in her jade eyes.

Oba nodded his head to the woman. "Many thanks," he said, gesturing at the dead Hanzo and the sinister weapon he had been prevented from using. "Even for a ronin, to use the poison of the nata spider is an honorless trick." He removed a strip of silk from beneath his belt and ran the rag along the length of his sword, cleansing the blade of mercenary blood. When he had finished, he tossed the stained rag aside, but made no move to return his sword to its sheath.

The woman smiled at him, an expression at once both coy and mocking. "Surely you are not afraid of a girl?"

Oba grinned back. "The one they called Hanzo wasn't wary of you. That was his last mistake. It is unwise to take your eyes off a ninja."

The woman's body became tense, her hand tightening about the grip of her knife, her eyes narrowing to the merest points. Challenge and anger rose to the surface of those glaring pools, the fury of a reptile dragged out from its dark cave to be scrutinized in the cold light of day.

"Don't bother to deny it," Oba told her before she could speak. "You didn't kill him by cutting his throat. Too sloppy. A stab between the ribs and straight into the heart. The Kokuryu clan kills its victims in that fashion. Slitting his throat was to make it look like the work of a hapless comfort girl." Oba's voice dropped its casual tone, becoming low and menacing. "Why is the Kokuryu clan here? Are you working for Torohata?"

The ninja smirked. In an almost blinding flash of motion, she sent her knife flying at Oba's throat. Almost as quickly, Oba raised his sword to intercept the deadly missile. The knife glanced off the edge of the blade with a sharp ping, clattering off to be lost in the fog. The samurai swung around, but the woman had made good use of his distraction. She had leapt back, her hands quickly digging through a sack of rice to retrieve the blackened length of a wakizashi shortsword. She dropped into a battle stance as soon as the blade filled her slender hands.

"Shintaro Oba, of the Sekigahara clan," the woman said, confidence in her voice. "You have come far to die alone. Better you had done your duty and died with your master."

"I have no intention of dying and the duty my master demanded of me made it impossible to perish with him defying the Shogun's tyranny," Oba replied in a growl. "Whatever your quarrel with Takegashi, or Torohata for that matter, I have no part in it. I did not come to Cripple Mountain to kill men. I came here to kill a monster."

The woman stared at Oba, trying to decide if the samurai spoke the truth. The grim resignation she saw in his features made her decide that no deceit hid in his words. Carefully, with slow deliberation, she returned her blade to its oversized sheath and set it down on the ground, then knelt beside it.

"I have no intention of dying either," she told him. "Looking at you, I find myself doubting my own ability. And I believe you when you say you do not serve Takegashi. Killing his ronin made that abundantly clear."

"Then the Kokuryu clan is helping Torohata?"

By way of reply, the woman bowed her head, almost touching her nose to the ground. "I am Yasune Meiko," she said. "If you have truly come to slay the monster, I will guide you to its lair."

Meiko led Oba up the steep slope of the mountainside. The fog grew thinner the higher they climbed, clearly exposing the wasted, blighted nature of the forested slopes. The trees were utterly denuded of foliage, their limbs dangling in the air like skeletal talons, their trunks pitted and splintered. Strange black burns spotted the wood, marks that looked somehow too unclean to be the work of lightning or fire. Slivers of bark jutted from the muddy ground like stakes, and it did not ease Oba's mind to see skeletons draped across some of the wooden spikes, half-buried in the greasy black mud of the mountain. He stopped counting after his sharp eyes picked out their tenth skeleton poking from the mud.

Ten skeletons, and not a skull among them.

"The monster's work?" Oba asked his guide, pointing to the eleventh skeleton.

Meiko nodded grimly. "The gashadokuro eats only the heads of those who trespass upon its mountain," she told him.

Oba stepped over to the body. He leaned down and ran his glove through the mud, soon uncovering a badly rusted *maebashi*. He held the steel visor up, flicking clumps of dirt from it. "This belonged to a samurai," he said.

"Cripple Mountain has long been contested by Torohata and Takegashi,"

Meiko told him. Even the presence of the monster has not stopped their feud."

Oba let the visor fall from his hand to join its headless owner in the mud. "No," he said. "I don't think even the most vainglorious lord would choose a monster's hunting ground for his battle. There is something more behind all of this." His eyes narrowed as he saw the deliberate, masklike expression that spread across Meiko's face. Her hands were hidden within the sleeves of her kimono, but Oba thought he could see the slightest hint of motion beneath the cloth.

The samurai lifted his hand in apology. "What they really want, does not concern me," he told the ninja. "I am here to find and kill the monster. That is all that concerns me."

Meiko's expression remained impassive, but Oba sensed a lessening of the dangerous tension within her. The ninja held some secret, something she would kill to protect. What puzzled him was why she hadn't already tried to kill him.

The petite woman turned away, walking with uncanny grace up the steep, muddy ground. "How much do you know of Cripple Mountain?" she asked him.

"I know that in my grandfather's grandfather's time, it was called Frosthome and the Doro Emperor built his summer palace upon its summit." Oba struggled to keep pace with Meiko, cursing the rough terrain.

"The Doro Emperor offended the gods of the mountain and in their rage they sent the fires of the earth dragon to consume his household. The palace was destroyed, the summit of Frosthome scattered into the winds. Five hundred feet of mountain vanished in the blink of an eye and when the earth dragon's smoke faded, Frosthome had become Cripple Peak."

Oba leaned against the trunk of a splintered tree, staring hard at the haunted, hideous landscape. "There are some who say the Doyen Kato sent demons to destroy the Doro Emperor and that they still dwell upon the mountain."

Meiko favoured the samurai with another of her frustratingly enigmatic smiles. "I should trust a member of the Sekigahara clan to know about demons."

Oba felt his blood boil at the barb. He tightened his hand about the hilt of his sword, glaring at the ninja. "I know enough to never listen to the promise of a demon. My lord learned the peril only too late. The Sekigahara owed their power to a pact they had made with a demon king. They would prosper, but only at the cost of the soul of the clan leader when he died. The lords of the clan were smarter than the demon, father always passing leadership of the clan to his son well before he died so that the debt would pass on to the next generation. For centuries, the trick worked and the souls of Sekigahara did not pass through *kimon*, the demons' gate."

The samurai shook his head and ground his teeth, remembering the siege of his lord's castle, remembering the arrow that struck down Katakura's son.

"My master was not able to pass lordship of the Sekigahara clan to another of his blood. When he died, his soul was forfeit to the demon. The last duty he charged me with was to track down this demon and force it to free his spirit."

So lost in the coils of shame and guilt had Oba been during his account of his clan's doom, he had allowed his carefully maintained caution to slip. Now, as he freed himself from memory's snare, he noted the sound of horses galloping up the slope from below. Meiko heard them too, he could see that, and she had probably heard them well before he did, drawing him into an angry explanation of his clan's shame to distract him from the approaching peril.

Meiko smirked and darted for the trees. Oba lunged after her, no longer feigning the clumsiness that had allowed her to so easily distance him during the climb up. The ninja quickly reached for the knives hidden in the sleeves of her robe, but Oba was quicker still, pinning her arms and crushing her lithe body against his. He held the edge of his uchigatana against her throat, then turned with her so that they could both watch the horsemen emerge from the fog.

There were at least a dozen of them, the sashimono banners fluttering from their backs emblazoned with the characters of the Torohata clan. No ronin, but household samurai of Mako Torohata. Oba doubted if they were a simple patrol. There was some purpose in their riding into the forest and he had a feeling he held that purpose in his arms.

"Your friends have come to escort you home," Oba hissed in the ninja's ear. "Call out to them. I will negotiate your release. All they need do is leave me alone to find the monster and they can have their assassin back."

Meiko's eyes were filled with scorn. "If they find us here, they will kill us both," she told him. "My clan does not serve Torohata anymore than we serve Takegashi. The samurai are hunting for the man who stole certain papers from their master's castle."

Oba watched the riders as they came closer. Clearly they were following the trail he and the woman had left. "The thief was another of your clan?"

"There are too many for you to face alone," Meiko stated.

Oba laughed. "Oh no! At least with them I know my wounds will be—"

The samurai got no further. A horrible ringing suddenly struck him, like the buzz of a beehive sounding inside his ears. The weird sound overwhelmed him, his grip on the ninja slackened and like an eel she instantly writhed free of his grasp. Oba shook his head, struggling to focus his eyes. He started to rush after her. The sound of terrified horses and frightened men from the slope below told him he could ignore the horsemen for a time. The ninja was his immediate problem.

Even as he made to rush after the fleeing fugitive, Oba froze. Meiko had not fled more than a few paces away. Now she stood as still and silent as one of the barren trees. Her face ashen, her eyes lifted — even the ninja could not hide the fear she felt.

Oba lifted his own eyes, following the direction of her gaze. Suspended in the fog, some distance above the trees, two immense blue lights burned like bonfires. He could see the eerie flames flicker and sway, shuddering strangely through the fog. There was a peculiar uniformity in the way they moved, but it was only when he felt the ground beneath his feet shudder and heard the crash of some great weight driving against the earth that he understood why the fires lurched and danced in such a manner. They were not fires, at least not true fires. They were eyes, eyes glowing from the face of some immense creature. The eyes of the gashadokuro, the monster of Cripple Mountain!

The sound of the horsemen trying to recover control of their frightened steeds came as a distant murmur to Oba's ears. His head pounded with the persistent, unnatural buzzing noise, his body trembled with the booming footfalls of the gashadokuro, his eyes were locked only on the immense shape striding through the fog, snapping trees as though they were twigs. He could see the shadowy outline of the monster's body through the mist, a gigantic man-like shape. He forced himself to look away from the monster, glancing instead at the ninja. Meiko's face was twisted with a terrific concentration, her scheming mind fighting back the fear evoked by the gashadokuro. Oba could see her move, move with such slowness that almost he thought he imagined the motion. She was creeping away, by inches, carefully retreating from the path of the monster's advance.

The crack of a tree toppling beneath the press of a titanic foot tore Oba's attention away from Meiko's strangely lethargic escape. His eyes returned to the shadow looming in the mist just as it emerged from behind the fog. The samurai's breath wheezed through slackened lips like an icy wind.

Legends held that the gashadokuro was a giant skeleton, animated by fell magic and fell deeds. Myth and folktale did not prepare Oba for the horror they clothed. It was gigantic, fifty-feet at its bony shoulders, each withered arm longer than a ship's mast. The hands that swung from each arm were big enough to crush an ox and each finger ended in a blackened talon wider than the head of an axe and thicker than a man's skull. Each bone of the gashadokuro's skeleton shape was held against the next by a thin glow of blue fire. Oba noted that the bones were not simply those of a man swollen to colossal size, but each was formed of dozens — hundreds — of normal sized bones that had melted and fused together in some unholy fashion. Each finger was a bundle of smaller bones knitted together, each rib was a swarm of normal ribs bound to each other. Atop it all was the monster's head, a leering skull as big as a peasant's hut, its teeth sharp and long like the fangs of a wolf. From the pits of its sockets, the blue fires danced and writhed, swirling with a dull intelligence both inhuman and malevolent.

The gashadokuro swung its head from side to side, its bony countenance somehow conveying an attitude of terrible observation, the stalking maliciousness of a hunter in search of prey. It took every scrap of strength he could muster for Oba to look away from the monster, to stare at the retreating Meiko. She had moved, there was no question of it now, but she had not gone far.

The samurai could see the sheen of fear-sweat dripping from the ninja's face, the eyes that had almost faded into blind mad panic. Still she maintained her control, moving only by inches and degrees.

Oba swung his head back around to the monster. Instantly the lurching horror snapped its enormity around, bending down, its skull glaring down at him. Oba's hand closed about the hilt of his uchigatana, but the samurai fought back the instinct to draw his blade. Something about the way the monster moved gave him pause, and he thought of Meiko and her slow fade from the gashadokuro's path. Every muscle in the samurai's body froze, even the rise and fall of his chest became only the shallowest suggestion of motion. The grinning skull of the gashadokuro swung from side to side, its bonfire eyes staring down, blindly groping for what had been seen and lost.

The samurai could feel a crawl of terror tingling up his spine as the monster persisted in its eerie search. Though it towered only a few yards from him, the gashadokuro seemed unable to see him. That it knew he was there, Oba could not doubt, but the gruesome horror's blazing eyes were impotent to find him. The samurai did not question whatever magical deceit hid him now from the monster. All that concerned him was how long it would search and how long he could endure the closeness of its abhorrent presence. Oba knew that only his lack of motion kept him safe, a secret he had discerned from observing Meiko. Like a great river toad, the gashadokuro's sight depended upon motion; whatever did not move was invisible to it. But he did not know how long he could maintain his rigid, self-imposed paralysis; how long he could fight down the urge to claw the spectral buzzing from his brain.

The gashadokuro's skull continued to sway from side to side, its actions almost mechanical in repetition. The monster knew it had seen something and its persistence was that of a demon waiting to pass through the gate of *kimon*.

Just as Oba thought he could endure no more, he heard a scream from the slope below. The gashadokuro also heard the cry, its towering body snapping upright as though it were hinged. More cries sounded and the monster took a shuddering step. Oba heard a shouted command and then the hiss of arrows flying through the fog. The missiles clattered like so many sticks against the grey bones of the gashadokuro, glancing from its body in every direction. Torohata's men had discovered the gashadokuro and sprung to the attack.

And in so doing, sealed their doom.

The gashadokuro stomped forward, each step causing the earth to tremble. Oba maintained his rigid pose, not daring even to blink as the skeletal horror thundered toward him. So near did it pass, that a bony ankle brushed against the samurai's cheek, drawing a bead of blood from his face as its sandy roughness grated past. Fear roared in Oba's mind as he wondered if the smell of blood would announce him to the monster. The renewed screams of Torohata's horsemen made it clear that the gashadokuro sought larger prey.

Through sheer force of will, Oba spun his body around, listening to the sounds of desperate combat raging below him on the slope. Through the thinning fog, he could see the horsemen charging around the gashadokuro, jabbing at its bony flanks with spears, slashing at its skeletal shins with katanas. The monster paid no notice to these feeble hurts, but instead reached down with its ghastly claws. A man screamed, the sound terminating in a gargled wail as his steel kabuto was ripped away, taking with it the head within. Like a glutton with a sweetmeat, the gashadokuro popped the gory trophy into its fanged mouth.

Oba did not wait to see more. Torohata's men were helpless to harm the gashadokuro, that much was clear to him, and whatever distraction they offered for the monster was not going to be a long one. Cold determination flared within the samurai's soul and he drew his sword, glaring back down the slope. He did not know the name or the shape of the demon that had enslaved his lord, so it was possible the gashadokuro was that beast of *kimon*. That possibility had drawn Oba to Cripple Mountain for it was one he could not ignore.

The samurai took a step toward the melee. Such a chance to attack the monster while it was unaware might never come again. Suddenly he remembered Meiko. A glance found the ninja near the edge of the trees, shuffling her body closer with each sliding slither of her feet. Not daring to turn and watch the monster, the ninja could not see the gashadokuro's battle, nor be certain that its attention was fixed down slope.

The woman decided Oba's course of action. Meiko knew the secrets of the monster; if there was a way to destroy it, she would know. It was no dishonor to die fighting the gashadokuro, but to fall without accomplishing his mission and freeing his lord's spirit was a shame Oba could not accept. With quick strides, each step threatening to explode his heart with fear, Oba rushed at the ninja. His strong arms coiled about her, pinning her hands and pulling her to him. Meiko started to scream, then bit down on her lip to stifle the sound.

"I think we should talk," Oba hissed in her ear. "And if I do not like your answers, you will wish I had left you to the monster!"

His threat made, Oba pulled the woman with him into the fog. Behind them, the death-cries of Torohata's men pierced the night.

Throughout the night, Oba drove his prisoner onward, not daring to rest until the gashadokuro and its slaughter of the Torohata samurai was far behind them. He had paused several times along the way to frisk Meiko's kimono. Secreted weapons littered their trail through the haunted forest: a score of needle-thin shuriken, half a dozen knives of all shape and size, a thin blowpipe that made the late Hanzo's weapon look as cumbersome as a siege engine, five egg-shaped bombs filled with the gods alone knew what kind of foulness, and a coil of hair-thin copper Meiko had worn wound through her hair, an innocent hiding place for a strangler's cord. Along with her ninjato, the cruelly edged wakizashi. Oba was confident the woman was unarmed now, but was prudent enough to still check whenever they stopped to catch their breath.

During one rest-stop, with the sun just peering out from behind the clouds and the grey fog withering into nothingness from its heat, Oba sat his captive down upon the splintered trunk of a tree that had suffered from the attentions of the gashadokuro. His stern eyes were pitiless in his scrutiny of Meiko's dishevelled appearance. Her hair hung in loose coils after his rough extraction of the copper garrote, her kimono was torn and tattered from the rough travel up the slope of Cripple Mountain, her face was stained with mud from the many times she had pitched to the ground or crashed against a tree in the dark. Oba might have been moved to pity the woman's discomfort if he were not already familiar with her cunning and deceitful mind. A man who felt sympathy for a ninja was almost as big a fool as the one who trusted a ninja.

"What is the Kokuryu clan doing on Cripple Mountain?" Oba asked without preamble.

Meiko glared at him, her lips curled with defiance. Oba smiled back at her, his face as cold as a winter lake. "Keep your tongue then," he said. "We will just wait here for the monster. When he shows up, we'll see how still you can stay with me throwing rocks at your pretty head."

Color drained from Meiko's face. She licked at her lips, glancing anxiously at the gaunt, barren trees all around them. "I cannot tell you," she said, her voice a whisper. "But I can show you."

Oba laughed. "None of your tricks, you'll tell me what your clan is doing here and how much it knows about the monster. You should understand I mean every word of my threat."

The sharp cry of some animal in the darkness of the forest made Meiko's eyes go wide with fright. She threw herself down from the log, groveling at the samurai's feet. "Do not leave me to the gashadokuro!" she pleaded. "I will tell you what you want to know. Has it not struck you strange that Takegashi and Torohata struggle so for possession of this accursed mountain? It is because there is gold within the broken peak! Wealth enough to awe even the Shogun! That is what the lords fight for and why they dare the wrath of the monster!"

Oba stepped back from the ninja's clinging arms, glancing suspiciously at the dark forest around them, listening to its brooding silence. "I see now. The Kokuryu clan is stealing the gold out from under the noses of the lords, using the monster to keep their armies off the mountain." He laughed bitterly. "Only the crooked mind of a ninja would conceive such a scheme!"

Meiko scowled at him, lifting herself from the ground. "The plan is that of the Shogun," she hissed.

Hate flared in Oba's eyes, old hate fuelled by guilt and shame. "Then I have two duties to perform ere I leave Cripple Mountain. First to kill the monster, second to keep that bloated spider Yoshinaga from getting even more fat off the mountain's gold." He looked again at the blackened forest, suspicious eyes studying every tree and rock.

"We should be moving," Oba said. "I don't trust this place. Take me to this mine of yours, then we will discuss how to kill the monster."

Meiko snarled at Oba, lunging for him. The samurai easily sidestepped and the ninja fell into the mud, spattering her face with grime and muck.

"If you are through playing, I am anxious to be moving on," Oba told her.

The ninja mustered what dignity her dripping face allowed her and glared at Oba. Slowly she turned, picking a path between the trees. The samurai followed close behind, just far enough away to draw his uchigatana should the ninja make a more serious attempt at violence.

He did not notice the little mark Meiko had scratched in the mud when she fell, the little symbol that was so very similar to the ones she had left all along their trail.

True to Meiko's word, they found the mine situated at the very summit upon a jagged plateau of shattered rock and mangled earth, vivid testimony to the fury that had destroyed Frosthome's peak. Yet all was not lifeless upon the broken summit. Oba was surprised to see the buildings of a village sprawled below him as he reached the lip of the crater-like expanse at the top of the mountain. He could see men moving among the closely-packed structures of mud and thatch, could hear the sounds of pick and hammer crashing against rock. A plume of dust rose from the crater wall just behind the village, rising above the mine like some spectral flag.

Oba did not study the village long, but cast his eyes toward a pair of wooden watchtowers at either side of the settlement. He could see great brass bells hanging from their roofs, and a sentinel posted upon each tower's platform. The samurai nodded grimly. Without a doubt, the guards watched for the monster, but they would just as quickly sound the alarm should they notice him and his captive.

"We'll have to circle around," Oba started to growl at Meiko. The ninja sneered at him, her dainty foot smashing into his leg with such violence that Oba feared she had broken his knee as he spilled onto the ground. Instead of pressing her attack, Meiko sprang back, vindictive triumph still twisting her pretty features. It was the only warning Oba had.

The samurai did not try to rise, but rolled across the ground. The unexpected move surprised the ambusher who had seemingly popped out of the earth to kill him, yet even so the attacker was quick enough to correct his ninjato in mid-strike, slashing a deep cut along Oba's side.

Oba's uchigatana sprang from its sheath in a blinding flash of steel before the ambusher could attack again. The samurai's sword clove through the man's waist, just above the rope that held a skirt of woven brambles over his dun-colored leggings. The ninja fell, cut in half by Oba's blade, writhing hands pawing uselessly at the earth while blood bubbled from his mouth.

Oba observed his enemy only long enough to be sure of his death. Then the samurai twisted around, bracing for another attack. Turning, he caught a spike-like throwing knife in his shoulder, the blade sizzling like a red hot iron as it sank into his flesh. He did not know where the woman had hidden the weapon, nor how long she had awaited the perfect opportunity to use it, but Oba was pleased to cheat her of her murderous intention. He ground his teeth against the pain, stalking slowly toward her like a maddened tiger.

Meiko retreated before him, yet her look of vindictive triumph remained set upon her face. Oba swung around, just in time to meet the attack of a second ambusher. Like the first, the ninja was clad from head to toe in a weird cloak and skirt of woven brambles and grass, only a narrow slit for his eyes betraying the man within. Lying motionless and patient upon the ground, he had blended perfectly into the terrain. Oba's sword caught the descending ninjato, swatting it aside with a ringing crash. Oba did not follow through on his attack, instead spinning back around. A third grass-cloaked ninja had sprung from the ground. Seeing the samurai prepared for him, the assassin's eyes narrowed and he sheathed his sword, in the same motion drawing a pair of star-shaped shuriken from beneath his covering of grass.

The sharp-edged shuriken flashed through the air. Oba cried out as they bit into his body, slamming into his chest. Like the knife Meiko had thrown, the wounds dealt by the shuriken burned with hellish intensity. The samurai glared at his enemies, guessing the reason for his hurt.

"Sniveling jackals," Oba cursed under his breath. "Fight me with honest steel, not poison and tricks!"

Meiko shook her head, her smile becoming even harder. "We do not intend to fight you, Shintaro Oba. We intend to kill you."

Oba's eyes narrowed with hate and it was his turn to wear a cold smile. "I should warn you. I have had dealings with the Kokuryu clan before." His hand fell limply away from his wounded shoulder, but when it reached his belt, all semblance of fatigue vanished. Swiftly, Oba drew from his belt the pouch containing the egg-shell grenades he had taken from Meiko.

"I know your tricks!" Oba snarled, hurling the entire pouch at the three ninja. The assassins covered their faces and recoiled from the missile, retreating as black smoke billowed from the shattered grenades. Oba turned and sprinted toward the village, hoping to lose himself among the peasants and miners, to think of a way to meet the menace of Meiko and her clansmen. The leg the woman had kicked throbbed painfully each time it struck the ground, and his breath came hot and shallow as his lungs fought for air. He could feel his blood almost seeming to boil, lancing threads of agony throughout his body. Fleeing from the ninja pumped their poison through him with hideous speed, but Oba knew that to fight them on their own terms would be just as lethal.

The samurai paused as he rushed down into the village. He had expected the villagers to scatter at the arrival of a bloodied soldier, or at least to stare and gawk. Instead, he saw faces watching him impassively, saw hands tightening about the hafts of picks, fumbling beneath tunics for triple-bladed sai and curved kama. A cold chill ran through Oba's mind as he realized the enormity of his mistake. The Kokuryu clan had not imported slaves or serfs to work the mine. Peasant rabble did not people the village — members of the ninja clan did.

Oba backed away, trying to look as menacing as possible with his uchigatana held before him in both hands. The villagers continued to slowly converge upon him, their own weapons at the ready. Oba reflected that these must be low-level members of the clan, otherwise they would already have surrounded and killed him a dozen different ways. It only made sense, for the clan would not send its master assassins to dig a hole. Even so, there were enough of them to cut him down however sparse their training. Whole, Oba might have relished such a confrontation, but with Meiko's poison already in his veins, he knew what would come would be less a battle than a slaughter. Butchered like a fattened pig was no way for a samurai to meet his ancestors.

Suddenly, the dull crash of an alarm bell thundered over the village. The ninjas' faces went pale, their eyes going wide with alarm. An instant later, Oba knew why as the supernatural, ghastly buzzing sound invaded his brain, the ghostly herald of the gashadokuro's approach. Like statues, the murderous villagers froze all around him, their eyes darting between the samurai and the distant watchtower. Some fingered their weapons, debating how close the monster was, wondering if they had enough time to settle their enemy before it drew close enough to see them.

Oba seized the opportunity afforded by the confusion of the ninja. He sprang past the nearest of his foes, pushing them into the mire of the village street. The samurai ducked the bladed head of a naginta one of the villagers thrust at him, then drove his shoulder into a man who came at him with a pair of sickle-like kama. The wiry ninja was sent flying by the blow, crashing in a spray of filthy water. Oba kicked the man's face as he started to rise, splattering his nose in a burst of blood.

Antagonized by Oba's violent escape, other ninja rushed toward him. A ninjato slashed across his back, only his armor keeping the blade from cleaving his spine. A sai punched through his forearm, only force of will enabling him to maintain hold of his sword. A claw-like grapple fitted to a slender chain of steel whistled out and wrapped about his leg, pitting Oba in an uneven struggle against the man at the other end of the chain to remain standing.

As abruptly as the violence of the ninja erupted, they became once more as still as statues. The alarm bell had fallen silent now, but in its place had come a dull, ponderous sound, the impact of a huge weight against the earth. Again and again, the thunderous footfalls sounded, the ground shivering with each step. With agonizing slowness, the ninja lifted their heads, staring up at the grimy sky above the village. Oba followed their gaze, knowing what he would see.

The titanic shape of the gashadokuro, even more hideous in the dusty light of dawn, loomed over the village like some primordial god of death. Its witch-fire eyes glowed weirdly in its skull, boring down with malignance and rage. Oba trembled as he saw the head sway back and forth, like a dog sniffing for a hidden bone. Sweat ran down his face as he remembered the last time he had stood stiff and still waiting for the blind monster to find him.

He would not go through such an ordeal again! Oba tightened his hold on his sword. He tugged at the chain wrapped about his leg. The ninja at the other end stubbornly refused to release his hold. Oba glared at him, then risked a look at the gashadokuro. He waited until the skull swung around, until the eyes were staring in his direction. The samurai put his full strength into another sudden yank on the chain. His enemy was not ready for the effort and was jerked off his feet. The ninja stumbled after Oba, then released his hold on the chain. White with horror, the assassin turned and shrieked as death reached down for him.

The skeletal paw of the gashadokuro closed around the staggering ninja with the fury of an avalanche. Oba could hear bones crack beneath the brutal grip. A spray of blood burst from the ninja's mouth as something ruptured inside, but he still had life enough in him to scream as the monster lifted him to its face. Oba saw the fang-ridden jaws of the skull snap open...

The samurai tore his eyes from the gory spectacle and flung himself down the narrow lane between the ramshackle buildings of the village. Fire pulsed through his body, but he ignored the pain, ignored it with the fatalistic determination demanded of his caste. He could feel the ground shudder beneath him, hear buildings splinter as the enormous bulk of the gashadokuro crashed through them in its pursuit of him. The discipline of these low-caste members of the Kokuryu clan was remarkable. They remained frozen in place even as the monster raged past them, not uttering a sound when its skeleton feet crushed them in its unseeing rage. They remained statues as Oba ran past them, only the hateful gleam in their eyes betraying the life within them.

For all its size and power, the gashadokuro's peculiar motion-based vision encumbered it. Oba would duck behind the wall of a hut, then emerge a moment later from the other corner, gaining a valuable instant of freedom while the monster sought to seize him where he had been instead of where he was. The samurai was not fooled that it was anything but a respite. The monster showed no sign of losing interest in the hunt, displaying the same single-minded obsession it had shown before. The ninja, dying beneath its feet in silence, were not going to distract it from its prey as Torohata's samurai had. The weathered buildings of the village offered no shelter from the monster's claws, it could knock them down as easy as Oba might swat a fly.

Oba's eyes darted to the plume of dust rising from the pit of the mine. A deep hole gouged in the earth, he could see no way that the monster's hand could fit in an opening only a little larger than a man, nor could he imagine it tearing through the rock of the mountain as easily as it had the decrepit huts.

The desperate plan decided upon, Oba ran toward the pit, knocking aside any ninja who stood in his path. The chill shadow of the gashadokuro fell across him, blotting out the sun. Oba dove as the monstrous claw of the skeleton reached for him, the fiend's talons slashing through empty space instead of his neck. The samurai rolled as he landed, then threw himself forward in another dive. Earth exploded behind him as the gashadokuro's claw slammed into the ground. Oba heard the skull's jaws snap angrily, frustrated in its effort to grind him into the earth.

The pain pulsing through his body was now almost unendurable. Oba felt the impulse to lie down and let the monster destroy him, but such a useless death enraged his very soul. The pit was near now, ninja miners ranged around it, their clothes caked in dust, an array of picks and hammers clenched in their fists. The assassins shivered in terror as Oba and the thing pursuing him closed upon them, but they knew that to move would bring certain death upon them.

Oba ploughed through the paralyzed ninja, pitching them into the dust, leaving them for the gashadokuro's feet to crush or spare as capricious fate decided. He lunged for the black opening of the pit without hesitation. He could feel the claw of the gashadokuro whip through the air above him as he hurtled down into the shaft of the mine. Cold darkness rushed up, enveloping him, blotting out pain and fear in the chill embrace of oblivion.

Pain flooded through Oba's body as awareness slowly returned to him. He could barely remember the impact of striking the bottom of the shaft. A dim suggestion of sunlight at the top of the pit made the samurai shudder to think how far he had fallen. He rolled onto his side, instantly regretting the maneuver, stabbing agony exploding within: broken ribs digging into his flesh and scraping his organs. He was more careful as he tried to move his limbs. One arm was snapped, hanging like a broken twig from his shoulder. His wounded leg felt numb, possessed of all the feeling one might expect from a boiled haunch of ox, but at least it moved when he willed it to do so.

The samurai took stock of his surroundings. Sputtering torches set into roughly hewn niches in the ragged walls of the pit did more to illuminate the mine than the feeble sunlight filtering down from above. There were no ropes or pulleys rising from the shaft, only a series of handholds gouged into the walls for miners to climb up from the pit, bearing their quarried ore upon their backs like beasts of burden. The dark mouths of tunnels spread outward in every direction, radiating from the shaft like the spokes of a wheel. Oba could feel the icy clutch of their black depths stretching out for him. Any ninja who had lingered behind in the mine would find a thousand places to lurk in ambush for him. Oba's skin crawled with the sensation of a knife sinking into his back.

The walls of the shaft trembled and a tiny stream of dust and rock rained down about Oba's head. The samurai took shelter in the mouth of a tunnel, watching as something huge blotted out the sunlight trickling into the mine. Skeletal claws the size of oxen tore at the rim of the shaft, trying to widen it so that the gashadokuro might reach down and claim its prey.

Oba removed a torch from its niche and turned back toward the tunnel. Better to risk the lurking blade of a ninja than the monster's mercy. At least with the ninja, he might take his killer with him when he died. Dragging his numb leg, his broken arm hanging limp against his body, his side afire with dripping pain, Oba started down the winding tunnel.

How many hours he spent wandering in the darkness, the samurai could not say. It felt like days to his pain-maddened senses, but cold pragmatism told Oba that even his endurance would have reached its limit long before then. He was nearly at his limit now, unable to focus his eyes in the half-gloom of the mine, his lungs choked by dust and the smoke of his torch. No lurker had set upon him, nor could he hear the sounds of the gashadokuro digging down to find him, both of which he took as good signs until he realized his wanderings might simply have taken him so deep into the earth that he was beyond the reach of both ninja and monsters.

Despair was just sinking its fangs into Oba's spirit when he saw the door. In all his wanderings through the tunnels, he had found only bare walls pitted and scarred by the attentions of pick and hammer. Here stood a sturdy door of solid oak, banded in iron and fixed to the rock with thick staples. Such a door a lord might fit to guard his treasure vault. That thought made Oba consider the purpose of the mine and the Kokuryu clan's presence on Cripple Mountain. He scowled at the thought of the all that wealth going to the Shogun. Only freeing the soul of his lord would give him greater pleasure than cheating the Shogun of his gold.

Oba tried the door with his shoulder, finding it stout and unmoving. The samurai tried to balance himself on his numb leg and set his torch on the floor. Drawing his sword, he chopped at the iron staples. The keen blade passed through the iron bands as though they were river reeds. The oak door groaned and sagged, then its own weight completed the job, ripping it free of its last moorings. With a deafening thud, it crashed to the floor.

Oba recovered his torch and staggered into the vault beyond the door. He felt somehow cheated when the glow of the light did not reveal piled gold and treasure. Instead, he found himself looking upon a little man sitting in a straw chair. The man was old, incredibly so, his snowy beard falling to his knees, his face an almost shapeless mass of wrinkles. He wore crimson robes daubed with fantastic symbols and a blue sash adorned with silver pomes of fluff circled his chest. The sharpness in the steely eyes that stared from the ancient's wrinkly face surpassed even the keenness of Oba's sword.

"Did the Kokuryu vermin forget to give you the key?" the old man asked, his voice high and strangely youthful, incongruous with his appearance. The elder smiled at Oba and made an expansive gesture with his hands. "The hospitality of Eiji of Cripple Mountain is yours just the same. And I think you had better accept it while you can. The poison of ninja is not wise to ignore."

The samurai felt a wave of weakness seize him and he crumpled to his knees. It seemed strange to him that he should succumb to his wounds just as the old man spoke of them, but such suspicions vanished as the elder left his chair. As he moved, Oba could see that the man's legs were missing, only empty robes hanging about his waist. Even so, the elder crawled across the vault toward him. The ancient's hands, clothed in paper-thin skin, probed Oba's wounds, kneading his mangled flesh. Oba could faintly hear the old man whispering into his beard, whispering words the like of which the samurai could not understand, words that were more like the hisses of serpents than the language of men. Gradually, Oba felt the burning agony in his limbs lessen and fade. When the pain had lessened enough, he summoned the strength to stare into the old man's penetrating eyes.

"What are you?" Oba demanded. "Why have the ninja imprisoned you in this place?"

Eiji chuckled, continuing to minister to the samurai's wounds. "Here is as good a place as any to keep me, I suppose. Even if there were anyone interested enough to look for me, they would hardly do so in the depths of a mine. As for why they keep me here, I am yamabushi."

The word lingered in the air after Eiji spoke it, seeming to echo of its own accord through the tunnels. Oba nodded with new respect to the old man. The yamabushi were hermit mystics, solitary wizards who sought the isolation of the wilderness while they mastered the black arts. The skills and powers of the yamabushi were known far and wide throughout Mu-Thulan, admired and feared by everyone from the lowliest peasant to the Shogun himself.

"I've been in these mines a long time," the wizard continued. "Years, I should think. Ever since the Kokuryu clan came to steal the mountain's gold."

"Why do they let you live?" Oba asked. It was a natural question. If nothing else, ninja were cautious; keeping a yamabushi alive and prisoner was an act of foolhardiness he found it hard to accept.

The yamabushi chuckled once more. "They know I can control the gashadokuro." The statement brought a look of shocked disbelief on Oba's face. "They are right," Eiji assured him. "You see, it was I who created the monster."

Oba's mind whirled. This wizard had created the gashadokuro. A thousand questions raced through his thoughts, but one rose more prominently than the rest. If Eiji had created the gashadokuro, then it could not be the demon he hunted, the fiend that had claimed his lord's soul.

"I've lived on Cripple Mountain a long time," Eiji continued. "Longer than you would credit, I fear." He pointed a crooked finger to the roof of the vault, gesturing at the surface far above. "That village was once home to honest folk, not a crumbling lair for ninja. They were peasants, honest farmers and hunters trying to claw a precarious existence from the mountain. They were so poor that neither Torohata nor Takegashi saw fit to claim them or their settlement. Yet even so, these poor people shared their humble charity with the old ascetic who lived in the forest. A ball of rice from the table of a peasant is a richer feast than the banquet of a nobleman.

"In my way, I watched over the village, keeping the attention of wandering ghosts and malicious tengu from their homes. But I could not protect them from the malice of the mountain itself. One day, a farmer tried to dig a new well and in his labors, he discovered the mountain's secret. The news that gold had been discovered on Cripple Mountain seemed to be carried upon the wind. No longer did Torohata and Takegashi ignore the forgotten village and the accursed mountain. Their samurai surrounded the mountain, guarding every approach to prevent anyone from stealing away with the gold each lord considered his by right of rule. The villagers could not leave the mountain, fresh seed for their fields could not be brought up to them from the farms below. While Torohata and Takegashi fought on the slopes below, those trapped upon Cripple Mountain withered and died in the agony of starvation."

Eiji"s eyes burned with hate as he remembered the scene and its cause. Oba was chilled by the malignity of the wizard's stare. "I could do nothing to provide for them, as they had for me. But when they were all dead, their skinny corpses strewn about their hovels, I determined that their killers would not prosper by such villainy. From each body I took the bones and with my magic I bound them into an engine of destruction and vengeance that would kill any who dared approach the mountain and the cursed gold within it!"

"But your plan failed," Oba said. "The gashadokuro serves the ninja now!"

The yamabushi shook his shaggy head. "It does not serve them, anymore than the mountain does. They simply know how to avoid its wrath. A ninja is subtle, he knows when to hide and when to strike. Their craft is such that even an old yamabushi, wise in the ways of gods and demons, may be deceived by them. They came and caught me and put me in this place. They cut away my legs to keep me here, thinking such mutilation would weaken even a yamabushi and make him safe." A malicious grin split the wizard's face. "But perhaps Eiji will still have the last word." He looked into Oba's eyes. "I will need your help, and I can promise only danger in return."

Oba thought for a moment, then nodded. "To keep the mountain's gold from the Shogun's coffers, even death would not be too steep a price to pay."

Eiji leaned over him, his claw-like hands pulsating with unnatural energies. Oba felt his skin writhe where the yamabushi touched him, the gaping wounds closing upon themselves like melting butter. "I will need your strength to win free of this pit," Eiji told him.

"You will need your strength to escape what follows."

Oba's body still throbbed with the icy echoes of Eiji's magic. His wounds had healed with supernatural speed, his bones had set and knit of their own accord. Even his blood was clean and pure, divorced from the poison Meiko and her clansmen had used upon him. His mind recoiled to consider the fact, but he had never felt stronger than he did now. The wizard's wasted frame, clinging to his back like some grotesque child, was an insignificant burden to his pulsing muscles as he climbed the wall of the shaft. Oba kept his eyes trained upon the dim disk of sunlight above him, dreading the bony claw of the gashadokuro to come reaching down for him. Whatever mastery the yamabushi had over the monster, he hoped it was enough to fend off such an attack.

An eerie silence clung to the walls of the shaft. It was only when he was nearly at the top that Oba's ears began to ring with the spectral buzz of the monster's presence. However long he had been in the mine, the gashadokuro had lingered, waiting for him. That was the reason the ninja had not returned to their diggings, still trying to escape the monster's attention. Oba was thankful in a way. The gashadokuro would keep any lurking assassins away from the pit. A light burden or no, the wizard was still slowing him down and he knew he would make a prime target for the arrows of the Kokuryu clan if any of the ninja saw him ascending the wall of the shaft. Oba muttered a prayer to his ancestors that the monster would keep his enemies at bay until they were free of the pit.

Oba could feel the earth shudder beneath his hands as he reached the lip of the shaft. A sharp cry rang out and he could hear the booming falls of the gashadokuro's skeletal feet. With a final burst of endurance, the samurai threw himself up the last length of shaft and pulled himself onto the surface. Instantly his eyes scoured his surroundings for lurking enemies. The crushed bodies of a few ninja who had been caught in the monster's path were smashed into the ground, but they were beyond threatening him now. Farther away he could see the ravaged village, many of its huts shattered into splinters. Several ninja were standing about its streets, still and silent as statues, their faces turned toward the giant skeleton that loped through the muddy lanes.

Oba could see a lone ninja fleeing from the monster. Abruptly the man froze, becoming rigid as a post. Instantly a ninja further down the street gave voice to a sharp cry and started to run. The gashadokuro's burning eyes swung from the ninja who had stopped moving and it began pursuing the new runner. Instantly Oba appreciated the cunning of the Kokuryu clan's ruse. They were leading the monster away from the mine by means of this lethal relay. Before the gashadokuro could close upon the second runner, a third took up the cry and started to sprint toward the edge of the crater. The samurai closed a hand around the hilt of his sword. As soon as the monster's threat was removed, the ninja would return to settle with him. He only hoped to take some of them with him when he died.

"Set me down!" snapped Eiji from behind him. Oba kneeled against the ground, helping to lower the crippled yamabushi to the earth. Eiji pushed the samurai's hand away and raised himself awkwardly into a sitting position. The wizard's eyes gleamed as he watched the ninja leading the skeletal horror from the village. "So they think they are clever?" he growled. "What do slinking assassins know of magic!" He turned and regarded Oba with some degree of guilt. "You must make the most of the time I can give you. I can control the gashadokuro only so long as I can give it enemies to kill. After that…"

"How can it kill what it can't see?" Oba asked, watching as the blind monster stomped obliviously past a small group of ninja. He saw that it was Meiko and the grass-cloaked killers he had fought before. The woman seemed less interested in the monster than in the two men who had suddenly appeared at the edge of the mine. Oba could see her lips moving as she whispered orders to her clansmen.

"We will have to fix that, won't we?" Eiji said. The wizard nodded grimly. "Yes, indeed, we will fix that…whatever the price." He bowed to Oba, then made an angry gesture with his arm. "Leave me to work my sorcery, samurai. There is no work here for you or your sword."

Oba started to protest, but his blood went cold as he saw the change coming over the yamabushi. Eiji's skin was darkening, becoming the color of soot, his hair falling from his head in bloody clumps. Loathsome words slobbered from his lips and when Oba looked at the wizard's hands, they were knotted into hawk-like talons. Still chanting, Eiji lifted his deformed claws to his face. Blood spurted from beneath his fingers as he dug into his own sockets, ripping and tearing at what they contained. Crimson tatters of pulp clung to the yamabushi's fingers as he lowered his hands. Where Eiji's eyes had been was only a dripping vacuity, but even as Oba looked in horror, he saw a flicker of light begin to grow in the depths of the gory wreckage, a light that soon blossomed into orange flames.

Shrieks sounded from the village, wails of terror that tore at the sky. Oba turned from the mutilated wizard and watched as the gashadokuro lifted a hapless ninja from the ground. It was not the one who had been luring it away, but was one of the unmoving grass-cloaked assassins. As the gashadokuro's jaws closed about the struggling man's neck and decapitated him, Oba saw that the fires shining from its skull had changed, losing their blue light and turning into raging orange flames. Eiji's magic had given the monster new eyes at the cost of his own. Now the ninja could hide from the monster no longer.

Oba caught the glare of Meiko's hate-filled gaze as she stared at him before fleeing over the edge of the crater. The other ninja were less calculating in their panic. Some brought a dizzying array of weapons against the gashadokuro, spears and grapples, arrows and bombs, all alike in their uselessness against the skeletal titan. Other ninja fled into the huts, desperately trying to find some manner of sanctuary from the marauding beast. Still others held their ground, staying stiff and still, hoping against hope that the monster would ignore them.

It didn't. The screams of the dying split the air each time the gashadokuro's claw came reaching down, tearing another ninja's spirit from its body.

The samurai watched the massacre impassively. Honorless killers, spies and thieves — the Kokuryu clan was beneath his pity. They did not even have enough dignity to die well. Oba eased his way through the now deserted street, striding boldly past the rickety refuges of the last survivors. The gashadokuro raged and slaughtered, its claws and fangs wet with blood. It had turned to the village now, ripping apart huts, shredding them in its hunt for its prey.

Oba held his head high as he stalked toward the monster. He felt a tremor of fear as the beast swung its skull about and glared down at him for an instant. But Eiji's promise held true. While there were still ninja in the village, Oba was free of the monster's wrath. The gashadokuro turned back around and soon an agonized shriek rose from the battered hovel.

Shintaro Oba marched past the rampaging behemoth. The Kokuryu clan were doomed, their scheme to fill the Shogun's coffers with gold finished. Eiji's terrible revenge would continue and the gashadokuro would protect Cripple Mountain from Torohata and Takegashi and all those who would steal its treasure.

Wherever their spirits had fled, Oba hoped that the peasants appreciated the terrible vengeance the yamabushi had invoked in their name. He knew only too well the weight of sacrifice and obligation. He hoped that when the time came for him to redeem the soul of his lord, that he would be equal to whatever ordeal his own vengeance would demand of him.

Daniel R. Robichaud was last seen venturing into the wilds of central Massachusetts, searching for the City of Lost Consonants. Long feared dead, missives have recently found their way back to civilization, telling stories of such dubious quality that they can only be sold as fiction. These are appearing is such diverse places as the Cinema Spec *anthology,* Alienskin Magazine, *and the* Malpractice anthology. *This source of irregular revenue funds semi-regular rescue missions, though none of these has yet succeeded in locating the elusive explorer. If you find this author, please lure him back to civilization with the promise of dark beer. Look for clues to his whereabouts in over seventy of his reviews of Dark Fiction at www.HorrorReader.com or at his irregularly updated blog OddLife (http://dark-towhead.livejournal.com). Ingenuity in the face of death is what differentiates man from beast. Employing cunning and cleverness whilst on the run for his life from not one but two gargantuans, Vasily the Voyvodin learns it is difficult to find an acceptable place to die.*

Vasily and the Beast Gods

A Tale of Voyvodin

by Daniel R. Robichaud

A man of sense does not dwell long amongst the shadow-crested peaks of the Uryl range, Voyvodin wisdom said. For when the winds come shrieking down those jagged slopes, they come from the unknowable darkness between the stars and can blow a man to madness.

These words echoed through Vasily's thoughts while he assessed the strength of his chains and rolling prison, endured the jackal-like laughter of his once-allies-turned-captors, considered the smoldering eyes of the girl-slave who had bewitched him to turn on his qasaq company, or swore dire vengeance against the dark robed figure leading them higher into the mountains. With every moment, he remained alert for any opportunity to secure his freedom.

Mutt-faced Barot banged his mead cup against the bars of the cage and then stepped aside. The scars across both of his cheeks made a cruel, savage smirk from even placid expressions. His face far from placid, he said, "I always knew a woman would be your undoing, Vasily." *One step closer, and I'll be the undoing of your throat.*

Of course, just because he grabbed did not mean he would catch the whip-thin man. Before the betrayal, Vasily had long admired the smaller fellow's speed and skill at both evading and delivering blows. Now, Barot was merely another talented enemy. "What is it about this scrawny slag? When shapely wenches await us and the fat purses this trek promises, why throw all away for..." Barot reproved the girl with a dismissive backhand.

Vasily remained mute. What could he say that Barot would understand? That this wretch, this girl called Katya, reminded him of the sister he had vowed but failed to protect when he was but twelve autumns old? Barot had sold his own kin for a little road coin.

"Silent with regrets, eh?" Barot chuckled. "Well, no fear. Your share will not go to the hands of these dogs. I'll entrust its safety." Barot trod ahead, leaving Vasily to brood.

Vasily's harsh face, scarred and battered by life's rough road, crinkled in irritation. A man of varied experience, he knew what lay ahead for him now. *A man of sense, huh?* He snorted and strained his strong body honed by ten autumns spent fighting other men's wars, but the chains were too strong for breaking. Idly he tugged on the bars, on the off chance that Barot's stench might have weakened the iron. No luck.

No stranger to either the blackest moods or the brightest mirths, always Vasily seemed the bearer of old sorrows. He had wrested crowns from dead men's brows, only to pass them along to the ambitious living; the throne held little allure for him. The road always beckoned.

The road…His first love, his deepest affection. Riding above it, chained in a cage wagon, seemed nothing short of blasphemy.

Tired with testing , Vasily studied the steel ring binding both his and the woman's chains to the cage ceiling. Only ropes held it in place. *Too many and too thick to snap before they would come for me, but a knife would make short work of—*

Of course, he did not have a blade of any sort. Another blasphemy.

Katya grunted like a hungry bear. She stared at him with a hot outrage, no different than when he had walked on Barot's side of the bars.

"There is no sense in hating me," he said. "The both of us are slated for slavery 'til death, now."

Vasily looked ahead to the robed man, the hairless twig of a sorcerer, shrewd source of coin for the qasaqs and leader of this expedition. The man called himself Gregori, and he was tall, nearly six feet, but emaciated. What few dealings Vasily had with Gregori had revealed the sorcerer to be little more than a bony shell, a husk around some cold, alien flame of power. Without it, Gregori would be a wizened corpse; with it, he was unstoppable.

"Perhaps not." This from Katya.

Despite Barot's dismissal, there was a fierce beauty to the woman. Hair lustrous as a sable, eyes like emeralds, she carried a kind of strength that many men could only dream of possessing. Hers was the tongue of the Chuckchi mountain folk, neither the fluid Voyvai of Vasily's steppe dwelling forbearers nor the stilted, formal tongue of the Muskovite city dwellers. It startled Vasily, for the woman had never actually spoken to him before, and it took him several heartbeats to realize she did not respond to his thoughts, but to his spoken fatalism.

He cocked an eyebrow at her, demanding explanation. She offered none, staring instead into the frosty mountains above and around them, as though she might divine the future from their peaks.

When the wind howled then, the hackles on Vasily's neck rose. Up here, the wind sounded like a living thing and that was eerie enough, but now…Now, Vasily detected something hidden inside that howl, carried upon it like ticks upon a hound. He turned to scan the slope that captivated Katya's attention. Ice and snow, rock and scrubby trees.

Are those slithering shadows more than plays of light?

A grin tugged at his mouth. This could well be the chance for freedom.

"Alarm," a qasaq called, but already too late. Death leapt up from carefully concealed hunting pits, emerged from the shadows of ice crusted stone, armed with broad bladed spears and skinning swords, wrapped in the white fur cloaks of their sacred bears, bodies painted an even emptier shade of pale by frost wode extracts. These were Chuckchi men, kin to the qasaqs' fair prisoner — yet they came not in the manner of a party bent on rescue but as one filled with blood rage, berserk and lunatic, and the winds came with them, roaring like the thirsty dead.

Surprise and blundering allowed the Chuckchi tribesmen a momentary advantage. Snow became bloody slush where qasaqs fell, but in time Vasily knew the tide would turn. Already, Gregori was channeling the dark power he wielded, and alongside the reek of sweat came the stink of brimstone.

"Keep the prisoners!" Barot shouted. One of the young qasaq men, a dark skinned Turk called Alexi, arrived outside the cage first, in time to fend off a savage attack from a pair of maddened Chuckchi. As he dispatched his opponents, he inadvertently backed into Vasily's reach, learning his fatal mistake only when the prisoner's hands caught his throat.

"Open the cage door, boy."

"N-Never!"

A sense of immortality is the province of youth. With the proper tension, Vasily aged Alexi into manhood. The young qasaq kicked a lever, and the cage door rattled open.

"Now, your sword."

Alexi complied, throwing the blade into the cage. Vasily shoved the boy forward into a pair of approaching qasaq. While that trio floundered, the Voyvodin grabbed up the discarded weapon and hacked the ropes binding chain ring to ceiling. It fell, and man was again separated from woman. Vasily held out a hand, a silent bid for her to join him. Katya hunched beneath her blanket wearing a mask of stern defiance, certain of eventual rescue by her tribe.

To Hell with you, then.

Vasily caught a whiff of ozone before rivers of weird green flame bathed him, lifting and flinging him out the cage. Fingers of fire traced ghastly burns across Vasily's torso and arms. He muttered a curse and found his feet, hazarding a single glance back toward the wagon. A spectral aura of translucent green wreathed nearby Gregori, a sorcerous fire that seemed not to discomfort its bearer but ignited any who approached. In the cage, Katya cowered, her certainty of Chuckchi rescue gone.

Vasily's heart went to her, and he found himself on the verge of rushing to her rescue. Cold reason stayed him. *What hope did steel and a strong arm or heart stand against witchcraft?*

Vasily fled, swinging his blade against an enemy he could dominate. A fighting madness consumed him and qasaq and Chuckchi alike fell before him as he ran.

Soon, he was alone but for the wind, like a bedeviling dog, snapping at his heels.

A racing heart slows in time. A runner's legs weary under the hot strains of exertion. Were he at top shape, fed properly over the last few days, rested, and not carrying twenty pounds of chains, Vasily might have gone for longer than an hour at top speed, and were the ground not so treacherous, his speed might have been enough to cover more distance than a single mile.

Not this day.

In under an hour, in less than one mile, Vasily collapsed to his knees, spitting great clouds of cold smoke, shivering beneath the dancing winds whose invisible fangs so easily chewed through his blood and sweat soaked garments.

If I do not find some shelter or at least the fixings of a fire... There was no need to dwell on the doom promised by such a situation.

He found himself on a narrow ledge. A scrubby tree offered little protection from the wind, though it did stand tall and straight despite the gales. A stone poised near the edge offered a little more relief, but the sheer rock wall of the mountain at his back guided the winds along his spine.

His legs burned. His lungs ached. This ledge seemed as fine a place to die as any.

Though not yet ready to surrender, Voyvodin wisdom insisted a man sit only in a place he would not mind being his grave. Vasily minded, yet his aching legs and arms would not carry him much further.

He stabbed his sword into the snow and leaned upon it. The discomfort would keep the winds and exhaustion from wooing him to deathly sleep.

The settling chill brought an indescribable thirst. Every gallon in the great, freshwater Black Lake could not quench such a thirst. After but a moment's rest, Vasily tried to push himself back to his feet.

A laugh answered his efforts to stand. Vasily's head darted side-to-side. "Who's there?"

No answer but malicious glee. Louder now, heartened by his confusion. "Answer me, damn you!"

Was this laughter real? A trick of the wind, perhaps? Or a broken mind?

A man rose from the far side of the ledge, defying a two hundred foot drop. His cheerful face was strange, too small for the egg-shaped head. Large, moist eyes and chubby cheeks gave him a nearly infantile quality. He settled his chin upon a pair of wrinkled hands, hands that lay upon the stone as though leaning on a table and not somehow suspending him in midair. The laughter paused long enough for the stranger to say, "And would you murder humor?"

"I'd end yours."

The stranger's mirth froze. "For such disrespect, my wife would take your tongue. Perhaps your eyes, too."

Wife? What manner of creature is this? Certainly not human, for it seemed equally careless of heights and wind; the fine hair upon its head did not so much as twitch in the gusts.

"And will you," Vasily wondered, "do as your wife?"

The stranger considered this a moment, and then laughed once more. "I think not. A man should have teeth, I say, and so armed he should not be afraid to use them. Are you quite near to death yet?"

"Not so near as you might— "

"Oh, but you *are*." The laughter suddenly grew poisonous. "Any moment now will be your last, and as I've a preference for warm meat." With that, the stranger began crawling over the rock, revealing new levels of strangeness.

No man at all, this being was like several men combined. Head to neck to torso was fine, but where a waist should have been was instead another torso, equipped with two more working arms. Another torso and set of working arms fitted under this. And another. Each neck stump fitted somehow beneath the previous ribcage, and each strange segment rocked slightly with the creature's movements. Six arms became eight, became ten… Still the thing came, enormous and crawling on a multitude of hands. The grin on its rubbery, infant-like face stretched wider than Vasily thought possible; that mouth became an enormous gash, revealing two rows of hooked, needle sharp fangs.

Seeing them, Vasily recalled the hushed tales of Little Grandfather, said to dwell in the Uryls, an eater of flesh and husband of the Yaga Witch. Little Grandfather was nigh invulnerable to weapons forged by mortal hands. Still, the tales spoke of the monster being bested…

Vasily blurted, "I've a challenge for you!"

Little Grandfather, so the stories said, had a weakness for competition.

The crawling, segmented creature reared back to eagerly wring several pairs of hands. "Truly?"

"This meat of mine is near cold," Vasily said, "and I think it would be tasteless. However, I pose we have a contest to get the blood stirring. If I lose, the meat will be warmest of all."

The quantity of slobber told Vasily that Little Grandfather found such a notion to be favorable. "And, if you are the victor, little mortal?"

"My life is mine," Vasily said, "and you'll answer one question."

"Greedy, aren't you?"

"Not at all. I simply know the value of my flesh. Do you see the muscle here in my arms? Large and strong."

"Stringy too, I wager," Little Grandfather countered, its face now as shrewd as a fat merchant.

"My skin is pliant—"

"Methinks it sun hardened."

"Then perhaps you yield without even hearing my challenge?"

"No." Eagerness filled Little Grandfather's face and body. Its eyes fairly bulged, its hands squeezed each other until the knuckles went white and cracked like dice in a roller's well. "Tell me your challenge."

Vasily quickly wracked his memory for any salient information. Little Grandfather was quick as a centipede, could climb like a cat and had the endurance of five oxen, but its arms, so shriveled and ancient, were individually weak.

"I challenge you to a feat of strength— "

"Rolling boulders?" Little Grandfather offered, its many hands — including some dozen pairs as yet unseen — clapping with glee. "Perhaps a rope war?"

In either of these, the vast number of arms would pose an unfair advantage. Even the little strength of each when offered in such abundance was more than Vasily could hope to counter, particularly as weary as he was.

"No," Vasily said, "a wrist wrestle." So as not to insult Little Grandfather, he added, "You may use any two of yours against one of mine."

Mirth vanished beneath a wave of fury. "Do you take me as a weakling? I'll match but *one* of my wrists to yours."

"Apologies, Little Grandfather."

The slobbering grin returned, now. "So, you know me? Then you must also know how the Devil's Forge Master Yakob made gauntlets to ensure my hindmost limbs would be stronger *than any mortal man's*."

The sinking in Vasily's gut confirmed that if he had known this, it had been forgotten. Little Grandfather noted the fresh beads of sweat on the Voyvodin's face and fairly cooed. "Already you warm for me! But not enough. Wearied by travel, are you? Well, I will not face a weakened opponent." From a pouch hanging around one of its waists, the creature produced a slender flask and tossed it into the snow at Vasily's feet. "Therein is a draught my dear wife prepared. One quaff can refresh a man like a good night's sleep."

Vasily took up the flask, unstoppered the top and sniffed the sloshing contents.

"Just one sip, friend," Little Grandfather said. "This brew is much too rich for a mere mortal."

The stuff was horrible, bitter as vinegar and thick as Syberian Elm sap. Vasily coughed at the sip he took. The mere notion of a second taste made him want to retch. "Many," he wiped his lips, "gratitudes, Little Grandfather." Still, the promised effect was granted. Weariness slid from him like an unwanted blanket.

~ Vasily and the Beast Gods ~

He returned the flask.

"Shall we have that contest, now?" Without waiting for reply, Little Grandfather continued forward, revealing the rest of its monstrous form. Two dozen different human torsos, mystically combined. Each set of arms was as shriveled as the last, but for the final two, which were sheathed in enormous bands of gleaming Soulsteel, stuff forged on the Devil's anvils in the Hell beyond the great Western wastes.

Vasily tasted the sour promise of defeat. Stronger than any mortal. How could he hope to win against this? Not in any honest competition, so how might he adjust the odds?

Vasily could not help but tremble before this enormous creature.

"Full of respect and fear? I like you, mortal! To again prove my generosity," Little Grandfather said, "I'll even grant you this: Ask your question and I'll answer it."

Vasily longed to ask *How might I best you?* However, such a question would violate Little Grandfather's patience. While certainly greater than that of the Yaga Witch — notoriously short tempered and prone to boiling offensive fools in butternut broth — Little Grandfather's patience had limits.

Katya, Gregori and the qasaqs occurred to him, then, and he blurted, "I traveled with a sorcerer and his girl-slave. They sought to reach the highest peak on this mountain, claiming it to be home to ancient treasure. What will they find up there?"

Little Grandfather laughed once more. "Why any Chuckchi child could answer that." The creature's eyes pinched shut in concentration before a litany fell from his mouth: "'The Ancients drilled deep, hollowing from peak to bedrock, and they filled the Uryls with sorcerous machines. From here, they decided the fates of kings and birthed the fires of small size, which burned deepest and scoured the world in That Age Forgot. On this peak, dwells the great Kaiynen-Kutho, charged to keep the sorceries imprisoned, that they might never wreck havoc upon the world again.'"

Vasily groaned. Kaiynen-Kutho? The God Bear, sacred deity to the Chuckchi?

Little Grandfather continued. "'Tis said the doors of his temple can be opened by blood sacrifice and ancient invocation. I'll wager the girl-slave you mentioned is to be the offering to Kaiynen-Kutho himself. Providing that the proper rites are followed, the great beast might allow passage into the heart of the ancient barrow. But I, for one, would not return there for all the rubies in Muskow."

Vasily's spirits slumped. Only a madman would seek out the gates to the Hidden Kingdoms of the mythical, inhuman Ancients. Seers and prophets and sorcerous masters of time, space and the demons that dwell within all matter, their knowledge was lost in the fires of the gods-sent Armageddon.

Any who sought to master those lost arts found a gruesome end.

To prevent further thinking about such insanity, Vasily desperately considered his surroundings. The mountain wall offered very little to help him. Likewise, the rock Little Grandfather used as a perch. Likewise, the scrawny but stout tree…

"Wait, wait Little Grandfather. There is too little space here for the both of us. Could you perhaps climb down again, to give us both some room to compete?"

Little Grandfather's eyes became cautious slits as it considered this request. "Do not attempt to trick me, mortal. Mine is the patience of stone, but mine is a greater wrath than even the Yaga Witch. I will hunt and have the lying hearts of those who think they have the best of me."

"I understand." Too late to change his mind now. Vasily could only hope that, should his plan succeed, Little Grandfather simply boasted.

Little Grandfather marched over the side and down until only its hind end and limbs remained on the ledge. For a moment, Vasily wondered if the creature would suddenly reveal a snake-like flexibility, bending around to observe the contest, but this turned out not to be the case. Little Grandfather's jointed body offered little sideways mobility, so with its hind end facing Vasily and its arm crooked at the elbow for wrist wrestling — bending in reverse, so when elbow touched earth, the thumb pointed toward ground — the infant-like face could see nothing of the actual contest.

Vasily stood stock still, speaking slowly to keep the nerves from his voice when he said, "You're too close to the edge. A hearty success would send me over the side, and you'd be out a good meal. Come closer."

Again, Little Grandfather offered a suspicious, "Remember what I said about trickery," but did as bade. "Now, face me!" The upside down hand, sheathed in its Soulsteel house, flexed and hellish steam slithered about it.

"We're still a bit close to your perch. If you apply just enough strength, you'll dash me to paste. I'd rather you chewed me, Little Grandfather. Come just two paces more."

"Fine, fine. Your meat had best be succulent, what with all this trouble."

"Oh, it will be," Vasily said, "if you win."

"How can I not? Are you ready?" Without waiting for the reply, Little Grandfather swung its arm in a crushing arc. The steel over its wrist connected not with a surprised or lax opponent but heavy resistance. Little Grandfather strained and grunted, but the resistance held fast. "What might, for a mortal. This will be a fitting match, indeed!"

Vasily skulked away. With luck, the stout tree would endure Little Grandfather's contest long enough for the Voyvodin to make his escape.

Vasily made good time along the trail he had taken. Fear can quicken a man's steps even past the point of exhaustion. Adrenaline and the Yaga

Witch's brew gave enough of a boost to carry him the mile back.

The ambush had ended in Gregori and the qasaqs' favor, but it had been a costly victory. Plenty of bodies littered the mountain trail, but not the cart. Wheel ruts in the snowy pass spoke a tale of movement made more for speed than caution. Based on the numerous dead, littering the earth like tree pollen in the springtime, Vasily wondered if the Chuckchi tribes had any able bodied men left.

The corpses offered an abundance of dry garments and weapons — he slid a quiver of three javelins across his shoulder — as well as freedom from the chains and the makings of both fire and food. In time, Vasily felt strong enough to follow the trail up the mountain.

All for my sister...for a woman who resembles her... It seemed foolish to the survivor in his mind, the Barot side of him. Even revenging himself on those who imprisoned him seemed little reason. *Let the mountain gods eat them!*

Foolish or not, he pursued his former comrades; foolish or not, he followed that woman, hoping he was not yet too late.

He heard the travelers before seeing them. Gregori was singing a strange arrhythmic song, punctuated by the woman's curses. They were camped on a plateau within sighting distance of the mountain's summit.

Slipping into a place of concealment, Vasily studied their camp from among snowcapped stones.

A pair of bonfires roared in enormous pits, and the smoke stank of seared flesh and oil. Only a handful of qasaqs — Barot included among them — remained in any kind of fighting shape, and even these appeared too weary to last long. Two men chained Katya to an altar stone. Struggle as she did, they worked relentlessly, never once looking back toward their singing leader. Gregori sat apart from the bonfires and past the altar, drawing the curved edge of a kukri knife across a whetstone.

Beyond even the sorcerer stood a thirty foot tall block of ice frozen across the face of the mountain. To Vasily's eyes, the dancing firelight illuminated stone too flat to be natural and revealed seams in the translucent, filthy freeze. Doors, they were. Enormous, yes. Concealed, yes. But doors, nonetheless, and old.

With no time for proper observation and planning and little time for a stealthy approach or one-by-one whittling away, Vasily considered his options. If the woman had looked any differently, he would have left altogether. Or so he told himself. It was no decision. He stabbed his trio of javelins into the snow, lining them up for quick and easy access, and began his one man assault.

The first javelin impaled the qasaq holding Katya's wrists. It was Alexi. The young warrior crumpled atop the altar, clawing at the gory steel head protruding from his belly.

The second javelin arrived while the qasaqs were still startled but calling alarms. The sorcerer's looking up and around was all that saved him from a killing strike. The javelin struck shoulder instead of throat.

The final javelin, aimed for traitorous Barot, bit ice and vanished into a snow bank.

The qasaqs brought arms to bear and quickly amassed into a protective half-circle, facing all possible directions.

Vasily grinned. *They expect another assault from the Chuckchi.*

This gave him the chance to close much ground before the qasaqs realized their mistake. Only after Vasily's sword drank blood and life, leaving one of the battle-worn and travel-weary qasaqs in a heap on the heat-leeching ice, did the others come.

Swords clashed, axes swung, but the blows came weakly and slow from demoralized, frozen hands.

Vasily could have recounted each of their names and strings of their deeds, so well did he know these men. Yet Gregori had proven a hard task master, and the mountain folk must have been relentless in their barrage of assaults. The qasaqs would neither seek nor accept mercy, though now they fought like passionate amateurs at best. They came like exhausted children, scratching from spite. The Voyvodin put them to bed, one and all, until only Barot remained.

"You'll not have me so easy, Vasily."

Vasily readied his sword, savoring the taste of sweat and blood upon his tongue, the battle fever in his head. His grin must have held something fearsome because the smaller man began to tremble.

Whip-fast, Barot came; panther-quick, Vasily met him. Their slashing swords spat sparks, cutting lightning-fast swaths through the air. Barot fought like a demon, frothing and cursing, but always on the offensive, pounding and cutting, trying to batter through Vasily's defenses. Then, Barot's boot found a patch of blood-slicked ice and his stability vanished. He crashed to the ground, and his sword slid into the nearby bonfire. The qasaq waved his hands between his face and the tip of Vasily's sword, wordless but begging for his miserable life.

"Fear not," Vasily said, "I entrust your coin will be wasted on neither slags nor dogs."

The sudden stink of ozone distracted him from delivering the finishing blow. Eerie green flame arched across the corner of his eye, and Vasily dove back from the worst of it. One fiery finger glanced across his face, scalding his cheek and throat and left eye, but Barot caught the brunt. He screeched as he roasted.

Finding his feet, Vasily again wondered what chance he might have against a sorcerer surrounded by flame. Though the blood on Gregori's shoulder suggested he could die like any other man, it did not make Vasily the one to finish him.

Suddenly, the entire plateau shook, and the air filled with the gritty din of some giant grinding his knuckles against the frosty earth.

Not a giant Vasily discovered. Those enormous blocks of ice and the smooth stone — now revealed to be iron — slowly swung out like matched sets of double doors, revealing a lightless passage that vanished into gloomy depths.

How—?

Katya, no longer chained, pointed one hand toward the doors, while alien syllables fell from her tongue. As both Vasily and Gregori — momentarily distracted from his Voyvodin opponent — watched, the woman threw up a scarlet-slicked second hand, presenting an offering taken from Alexi's open wound.

Beyond the clamor of ice and iron grinding through snow and ice and gravel, Vasily heard new sounds. Through those doors, or perhaps beneath Vasily's feet, came the crackles of lightning, the groan of age worn gears, and above all, the relentless pounding of one thousand hammers at work on steel bells. It filled him with a kind of terror. *What inhuman hands might still be wielding those hammers after unknowable centuries? What eyes might see through such impenetrable darkness?*

"A fine, final sight, eh?" the sorcerer asked, "Sounds and sights of Ancient glories before you die? Few men could attain anything more enviable."

At the stink of Gregori readying his next assault, Vasily raced for the open doors. If he might lose himself in the darkness inside…

Though the sorcerer's footfalls followed the Voyvodin, none of the sorcerous flame did. *Perhaps he desires to do no damage to the treasures within.*

Vasily reached the threshold the same moment he discovered a new sound from within. A strange reverberation. A string of recurring tremors. If the doors opening had been a giant's knuckles grinding across ice, then these must be that titan's footsteps, steadily approaching the moonlit outside world.

Footsteps.

Cackling like some victory drunk loon and caring not one whit about the hammers, Gregori continued his relentless approach. Vasily could smell the nearing reek of the sorcerer's protection.

Between a madman and the unknown, Vasily chose the evil he could see. He spun on his pursuer, sword at the ready.

Knife held high, Gregori stopped some ten feet away. "And now," he said through a sneer, "you die—"

Thunder pounded from within the darkness, freezing the sorcerer's smile. Gregori's eyes pulled away from Vasily, past him, above him, ignoring him for something new and startling. A sudden gust, stinking of time and decay, swept around the two men.

Vasily hazarded a glance back and froze.

A paw had emerged from the dark. Wider than Vasily's shoulders, with ebony claws longer than his legs, it clomped down against the stone floor. Thunder rumbled through the chamber.

Even as the Voyvodin gaped, the ankle rocked and the enormous leg became visible. Covered in thick, dark fur but for patches — *Diseased?* — where only silvery flesh gleamed, it stretched up into the darkness some fifteen feet overhead.

Vasily stared upward, silent.

The bottom of a muzzle appeared above Vasily's crown. More brown fur, more patches of shorn silver flesh. A twitching black nose wet with some kind of viscous mucus.

Next, a full head emerged from the stygian depths, bear-like but immense. Broader than the cage wagon, it housed two horrible, yellow eyes large as tower shields, the orb of the left eye oddly shattered, ruined by a spider web of cracks. Crafty intellect flared into purest hatred when they beheld Vasily and Gregori.

The muzzle split into a toothsome maw, and a fresh blast of stinking wind emerged along with a roar of such rage that surely even the mountain would bow before it. Kaiynen-Kutho, this must be. The God Bear, himself. Enraged and terrible.

Vasily's strength nearly fled his limbs. He remained standing only through some miracle of self control.

Gregori, on the other hand, spoke the language of magic in terrified squeaks. Stronger flames must have wreathed his body, for the increased illumination revealed more of the great beast in flickers. Revealed the descending underside of the God Bear's other paw.

Instinct took over. The Voyvodin ducked underneath the heavy swipe, then dodged away from a savage second. The paw slammed the frozen earth with force enough to make the mountainside shiver.

"Run!" Katya shouted. A good idea, but first he had to evade the God Bear's fury.

Vasily could dart around Kaiynen-Kutho's frenzied claws for only so long. Finally, one struck him.

The Voyvodin had once seen a swimming man's skull split beneath a warship's prow. This blow was enough to likewise devastate the fragile human form, had Vasily not rolled with the impact, distributing yet diluting its effects.

Thrown from the doorway, he skittered across the ice, not stopping until nearly all the way to the altar. His ribs felt as if a hammer had been taken to them; likewise his pelvis and neck and face, his arms and legs. Nothing immediately life threatening, though salty blood enriched the saliva filling his mouth. As soon as he reached a place of safety, he vowed to take closer stock of his wounds. Until then, Vasily gritted his teeth against the pain coursing through every bone of his body and pushed himself upright.

He staggered to Katya and unchained her legs from the altar. "We must get away."

"Not," she said, breathless and pointing at the sorcerer's faltering strength, "yet."

Voice little more than a mouse peep, Gregori said "You…You will obey me, beast."

In response, enraged and snarling Kaiynen-Kutho leaned down with jaws spread.

The sorcerer's commands became terrified gibbers.

The jaws snapped shut. Swallowed. Kaiynen-Kutho then unleashed a third roar before turning to behold Vasily and Katya.

The Voyvodin whispered curses, and Katya caught his shoulder with a desperate squeeze. "Venture no further than this," she whispered. "Make no move, or you will call His attention."

"I think," Vasily whispered, "I've already invited that damnation."

The mighty God Bear took a single step from his den, and Katya's eyes widened. She furiously mouthed words foreign/unknown to Vasily. *Prayers perhaps? Enchantments? Protections? Curses in Kaiynen-Kutho's name?* Whatever she attempted, it did not stay the behemoth from taking another step.

Then, a new voice cracked the air like a horsewhip. "And so I find you, betrayer!"

Vasily's spirits sank even deeper, when he recognized that irritated snarl before the speaker's many limbs carried it up and around the peak.

Kaiynen-Kutho paused when he heard Little Grandfather scuttling over the doors of his lair. The mighty head rose, and a new surge of fury given voice spilled from the gargantuan bear-god's mouth.

"The mortal man is mine, Kaiynen-Kutho!"

The God Bear either did not understand the words or did not heed them. He stood upon hind legs — towering over creation, this king of all kings — and pawed at Little Grandfather. Catching hold, Kaiynen-Kutho then drew this prize into his enormous jaws. Fresh gore joined Gregori's crimson on the God Bear's fangs.

Little Grandfather screamed curses but did not yield. Its mighty rear limbs, adorned with steaming Soulsteel gauntlets, pounded against the bear's midsection. Kaiynen-Kutho snarled and squeezed. Little Grandfather screeched but struck yet again. Reddish-black ichor from two godlike beasts splashed across the ice.

Over the sounds of furious combat, the unseen hammers inside the mountain continued to pound, inviting but sinister.

"Can you close them?" Vasily demanded. Katya's face registered only confusion. "Close the doors, Katya. Trap the both of them inside."

She drove both hands into dead Alexi's gut and wrenched out fists filled with blood and viscera. These she tossed into the air and spat mouthfuls of alien syllables. The doors began to grind their way shut.

Too slow, Vasily realized. *The God Bear will easily escape!*

However, at the sound of the door's motion, mighty Kaiynen-Kutho again dropped to all fours and started back into his dark lair, dragging Little Grandfather with him.

Little Grandfather did not go without protest. It made even more frantic attempts to escape the jaws and claws of the God Bear, though these efforts produced no more successful results than before. As the behemoth dragged it into the darkness, Little Grandfather spat, "A thousand curses on your head, Voyvodin! May snow leopards bite you! May the World Serpent swallow you! May your feet never settle in one place for longer than—"

The slamming of the doors silenced what followed, once more sealing monsters and mysteries behind iron and ice.

"What riches lay in there?" Vasily whispered.

"No riches but death," Katya said, bringing up another handful of Alexi's blood. "The infernal craft of the Ancients is forever guarded by the tireless Kaiynen-Kutho."

The winds blew, carrying the cackles of insane gods.

Vasily prodded the fire to keep it strong and remained ever watchful for any sign of activity, either from the massive doors or deep shadows. Katya sat beside him, head upon his shoulder, arms about his waist, watchful as well.

Thus would they pass time until dawn, when he would see Katya back to her people and then travel as far as he could from this place of bear gods and relentless hammers, of ancient sorcery and maddening winds, of vengeful monsters and ice. The world waited and the qasaqs' coin purses would take Vasily far from here.

Sitting quiet beside this proud Chuckchi woman, the Voyvodin thought: *This would be a fine place to die, were it not so blasted cold.*

Jeff Draper writes heroic fantasy fiction in the vein of David Gemmell and Greg Keyes. He's been published by The Sword Review *(now* MindFlights*), the anthology of heroic adventure* Return of the Sword, *and* Abandoned Towers. *Married with four kids in the Seattle area, he lives a busy life of work, church, more work, family time, household chores, some more work, and the Marine Corps Reserves. Follow the writing side of his life at his blog, Scriptorius Rex, at http://scriptoriusrex.blogspot.com. Jeff's tales — those I've read — evoke powerful emotions and thoughtful consideration. They are built upon brutal truths that deliver believable action because they put the reader smack-dab in the midst of traumatic events. In this instance, rage is a formidable ally...until it begins to consume a man. The hero here has the opportunity to define more than just his name.*

Thunder Canyon

A Tale of the Mountains

by Jeff Draper

Rath slid a knife between the guard's ribs while holding the man's mouth shut from behind. The body jerked and kicked. Rath pulled back, feeling pain in his fingers. Blood rushed out around his knife hand as he lowered the quivering body to the wooden planks of the sentry's stand, working the blade back and forth. He flexed his other hand and only then realized that the guard had bitten him. Breathing in deeply, Rath pressed his wounded hand into his thigh and then searched out the other sentry. His revenge had begun.

The night cloaked his movements and the cold wind whistling down the mountain canyon covered the few sounds he made. Rath skirted around a line of huge stakes made from entire tree trunks set deeply into freshly broken soil. Years of hunting had made him used to stealth. A frontier village life with bandits and criminals had made him used to death. This was different.

Rath paused and took a cloth out of his pocket, wrapping it around his throbbing left hand. He should have remembered gloves. Moving around the enormous cage, he started up stairs of raw red pine to close in on the next sentry. Halfway to the landing a step creaked under his weight. At the same time a deep huffing sound came from within the wooden enclosure, like a giant bellows with a shovelful of gravel thrown in. Rath froze, bloody knife in hand, while the guard glanced to his right but did not look behind him. Coming up the rest of the way, Rath finished him off just like the first, only this time shoving him forward into the railing to prevent the body from thrashing.

Laying him out and withdrawing the knife, Rath looked down the canyon at the ramshackle buildings clinging to the rocky walls and scattered around the dry, dusty ground. Once a river leading out of tired, rounded mountains, the canyon had long ago dried up. Most of the lower buildings were made of local stone with squat, utilitarian features. Along the sheer canyon walls ran an extensive scaffolding system of wood and rope that supported all manner of construction. Some of the buildings even reached the top, nearly a hundred feet up. Several lanterns and hooded candles swung on poles or illuminated windows. No one else moved about at this time of night.

Rath cleaned his blade on the dead man's furs. He smiled. The trembling in his stomach had disappeared when the first drop of his enemy's blood hit the dirt. Three days before he'd rounded the bend on the road home to see smoke clouds in the sky. Frantic moments flew by as he spurred his horse and then his world collapsed when he saw his village and his smithy a smoldering ruin. Heather, his wife, newly wed and bright as sunshine, lay covered in rubble, a blackened, stinking corpse. He'd stood there, looking down at the body he'd courted since childhood, a body he no longer recognized. Since that moment, all he had thought of was killing.

While he worked he watched the source of the strange noise within the cage. The bars next to him rose fifty feet up and nearly spanned the entire width of a narrow choke point within the canyon. Inside sat what looked like a great boulder perhaps twenty feet high and just as wide. Rath watched it, seeing the outlines of its arms and legs, its bowed head. The imprisoned Wen Quaar warrior sat sleeping and, thankfully, occasionally snoring. He didn't know how it had ended up behind bars and didn't care. They were known for bad tempers and that was useful right now.

Rath finished with the blade and started tying the cloth to his hand. Another huffing sound came from beside him and he glanced over. A giant head, as tall as a man, turned and looked down with glowing red eyes. Rath scrambled backward, pressing up against the railing. The Wen moved forward, with a grinding sound like stone on stone, until its face was against the bars. "How many of those can you kill?"

Rath knew the legends and the traders' stories. He'd heard the reclusive stone giants could speak but had never actually believed it until now. "What?"

The Wen turned to look at the camp. Its voice was surprisingly quiet, barely heard over the gusting wind, but deep and resonant. "Is there enough iron in your spine?"

Rath was at a loss for words. He tried to make out any kind of expression on the huge, stony face but saw only darkness against darkness. "I'm going to kill as many as I can." He turned away, looking for any sign of alert.

"Will that satisfy you?"

"Maybe. Actually I…I was about to free you."

Rath heard a quick fluttering rumble and realized the thing laughed at him. "Free me, little one? So I can enact your revenge for you? I think that's a bad plan. Your kind is smarter than that. I have my own revenge to enjoy. Yours would have to wait."

"How do you know I'm looking for revenge?"

"You reek of it."

Rath stood, looking the Wen in the eyes. "Listen beast, these raiders are savages. They came down from these mountains and slaughtered my village, my wife, and I will slaughter them. I will keep killing them until a river of blood flows down this canyon."

The Wen regarded him for several moments. "There is plenty of iron in your spine. What is your name, little one?"

"Rath."

Again the Wen laughed. "In my language that means great anger. Brutal and unrelenting."

"After tonight it will mean the same thing in my language."

The Wen made a sound that resembled the purring of a giant cat. "We have similar natures tonight. Both of us exist to kill."

"So if I let you out of this cage we can work together?"

"Little one, I am not imprisoned by this cage. It is merely to comfort my tormentors' hosts. I could break these bonds with a shrug. Your raiders have taken up with a klatch of warlocks. Their magic imprisons me. They travel the mountains and capture us. In the morning they will pierce me and drain my blood. They will bathe in it and drink up its power. You must crush the amulet worn by their leader. If not it will be my blood that forms a river."

Rath looked around at the guard platforms and just now noticed the ceremonial look to them and the cage. "What's in this amulet?"

"The bones of my brother. The spears of these guards are made of the same. They are the only things that can open me."

Rath grabbed the spear, standing in a bracket beside the body. It was made of stout wood, braced with undecorated bronze and tipped with an oversized iron head. He ran a finger along the edge. It looked like regular metal to him. "This is Wen Quaar bone?"

"There is iron in our spines."

Rath smiled and set the spear back. "So where is this warlock?"

"The large tent on the other side of the camp. There are eleven warlocks. Each one has a tent and a servant."

Rath could see nothing but the darkened cluster of buildings ahead of him. A thought occurred to him. "You really trust me to do this?"

The Wen nodded its head but then said, "I have few options."

Rath raised his eyebrows and breathed in deeply, setting his mind to the task. "Do these wizards die like regular men?"

"I've opened many. But many more keep coming."

Rath ducked under the rail and lowered himself to the ground. "That didn't really answer my question," he muttered.

With a grinding sound the Wen Quaar leaned down. "You will have to be more quiet, little one. You will not have me to cover your sounds."

Rath stopped, made to say something, but then changed his mind. "Why ask my name and then continue to call me little one?"

"It is a deep honor to call someone by their name. I have not yet earned that right."

Rath blinked, taken aback, then shook his head slightly and moved off into the camp. None of the stories he'd heard about the Wen Quaar seemed to be true. He hoped the giant could shed its easy temperament and fight.

Darting over to the side of the canyon, he picked his way around some boulders until he got to the first building. It was a stout little storage shed. He paused by the doorway, then went inside.

His original plan had been to kill the sentries and set the Wen Quaar free, hoping to rouse it and kill as many raiders as he could in the confusion. He had never given thought to infiltrating the camp and assassinating a few select leaders. Now he considered it while silently moving around in the shed. He'd discovered that the raider leader was called Skurge and he had many deaths to answer for. The trapper camps and miners had long ago begun giving him tribute but when that ran out, he'd started raiding further south. The local lords did nothing, leaving the villages to fend for themselves. Well, now with Heather dead, the village a smoking ruin, and friends and family carrying lanterns in the Great River Above, Rath *would* fend for himself. Tonight there would be justice and revenge. But most of all, there would be death.

He found a few big furs in the style the raiders wore. Rath grabbed one and swung it around his shoulders, hoping it would be enough in the dark. Assuming a slow, comfortable gait, he walked straight down the central cart path through the camp. Gusting wind tussled his disguise as he walked and his boots crunched on the sand and gravel.

He soon passed a larger stone building built back against the canyon wall. The space in front of it appeared to be a gathering place, clear for fifty feet until an impressive two story stone building rose from the ground, its second level connected by rope bridges to the catwalk and scaffolding that held up the rest of the buildings. He marked it as important but turned his attention back to the large structure he walked along. The sounds of snoring told him it was some kind of barracks.

Rath kept his feet quiet against harder packed dirt as he approached the corner of the building and stopped when he heard low voices. It sounded like two men, early risers having a casual conversation in the confusing language of the mountain tribes. He thought he smelled a warm savory scent, probably the blood tea these barbarians stewed. Rath's nose wrinkled and bile rose in his throat. The tea, actually more like a gravy, was supposedly made with whole rock lizards.

From their slow conversation, they didn't appear to be in any hurry to get anywhere. Rath was no expert, but they didn't sound close enough to kill quickly — and that meant he could do it but it wouldn't be quiet. He turned and listened to the window next to him, not hearing anything but sleeping men.

Remembering the first two sentries, Rath thought back to something a burly, boastful hunter had once told him. *Men don't die quietly. They just don't.* Rath adjusted the cloth tied around his wounded hand. He would have to make the best of it. Glancing at the sky, lighter now against the sharp canyon walls, he realized he had misjudged the time. Dawn would be coming and others would be rising.

Rath rounded the corner with his knife behind his back. Two men sat on a long bench about halfway down the wall. They looked up as he walked toward them and muttered a greeting. Rath repeated it as best he could and kept approaching, his steps agonizingly slow. The distance just couldn't close fast enough.

The nearest man sat up a little straighter and asked a question. Rath had four steps to take before he could kill them. Too far.

Rath doubled over and made a groaning sound, hoping it would gain him an extra step. The men muttered something and chuckled. Rath rose up and his knife flashed. The first man's throat burst open and a fountain of blood shot up. He kicked his legs and let out a choking gurgle but otherwise slumped back soundlessly. The second man had just started taking a drink and jerked away, spilling the disgusting brew all over his chest. He sputtered something and died when Rath jumped forward and shoved his knife through the man's neck, clamping his head down and forcing his chin to his chest. *Can't scream when you have no throat.*

Rath looked around and listened while he set the two bodies upright as if they were sleeping. Dragging them across the gravel would make unexplainable sounds and take too long. He had to rely on deception and move on to the tents, just visible past a long row of stone and wood buildings. Rath finished adjusting the dead men and followed a path behind the buildings.

Must move quickly. The enormity of his situation dawned on him now. Alone amidst his enemies with only his wits and a long knife as his weapons, time was not his ally. Dawn approached and the camp would begin to stir. There were easily over a hundred men here. The number of dead bodies he hoped to pile up began to dwindle in his mind, replaced by the sight of his own body on top of the pile. Rath clenched his teeth and remembered why he'd come in the first place, wondered if any of the dead behind him had laid a hand on Heather.

He crossed underneath several thick posts and beams holding up the buildings above him, moving behind stables strong with the scent of manure. Beyond this sat another large storage building that smelled of metal and leather; beyond that, a double row of tents.

Rath stopped at the back of the storage building, leaning against the rough stone wall. The light had definitely increased. The closest tents were dark, tied down tight but still billowing in the wind. Made with the vibrant colors of eastern traders they were not the standard bland canvas of the foothills. He thought he heard movement inside the closest one.

Rath walked behind the tents while keeping an eye on the rest of the canyon. On one of the upper levels a raider came out of a doorway and took one of the hooded lanterns back inside. Rath tried to maintain an unhurried walk but fear drove him to pick up the pace. He rounded the row and saw the last tent, about three times the size of the others. A dark pennant with a light colored ring in its center snapped back and forth on a tall center pole.

Behind the tent rose scrub brush, rocks, and a ladder that led to a sentry's post at the lip of the canyon. The sentry stood unmoving, hopefully as inattentive as the fools Rath had slain earlier. Rath looked at the tied down door flap and considered his options. None of them seemed to be a likely success. He steadied his nerves, cast a final glance at the sentry, tightened his grip on his knife, and walked forward.

Without slowing his stride, Rath slashed the tie down and pulled it open. The fabric whipped back and forth in the wind as he walked in. Darkness wrapped around him and he could see nothing. From his left he heard the movement of bedclothes and a surprised grunting. He swung around and plunged his knife down into the noise. The man did not die quietly.

Thrashing and coughing, he knocked over a night stand and Rath heard the sound of breaking glass. He plunged the knife down again and felt it slide through flesh until it hit bone. He turned quickly and took a step into the center of the tent, listening. More noise off to his right. A lantern shade was pulled up and light filled the tent. Laying among several pillows and furs was a half naked man with a shaved head and red tattoos. Around his neck was a crystalline container on a leather cord.

Rath leapt forward. Never let a wizard talk.

The warlock held up his hand with fingers widely spread. He barked out a few words and Rath felt himself slowed, like moving through water and then like moving through tangled vines. He tried to swing his knife but his arm would not obey. Frustrated and helpless, Rath snarled and tried to push forward again. Nothing. He was locked up and motionless right at the foot of the man's low bed.

The warlock smiled and slowly rose to his feet. He stood slightly taller than Rath and wore nothing but linen breeches. Red tattoos crisscrossed down his chest. He looked Rath over before speaking in a thickly accented voice. "Assassin? I thought you had welcomed us. We gave you the strength to make your new raids and you have prospered. Now you wish to end our bargain?" He stared into Rath's eyes. Smiling with the confidence of a cat gloating over a mouse in its claws, he continued. "I will remind Skurge who has the power here. I can kill any of your kind with a thought. I am linked to you all through your chief's agreement. You are a fool. You are all fools and I will kill every one of you. But you first."

Rath felt himself pushed to his knees by invisible hands. The warlock drew in a breath and chanted a few words. He raised both hands in some kind of pattern and spat out the last word. Rath felt the pressure holding him dissolve away.

Arms free, Rath launched himself upward and drove his knife into the warlock's belly, forcing it up into his lungs. The man flailed about and tried to grab Rath's arm, the shock of the failed spell evident on his face. Rath drew close enough to smell the warlock's dying breath. "I'm not one of them," he whispered.

Rath grabbed the amulet and whipped it over the warlock's head as the body fell back onto the bed. Holding it up in the dim light, he examined the bits of iron filings held within the thumb sized crystal. They looked ordinary enough. He glanced around for something to smash the amulet with, barely noticing the hot blood dripping off his hand and blade. He found nothing except a patch of flat, rocky ground. Putting the amulet down, he raised his knife and brought the butt end down hard. Crystalline shards scattered across the rocks.

A roar like thunder sounded from the other side of the camp.

Rath ran to the tent flap. Pushing through, he saw another warlock standing with his servant. Both looked away from him but had clearly been coming to investigate the noises within their leader's tent. Rath swung his knife in a wide arc and drove it into the warlock's ribcage. He pulled it out, not caring about stealth any more, and jumped forward to stab the surprised servant in the chest. With a backhand he slashed open the staggering warlock's neck.

The bodies dropped to his feet and he looked up to see what had drawn their attention. A cloud of dust and splintered wood billowed up at the far end of camp, a dark figure leaping from its heart. Silhouetted against the grey sky, the Wen Quaar rose up and arced down, seemingly suspended for a moment at the apogee of its leap. Another furious roar echoed through the canyon before the beast came crashing down into the open space in front of the barracks.

The sleepy camp erupted in noise and confusion. Rath saw people staggering out of the various buildings around him but didn't move as he watched the Wen raise both arms and slam its fists through the roof of the barracks. Pulling back huge sections of timber and slate, the beast ripped it open like a bear tearing open a fish.

One of the nearby tents opened and the warlock inside saw the loosened Wen Quaar. He turned and took a few running steps toward his leader's tent. Seeing Rath standing over the bodies of his brethren with a bloody knife, the warlock brought himself up quickly, skidding on the gravel, and shouted something in his own language. Rath dashed to the right, behind the tents, and ran toward the first level of buildings along the base of the canyon wall.

The Wen's roar filled the canyon again, closer this time. Rath stopped at the corner of a building and looked back. The Wen dropped into the middle of the tents not twenty feet from him. The ground shook as a blast of air whooshed past Rath's face, causing him to blink and turn away. Dust dropped from the walkways above him. Rath turned back, clearing his eyes, and watched as the Wen pounded the ground on the other side of a tent with a powerful downward punch. It struck down with its other huge fist and brought both hands up with dark liquid and squishy bits dripping off them. It started swinging its arms back and forth, ripping tents out of their stakes and scattering the warlocks. The Wen Quaar could fight.

The wanton destruction so enthralled Rath that he almost forgot what he had come to do. The door next to him opened and reminded him. A raider burst out, running past him with a heavy spear in hand. Rath jumped forward and plunged his knife downward though the man's shoulder.

Rath saw the spear hit the dirt and thought about grabbing it but figured his knife would work better for the close fighting that was about to happen. When he looked up he saw that the tents were all down, several bodies were splattered against the ground and the Wen was turning toward him and reaching out. Rath suddenly regretted his disguise, raised his hands and shouted, "Wait! Wait!"

The massive open hand shot past him and smashed through the doorway. Pulling out another raider with a spear, the Wen twisted and threw the man, screaming and kicking, into the third level of buildings on the other side of the canyon. The body crashed into another raider and they both broke through a wooden wall.

The Wen turned back and drew close, its skin dark and rocky, its expression clouded by shadow. "Watch your backside!" Then the huge beast stood and leapt to the other side of the canyon, crouching low and punching a scurrying raider through a stone wall.

Rath heard boots clomping along the walkway above him. A nearby ladder shook as a raider jumped on and started climbing down. Rath moved without thinking. Dashing to the base of the ladder, he drove his knife into the man's broad back. The man arched backward and dropped the spear, Rath stepping aside to let the body fall. He looked up to see another raider grab the ladder. Rath picked up the spear at his feet and struck upward through the man's groin. With a spasm and a gurgling yell the man slipped off the ladder and impaled himself as the butt of the spear planted firmly into the dirt. Rath blinked in surprise as the skewered body landed at his feet, caught a glimpse of the raider's eyes, then thought: *More*.

The Wen continued to slam away at the buildings clustered onto the other wall of the canyon, shouting things in its own language. The entire camp was awake, shouting and running. Rath climbed the ladder, knife again in hand, and got up onto the walkway. He stalked forward, searching out a way to get back to the impressive building at the center of camp.

He'd killed ten of them so far. That wasn't enough. Seeing three or four raiders clustered around the nearest building, he unleashed himself.

Running down the walkway, he charged into the first, swinging and striking him solidly in the chest. Rath kicked the next one and pushed him backward then shoved the dead body in his hands into another. Spouting blood followed his blade as it withdrew and swung through the air to slash through a blocking forearm before raking across an undefended gut. One of the raiders brought his spear up but couldn't use it properly in the tight confines of the walkway. He swung it like a quarterstaff and caught Rath alongside the head, ripping a gash open above his ear.

The man he'd kicked pushed himself up off the railing and reached out. Rath avoided the wrestling grab and swung upward with his knife, scoring deep into the ribcage. With a yell, Rath shouldered into the last man and knifed him in the chest. Again and again he drove the knife in, willing the man to fall, to die. *To pay.*

When the body slumped to the deck Rath stepped back, breathing hard and drenched in steaming blood. A cacophony from terrified horses ripped through the canyon. The Wen had found one of the stables and smashed one end of it open. A raider on an upper walkway threw one of their slender hunting spears but it glanced off the Wen's stony hide. The beast quickly reached up, grabbed the man, and bit off his head. Spitting out the head like a cherry pit, the Wen turned and cocked its arm back. With a barely coherent shout, the beast threw the body up and clear of the entire canyon, as if trying to land it on top of the mountains.

Rath watched for a moment as the beast kicked a shed and shattered it. He wished he could kill like that. Then he turned and continued down the walkway. Shouting and running raiders were on the level above him and he rounded another building stilted up against the wall, its door swinging open in the wind. Ahead of him a rope bridge with a slatted wood walkway stretched across an open span, too wide to jump. It was the building he'd been looking for. A leader's house if he ever saw one.

Rath ran for the bridge. Two raiders stood at the other side with ready spears and fierce looks. Since they didn't run like the others he figured them for bodyguards of some type. They shouted at him but he kept running across the wobbly boards. As he came toward them they thrust both spears out and started screaming. Rath kept charging, straight into the points of steel.

At the last second, Rath twisted and knocked one spear out of the way with his knife. He felt the other spear slice along his ribs, biting into the furs clasped around him and tearing them off. Rath shouldered into one guard and struck his knife deep into the leg of the other. The guard he ran into lost his footing and both tumbled to the deck. The spear caught in the railing and spun out into the open air. They grappled, Rath pinning the man's arms with his body and driving his knife up beneath the exposed ribcage.

Rath looked back to see the other guard clutching the inside of his thigh with both hands. Red blood spurted like a fountain from the wound. The man's actions slowed; he'd be dead in a few more seconds but Rath didn't wait to see it. He staggered to his feet, temporary disguise gone, with blood running down his face and side. He wasn't sure how bad his wounds were so he drove himself forward before he bled out like the whimpering man at his feet.

Rath walked around the corner of the large building. Two more guards ran at him. With two strikes they were dead and dropping to the walkway. Rath pushed his way through the door.

Across the sumptuously appointed room — the best of their thievery on the tables and walls — the raider leader, tall and broad, strapped on a bronze breastplate. He looked up. Rath filled the doorway, a billowing cloud of dust roiling behind him as the Wen buried the barracks beneath a whole section of the camp's suspended framework. Skurge went for his sword, lying on the table behind him.

Rath vaulted forward, covering the distance before the leader could turn back. Rath's knife crossed and stabbed into Skurge's forearm. He brought his other fist up in a punch that knocked the man back. Rath kept driving and shoved him against the wall, knocking over the table and scattering trinkets. The sword fell onto the expensive, now bloodstained, carpet. Rath brought his knife up under the leader's chin and held it there, pressing ever so slightly into his neck.

Skurge froze, straining, as if trying to withdraw through the wall. Anything to ease the pressure of the blade and stop it from cutting the most vulnerable part of his throat. Rath leaned in close and slowly shook his head. "Be still," he whispered.

Outside, the Wen roared again and smashed something.

Sweat ran down each of their faces. Rath looked into Skurge's eyes and saw the fear that dwelt in the heart of all evil men. "I'm not going to kill you yet even though I should. I should slice you open and be done with it. But that's not good enough for me. You're going to suffer first."

"Who are you?" whispered Skurge.

"I'm from the village you destroyed three days ago, next to the small lake." Rath reached with his free hand and grabbed an oil lantern that was hanging on the wall. "You're going to burn slowly, just like my wife in the smithy."

"Smithy?" The leader clearly didn't speak enough of Rath's language to understand.

Rath boiled over, frustration mixed with rage. The bastard had to know why he was suffering! "The blacksmith, you dog! The forge! The fair haired woman there! She was my wife and you killed her!" Tears burst and Rath screamed in fury at Skurge's face. "We were married only two weeks! Two weeks!!" Rath raised the lantern and shuffled his feet to gain a good balance. The tip of his knife barely sliced into the raider's throat and drew a trickle of blood. The man winced and tried to draw back further. Terror filled his eyes and made him shake.

"The sunshine hair? We did not kill her," pleaded Skurge. "We sell her to slaver caravan yesterday."

Rath paused, vaguely aware of the beast shouting and breaking things. "I don't believe you," he said, but his voice wavered. Heather was the only blonde haired woman in the village. "The—The body was there in the rubble."

"Someone else. We kill her and take the sunshine hair. Very valuable."

"What?" Rath stared into his eyes for a few moments and suddenly felt sick in his stomach. So close to killing, now he needed the man. Desperation crept into his voice. "What slavers? Where are they?"

The leader looked to the door and Rath heard footsteps. He turned back to see two more raiders coming through, one with his spear up and ready to throw. Skurge pushed Rath's arm away as the raider threw his spear. This close, he could not miss. Rath let go of the leader and spun to the side. The spear hit the lantern and knocked it free, spraying its contents on the wall. Flames erupted and Rath kept moving, finding a door leading outside and taking it.

He had been ready to die. In reality, he'd been looking forward to it. Knowing that his fury would ebb away eventually, he had planned on using it for as long as he could before succumbing to the flow of the Great River and joining Heather in the march of the heavenly lanterns. Now, in an instant, he knew that things had changed. He leapt for the bridge that led further down the encampment.

Now he had to live.

Out of the corner of his eye he saw that the Wen had moved back down away from him, swinging a long timber like a club. Rath saw raiders scurrying about on the various levels ahead of him. He started to panic. He couldn't see an easy way out of this.

Halfway across the bridge another raider dropped down from a higher level and shouted words Rath couldn't understand. He stopped. He looked back and could not see the leader and his guards through the smoke billowing out of the windows and doors. Returning to face the raider, Rath saw the man cocking his spear arm back to throw. Rath couldn't go forward and couldn't go back. He didn't think he could get over the rope and jump to the ground below quickly enough. He was dead.

From over his shoulder came the timber the Wen had been using. It speared through the air and struck the raider just as his arm came forward. Thick as the man's entire chest, the timber caved him in and shoved him through a wall.

Rath swallowed, gripped with fear. He ran on shaky legs to the other side of the bridge. The Wen had saved him again. The beam lay across the walkway so Rath took a ladder up to the next level. When he got to the top he saw that a long walkway ran down almost the entire remaining length of the camp. It was clear. Rath started running.

Behind him he heard a change in the Wen's onslaught. A choking sound and the heavy thud of the beast hitting the ground. Rath glanced back and saw the beast on its hands and knees with the raider leader swinging around on a heavy spear that lanced down into the Wen's shoulder right at the base of the neck. Skurge scrambled to sit on the back of the Wen's head and pushed down on the spear. The beast collapsed into a heap, sprawled out on the dirt in front of the barracks.

Rath staggered to a halt, unbelieving. Skurge wrenched on the spear again. New fear washed over him and Rath turned and resumed running until he heard the Wen gasp for air and call out.

"RAAAATH!"

Stopping as if hitting a wall, Rath turned and saw the Wen reaching up toward him. Its rocky hand wavered and then curled up. The beast dropped flat on its face. Slowly reaching back and trying vainly to get at the raider leader, the Wen let out a great breath. Dust clouds surrounded its head as the giant continued to sputter and gag.

The way was still clear. Rath could run. He could find the slavers and free his wife. But with another look at the struggling Wen, he knew he could not let the raiders win. Fury returned to him and iron filled his spine.

He had just passed a crane that had broken free of its mooring. Pushing the long arm out into the canyon, Rath grabbed the ropes running from the tackle and jumped off the railing. Wind caressed him as his body fell weightless for a moment before the swing of the crane and the ropes directed him out and back toward the open area where Skurge kept trying to work the spear deeper. As he swung over the wreckage of the barracks he picked up speed. When he thought he was going to swing too far back out of the way, Rath let go of the ropes and flew feet first into Skurge's chest.

They both spilled out onto the rocks, Rath landing mostly on top of him but still the impact knocked him hard. Gravel ground at his arms and legs and back. His head bounced off Skurge's legs and they both rolled to a stop. Rath, groggy and disoriented, at least knew what he had to do. He got up and staggered on injured legs to the spear sticking out of the Wen's shoulder. In the dim light of morning mixed with the glow of burning buildings, Rath pulled.

He felt the spear start to give and he pulled harder. With a sudden release it popped free, followed by a gout of black blood. The thick liquid shot up and covered Rath, drenching him. Rath staggered backward. He saw the Wen turn its head slightly and look at him with those glowing red eyes. "Bathe in the river," it whispered.

Then the Wen closed its eyes and relaxed with one final breath.

Rath's skin sizzled everywhere the blood touched him. He wiped his eyes and face, felt his legs buckle and he leaned against the Wen's sticky shoulder. All around him the sounds changed. He felt the wind on his skin, felt every bump and crevice of the Wen's rugged skin against him. His vision became crystal clear, everything he saw he somehow saw completely, like it was illuminated from all directions and he could focus on any part of it.

His mind cleared and Rath stood up. A raider ran at him with a small hand axe. Rath watched him come up, saw every flutter of his clothing, every ripple of his muscles. The raider swung a leaping overhand blow. Rath whipped an arm up and blocked. He felt the raider's bones shatter and the arm deform around his. He punched straight out into the raider's face. Rath felt the skull cave in and saw blood shoot out around his fist. The rest of the body kicked forward as the head stopped. It bounced off Rath like paper and dropped to the ground.

Another raider ran at him, lunging with a spear. Rath broke the spear and punched the man in the chest. Ribs broke and sternum splintered. His legs flew out from under him and the body dropped next to the other.

Another raider ran at him, leaping over Skurge's body. Rath killed him with one strike to the face.

Sound from behind him. A raider jumped off the Wen with arms outstretched, trying to tackle him. Rath batted him aside, nearly folding him in half with a swing that connected solidly under his arms.

Rath heard a slip of a whistle, different from the wind, and knew a spear flew toward him. He flicked his head to look but already knew where it was. His hand swung up and broke the shaft right behind the spearpoint, which tumbled twice while passing his ear.

Two raiders ran at him with knives. He stepped forward and killed one, knowing he could ignore the other. He felt the knife blade strike his shoulder and glance off. He saw, no, he somehow felt, the man's expression change from rage to shock to horror. A backhanded slap crushed his skull. Rath's other hand shot up and caught a thrown spear before it struck his face. He broke it with a flex of his fingers.

Rath stopped. He saw, heard, and felt everything around him. *Everything.* The heat rising off the bodies at his feet, the wind as it made his hair sway, the sounds of running feet fading into the distance. He breathed in deeply, smelling the burning wood, bloody dust, and fear-stained leather. Other than the crackle of fire and the clatter of doors swinging in the wind, Rath was alone.

While he stared up at the bluing sky, he sensed movement to his left. Skurge inhaled and pushed himself to his knees, still facing away. Rath stretched his fingers, preparing to leap over and grab the man.

He sensed another movement and heard the unmistakable sound of grinding stones. A mighty hand swung across his field of vision, grabbing the raider leader as he struggled to stand. The Wen had him firmly grasped and Rath saw the stony muscles begin to contract. "No, wait!" His voice boomed out of his lungs — a fraction too late.

The giant squeezed. Skurge did not even have time to scream before he died. His eyes bulged and blood erupted from his mouth. Skin split and streams of blood spurted out between rocky fingers. Then the Wen opened its hand and let the crushed body slump to the ground.

Rath watched the body leak fluid out onto the dirt. With it seemed to go his hopes of finding Heather. "He was going to tell me where they sold my wife."

The Wen coughed and began to gather itself up. "You said your wife died."

Rath turned and stared up at the huge Wen Quaar. "I found out otherwise. She's still alive. Sold to slavers."

The giant got to its knees and sat back on its calves. It stretched its head side to side. With more light, Rath thought it looked different, not as intimidating. Just an oversized, hulking man with a flat face and grey, stony skin. "I thought you were dead."

The Wen poked at his wounded shoulder and tried to look down at it. "There is still iron in my spine." Rath watched him examine his wound. He'd somehow always thought they were made completely of stone. Something else not true about the giants that walked the edges of civilization.

The Wen stood and looked up and down the canyon. "No one left to kill."

Rath glanced around at all the bodies. Then he realized that his senses were returning to normal. He looked down at his blood covered arms and torso and noticed that his wounds had healed up. "That was amazing. Do you see and feel like that all the time?"

"Yes." The Wen turned and studied the wreckage around them.

"I, uh…Could I know your name?"

The giant's head turned toward Rath. He couldn't be sure, but he thought he saw the faintest upturn of a smile. "Cairrg."

"Kerreg?" asked Rath, trying to get his mouth around the resonant way the Wen spoke.

The giant nodded. "Close enough."

"Well, it's been an honor to fight alongside you."

Cairrg looked up at the edges of the canyon, speaking as he watched them. "Wives are important to your kind?"

"Very important. She's everything to me." Rath suddenly felt empty at the thought. Helpless. He realized the rage was gone. The memories of her face, her smile, attacked him. Tears ran down his cheeks. "I've loved her all my life."

The Wen thought for a moment. "Love I do not understand. But I do understand important." He lowered his arm and extended his hand like a ramp. "Climb up, Rath. We have much ground to cover."

T.W. Williams writes fantasy, science fiction, and horror from the northern Chicago suburbs. His works, including other tales of John Humble, have appeared in several magazines and anthologies. More about his published works and future plans can be found at http://sites.google.com/site/twfiction. He and his wife, Lynne, have five children and a very vocal Bengal cat. What traits and proclivities will a man follow and discard when survival is at stake? Pride has no place amid battles of life and friendship; nor does prejudice. John Humble — though by no means a vocal example of his surname — is yet still a man of humble confidence whether leading the charge or tumbling his way into the fray. The shadow a man casts is sometimes the largest of the behemoths in his life.

Where the Shadow Falls

A Tale of John Humble

by T.W. Williams
& cover art by Didier Normand

The Lictian huntsman cringed as the relentless tide of the griffin's shadow rolled across the high plateau.

Her shrieking crescendo split the air, causing him to crouch lower behind the boulders he hid behind. She was on the hunt. He had sought her for weeks; now any place that wasn't *here* was a better place to be.

Despite his dread, he didn't flee. Any death she could visit on him would be violent but mercifully quick. The ones who had sent him would be neither merciful nor quick if he failed. And he would be just as dead.

A stone's throw below him a giant bear rose on two legs to sniff the air. *Twelve feet tall,* the hunter judged, watching the silver tips of the umber fur bristle as the bear detected the griffin's scent.

The Lictian licked his wind-chapped lips. He understood the ways of bears and knew that the grizzly, roused from hibernation, would be in a foul mood. He imagined the confusion and anger in the tiny ursine brain giving way to panic.

As if their minds were connected, the bear shook its head then dropped to all fours, tearing through the chokeberry and cliff rose at a speed belying its size.

The hunter prayed silently to his animal gods, caressing the matted wolf skin draped across his shoulders as he watched the massive bear flee. The thunder-shriek crashed again, swaying the fir trees, shaking snow from the slopes.

As the bear charged downhill, the griffin's shadow stretched out to envelope it. The bear dodged into the sunlight, skidded, slammed against a boulder.

Its retreat cut off, the huge grizzly thrust itself up on its back legs again, a howl of defiance rising in its throat. The roar died abruptly as the griffin's gargantuan paw batted the bear against the cliff face, breaking its back. Claws like crescent moons lifted the limp form so she could tear it apart with her raptor's beak.

She screamed triumph, rattling the mountains again. The sound penetrated the Lictian's bones, and he shivered at the thought of the report he must make and the trap he must then prepare.

Abomination. He silently mouthed the word and curled himself even smaller, listening to the sounds of the griffin feasting.

The rain was warm; he hadn't felt the blood on his face.

It wasn't until John Humble got back to his tent that he realized he had been nicked right at the hairline. That Lictian bastard's slingshot had found its mark. The clotted blood began to flow again as he pushed dark, curling hair out of the way to clean the wound.

That's what you get for being a big target.

Comrades blathered about his size, but he paid them little heed. He figured the space between his sword and the foeman's gut was all the measuring he needed.

John dabbed at the gash as he stripped. The camp slaves had readied the biggest tub of water, and he wedged himself in with a sigh. *Not big enough, but what was?*

If the battle was won, the mercenaries were expected to go straight to evening services, wounded or not. Flowing blood honored Achta, the priests said.

The others went; John stayed.

Fair compromise. If not for me, we'd have lost today and no one would be bowing and scraping before her. Taking the duke's silver is one thing, but taking his goddess? He grimaced. *This hot bath is the only thing I worship.*

His stomach rumbled as he tried to get comfortable. Battle always made him hungry, and any involvement with the gods always gave him a sour gut. Achta's greed knew no bounds; she was a taker who did not abide losers.

At least she and I agree on that.

As he drowsed, a shadow fell across the tub. One of the priests, a thin crow of a man, stood in the tent opening, dark eyes agleam.

John cupped his hands to splash hot water in his face, then broke wind, causing the water in the tub to burble. *That for the priests and their precious Achta.*

"So, John Humble" — the priest made his name a curse — "I find your big carcass soaking in the only hot water north of Greensward while the duke is still stinking in his battle leathers!"

"Save your breath," John said, rising and pulling on breeches over damp skin, amused that the priest looked away. "We were outnumbered. If I hadn't charged and killed their chieftain and both his lieutenants—stupid, that, bunched like gossiping women—they might have rallied."

"Achta garbed you in her bloody robes of glorious terror. That's why we won," the priest said, scowling, his spider-like fingers skittering across his shaved scalp.

If he's aiming for menacing, he isn't making it much past pouting. John stared hard at the priest and was rewarded with a flinch.

"You think a foe's guts shrivel like a nightcrawler on a hot stone when they see you coming," the priest sneered. "It's not you, though. It is the goddess."

It was John's turn to scowl. "The duke believes in Achta. Be satisfied with that."

"It is not about believing, John Humble. It is about perceiving," the priest said. "Big as you are, you are one man, and mortal. The Lictian clans have us outnumbered; our spies say they are scheming again. We will need the goddess before this is over."

I felt mortal today, John admitted. When the red mood was upon him he was reckless, and Ran Archer, Wil Cooper and the others had saved his hide after he charged into the narrow pass a dozen strides ahead of everyone else.

Not that I wouldn't have won. It just would have taken a bit longer. After finding the forty-seven women and children of Thorn Rock spitted, burned and gnawed on, I'll give all the time that needs to be given.

The priest's bone-thin fingers danced along his pate again. "You should make an appearance at the service. Men look to you."

"I look to me," John said, pulling on his boots. "Let the men look to the duke and to Achta."

The priest waited, staring at him.

"I'll come," John said through clenched teeth. Comrades stuck together, whether or not their leaders were idiots. "But be clear on this: It's not for Achta's sake." *Nor the duke's. Nor mine.*

As he trudged to the worship pavilion, the warm breeze that had swirled constantly through camp for the past few weeks blew away the last few raindrops.

"Achta's breath," the priests called it: The hot breath of war. Summer's brown, brittle months were near. Months of blood and smoke and sweat. The skirmishes of the wet season would blossom into full battles in the summer heat.

A feral grin flitted across John's face, but no humor shone in his hazel eyes. It would be good to hack Lictian flesh again. After Thorn Rock, he figured he didn't need an excuse.

He shouldered his way into the crowded pavilion. The priests were chanting again. The duke and his aides stood up front, eyes glassy with adoration. John's attention drifted, and he found himself looking at the statue of Achta.

She wasn't much to look at.

If a worshipper was seeking some smooth-carved, white-marble beauty like the ones that the Southers put in their temples, Achta wasn't it. She sat on her jagged black pillar, staring doom. The sculptors carved her spider's legs so that they draped over the pillar's edge in front and rose above her body behind — it looked as if she was ready to spring down among the worshippers.

Instead of the fanged monstrosity of a spider's face, Achta's curving body narrowed to a woman's torso and head, and in that feature she was as beautiful as anything a Souther could dream. Shining ebony, with rubies gleaming from her eye sockets, from the points of her teats, from the tip of each leg.

The emotion in the big tent was as thick as the incense in the air as the chants rose and fell. John's mind as well as his lungs wheezed for relief. She was Achta. She was Goddess. She was War. He bowed his head to hide a yawn.

Without conscious intent — though who knows how gods manipulate men — the yawn caught in his throat and John Humble belched loudly, shattering a silent, solemn moment.

Four burly men woke John from sound slumber, pinning his arms as two priests looked on.

"The duke has had enough of your disrespect. You will fight no more this season, sell-sword," one of the priests said as their henchmen pulled cords tight at John's elbows. The other priest, the crow-like one, smirked.

"Had I been awake," John croaked, his voice rusty with sleep, "it would have taken eight of you stinking lickspittles!"

Other men, priests mingling with them, held back Archer and Cooper.

John shook his head slightly. No need to get them mixed up in this. "Meet me at Three Goats Tavern in the fall," he told them. "Bring silver; I'll be thirsty."

Without another word, the priests and their lackeys marched him to the edge of the compound and shoved him tumbling down the slope, tossing his sword and boots after him.

John staggered to his feet. Flexing shoulder muscles and biceps, he snapped the cords. He thought about charging uphill to get the pay he was owed, but, big as he was, two hundred-to-one odds were bigger.

By the time he pulled on his boots and adjusted his sword, the hot wind had risen again, blowing grit in his face. Turning away from the swirling dust,

John eyed the mountains, their crowns glinting with snow. *North, then.* Cooler there, and places he'd never seen. Long fingers of deep shadow seemed to beckon him.

He hitched up his breeches and started walking, not bothering to look back. Any Lictians he found better pray to their animal gods and move out of his way.

The griffin padded on her lion paws, restless in the high meadow. She might have flown to her aerie, nestled in for the night, but she was hungry again. The morsel of the grizzly was a distant memory, and for almost three weeks she had caught nothing, last feasting on rotting scraps of an elk even the scavengers had spurned.

Her hunger had grown with her each season for the last three centuries. In the last decades, as her sight failed, she had become insatiable.

The griffin's diminished vision made the blue tints of dusk the same as darkness, and a mixture of sadness, anger and frustration shook her massive frame. Her leonine ears twitched. Nothing nearby. If she wanted food, she'd have to go seek it.

Swirls of snow chased each other across the withered grass. Below, she knew, it would be rain, the last rain for months. Preening her shoulder feathers with her wickedly curved beak, she crouched and launched herself skyward, her wings flapping mightily, taking advantage of the powerful leap.

She burst through the clouds, her shadow long in the sunset, rippling over the snow-capped mountain peaks. Soon it would be summer, and the slanting rays of sunshine made her old bones feel good.

The glitter of her hoarded gold and gems had lost its allure as the centuries dimmed her eyes, and she gave little thought to the kings' ransoms, once so jealously guarded, that lined her nest. She did, however, miss swimming in the colors of the sunset sky.

Tilting a wing, she tucked in her forepaws and rode an updraft, turning until her opaque eyes faced the sun's warmth. Her powerful wing strokes carried her higher still.

"It's not a cliff," John Humble muttered between clenched teeth. "Just a steep slope." The distinction failed to cheer him.

He glanced over his shoulder, watching his elongated shadow against the ravine's far wall. Beyond the narrow canyon he climbed, others stretched parallel, as if giant claws had rent the earth.

He had climbed steadily all day, stubbornly following the rough natural path upward through the canyon. The higher he had climbed, the narrower it had become. Now he inched along, chest flat against the rock, heels sometimes hanging into space.

John paused and worked his mouth, trying to generate some spit as he watched the evening's first stars wink into existence. He had last drunk from a rivulet about midday. He reached for his next handhold when an unearthly sound — a great cat's roar interwoven with an eagle's piercing *skree* — echoed through the ravine.

Nothing this side of legend could have made that noise.

Startled, he overreached, and the rock he was stretching for gave way, pulling his leading foot off the ledge. He fought for control, willing his muscles still. Just as his right boot regained a tenuous toehold, a spasm rippled through his left calf muscle. John jerked backward, falling through the night air.

His body scraped the canyon slope as he tumbled, flaying patches of skin. Fingertips tore as he tried to slow his descent. A burst of pain heralded both impact and unconsciousness.

John woke to the sensation of cool air caressing his face and opened his eyes to see the tops of fir trees a few feet below, their clumps of needles green-black in the predawn light. His left arm, pinned underneath his belly, was numb, but he couldn't tell if it was broken or merely deadened by his weight. His right arm dangled into space, the back of his hand brushing fir needles.

Face down on a ledge. How wide?

Cautiously, knowing his left arm would be no use, John tried to draw his knees under him.

Not wide enough. He overbalanced, barely bringing his arm up in time to shield his face as he plunged headfirst into the fir trees, falling again.

This time the journey was short, as he bounced from tree to tree, limb to limb, ending with a long, skin-tearing slide along rough, knotted bark. He had rotated and twisted as he fell, so he hit the forest floor back first, and the air left his lungs in a gasping whoosh.

He rose dizzily, every bruise and scrape aching. His left arm felt like it had been jabbed with stiletto tips. *Not broken, then.* With his heart in his throat, John suddenly remembered his sword. His hand flew to his back and felt the wire-bound leather hilt. *Safe. Two feet on the ground, battered but breathing. My luck's turning.*

Kneading his upper arm, he shook conifer needles out of his hair — and heard voices. John swore inwardly. His luck had turned, verily: Turned ill.

A stray image of Achta flitted through his mind. *No, by all the gods above and below. She is not the author of my misfortunes. If I believe that, then I have to give her credit for the good, too, and that I'll never do.*

The thick accent was unmistakable. Lictian. He hoped they were pilgrims or a group of traders — though what Lictians traded in besides death and violence he had no idea.

John's eye caught the glint of spearheads, shafts leaning against trees not far from where he stood. Not pilgrims or traders, then, but not enough weapons for a war party. *Scouts, or foragers.* As if to confirm the thought, he heard cattle lowing.

He crouched, feeling naked behind the slender fir. There was no underbrush, nothing but a thick layer of fir needles underfoot. The sun had peeked above the canyon wall, filling a clearing in the trees ahead with light. Bands of sunlight and shadow were his only camouflage. *Unless a Lictian looks right at me.*

John stifled an oath as his raw thigh brushed the tree trunk. *Naked? Skinned was more like it.*

He let out a cautious breath, trying to ignore the warm trickle running down his left leg. It took his battered brain a moment to realize it wasn't blood. It took the Lictian soldier pissing on the tree a moment too long to realize he wasn't emptying his bladder on a stump.

John whipped out his sword and hewed the Lictian across the chest. The man fell, mouth agape and bubbling crimson, without uttering a sound. The stench of death-loosened bowels mingled with the smell of his urine.

"You should have had a longer weapon," John hissed. *Close call. Too close.*

He breathed shakily and bent down to wipe his blade on the Lictian's tunic — and the man rose howling and thrashing, clenching John's sword arm in his death throes. The woods echoed with the gurgling screams of the Lictian who was dead but did not know it yet.

Tearing his hand free, John kicked the man aside and raced into the clearing, his booted feet silent on the fir needles, aiming for the spears. Three cattle were tied to a stake in the center of the clearing, shuffling nervously and lowing louder as they caught the scents of blood and death.

"Come on, you curs!" he shouted. The remaining Lictians, six of them — *No, eight, damn my spinning head!* — edged around him in a semicircle. A few of them had daggers, but without their spears, none seemed willing to chance the three feet of steel John waved at them.

He backed slowly toward the cattle, thinking to use them as diversion or shield if any of the Lictians rushed him or chanced a dagger throw.

Suddenly, he was falling again, as needle-strewn matting gave way beneath his feet and sent him plunging into the pit below.

The evening's hunt had gone sour; the mountain goats too small and spry.

The griffin was in a foul mood, her hunger and anger scarcely tempered by the dawn. Her feeble eyesight could pick out blotches of color, but it was her tufted ears that picked up the sound of cattle bellowing.

As she wheeled in a wide arc, homing on the sound, a memory of stalking the great pachyderms of the East flashed through her mind: Tender flesh under thick, wrinkled skin, chest of gems and gold carried off, the screams and curses of the puny rajahs and their guards who never had been more than irrelevant.

She sensed men now, felt the odd emanation they called magic. That only served to deepen her anger. Men and their sounds. She understood them well enough, had learned their babbling words over the long years. Pointless then; still irrelevant now.

With powerful back-beats of her wings, she slowed her descent as the blurred shapes resolved into bovine form. Too paralyzed to move. She was used to that.

Screaming her roar-shriek, the griffin dove, claws extended, for the small cluster of steers.

John Humble groaned and propped himself up on an elbow. He squinted at the rim of the pit some twenty feet above him. Diffused light through the matting made the dimensions murky.

He heard the Lictians' harsh laughter above and caught a word that sounded like "monster" as they threw fresh branches over the hole he'd made.

When I climb out of here, I'll show them monster.

John resisted the urge to curse them. Perhaps if they thought him dead, he'd have a better chance to escape. Judging by the thick muck on the ground, he guessed they'd been working on the pit during the rainy season. His bones at least should be grateful the ground was saturated. He rolled to his knees.

Something gleamed across the pit. His sword, he realized, clambering to his feet and weaving between tree trunks toward it. *Tree trunks?* Sharpened stakes, each as big around as his thigh and far enough apart that he had fallen between them. *Whatever those Lictians are hunting, good thing it's a lot bigger than me.*

He hefted his sword. The blade was sound and straight, the hilt firmly attached.

Third time pays all — no more places to fall.

With a thundering crash and ungodly scream, his world caved in.

Instinct forced John's battered muscles into action. He dove aside as something heavy smashed into his back, hurling him against the pit wall, which was not nearly as yielding as the ground. Thunder filled his ears and he fought to remain conscious. And won. Barely.

Something as ponderous as one of the great jungle pythons lay across his chest and John pushed against it. To his surprise, it moved, lashing him in the ribs and forcing what little breath he had left from his lungs.

Lion's tail, his brain said as he gasped for air. He knew for certain he was addled. There had never been a lion born that could wear such a tail. Diving under the tail's next swipe, John scrambled to his feet. He was tempted to rub his eyes. He stood near the hindquarters of an enormous tawny cat. If the cat had been on its feet, he judged he could have walked under it without crouching.

The beast was lying twisted, half on its belly and half on its side, and its great flanks were heaving like a blacksmith's bellows. Great gory swaths striped its hide where the stakes had drawn blood. The creature was gouged, not pierced, John realized, marveling that something so big could twist its body like a back-alley tabby and miss all the stakes. *No*, he amended. Many of the stakes, loosened in the muddy ground, had been knocked over like straws.

He eyed the huge claws and, as quietly as he could, stepped sideways, putting a stake between him and the jagged scimitars.

Wrong. Twice wrong. Not a cat, and not unscathed.

From his new vantage point, he saw that a stake had lanced through the griffin's right wing, pinning it.

"That's not a myth," John said under his breath. "It's a nightmare." The eagle head turned and a huge golden eye glared at him. The lion's body trembled. *Like standing beside a volcano.*

"I am not your enemy," he said quietly, keeping his sword pointed down. The creature continued staring at him, her ears twitching as if she understood his words. Her great muscles remained coiled, but the trembling diminished to an occasional shiver. "Save your ire for those who put you—put us—here. If we work togeth—"

Lictian croaking interrupted him.

"Fool! You set the stakes too far apart! Now, instead of a sacrifice for the Chaz'pe'pah, we have a live Abomination! A pit trap for a winged beast? Idiot!"

"Bu-but the p-p-pit was narrow enough to force her wings furled…and we had but a few weeks," a voice quavered. "And the rains, the rains were heavy, and…"

The huntsman's whining faded as John's thoughts whirled. *Chaz'pe'pah.* Magic-users. If there was one thing he loathed more than Lictians, it was Lictian witchy-men. He thought of the rune-carved stakes impaling the Thorn Rock villagers and his hands tightened on his sword hilt. *I hate magic.*

No mention of me. Now, if the griffin would just ignore me as well… The aquiline head had drooped, but one ear was cocked, as if the griffin listened to the Lictians' words.

A different Lictian voice rasped.

"This fool of a huntsman will be our salvation, brother. The Abomination is weakened. The magic we summoned to help destroy it will now control it instead! We have amassed twice their men. Having a griffin, Abomination though it might be, in our vanguard, will seal their fate! We will sweep the dung-eaters from our hills forever!"

The Lictians' cheers turned to screams as the griffin lunged upward. She settled back down with half of the Lictian huntsman in her beak. With a single shake of her head, his still-wriggling torso disappeared down her throat.

"Good girl," John said softly. "I guess you share my view on magic. And Lictians."

He pondered his options as he looked into the clouded golden eyes, eyes the size of barrel tops. He could have sworn the griffin winked.

Better to be an ally than share the Lictian's fate. Feeling the fool, he explained his plan to the beast.

John looked down at his sword, trying not to think about the blade's keen edge and what he was about to do. Exhaling explosively, he swung the blade into the stake piercing the griffin's wing, gritting his teeth as the blade chunked into wood just above the wing. Her shriek a thousand swords grating against armor tore through his skull. He swallowed hard — only the thudding of his heart was proof it hadn't stopped. *Focus! A missed stroke means unpleasantly permanent consequences.*

He hoped the chanting of the witchy-men would disguise the sound of his work. The griffin, whether in pain or understanding his intent, roared and shrieked until John's ears rang.

Chopping through the stake was one thing. Yanking it through the griffin's wing was another — and potentially fatal. John grimaced. He would either die in the next heartbeat in this muddy pit…or not.

Where the shadow falls, and when, is not worth fretting over. Life must be lived, and the only way to anywhere is through, not around.

Bunching his great muscles, he tugged the stake with all his might. As the wing slid free with a scraping, squelching sound, the griffin bounded into the air, her pained roar filling the pit, only to fall back heavily, gouging her forepaw on the stump John had hacked off.

She glared near-sightedly at John. A spark kindled in her occluded eyes and anger rumbled deep in her chest.

"Easy, easy," he muttered, pulling off his shirt and tearing it into strips. He slathered mud over the pieces of cloth and bound the injured paw as best he could. "Keep still, if you please, and let me tend to your hurts."

If you please? Being polite to the beast seemed absurd — but no more so than nursing the monster in the first place.

Hours later, John wore nothing but boots, codpiece, sword harness and muck. He had slathered handful after handful of mud to patch the griffin's bleeding. His breeches had plugged a particularly nasty wound on her back.

She lay quiescent, as if his rough ministrations had worn her out. Likely she had never had to tolerate a man's touch before.

Above them, the afternoon sun shone into the pit. The monotonous chanting of the Lictian spell-casters had increased in volume, hard and bright as the sun. A sickly chartreuse fog was gathering over the pit, and John eyed it sourly. *I hate magic.*

"You should leave now, if you've the strength for it, before their magic net is woven tighter," he said, reaching up to stroke a wingtip. "And thank you for eating that Lictian. One less for my sword."

The eagle head turned. A big eye narrowed and she tilted her head. He got the impression she was amused. Without a sound, she rose on all four legs and bounded into the air. The leap took her above the pit's lip with enough clearance to unfurl her mighty wings. The spell-fog shredded into sickly green tendrils, blown away by the hurricane force of her wing-strokes.

John heard with satisfaction that the witchy-men's chanting had changed to shouts of alarm. *Now to shinny up one of these stakes and climb out of here.* Lictian screams rent the air. *Perhaps she'll leave me a few.*

Before he could move, a gigantic paw dipped into the pit and a single claw hooked under his harness. He was high in the air before his startled shout rang through the canyon.

John had ridden in sea-going ships smaller than the griffin's nest. He stretched to peer over the edge, slipping on one of the mounds of gold and gems littering the nest's bowl. "Littered" was the only way he could describe it. The treasure was scattered about and trodden underfoot — mingling with a charnel house's worth of bones — as if it meant nothing more than pebbles or dirt.

You'd have to be a griffin to get here, he thought. The nest rested atop the flattened top of a sheer peak, high enough that he watched clouds scud by below. He slid down the side of the nest and sat down. The griffin had settled on her haunches and was cleaning herself like any cat would — except that she preened not with her tongue, but with a beak longer than he was tall.

The rent in her right wing was nearly healed, though it had only been yesterday that they had escaped the Lictian trap. *Why shouldn't the griffin have recuperative powers that matched her size?*

John realized she had stopped pecking at her fur and was watching him. Her gigantic curved beak swooped down without warning and pushed a pile of jewels into his lap before he could even flinch. He suddenly remembered how naked he was.

He looked into the filmed eyes. "I don't want your treasure," he said. "I think we're quits."

A noise like grating metal mingled with the shrilling of escaping steam issued from the griffin's throat.

"Well, maybe one then," John said, selecting a topaz. It was the size of a plum and glowed with golden light. "To make up for my season's lost wages—and to remind me of you."

Thinking of his former comrades, he pictured the massing Lictians. Even without the griffin, they vastly outnumbered the duke's men. The seed of an idea blossomed.

He reached over and placed a hand on the griffin's unbelievably massive forepaw.

"If you really want to reward me," he began, "what do you think of visiting our old friends the Lictians..."

Plumes from scores of Lictian campfires rose in curling white pillars into the still evening air. At least four hundred men spread across the broad plateau. Unbidden, an image of Thorn Rock's smoking ruins and impaled bodies flashed through John's mind.

Four hundred-to-two odds seemed just fine.

Swooping low, the griffin tilted a wing. John rolled off her back at the camp's eastern edge. Startled sentries screamed and ran, only to fall to beak and claws as the griffin shrieked a battle cry before spinning away. She would circle and come from the west, John knew, so the fading sunset was at her back, affording her a little light.

Meet you in the middle. This time, the grin reached his eyes.

Loosing a wordless cry, John unsheathed his sword and sprinted through the camp, heading for the tallest tent, where he figured to find the witchy-men. Any chieftains in the way would be a bonus. He hacked as he ran, his flashing sword adding to the half-asleep Lictians' confusion. Shrieks of terror and vengeance blended in macabre harmony from the camp's west side.

A chieftain wearing a wolf's head atop his own, the pelt trailing down his back, peered from the entrance of the big tent, trying to see what the commotion was. Without breaking stride, John hewed him down and leaped into the tent. The man's gurgling death-scream alerted the others, and hastily aimed blasts of mage-fire scorched John's hair and dazzled his eyes. The canvas behind him blossomed with green fire.

Blinking back tears of pain, he discovered two other chiefs standing between him and the witchy-men. One wore a bear's head, the other that of a mountain lion. They attacked simultaneously with axe and spear.

John parried the axe blow on his sword blade and, timing it closely, twisted inside the spear thrust. Shoving the axe-man away, he rammed the hilt of his sword into the face of the cougar-clad man and heard the crunch of broken teeth. The man staggered backward and screamed as a bolt of energy from one of his own witchy-man caught him in the neck. He flopped to the floor, shuddered twice, then lay still.

Diving forward, John thrust his sword into the witchy-man's gullet before the man could utter another spell. Sensing the axe-man's charge, John whirled, bringing his sword in an arcing overhand stroke and cleaving the man's head in a blow that started between the bear's eyes and ended at the Lictian's chin.

The remaining two witchy-men shouted ineffectual spells and fled. John's sword stroke carved one through the neck, half-severing his head. The other dodged out of the tent, wailing. His high-pitched shriek ended abruptly.

John stepped out into a maelstrom of fire, motion and hoarse screams. The griffin sucked in the witchy-man's dangling leg and blinked at John.

"Now, now, you'll only make her angry," John rasped as a spearman loomed out of the darkness, lunging toward the griffin. He thrust a shoulder into the Lictian to spoil his aim, then sliced him across the belly. The man fell, gushing entrails.

"Don't stand around and eat when there's work to be done," he told the griffin. "If you please."

She winked at him again, and with beak and claw and sword, they routed the remaining Lictians, though sheer terror was their greatest weapon.

Dawn found them amid the charred ruins of the camp. John munched on jerky and stale bread, washing it down with raw red wine, three other wineskins at his feet. He had given up trying to find a Lictian whose clothes would fit, wanting no part of their animal pelts.

The griffin broke her fast in her own way.

"The best part," John said, declining once again the griffin's offer of a choice Lictian thigh, "is that the duke has paid good silver for men who will sit on their arses all summer and not swing a sword once. I'd like to see the duke try and get his money back!"

He reckoned the duke and the priests and Achta would have an unhappy summer — though not as unhappy as the Lictians.

He looked over at the beast, meticulously cleaning herself again.

If he was ever going to worship something, it would be the griffin rather than Achta. The spider goddess was merely an idol, an idea; an excuse to cloak ignorance in darkness and mystery. The griffin was neither myth nor monster; she was the most real creature he had ever met. And though she was forced to live in darkness, she found a way to endure.

"I have heard some say darkness is evil and war is evil, but if the former is true, then no man would ever wake fresh from a night's rest, and if the latter is true, then no patriot has ever been a good man." The griffin stopped preening and canted her head toward John. He started, realizing he had spoken aloud.

She winked at him, then screamed agreement and victory. The mountains thundered in echoing reply.

INTRODUCTION BY **MIKE RESNICK**

Michael H. Hanson's

SHA'DAA

Tales of the Apocalypse

Edited by Edward F. McKeown

http://www.cyberwizardproductions.com/altered/shadaa.html

*New from Altered Dimension's Press!
Get it. Read it. Experience it!
You are warned. The Sha'Daa IS coming!*

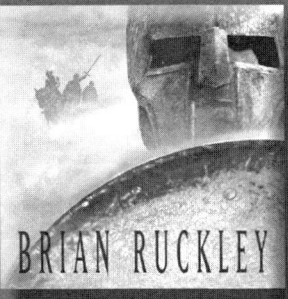

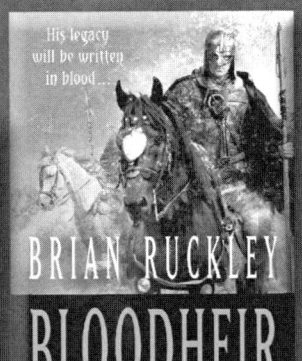

Black Gate
MAGAZINE

The Best In New Fantasy Fiction

4 issues/year
$29.95

Art by Bruce Pennington

WWW.BLACKGATE.COM

Featuring characters from the
best-selling Gotrek & Felix series

WARHAMMER

Buy this
book or read
a free extract at
www.blacklibrary.com

GREY SEER

BY C·L·WERNER

A THANQUOL & BONERIPPER NOVEL

COMING APRIL 2010

Rogue Blades Presents

Roar of the Crowd

150,000 words of the original massive multiple player games!

These are the tales of ancient cultures locked in mock battles of deadly intent; of forgotten generations playing violent games in lieu of warfare; of individuals vying to the death for the favors of rulers and lovers. These are the tales of the games where winning is survival – and where the crowd determines all. These are historically real games* from real cultures, but **fantastical elements are required!** The crowd must be involved: Either the game carries into the crowd or the crowd overwhelms the gamers.
The crowd is the key: your story cannot be told the same minus the crowd.

Featuring:
Mongolian horse polo ~ Mayan pokolpok ~ Assyrian, Egyptian, Hittite, Roman, Byzantine chariot races ~ Greek pankration ~ Celtic & other cultures' mock land battles ~ Roman mock sea battles ~ Medieval melees ~ Iroquois tewaarathon ~ Zulu donga ~ Indian silambam ~ basically any ancient war game or game of violence ~ **NOTE:** Individual battles, ala Renaissance duels, Roman gladiators, and Medieval jousts, will be considered so long as the parameters of the anthology are met. **FURTHER NOTE:** These individual battles are not the priority – IF I accept any such tales, there will be only one of each style game. This is not so of the multi-player games.

Word Count: 5,000-15,000 words ~ no less, some leeway with more
BIG DIFFERENCE IN 2010: This is a word count anthology, not a story count.

Submissions open: August 1 – November 31, 2009

Submissions will be read en masse from December 1 to 31, 2009,
and all stories will be rejected/accepted in January 2010.

Roar of the Crowd
Coming April 21, 2010 to all fine book sellers
Or order direct from RBE at www.roguebladesentertainment.com

*The games must be legit. Either on the list provided above, or you must provide evidence of the existence and culture of whatever game you're writing about. Because the games have to be 'real,' that includes their culture and their people. Now that could mean all sorts of things…
This anthology **will NOT** be simply historical adventure fiction.